## Praise for *Offspring*:

"I was swept away by Scott Appleton's en[g] achieved the rare feat of creating strong, un follow their own path instead of trying to r Many books claim to be 'in the tradition of L.... and Tolkien, but Appleton has earned that distinction by blazing his own path in modern fantasy. I look forward to more books by this original author."

— **Julie Dick** (age 19 from Wisconsin)

"I was overjoyed to be given the opportunity of reading *Swords of the Six* in pre-release. Then I read *Offspring* electronically and tore through it just as fast if not faster than any other compelling book I've read. I was completely engrossed in all aspects of the story, from Oganna's young childhood on up to the tough trials she has to face. Of the whole book, one thing I couldn't get enough of, the Megatraths! So intuitive and natural. Scott Appleton is fantastic in his storyworld blending and his aptitude to create trends, not follow them. *Offspring* is chock full of awesome storytelling completely free of typical fantasy cliches. I followed the book breathless to the end when it. . . . oh man. I can't ruin it for you all. I have one caution for readers... do NOT pick up this book if you intend on getting anything done in the next 12 hours. It's dangerous."

— **Leighton Hajicek** (Missouri)

"As the next book in the series started by *Swords of the Six*, *Offspring*, by Scott Appleton, delivers another action-filled story. Containing huge battles, lonely vigils, incredibly imaginative creatures, and the forces of light and darkness clashing in a tangible way, *Offspring* is a welcome addition to the fantasy genre."

— **Sam Jenne** (age 17 from Oregon)

"Scott Appleton truly writes from the heart. The story he has created is wonderfully magnificent. The beautiful spiritual themes woven throughout blessed me. I cried with the characters and rejoiced with them and felt like I was there with them every step of their journey. Forewarning: this story is not a story for the faint of heart, but is a story of the heart."

—**Ryan Paige Howard** (California)

"What drew me into *Offspring* is how it's not at all like our world in appearance, but in an allegorical sense it is like our world in every way. Few authors can write like Scott Appleton. . . . This book took me into the world of *Offspring* and I finished it in just one weekend. It has some of everything: adventure, humor, suspense, and a little bit of romance."

—**Josh Ryner** (age 12)

"Appleton weaves an exciting story with an imaginative world, unforgettable characters, and a suspenseful plot. I found myself lost in the story and did not want to put it down. A definite keeper and a solid follow-up to *Swords of the Six*!"

—**Joseph Ely** (age 15 from North Carolina)

"Oddly, the only fantasy books I really seem to find in bookstores are the Narnia books by C. S. Lewis. If you're over the age of 17, and are looking for a more mature Christian fantasy novel, then check out Scott Appleton. The characters in *Offspring* are deep. . . . it was as if the author actually interviewed his characters as he was writing the novel; kind of reminded me of old friends sitting next to you and telling you their story. The plot of this novel is a lot more intricate than the first novel. The story is bigger and more epic in scope—a hybrid style between the action-packed cinematic writing of R. A. Salvatore, and the morality of J. R. R. Tolkien. Perfect for sitting in the living room after a hard day at work. The story may be Christian, but it would appeal to anyone who loves a great fantasy book well told.

—**Jake Scholl** (age 19 from Idaho)

"Scott Appleton tells stories like no other. And *Offspring* is a tale of wonder that will keep readers daydreaming about its imaginative characters, creatures, storyworld, and mystery long after they close the book."

—**Jill Williamson,** Christy Award-winning author of *By Darkness Hid*

THE SWORD OF THE DRAGON SERIES · BOOK TWO

# OFFSPRING

LIVING INK BOOKS
Writing Worth Reading™

## SCOTT APPLETON

*Offspring*
Volume 2 in **The Sword of the Dragon**® series

Copyright © 2011 by Scott Appleton
Published by Living Ink Books, an imprint of
AMG Publishers, Inc.
6815 Shallowford Rd.
Chattanooga, Tennessee 37421

This is a work of fiction. Names, characters, places, and incidents either are the prod-
uct of the author's imagination or are used fictitiously. Any resemblance to actual per-
sons, either living or dead, events, or locales, is entirely coincidental.

| | | |
|---|---|---|
| Print Edition | ISBN 13: 978-0-89957-861-3 | ISBN 10: 0-89957-861-6 |
| EPUB Edition | ISBN 13: 978-1-61715-261-0 | ISBN 10: 1-61715-261-7 |
| Mobi Edition | ISBN 13: 978-1-61715-262-7 | ISBN 10: 1-61715-262-5 |
| E-PDF Edition | ISBN 13: 978-1-61715-263-4 | ISBN 10: 1-61715-263-3 |

First Printing—September 2011

THE SWORD OF THE DRAGON is a trademark of
AMG Publishers.

Map Illustration by Nichole White

Cover illustration by Kerim Beyit

Cover layout and design by Daryle Beam at BrightBoy Design, Inc.,
Chattanooga, TN
Interior design and typesetting by Kristin Goble at PerfecType,
Nashville, TN

Edited by Rebecca L. Miller, Christy Graeber, Jennifer Salveggio,
Bonnie Appleton and Rick Steele

Look for *Key of Living Fire*—the next book in
**The Sword of the Dragon** series, releasing spring 2012

Printed in the United States of America
16 15 14 13 12 11 –B– 7 6 5 4 3 2 1

**For Kelley,**

The star in my life
Who fell from the sky to
Perfectly complete me

# CONTENTS

# PRONUNCIATION GUIDE

Ar'lenon: ar—leh—non

Burloi: bur—loy

Crysallis: cri—sal—is

Gabel: gabe—el

Garfunk: gar—funk

Gwensin: gwen—sin

Hersis: her—sis

Linsair: lin—sayer

Mazmodel: maz—mo—dull

Megatrath: meg—a—trath

Netroth: neh—troth

Nostravium:
    nah—stra—vee—um

Osira: oh—sigh—ruh

Poonie: pooh—nee

Razes: raze—ez

Resgeria: rez—geer—ee—uh

Vectra: vek—truh

Veil: vale

Vortain: vor—tane

Yimshi: yim—she

BORLOI
Necroth
and the Citadel of
Ar'lenon
N
W
E
S
The Northern Desert
The Sea
of
Serpents
Fort North
The
Waterfall
Ganning's
Place
Ilfedo's House
Crysalis
The Western
Wood
Honer's
Home
Ombre's
Abode
The City of
Gyensin
Coastal
Town
The
Hemmed
Land
Borderline
RESGERIA
The Endless Wall

# PRELUDE: THE ANGEL'S PROMISE

*fter Prince Brian fell to the traitors, the dragon prophet arrived on the battlefield . . . too late.*

The white dragon's teeth knifed into Clavius's body as it raised him high off the ground, breaking him in half. The traitor's sword clattered to the ground as the dragon's claws raked the earth, breaking stones as he faced the next traitor: Letrias.

Auron stood nearby, unable to move; his mind begged him to escape while the moment allowed, but his body refused. The dragon's lips parted, dripping the blood of Auron's former accomplice onto the stones. Flames roiled in the dragon's half-open mouth, and Letrias's eyes widened with fear.

Letrias dropped his sword and spread his hands. Energy sizzled along his palms. His lips trembled. "You are not all-powerful, Albino. Hermenuedis is more than a match for you . . . and he has taught me"—bluish light amassed between Letrias's fists—"how to wield mighty *power!*"

The energy shot from Letrias's hands in the form of bolts that sped toward the dragon's chest. But the energy passed through the scaled creature's body as if it was not really there, as if it had no physical presence.

Dark clouds rolled overhead, joining each other until the sunlight faded.

Albino the dragon spoke. "I will waste no more breath on you." He drew back his head and fire streamed from his mouth.

A cloud spiraled to the ground and a dark humanoid entity passed from the heavens to the earth, landing betwixt Albino and Letrias. He crouched for a moment, then straightened like a bird prepared to take flight. The wind played along the Art'en creature's back, ruffling the feathers of its voluminous, furled wings. Auron swallowed, recognizing the wizard Hermenuedis.

The Art'en held out a black sphere that absorbed Albino's flames, swelling to the size of a boulder.

The white dragon's hard gaze riveted on the wizard, and Hermenuedis flapped his wings as the flaming barrage slid him backwards. The dragon took a step toward the Art'en.

The Art'en wizard would lose this battle . . . and the white dragon would come after him next. Auron turned and ran. His sword grew heavy in his hand and he dropped it like a lead weight.

The dragon roared and the ground quaked. As Auron fell, he glanced back.

Albino rose in terrible majesty and flung a black dragon down the slope, its dark body digging a rift in the hard earth. So, Valorian had joined the battle.

Auron stumbled to his feet and raced eastward. For five days he fled. The sky remained cloudy, and rain pummeled him night and day. Eventually he found shelter on the forested slopes of a mountain. That night he fell into an exhausted sleep. But something cold pressed against his throat. He opened his eyes. The tip of a stone dagger played at his throat.

A familiar face stared at him over the blade. The clouds must have thinned, for moonlight fell through the trees. "Letrias? You're alive! How did you survive?"

Letrias clamped a hand over Auron's mouth and withdrew the crude weapon.

"Silence, Fool!" Letrias's gaze darted about the trees. "Someone has been following me."

At that moment a fair-skinned man with blond hair stepped from behind a tree. Letrias bounded to his feet, prepared to run. The man raised a hand and said, "Stay in thy place. I know who thou art, Letrias. And I know thy companion Auron."

"I don't know how you found me, but I'm warning you—" Letrias eyes widened, and Auron's own body froze in place. There was nowhere he could look except at the stranger.

The man's body glowed with holy light. It hurt to look at him. The heavenly being's eyes blazed like small suns from his glorious face. Spotless white robes covered the man from head to toe, and his hair radiated light as golden as Yimshi's rays.

"God, the one and only ruler of the universe, has seen thy wickedness and the innocent blood you shed. Thy deeds will be returned upon thy heads. This night He has sent me to deliver a message and a curse, for in turning from his holy law you have brought His wrath upon yourselves.

"Thus says the Lord: 'I tarry for the redemption of the wicked, I plead for their souls. They shall not find rest—for wrath abides upon them. Age shall not change their bodies; they shall see the years pass and remember their sins until they repent or fall upon the sword of the righteous. I am the Lord. I Am forever.'"

The angel vanished. Letrias ran into the forest.

Trembling, Auron stepped to a tree and leaned his forehead against the rough bark. He should have listened to Albino and followed after righteousness; now he had fallen beyond redemption. Killing the prince should have secured for him a place at the side of the all-powerful Hermeneudis. But, if what he'd last seen of that wizard's battle with Albino was any indicator, the wizard would be fortunate to escape with his life. He scraped his skin along the bark, warm blood dripping down his face. He should have stayed on the side of the prophets.

A hundred years passed. In his heart it felt longer. Believing himself to be beyond redemption, he let the power of guilt solidify his rebellion against God and harden his conscience.

At the end of the hundred years he set out, eastward, to find the last remaining wizard, that pupil of Hermenuedis: Letrias.

⁂ ⁂ ⁂

"Letrias, a stranger has come to the valley." The stump of a man cowered before his master and bit his thumbnail.

Letrias regarded the man in silence. His slender figure would have deceived any stranger into believing him weak, but in his hand he held a metal staff. At its head the dark metal separated into several bands that wrapped about a small orb. He clanked the staff on the floor and calmly eyed the penitent figure. "Do not let your lips quiver, Mazmodel. Tell me what you know."

"Forgive me, mighty one . . . I"—the little man bit his other thumbnail and kept his gaze to the floor—"the stranger reported he knew you—a long time ago."

Letrias looked over Mazmodel to the massive chamber doors, then stepped down to the man's level. "Place your hands on the stone."

Trembling, the little man positioned himself on all four limbs with fingers splayed.

Letrias walked forward and landed his booted foot on Mazmodel's hand. The man cried out, but Letrias stepped past him, not even glancing down. "Ah, Mazmodel." Letrias laughed. "You must always be ready to give me a quick answer. Otherwise, if your usefulness is at an end, I will have no choice but to remove you from my protection—and your daughter as well.

"Now, tell me, who has come to my valley."

"He said his name is Auron." The little man's lips trembled. He spat on the floor as if to ease tension.

Letrias lifted his staff. It thrummed a deep tone that filled the room, and harsh, unintelligible whispers joined in—an otherworldly, evil sound that bespoke condemnation. Letrias laughed and faced Mazmodel. The evil he had fostered in his soul these thousand plus years had given him what he'd always desired: power.

Mazmodel's body rose off the floor until his limbs hung loose in mid-air. His toes dangled two feet off the stone. Tears sprang from the man's eyes.

"So, Auron has returned to me." Letrias smiled while the power of his staff continued to hold his servant a prisoner. Swift-flowing lava spilled from a nearby hole in the rock wall, flowing through a channel carved at the wall's base to his side. The molten rock curved against the back wall and streamed past him on the other side, forming a perfect U of hot liquid glowing orange-yellow.

Forcing all his fingers into his mouth, the little man stuttered, "I . . . I, he . . . he is . . . Auron wants—"

Letrias angled his ear toward the chamber's twin doors. A familiar presence entered his perception, and a smile creased his face. His leather clothes creaked as he lowered his staff to the floor. "And I had thought he, too, was dead."

Letrias let the staff's power drop the little man to the stone floor. Perspiration rose on the man's forehead and dripped down his cheeks. He took his fingers out of his mouth and licked his lips. "P . . . please, Master, I . . . I . . . I . . . you pr . . . promised"—he choked on his words—"promised me home."

A chorus of muffled hissing and unintelligible words arose in the shadows behind Letrias. "Home? You were warned against mentioning this in my presence." Letrias sighed. "Your fate is in my hand, Mazmodel. As is your daughter's. You are my trophy—though a disappointing one you have proven to be. You are my trophy of war, a constant reminder that piece by piece Subterran is falling into my palm. But your pleas weary me."

At that moment the chamber doors lumbered open. Two wizards wielding scythes entered, their bodies garbed in heavy black leather. They stood aside as four broad-shouldered men shuffled inside bearing a man on a litter. Each of the litter-bearers held a wizard's staff and wore black cloaks.

Letrias addressed Mazmodel without looking back at him. "If the whole land of Nostravium is filled with idiots such as you, my followers will feast on their corpses."

The staff's head glowed harsh-gray, and energy blasted from it into the little man's chest. Letrias ambled over to the litter as Mazmodel's body crumpled to the floor.

Letrias glanced at the litter and the man that lay on it. Auron's sand-encrusted face returned his gaze. "At last you have come. Welcome to the Valley of Death!" He frowned. "What has it been, Auron? Only a thousand years? Age has not touched our bodies, nor has time dulled my memory. Xavion is long dead and forgotten, and his master has not appeared, nor have I heard rumor of him in all this time."

He leaned on his wizard's staff, letting his dark eyes return Auron's weary gaze. "If you have come to serve me, then I will save your life."

Auron coughed and then growled, "Didn't I come all this way?"

Letrias said not a word. He played his fingers along the staff's smooth surface.

"For these thousand years I have searched for you, Letrias. I have not forgotten your promise to teach me . . . to teach me as Hermenuedis taught you."

Letrias stood back and swung his staff through the air toward the litter. The wizards holding it stood still as stones. Auron's eyes opened, and he started to cry out. The staff knocked him full in the chest, causing him to spit bile, and the litter shattered into billions of tiny fragments. Auron crashed to the stone floor.

"Do you want power, Auron? Or do you seek to evade the fate God decreed for you and I?" He knelt in front of the man. "A war is beginning—no, it has started already—a war against all who embrace the Creator and his prophets. And we know whose side must win if we are going to survive."

Auron struggled to his feet, and Letrias rose before him, looking down upon him. Auron seemed so weak. No, Letrias decided, he was pliable—ripe and ready to receive instruction. This former member of the Six had potential in the ranks of wizardry.

Grabbing Letrias's shirt-front, Auron sought to steady himself. But Letrias captured him in the powers of wickedness and suspended him in the air as he had Mazmodel.

His gaze on Auron, Letrias commanded the staff-wielding wizards that had carried the litter. "Seal the doors as you leave."

The dark-robed men turned to the door, and one of them stooped to grab the dead little man, Mazmodel.

"Did I ask you to do that?" Letrias raised his eyebrows and eyed the man out of the corner of his vision.

The wizard swallowed hard, withdrew his fingers from Mazmodel and bowed, eyes wide as apples. "Please, Master, forgive my presumption."

Letrias pointed his staff at the man and lowered his brow. "Forgive?" Electric current snaked from the staff's base toward its head. "Forgiveness begets weakness." He thrust the staff at the man's head. "And God knows I never believed in helping or preserving the weak." Energy bolted from the staff. Before Auron could blink, another body lay beside Mazmodel, the other wizards exited the room, and the doors thudded shut.

Letrias knew he had placed Auron in a fragile position. He had treated him as little more than a servant. They had once been friends, but today he must become one of many. He must see that he was not special, that he was a tool through which Letrias's power could be exercised. Letrias chuckled as Auron sat in front of him. The comradery of the Six no longer applied. People must live and die at his pleasure.

Letrias read fear in Auron's eyes. He would need to drive that out of him—especially the fear of God—if he was to be a capable vessel.

Auron would need an instructor who feared neither man nor beast, neither angels nor God himself. Unfortunately the battles to the east of the valley kept his prize pupil, the Death Knight, occupied. Only one other wizard currently residing in the Valley of Death possessed a similar fearless devotion to sorcery and to Letrias himself.

Wiping his dirty face with a shredded sleeve, Auron glanced at the ceiling.

Stooping next to him, Letrias nodded. "Yes, Auron, I do believe it is possible to escape the wrath of God. I have for a thousand years. The curse which his angel pronounced upon me has turned into my greatest ally. And one day soon I will be stronger than any man or creature that roams Subterran; I will be beyond even Albino himself. The Grim Reaper will envy me and Valorian will arise. That black dragon will call me his brother, while the world falls under the sorcery I now teach."

He pulled Auron to his feet. "Stay in my shadow and all will be well."

❧ ❧ ❧

Auron felt the bars of his heaven-bestowed prison rise around him. "I will stay in your shadow, as ageless as you, but I will serve in exchange for protection." He looked up at Letrias, noting for the first time that the wizard wore a turban-like headdress.

"Very well then, you *will* serve me. But I have no need of another pupil; you will learn from another." Letrias marched to the exit doors and touched them with the head of his staff. They immediately opened.

Down a long, high corridor they walked until they stopped at an arch opening into a large chamber. Auron followed Letrias inside past a fountain spouting lava. The heat drove him against the wall, but Letrias dipped his finger into the molten rock, pulled it out unharmed, and laughed. "Yes, not even an angel will dare tread me beneath his feet now."

The chamber opened into a cavern, and the floor slanted steeply for a few hundred feet. Lava rivulets spilled down the stone walls. The heat was nearly unbearable. But Letrias pointed his staff into the cavern to an arena far below. Armed men battled one another inside it. Sparks and bolts of energy abounded, passing from staffs the men wielded. Auron coughed as he inhaled sulfur, but he growled, fighting it. He stepped forward, planting his feet next to Letrias, and crossed his arms.

Two wizards rushed a hulking one, but the latter swung a metal rod against their chests, dropping them.

"Ah, see the power that I now wield!" Letrias spread his arms as if embracing the combatants. "I have built an army, an army that communes with the spirits and receives power from them. This is no mere force of men, these are wizards. Their power is less than my own, but combined they are formidable."

The thought of all these men communing with evil spirits and learning magic from Letrias chilled Auron. Not that he, with his God-bestowed curse, was better than they. In fact, this is why he'd come. He would learn and learn well. He would sell what remained of his soul if it brought him power.

Suddenly the arena calmed. The wizards formed a circle and a giant of a man emerged from the shadows to stand at their center. When he raised his sword in one hand and a staff in the other, the wizards attacked. But he batted them back like so many urchins, his body glinting as if covered with protruding blades.

"Meet Razes, a master among my followers. Your new master. Do not cross him, Auron, for he would end your life. Learn from him what you came to learn from me." Letrias slipped his hands to the base of his staff, and slammed its head into the ground.

Auron felt, more than saw, the burst of lightning that seemed to erupt from the point of impact. It threw him against the chamber wall. When he looked up, Letrias had engaged in a duel with another wizard who'd emerged from behind. It lasted moments. Letrias stabbed the wizard through the heart and then stood over the body. "A waste." He sighed and walked out of the cavern.

Auron was left alone. He descended toward the arena, wary of introducing himself to the giant . . . but knowing he must.

# GUARDIAN OF THE
# DRAGON'S OFFSPRING

G raceful, gentle, the great white dragon settled into the woodland hollow. He angled his bony face down at the hollow's border, at the shelf of stone which concealed the faithful guardian. Without being bidden, as if he'd sensed the presence of his master, Specter came out of the narrow opening to the cave. He'd been here ever since Dantress had chosen to become a wife.

"Master." He bowed to the majestic creature, leaving his cavernous gray hood over his head. Early morning darkness flooded the depressed clearing. Not a single owl made a sound and no bats hunted insects. It was as if they were afraid of disrespecting the mighty beast standing in the hollow, so held their voices and listened instead.

The dragon's arm muscle rippled as he crouched closer to the man. "Give me your hand, Specter."

"I would prefer not, my Lord."

"No?" The dragon growled. "Of what use will you be without the full function of both of your hands?"

"It is not a crippling injury." Specter extended his scarred hand, clenching and then opening his fist. "And it is a scar I will be honored to keep, for it is the price of a life saved, a life that one day might save humanity from the evil of the warriors who turned. Warriors that I trained."

Smoke wafted from Albino's nostrils. It settled around Specter like a fog. And the dragon gazed intently into the man's hood as if he could see his blue eyes. "Do not think that I have forgotten that day, my friend," he rumbled. "Time has not wiped away the blood spilled by Letrias's treachery, nor has justice been thwarted."

"One, my master"—Specter couldn't suppress a growl—"only *one* of those traitors met with the fate he deserved." He clenched his fist. "And he did not even have the honor to seek that death in combat. Instead . . . instead he committed suicide."

"And for that you condemn him?" the dragon asked thoughtfully.

Specter was silent for a while. The sky lightened in the east. The stars winked out one by one. The brightest ones remained visible a tad longer, twinkling even as the velvet sky turned blue around them. At last he whispered, "I loved them like brothers, trained them like sons. Kesla, why him? He had a family. I would never have questioned his loyalty. If one of my students were above reproach . . . it should have been him."

The dragon flexed his wings and then folded them to his sides. His long tail twitched, and the scales on his neck rippled forebodingly. "Listen to me my friend." The dragon hesitated. The man's cloaked head had tilted toward the ground. "Xavion?"

Specter looked up at his master.

"Xavion, I think it is time you know the truth . . . the *whole* truth of who lived and who died and why."

� � �

Kesla fitted his scabbard to his side and hugged his wife. His three boys and two little girls hovered behind their mother. His eldest son was almost twelve, the youngest no more than five. The girls were seven and eight. The children waited until he released his wife, then they clamored for their turns, hugging him until he laughed. They laughed with him, filling the log cabin with the joyful noise, and he smiled as he unfastened the last of his little girls' arms from around his neck. He stood her on the floor, tousled his boys' hair, and pecked his wife on the cheek.

"Go now!" She laughed with him. "I love you, too. Now be off with you. You have a goodly long distance to travel . . . it was your choice after all to build so far from the dragon's lands, and you must join Xavion.

"Be safe. You'll be in our prayers . . . as always." She pecked him on the cheek and shoved a glowing iron lantern into his hand. The light warmed her face as if she were an angel. In a way, she was; she was *his* angel.

Leaving the house with its smoking chimney and long, rough-hewn walls behind him, he set off down the dark, narrow path. The white cape flowed behind him. He jerked his head toward the sky, opening his nostrils to the fresh, cool air. The innumerable stars shone above him. On both sides of the trail the trees rose protectively, a border of soft, thick grass carpeting the edge. It was the night of new moon. Darkest night of the month.

The trail wended through the forest, a lonesome path, but his by choice. He could have had a mansion in Emperia, under the direct protection of the great white dragon. But he'd fallen in love with this forest on one of his travels, and here he had determined to build his family's future. The trees were straight, tall, and sturdy, with little forest undergrowth. Deer abounded, though he did not care much to hunt them, choosing instead to lie in his back yard and watch the woodland creatures graze without fear. Thankfully, his wife sympathized with his sentiments.

But on this night he sighed, realizing that it might be a long time before he could return home. The war against the wizards seemed to continue without end. Though the addition of the valiant prince of Prunesia to the dragon warriors' ranks had given him a small measure of hope.

And so he strode swiftly down the trail, unconcerned for the dark clouds that rolled without warning from the south to cover the stars. An exposed tree root caught his foot, and he fell forward. The night turned darker than it should have been, and the air around him bit with a sharp cold uncharacteristic for this time of year.

Turning to look at the sky, Kesla's heart beat with twice its vigor. His blood ran cold and sweat built on his palm as he reached down to check for his crystalline sword. Fear stabbed him with the force of a thousand blades as he heard a screech, as of an eagle on the hunt, but with far more volume. The screech echoed in the forest, rebounding from tree to tree, surrounding him with its dark cruelty.

Kesla spun on his heel and raced toward his house, sliding his pure blade from its sheath and holding it wide. The lantern in his hand became a burden, and he dropped it, shattering its chimney.

The clouds gathered above his house as he ran. They swirled, tornado-like, descending from the sky as if gravity forced them to fall. Something shaped like an oversized falcon dove from the midst of the swirling dark mass, dropping with incredible speed as if to catch its prey.

A sizzle of energy built inside the clouds, glowing green. Kesla gasped and picked up speed. A single bolt of green lightning followed the falling form. The strike exploded into the cabin roof.

Such was the force of the blast that the paned windows shattered outward and the stone foundation trembled. The shockwave forced Kesla's arm over his eyes, but he ran to the front door, catching a glimpse of the falcon-like form again as it dropped through the hole in the roof.

Kesla burst into his house. The walls were charred; the fireplace was cracked and smoking; the floorboards which he had so carefully laid out were broken and twisted.

In the darkness and amidst the ruins, Kesla's eyes confirmed his greatest fears. A breeze swept through the broken walls, whipping his white cape around his legs. It blew smoke over the crumpled, soot-covered bodies of his wife and children, their sides heaving shallow breaths.

Clouds of smoke billowed around a creature crouching behind them. Its twin black-feathered wings spread over and around them. Its eyes, glinting like gray-green metal, glared at him from the leathery face of a man. Black leather covered its entire body.

A flame grew in the ruined fireplace and flickered on the face of a smooth black sphere in the winged man's hand.

Kesla longed to rush forward. To gut the creature with his sword and feed it to the ravens, but he knew the foolishness of the thought. He knew his limits and fighting this creature would be as useless as beating his sword on a boulder.

"Good, you have restrained yourssself, Warrior Kesssla," the creature hissed. It spidered its fingers through the air over the prone bodies.

"Leave my family be." Kesla felt his sword hand shake, knew that it showed in his voice, too. "Whatever you are here for they are of no use to you."

"No?" The wizard Art'en lowered his black sphere until it almost touched Kesla's son.

Kesla's knuckles whitened as he wrung his sword's handle. Its blade glowed with pure white light.

The wizard laughed, high and birdlike. "But you are wrong, my dear warrior. They are *very* useful to me. So long as I hold them in my power . . . *you* will do as *I* sssay."

"No . . . no I would never." But even as he said it, the wizard touch his wife's cheek with an icy finger, and Kesla knew his declaration wasn't true.

"Oh, but it won't be so hard as you think, my dear, dear warrior . . . only a sssmall favor I ask. Just one . . . and then you can have your family back safe and sssound. Not a scratch." The wizard cackled, spreading its arms. "I promisss!"

Kesla swallowed, his eyes burning with tears that begged to be shed. "Wh . . . what do you want of me?"

"Not too hard a thing, my dear warrior. I asssk for one life in exchange for many." It pointed at his wife and children. "For some time now Letrias has been my servant. With my help he has enlisted the aid of your fellow warriors, members of the dragons *trusted* Sssix!

"Your captain need not die, unless he interferes with your mission. But the prince of Prunesssia . . . ah! I want his blood sprayed across the path by your own sssword!

"Do this thing and then come to me at Al'un Dai. If you succeed in thisss deed then I will keep my end of this arrangement: I will return your family to you healthy and sound and leave you in peace from that time forward.

"Double-cross me, or fail to kill the prince, and your wife's carcass and those of your children will hang on the temple until the fowl pick their bones clean and until time turns them to dussst."

The smoke whirled around the Art'en's giant figure, hiding him and the bodies from view. When it cleared, the wizard and his victims had vanished.

Kesla fell to his knees and beat his fists on the floorboards. "No! I will not do it! I will not betray him." But his wife and children filled his mind. He would do anything, become anything if it meant saving their lives. The prince must die. One simple act, one horrible deed, and life could return to normal.

He threw aside the pure white garments that set him apart as a warrior in the prophet's service, and donned a black cloak, deeply frowning all the while. His sword's blade glowed with only a faint light, as if reflecting the condition of his soul.

He left his home and journeyed into a foreign land far south of Emperia. On a plain of stone he waited beneath a cloudy sky until Letrias, Hestor, Clavius, and Auron marched out of the north. Letrias took the lead, the edge of his mouth twitching a sneer. "You see now, my fellow traitors, not even the mighty Kesla is above corruption."

"Silence!" Kesla shoved Letrias to the ground and stomped on his stomach. "As always," he glanced at the others, "you will follow my lead. Let us be done with this . . . and quickly."

"It was I that made contact with the wizard Hermenuedis." Letrias thrashed from under Kesla's foot and stood, dusting himself. "He holds me in high favor. Don't forget that and your family will be safe."

Kesla fisted the thin man in his jaw. "Why you . . . You told the wizard where to find them!"

"Nothing else would have turned you," Letrias said.

Kesla drew his sword and grasped the warrior's shoulder, prepared to thrust him through. But electricity sizzled out of Letrias's hand, blasting him to the ground. The other warriors grimly watched, though Auron almost smiled.

"I can kill you now and leave your family to die." Letrias pulled Kesla to his feet. "Or you can lead us to Xavion and the prince of Prunesia, and your family will live. My new master has left the choice entirely in your hands."

Kesla chose to continue on his path, vowing that, when all was set right, he would hide his family and find and murder Letrias. A couple of days later, he and the other traitors spotted the prince. Leading them into a cave, Brian brought them face to face with the mighty but wounded captain Xavion. They had met the wizard dragon Valorian in battle and lost. As Kesla fell upon the young man and the old, his heart seemed to die within him. Everything he believed in was epitomized in Xavion, yet everything he loved would die if the prince did not.

He thrust the prince through and wept over the still body. A roar filled the heavens. Looking up, he saw his former master, the great white dragon, coming in all his fury. In the dragon's wake the clouds divided like water.

For the first time ever, Kesla felt afraid of the powerful creature. It landed with such force on the stony battlefield that the ground split.

Albino raked his razor claws down Hestor's front, spilling his organs onto the ground. As Clavius started to flee, he roared, then caught the man in his jaws and snapped him in two. Next he wheeled to strike Letrias.

The wizard pupil vainly cast bolts of lighting from his hands that passed through the dragon's body. Albino pulled back its head, spraying such vehement flames that the dirt turned to glass.

Without warning, the Art'en wizard Hermenuedis fell from the sky with a screech and landed betwixt his pupil and Albino, sparing Letrias incineration. The orb in his hand grew in size and absorbed Albino's flames until it became as large as a boulder.

"Be gone, cursed artifact!" Albino roared. He stretched out his claws toward the orb and flexed them but did not touch it. The orb burst into a billion fragments.

Kesla stumbled back. He dropped his crystalline sword and stared at its blade, now stained with innocent blood. His tears burned on his cheeks.

He glimpsed Letrias standing behind the Art'en. His face paled ghastly white as the dragon swung its tail around, cracking it into the Art'en. "Hermenuedis," the dragon rumbled, "you have carried your wickedness to its final day!"

"No, Albino, thisss day isss mine!" the wizard screeched.

Suddenly, a large black dragon shot from the heavens aggressively toward Albino. With teeth bared, he attacked, but he passed through the white dragon as if through air. Albino grasped him with his claws and flung him down the slope. The black dragon's body furrowed a canyon in the ground as it skidded to a stop. Kesla recognized the beast as the wizard dragon Valorian he had seen on several battlefields. The creature was a foe of power beyond that of the average sorcerer.

Kesla did not wait to watch more of the conflict. He raced south as fast as he could toward Al'un Dai and his family. When he at last arrived, he found that he had not been fast enough. The Art'en wizard, wounded from his encounter with Albino, had taken refuge in the temple fortress, but the dragon had followed. Fire gushed from its mouth, and it called lightning from the sky. It broke the temple walls and cornered the Art'en, at last, in one of the great halls.

Rushing past the raging beast, Kesla stumbled through the rubble, becoming increasingly desperate as he searched in vain for his wife and children. As he leapt a pile of rubble he spotted an opening in one of the tower walls. The dragon's tail swept rubble over his head and he ducked, glancing across the court-yard. The tail crushed Hermenuedis into another tower.

The wizard stood again, the battle renewed as he fought for his survival. Kesla barely saw or heard all that happened around him. In the gaping hole left by Albino's attack in the tower wall, he saw the bloodied bodies of his wife and children trapped beneath fallen debris.

"No!" he screamed as he raced to them and frantically pulled away the stones lying on top of them. But the great white dragon continued to pour out its wrath on the wizard.

Kesla pulled his beloved family from the ruins and lay their bodies on the floor of an untouched tower, hoping to keep them safe. At that moment the dragon crashed through the wall, his claws ripping Hermenuedis's wings from his back while his teeth cut the Art'en's skull. The wizard's screams reached a pitch far more disturbing than anything Kesla had heard yet.

Finding a hatch with a stairs beneath it in the tower floor, he took the bodies of his family into the dark sublevels of the temple and buried them with a broken heart in the alcoves of a large, stone chamber.

In the midst of his despair a beautiful woman inhabiting the temple's sublevels came to him. She consoled him, soothed him. And in his loneliness he turned to her and lost himself to her. Even when he learned that she was the mistress of the dreaded Art'en wizard, he did not leave her. She taught him some of her master's dark arts. In particular she brewed a potion for him to drink, which left him with eternal youth. Eternal, that is, as long as the world, or he, lived.

⌘  ⌘  ⌘

"When my daughters brought word that Kesla had slain himself on the sword of his captain, that is, on *your* sword"—the dragon sighed—"I wept in secret. For had not I been to blame for the death of his family? Was it not I that was so bent on slaying my enemy I neglected the innocent?

"To my shame, I *am* to blame for his fall as much as he. And if I could do it all over again, I would have driven Hermenuedis to humiliation and not have scattered his followers to the four winds. Now his evil spreads across Subterran more surely than it did before. For Letrias with Auron evaded capture that day and hid from me, so that for many years I knew nothing of their whereabouts.

"Only Dantress's child and the sword that I have given to Ilfedo can cleanse the stain of that day from my conscience."

Specter shook his head. "Forgive me, master. My words were spoken out of ignorance and nothing more."

The dragon blew gentle clouds of smoke from his nostrils, filling the hollow, then its white-scaled sides shimmered and it became invisible. "A child approaches this hollow," the dragon explained, "You would do well to follow my example, Specter."

Specter chuckled softly. He waited until the head of a young boy appeared at the hollow's rim, let the youth spot him for only an instant, then caused his robe to shimmer with light, rendering him as invisible as the dragon. "There are more people in this region than there were before Dantress's pregnancy," he said, watching the boy looking with mouth agape at the spot where Specter had been.

"Yes." Albino blew a greater cloud of smoke into the air, veiling his face. "The Hemmed Land is about to change. Its people were leaderless, but now they are taking respectful notice of the young woodsman that saved the coastal people from the Sea Serpents, and they have heard that he cleansed this wilderness of the man-hungry bears. More settlers will come; it is inevitable."

The dragon's pink eyes stared blankly, as if seeing something beyond the man's range of vision. "The Sea Serpents have again invaded, this time in greater numbers."

"Master, let me deal with them," Specter said.

"No, I did not give that task to you and, though you are strong, my friend, I cannot risk losing you in that battle. It is up to Ilfedo and my daughters who remain to deal with those creatures."

"But if you would not send me for fear of *losing* me, why send them?"

"Because, my friend," the dragon rumbled gently, "though you are strong, Ilfedo is stronger. And though you have the gift of invisibility, Ilfedo has the gift of the sword of living fire, with which yours cannot compare. No, you must remain in these forests and watch over my offspring."

Lifting his head to gaze at the trees surrounding the hollow, Albino said, "The boy is gone.

"Here, take these and keep them safe until they can be given into the hands of my offspring." The dragon opened the palm of his other clawed hand. Therein lay the rusted sword of Xavion and the blade boomerang Dantress had retrieved from the fields around Al'un Dai.

Specter took the weapons into his arms with near reverence. "I will do as you ask."

Both he and the dragon dropped the shrouds of invisibility and regarded each other with sober resolution.

"Ilfedo will soon leave his home to seek out the Sea Serpents." The dragon snapped out his leathery wings, sending a wave of air across the woodland clearing. "He will soon know the extent of the power of the sword I gave him. At least, that is, the extent of its power when wielded by him.

"I wish you the full blessings of God." And with that the dragon crouched, digging his claws into the ground, and launched himself into the distant western sky.

❈ ❈ ❈

Stepping noiselessly between the trees, Specter stood in the hillside clearing. The early morning sunlight settled over a group of about forty people. Their soiled apparel and disheveled hair, and the assorted bags and other items lying about them as they slept, seemed to indicate they had made a sudden and hasty trip through the wilderness.

Children curled under blankets with the men and the women. Their breathing seemed ragged, uneasy.

Ilfedo's house stood behind them on the hill, silent and lifeless except for two white birds. Specter saw the sunlight glint off the birds' silver beaks, and he sullenly directed his attention to the northwest corner of the clearing where six figures emerged from the forest, one of them with not one sword but two hanging at his side.

The woodsman and five identically dressed women stopped at the clearing's border, looking upon the sleeping group. Ilfedo, cradling his child in his arms, took a step toward his sleeping visitors. Another group appeared on the opposite side of the clearing, and Specter recognized a few of them.

Ganning walked with a decided limp as he skirted the sleeping individuals. Fast on his heels strode Honer. He was a taller fellow with sandy-blond hair and very broad shoulders. Behind him marched Ombre, a gray fur coat on his back. The head of the dead wolf hung limp over his back like a hood.

Two women accompanied them, one following Honer. The other lingered at the eastern boundary of the clearing, her eyes darting from one prone individual to the next. At last, she too skirted the group and followed Eva.

Specter closed the distance between himself and Ilfedo so that he could better hear what transpired. As he approached, he got his first peek at the dragon's offspring asleep in her father's arms. Peaceful and beautiful she looked. Wrapped in a soft white sheet, Oganna slept with her mouth open.

The air that morning was warm and gentle.

"Ombre, Honer, Ganning." Ilfedo accepted a hug from each of his friends and then smiled through his tears as Honer's wife stood on tiptoe to kiss his cheek. "Eva."

"Is this . . . ?" Honer's wife looked at the infant with tender blue eyes. Her blond hair fell over her eyes and she brushed it back over her ears with her fingers. "Is she yours, Ilfedo?"

Choking on tears, Ilfedo nodded, kissed the infant's forehead and then held her out to the woman. Eva accepted the bundle as if it were gold. "She's beautiful!"

For a little while Ilfedo's friends and their wives fawned over the child, then Ombre stood aside and raised his eyebrows. "Ahem, Ilfedo?" He swept his arm toward the five sisters standing like living statues half-a-dozen yards away. "You haven't introduced us."

"Of course." Ilfedo wiped his face with his sleeve, smearing dirt through his tears. "Please," he said to Caritha, "do come closer."

One by one he introduced the sisters of his deceased bride, giving each a warm smile. At once their faces relaxed. His friends and their wives introduced themselves in kind and welcomed the sisters into their circle.

"You will have to join us for tea sometime," Eva said, rocking the baby in her arms.

"Thank you for your kind invitation." Caritha inclined her head for a moment toward Eva. "But we are here for the child, to raise her and protect her."

"Protect her?" Eva said. "Protect her from what?"

Specter caught Ombre watching Caritha throughout the conversation.

Aroused by the chatter, the people encamped in Ilfedo's clearing stood and ran toward him. The five sisters moved into position between Ilfedo, Eva, and the people, their purple skirts swishing over the grass as if they floated. Reaching down into their skirts they parted a hidden fold in each of their garments and drew out their rusted short swords.

The people stumbled over each other as they came to a sudden stop in front of the sisters. Ilfedo raised his hand and shouted, "Lower your weapons and let these people speak."

Laura stabbed her sword into its sheath and folded her skirt to hide it. Evela and Levena relaxed, sheathing their weapons, while Rose'el frowned, then shrugged her shoulders and followed suit. Caritha started to do likewise. She pulled the fold of her skirt aside, revealing the sheath, but a rugged woodsman leaned close to see and she angled her blade toward him.

Ilfedo shifted his gaze to only her. "I command you to do this if you wish to remain with me."

She retreated a few steps, hiding her rusted blade in the folds of her skirt.

"We are refugees from the coast," the group's spokesman said, fiddling with his soiled brown beard. "The Sea Serpents are back. Nowhere in the Hemmed Land is safe now. Nowhere! They're killing everyone they find, and we can do nothing to stop them.

"Please." He and the rest of those assembled dropped to their knees. "We have heard that you are a great hunter and that you slew the serpents who came before. Please! Come to our aid. Kill these creatures, and we will give you anything you ask!"

Ilfedo wiped his face with his hand and pulled the man to a standing position. Resting his hands on the bearded man's shoulders, he turned to Honer's wife and looked at his child. "Will you watch over her until I return?"

"Of course," Eva replied.

Caritha spun toward Ilfedo. "What? No, Ilfedo! We will watch over her—"

He shook his head. "I need you to come with me. I can't do this alone."

She looked stunned. Nevertheless, with a slight bow, she promised her help.

"Rose'el, Evela, Levena, and Laura . . . you're with me as well," he said.

Evela smiled a bright little smile that made Specter feel warmed from the inside out. Rose'el harrumphed and crossed her arms. Laura said, "Yes, Ilfedo." And Levena curtsied.

"Good." Ilfedo took off his extra sword, the one that had been a gift from his parents, and ran his fingers over its pommel. "Then we will head to the coast. . . Don't worry," he said to Evela as she looked at the ground, "I won't let any of you come to harm." He opened the door to his home and leaned his extra sword against the inside wall. Closing the door, he glanced over the expectant faces of the coastal people and at his faithful friends who stood by.

"What about us?" Ombre frowned, then nodded at Honer and Ganning. "You are going to just leave us behind on this one? I thought we were your closest friends."

"And so you are." Ilfedo looked at the eastern sky, breathed in deeply. "The serpents are intelligent beasts. If they have already invaded the coast, then it is likely they have penetrated the forests as well. It will take some doing to scout the entire region, but if you three work together and organize the locals into search parties, we should be able to make sure none of those belly crawlers is left behind.

"What do you think, Honer, Ganning?"

The men nodded. "If you think that needs doing. We'll see to it."

Within an hour everyone had prepped for departure. Ilfedo set out first, leading the five sisters east. Later, Ombre headed northeast, while Honer and Ganning banded together and went southeast. The refugees remained, per Ilfedo's instruction, encamped in his yard for the time being.

Specter followed Honer's wife south through the woods until she led him to a large cabin. Three young children greeted her at the door, oohing and ahhing over Oganna. Eva instructed them not to touch the baby and entered the house, closing the door behind her.

Contenting himself with standing by a rectangular window by the door, Specter watched through the glass as the woman sat in front of the fireplace in a rocking chair.

One of the children, a little boy, ran outside. He cut across the lawn in energetic bounds with a pail swinging from his hand. A wooden shelter with three sides, and a sort of stable attached to it, had been built a little distance from the cabin. Specter smiled at the sounds of goats crying, especially when a young lad exclaimed, "Hold still, Bella! Do you want the baby to starve? There . . . I didn't think so." He raced out of the stable and back into the cabin, the bucket partly filled with milk.

Leaning on his scythe's handle, Specter listened to Oganna's cries. Honer's wife, Eva, started to hum, and the child quieted. He smiled again. The child was in good hands.

# RISE OF
# THE LORD WARRIOR

An oak tree's leaf bowed toward the forest floor, gravity tugging at the pearlescent bead of cold moisture forming on its green tip. Miniscule droplets on the leaf's surface merged with one another, gathering into a single rivulet that fed the already precarious bead until its weight surrendered to nature's force.

Rays of Yimshi's sunlight split as it descended through the calm air, dappling colors over its translucent surface. The sunlight winked through the tree branches, appearing, fading, following the droplet as it fell, until it struck a metal blade, honed sharp. The droplet's molecules ripped apart, a few flying into the air.

Ombre looked at the long, straight blade of his sword. His gaze lingered for a few moments on the point where the dewdrop landed. But his real focus was elsewhere. His ears were attuned to the silence in the forest. He'd encountered a trapper, and together they had fought and slain a Sea Serpent. Now they were scouring the trees for any more that might have ventured this far inland. No chipmunks, no squirrels, no rabbits, no birds. He scanned the closely spaced trees for anything amiss.

"Garfunk thinks this's silly!" a voice suddenly said from behind.

Turning to face the trapper, but keeping both hands on his sword's leather-wrapped handle, Ombre shook his head at the man.

"What, so you think thar may be another Sea Serpent out here?" The trapper turned his black eyes from Ombre's frustrated gaze and faced the broad base of an oak tree. He made a sucking sound with his mouth and shot a dark wad of spittle at it. "Yeps . . . this's silly. I've been trappin' this part of the wilderness nigh five years. Garfunk thinks this's a waste of his time." He crossed his thick arms over his broad chest and stood with his legs set wide apart, bringing his height, which was still rather insignificant, below Ombre's chest. "Thar's no serpents here," he said through his grizzly, black beard.

"If there aren't, then you've no need to worry, Garfunk." Ombre raised his eyebrows. "And if there *are*, then you are going to put us on the short end of the fighting stick by alerting every critter from here to the sea to our presence."

"Bah! Garfunk thinks not!" The trapper shook his head and seemed amused. "Go on, young one . . . Garfunk's takin' a nap." With that, Garfunk sat on the ground, where he'd spit, pulled his coonskin cap over his eyes, and rested his hand on his belt, just above the row of hunting knives he had sheathed there.

With a sharp, long whistle the trapper pierced the silence. As Ombre twisted his finger in his ear, trying to get rid of the high-pitched ringing now playing havoc with his sense of direction, an old basset hound trotted through the trees, then howled and lay next to its master.

"Thars Garfunk's boy." The trapper patted the dog's head. "Just a smidgen nap, I promise," he said to Ombre.

"Garfunk!" The ringing in Ombre's ear had finally stopped. He lowered his sword, backed up to the tree, and kicked the trapper in his leg.

"Yow!" The trapper leapt to his feet. His foot landed on the dog's tail, and it yelped, rolling to its feet as well. Both dog and master looked up at Ombre, neither hurt, but both with wide eyes.

Ombre sighed and shook his head at the man. "Come on." He pointed his blade into the forest. "We've got a lot of ground to cover."

Behind him he heard the trapper muttering as he followed, though with a new note of respect in his tone. "Now thars a feller that'll get *us both* killed. You all right, Boy?"

His dog whined and the trapper seemed to take that as a yes.

"We'll be takin' a nap . . . just not yet. Ombre's got the idea to hunt some serpents. C'mon," he said with vigor, "mustn't disappoint the man."

Hours later, when the trapper started complaining again, Ombre left him and his dog to nap while he proceeded alone. The sunlight fell through the trees in perpendicular rays. It had to be about midday.

He'd left the trapper a good half mile behind. Now he stopped and sat against the rough bark of yet another broad oak. This part of the forest was not as hilly as where he and Ilfedo lived, and the trees were almost exclusively oaks with the occasional exception of a white birch or maple.

The forest was silent. He pulled the head of his wolf's skin over his forehead, cushioning his skull against the unrelentingly hard bark.

He thought back to the other day when Ilfedo had returned to his home without his wife, cradling his child in his arms. Ombre had never seen his friend so broken up. Not even the death of Ilfedo's parents had left a wound as deep as Dantress's loss.

With a twinge of guilt, Ombre remembered struggling with jealousy when Ilfedo returned to the Hemmed Land with his beautiful young bride. Not that he'd wished to deny his friend happiness, but Ilfedo and Dantress's bond prevented him from maintaining the close brotherly relationship he'd had with Ilfedo before.

All had changed for a period of less than a year. Now Ombre wished that he'd willingly sacrificed his adopted brother. How could he not have? Dantress was the most exquisite, delightful creature ever to step foot in their tiny corner of the world. Subterran had been brighter for her presence.

Now she was gone, and he could only imagine the depth of sorrow Ilfedo bore. To have loved so deeply, yet for such a brief time . . .

Ombre rested the hilt of his sword against his chest, the point of it stuck in the grass at his feet.

He couldn't help wondering what Ilfedo was up to at this moment. He chuckled to himself, thinking that once again his friend had the beautiful woman with him. Or, rather, wom*en*.

Why couldn't Ilfedo have sent a couple of them with Ombre? Actually, it seemed odd that Ilfedo had taken them along at all. They were surely going into battle. Then again, all five of the sisters had been armed and seemed to wield their swords with practiced ease.

He'd caught Ilfedo sparring with his wife once, not long after the wedding. Dantress had surprised him with both her agility and her reflexes. In fact, he doubted that he could have bested her in a duel. Ilfedo had done it without too much difficulty, but Ombre . . . no. She'd possessed a mastery of the sword that was inexplicable for one so young and so feminine. Maybe her sisters did as well.

He let the silence of the forest envelop him and closed his eyes. Sometimes when he closed his eyes, his other senses became more alert. Now his ears picked up the faint clopping of hoofs on dry leaves, the sound of running water, and a child's playful laugh.

A child? Curious, he opened his eyes and looked around. Seeing no one, he stood and crept in the direction from which he thought the laughter had come.

Again the child giggled. This time he spotted her, dipping her small feet into a clear stream running through the forest. He couldn't see her face, but she had long red hair and was no more than three feet tall. If he had to venture a guess, he'd say she was so no older than eight.

Nothing seemed remarkable about his discovery until a stallion appeared behind the child and nuzzled her. With a broad grin spreading across her rosy cheeks, the child turned. The stallion lowered its head, letting her run her fingers through its silver mane.

Ombre walked closer, fascinated by what he saw. The animal was magnificent. Never had he seen its equal. Its body rippled with muscle, and it looked at the child with eyes that glinted silver and ocean blue.

The stallion raised its head in Ombre's general direction. The muscles beneath its pale-gray body rippled as it pawed the ground with a silver hoof.

At first Ombre thought he'd been discovered, but a long black, scaled body slid through the forest growth ahead of him. *A Sea Serpent! They* have *come inland!* Before he could react, the stallion charged through the trees. Rising with a scream, it bent its forelegs and struck the serpent's body with its sharp hooves.

The forest around Ombre erupted into chaos as the injured serpent's black head rose from behind several bushes. Its white eyes targeted the stallion, its fangs framing its gaping mouth.

With the serpent's blue blood now dripping from the tips of its silver hooves, the stallion reared. It whinnied, wheeling to face its opponent.

The little girl screamed.

Ombre spotted another pair of white eyes rise from the opposite side of the stream. Another Sea Serpent come to join the hunt. It pulled back its head, its open mouth twisted into a snarl.

With his sword gripped in both hands, Ombre leaped over the first serpent. Racing to the stream, he splashed into it just as the second serpent struck. As it brought down its head to strike, he slipped his blade between its fangs, ripping into the roof of its mouth. The sword passed through the serpent's mouth and rose like a horn out its snout.

The serpent's blood ran in blue rivulets down his blade, and Ombre yanked the weapon free. The little girl dashed to him and wrapped her arms around his midriff, screaming in terror. He tried to calm her, but that was difficult to do with the Sea Serpent's monstrous head only a foot away.

Behind him the stallion screamed. It would be a shame if such a fine animal were poisoned by the Sea Serpent, but he dared not look because a third serpent rose from the forest floor.

Its tail whipped through the air, crushing his shoulder and sending him crashing into the water. He rolled to his side to protect the child from the fall, and the pebbles in the shallow stream bruised his arm and side.

As he fell into the stream, he pulled the sword with him. It left a hole in the second serpent's snout.

The serpents hissed as they loosened their jaws and struck at him . . . and the little girl.

Sitting up in the cold stream, he pulled the child out of the way and lifted her to the opposite bank. Rolling onto his shoulder, he evaded the second serpent's attack. The third serpent almost nailed him with its venom-dripping fangs. Ombre climbed to the stream's bank, raised his sword over his head, and brought it down with such force on the serpent's skull that it erupted, spilling its brains all over his hands and arms.

Fighting a revolting stomach, he slashed at the remaining serpent. His blade sliced its jawbone, and he followed through with another cut that left half the creature's mouth hanging useless.

As the creature twisted on the ground, Ombre stood to his feet. Pointing his blade at its head, he waited until it twisted into a convenient position and thrust through its brain. It stopped writhing.

The little girl splashed through the stream and clung to his waist. He rested one hand on her shoulder, his sword in the other as he turned around to find out what had become of the first serpent.

It lay on the ground nearby, the stallion's hooves had left innumerable marks on the vile creature's body so that its blue blood now painted much of the forest floor. But the creature wasn't dead. Gray shadowed its usual white eyes as it stared up at the rearing stallion. Its head, held low to the ground, jerked from side to side.

Suddenly a dog howled from the west, and Garfunk the trapper ran out of the trees from behind the wounded serpent, a long hunting knife in each hand. The serpent, already weakened, slowly twisted toward the new threat.

Garfunk's basset hound bayed from a safe distance while its master stabbed his armament of hunting knives into the serpent's head. When Garfunk backed off and stood with legs set wide apart, he crossed his arms over his burly chest. At least half-a-dozen knife handles crowned the Sea Serpent's head. And it fell moments later.

Ombre lowered his sword, breathed deeply of the cool, moist morning air. The little girl sobbed quietly. Nothing of her face was visible, only her red hair as she smothered herself in his soaked shirt.

He looked down at her, wondering how best to calm her. "You're going to be all right," he said, patting her head.

A soft snort made him look up. A pair of large, round blue eyes returned his gaze. The little girl's stallion protector. A breeze toyed with the stallion's silvery mane. Its eyes swam with the beauty of an ocean, deep and blue. Yet it seemed that strands of silver swam in that ocean, demanding something of him.

But what did the horse want? The child released his waist.

The stallion bent its legs until it crouched to the ground. The little girl grabbed a fistful of its long, silver mane and jumped to its back. It stood, snorted at Ombre again, and galloped away, avoiding the trees with gracefulness and vanishing like a phantom. The only evidence of its existence were the prints of its silver hooves in the dead Sea Serpent's body.

"You know," Garfunk pursed his lips, letting out a shrill whistle of amazement. "I thinks I've seen everythin' . . . but I's never seen a horse like that." His hound trotted up to him, and he sat on the enormous serpent carcass, punched it with his fist. He nodded at Ombre. "That thar was some good swordfightin' you did. You just 'bout killed these things yerself!"

"I'll take that as a compliment." Ombre rubbed his bruised side and looked to the east through the trees. "I think we've covered all the territory around here, that is, us and the other hunting parties. We're not far from the coast now. Are we?"

"I've been trappin' these forests a long time," Garfunk said, rubbing his hand along the serpent's skin as he sat on it. "Garfunk never thought to see one of these things inland." He stretched out on his back, atop the serpent, and closed his eyes. He jabbed his index finger eastward. "You'll find the coast thataway."

Ombre sheathed his sword. "I'll see you around, then." He jumped the stream and waved his hand without bothering to look back. "Thanks for your help."

❈ ❈ ❈

Ilfedo let the tree branches slide across his face as he stepped out of the forest. The air was still, the morning quiet. Dew from the branches moistened his forehead, and he didn't bother to dry it. The moisture felt good, refreshing.

Not a single cloud graced the blue sky. Beginning where the forest ended, the field where he walked rolled east to a distant line of white sand washed by the gentle waves of the Sea of Serpents. That vast body of water, in turn, stretched all the way to the eastern horizon. He imagined that the water beyond the horizon touched undiscovered lands full of green, rolling hills. Places he'd often wondered and dreamed about after his first visit to the coast when a youth.

Off to the side a walled town stood by the sea, and smoke rose straight to the heavens from several of the buildings. Ilfedo glanced over his shoulder. The five sisters emerged from the trees in a row, their dark eyes staring back at him intently, enduing him with extra strength.

Beckoning for them to follow, he set a brisk pace and made his way to the town's west gate. To enter, he ducked under a fallen beam and sidestepped one of the gate's twin doors, which had fallen to the ground. The sisters trooped after him, practically dancing over the rubble.

Inside, hard cobblestones paved the central street leading through the center of the town to its eastern gate. Those doors lay in pieces on the ground, as well, having fallen inward from the wall and onto the street.

The homes and businesses on either side still stood, but the town was silent as a tomb and seemed almost as cold as one, too.

"I want all of these buildings checked. Caritha, Rose'el, and Laura"—Ilfedo pointed to a street leading north—"look in that direction."

Caritha reached into her skirt, through a fold in the outer garment, and drew out her rusted sword. The blade glowed with a faint light. She held the weapon in one hand, acknowledged Ilfedo's order with a slow nod, and walked up the north street.

Following close behind, Laura drew her sword as well.

Rose'el shook her head, muttering something like, "Here we go again," and followed. She drew her sword, its rust screeching against the sheath.

"What about us?" Levena's eyes searched his face.

Beside her, Evela stood with her hands clasped over her bosom. "Give him time to think. He has dealt with these creatures before . . . surely he knows best what to do now."

"I *have* dealt with these creatures before." Ilfedo reached to his side, slipping his hand over the cool pommel of the sword of the dragon. For a moment he considered leaving the remaining two sisters to watch the main street. But he could hear the crackling of fire in several nearby buildings, their wooden walls feeding the blaze. He'd feel better if he kept his wife's kin in sight.

"Come with me." He forced a smile as he spoke, but it was a weak smile, one borne of necessity and not from his heart. That part of him still ached, trying to cope with the loss of his dearest love.

Casting aside his inner grief, he set off toward the southern end of town. At each building he expected to see a pair of white snake eyes peering around the stone foundation. If he found one of those foul creatures, he would channel his grief into his sword arm . . . and heaven help the serpent that dared stand in his way.

The buildings burned around him as he made his cautious way through the streets. Most of the buildings were single-story structures; some rose a couple floors higher than that. In places, the cobblestones had been stained red with blood not yet dried. But nowhere did he see any bodies.

Turning into a side street leading to the southeastern corner of town, he climbed a pile of rubble, stones mixed with wood. He stood on the rubble and gazed around. Behind him Levena and Evela murmured, "Take care, brother."

Few of the buildings remained intact. Gaping holes had been punched through most—holes large enough for a horse to walk through. Telltale bits of black leathern snake skin ringed each gap and mixed with the rubble. He crouched and extracted a black scale from under a stone.

As he turned it over in his hand, rage built within him. The rough snake skin scraped over his palm. Curling his fingers into a fist, he crunched the scale, paying no heed to the pain it caused as it bit into his hand.

Not bothering to warn the two women with him, he dropped the snake's scale and bolted into the nearest hole. Smoke stung his eyes, roiling around him. Rubble crunched under his feet; flames spread up the stairway and over the floors, threatening to burn him. But he pressed on through the building, past a table broken in half and chairs burning around it. He trampled a burning pair of curtains on his way out the back of that house. The alley led to another serpent-sized hole. He wound through that building and the next and the next.

He stumbled over an anvil in a smaller building, its long roof now smashed by some creature. Picking himself up, he gritted his teeth and skirted the blacksmith's forge. The forge itself appeared undamaged, but the rubble had fallen into the blazing fire. A wall of flames spread from the forge, churned along the wood walls, splashing against what remained of the splintered ceiling.

With a burst of speed, he ran through the flames, reaching the other end of the blacksmith's shop unscathed. The thick wall of wood had also been smashed through by something that had left three-foot-long strands of black-scaled skin hanging across the opening. The strands flapped back and forth as the fire within the building sent waves of heat against them.

Parting the strands of snake skin with his hands, he darted through the wall. He stepped out of the shop into the six-foot-long bed of a wagon. But one of the wheels was missing and the other was ringed with flames, leaving its bed angled sharply toward the street.

He slid down and landed on the street. With cobblestones once again under his feet, he stood in front of a large, four-story building. No fire burned along its walls, no smoke rose from the shakes covering its roof. Unlike the surrounding homes and businesses, it appeared relatively untouched, except that where a set of double doors had marked the entrance before, there was now a hole higher than his head and broader than a rowboat. The double doors lay splintered into large pieces on the stone steps leading up to the building.

"Ilfedo, what's wrong," a timid female voice said from behind him.

Without looking at her, Ilfedo took off his bearskin coat, dropped it onto the ground. "Stay here, my sister," he said, firming his mouth in grim determination.

"But . . . you are not going in . . . *alone?*" Evela's voice rose to a high pitch, and he heard her take an uncertain step forward.

"No!" He turned and set his hand on her shoulder. Behind her Levena rushed to catch up with them.

Evela bit her lower lip, her eyes wide with fear.

The path of ruin led here, to this building. Whatever waited within . . . he would face alone.

"Do not fear." He would risk no life except his own on this venture into the jaws of death. "I must do this alone." He let go of her shoulder and resolutely faced the hole in the building. The morning sunlight streamed from behind him through the billowing clouds of smoke but did not illuminate the building's interior. The fires heated the air so that it felt as warm as a clammy summer day.

Up the steps he went. Sweat beaded on his forehead. Not only was the air extra warm, but knowing what he was hunting brought to mind his close encounter with death that first time he'd faced the Sea Serpents.

His fingers inadvertently reached under his loose shirt to his right shoulder. He ran his fingertips over the parallel scars embedded there. A reminder of just how close the Sea Serpent had come to killing him the last time he'd faced its kind.

While waiting for his eyes to adjust to the darkness of the building's interior, he stood still in the deathly silent room, trying not to make a sound even though the dust begged him to sneeze.

At last his eyes adjusted to the dimness. A carved wood pillar twisted from the floor to the ceiling a dozen feet above his head, supporting an impressive arch upholding the story above.

Three portraits hung on the dark, stained walls. Judging by the fine apparel and aristocratic poise of the subjects, he guessed they were the town's mayor and other political leaders.

He peered into the gloom toward the middle of the room. Uncoiling beside an enormous stone fireplace against the back wall were six forty-foot serpents. Their eyes were closed, else he would have seen their whites. Their bloated bodies undulated in an unnatural way devoid of rhythm. Bumps appeared as if from inside. Ilfedo knew, beyond a doubt, that some of the townspeople were suffering a frightening death, drowning in the snakes' bellies.

He reached down to the sword at his side. This day, he would spill their blue blood over the place of their feast! "Rise, you devils! And let us have at it!"

The serpents roused, their wedge-shaped heads lazily rising from their tangled mass. Their white eyes startled open, fixing him with haunted gazes. Their tails twitched as they attempted to move their burdened bodies.

Ilfedo reached to his side and grasped the two-handed grip of the sword of the dragon. He drew it from its scabbard as easily as if it had been oiled and with both hands held the blade, pointing it toward the ceiling. The flames within the shiny metal spread out, twisting to entwine it.

The flames spread from the sword, up his arms and over his body. His muscles grew taut and his shoulders squared with extra strength. As quickly as the flames covered him, they now receded, returning into the blade but leaving him adorned with armor of white light. Indeed, flames danced inside the armor that replaced his former clothing as if telling of a realm beyond his reach. He stepped into the heart of the room, his armor flexing with his movements with such ease that he could have forgotten it was there.

His awareness of the room around him, around the armor, deepened as if it were an extension of his senses. The sword and his armor lit every dark corner.

The serpents locked their eyes on him. Their forked tongues twisted out from between their fangs.

Before they could advance or retreat, Ilfedo fell upon them. He thrust his flaming blade into three of the serpents' brains and slit the next one across its throat. The sword in his hand cut through the snakes as if they had been made of cheese.

As Ilfedo raised his sword to strike the remaining Sea Serpents, they regurgitated their prey. Coughing and choking on their own bile and that of the serpents, a dozen men, women and children sprawled across the floor. Some got up on their hands and knees to escape the filthiness around them.

A few victims remained prostrate in the puddles of brightly colored liquids that reeked like rotting animal corpses. Ilfedo clenched his jaws, breathing rapidly. His fists wrung the handle of his sword even as his eyes looked away from the survivors and burned into the serpents.

Rid of their burdens, the remaining serpents snapped their jaws at one another, untangling from one another and sliding across the floor, to face him with their ghost-white eyes.

"Come, you vermin!" Ilfedo yelled as he started forward, swinging his sword wide. "Face me! Fight! I would have it no other way!"

The serpents drew back their heads out of his reach. Their mouths hissed open, their fangs shining white, drops of venom forming on the tips.

In that moment, as the creatures rose in all their hideous strength, Ilfedo wished the flames burning in the sword of the dragon would reach out, burn into the creatures. An impossible feat, but somehow it now seemed viable.

As the serpents prepared to strike, he took a couple steps backward and pointed the blade's tip directly at the creatures' white eyes. Flames emerged from the weapon, forming a torrent of twisting yellow and red tongues that gathered strength and threw themselves through the air.

Ilfedo felt his will merge with the sword as if he were in its blade. He gathered the sword's power as if from an unfathomably deep well and threw it—threw himself, his strength, his wrath—against his opponents. His mind felt connected not only with his body but with the sword as well, enabling him to step to the side as one of the serpents avoided the shooting flames and snapped at him.

The other serpent fell, smoke curling off its head.

When the last serpent attacked him again, its fangs scraped across his shoulder guard but did not pierce his armor. The scraping of the fangs across his shoulder guard sounded like music to his ears. He held onto the sword with one hand and dug his armored fist into the serpent's eye with the other.

A scream tore from the serpent's throat, a sound halfway between an elephant's roar and a Nuvitor's cry. It pulled away from him, shaking its head, trying to reacquire its target with its uninjured eye.

Again gripping his sword with both hands, Ilfedo approached the creature and swung. The blade cut through the serpent's scales and burst its veins. Blue blood painted the walls, spraying the survivors. The blood struck his armor and steamed off it, leaving it as clean as when the dragon first gave it to him.

Around him the survivors stood to their feet. They gazed upon him with eyes wide and mouths agape.

"Who are you, *warrior*?" one man asked. The others gathered around Ilfedo while a few lingered to look at the bodies of those who had been less fortunate.

"I am no one of consequence." Ilfedo sheathed his sword. The living fire retreated off his body, returning to the sword. He tried to walk toward the door, wishing to get away from the admiring gazes directed his way.

"Wait!" one man said. He stood in Ilfedo's way and swallowed hard. "It's you again. Isn't it?"

"It's who?" the bearded man asked. "For the sake of all that is just, man, who is this?"

"Ilfedo! Ilfedo Mathaliah, the Sea Serpent slayer! I saw you." The man pointed at Ilfedo. "I saw you at The Wooden Mug . . . it was *you*."

Suddenly five figures filed into the room, brandishing glowing orange-red blades. The sisters, led by Caritha, faced the group.

Their sudden appearance imposed confusion on the survivors, enough confusion to let Ilfedo walk toward the doors unhindered. But before leaving he turned to the survivors with the sisters flanking him on both sides.

"Our land cannot continue in this way without falling prey to the world around it," he said. "Something must be done and, if no one else will strengthen us, then I will."

Uncomfortable nods followed his words as the bedraggled townspeople looked from the sisters to him and back. But the man who had first addressed him stepped forward, his face solemn. "Your reputation precedes you, Ilfedo. By killing the Sea Serpents you proved yourself brave and cunning. And in not asking much of the people whose lives you saved, you proved yourself wise." He dropped to the floor on one knee, head bowed. "Ages ago, as you know, our people followed a Lord, a warrior superior to all and envied by none. It is time for us to do the same and follow you as Lord Warrior."

Each of the survivors knelt before him, pledging themselves to him. The floor seemed to spin and Ilfedo stepped back. Him, a new Lord Warrior?

The five sisters did not bow, yet they watched him as he nodded to the people. It made sense. A Lord Warrior was needed, and no one else could fill that role. Only a short time ago he'd have thought this impossible. Now these people knelt before him, and he reached out, embraced the idea.

He did wish it. For the sake of his daughter and all children within the Hemmed Land's borders growing up with the knowledge that the Sea Serpents and many other creatures might, at any time, encroach upon their heritage and possibly take their lives.

He looked at the sword sheathed at his side. It offered him a chance to become a greater warrior than ever the Hemmed Land had seen. This weapon was the key to his future.

Except he no longer had a future, not without Dantress. His heart rent within him as he recalled the face of his beloved wife. So young, so beautiful, when she was torn from him. His future had died with her.

*No,* he cursed himself. He had loved completely, without reservation, and it had cost him his joy. Maybe he didn't have a future, but he did have the responsibility to build one for his child. Oganna was all he had that mattered. He would build a hedge of protection around her that nothing could penetrate.

He addressed the townspeople. "If you will follow me, then remain here and wait for my return. The Sea Serpents must be forced back into the sea from which they came, and I intend to make certain they never return.

"Your town is in shambles. Go! Put out the fires, clean your streets, tend to your wounded, and bury your dead. I will return."

Without looking back he exited the building. On the ground near the steps lay his bearskin coat. He left it there, left it in the dust. Behind him the sisters kept pace, their swords still drawn.

Ilfedo headed south, out of town. The fresh sea breezes cleaned the smoke from his lungs. The clear blue sky tempted his eyes upward, but he ignored it. His gaze searched the fields along the coast, looking for signs of other serpents.

Once, he ventured to look back at the town, now receding into the distance. Only scant wisps of smoke wavered above the buildings, a good sign that the townspeople were following his instructions.

He sighed. By accepting the title of Lord he had allowed himself to become an icon, a hero to the people. This would change his life forever. No longer would he be able to hide out in the wilderness. His name would be known, the tales of his deeds told, his prominence assured.

Ahead lay a life far different from that which he'd come to love. But sometimes change—even this sort of change, destructive as it seemed to him—was necessary.

Leading the five sisters along the coast, he pressed southward in search of other Sea Serpents.

⚭ ⚭ ⚭

A gust of wind struck Seivar, and he angled his white-feathered wings to take advantage of the updraft. The air carried him a little higher, just enough to skim the top of a high oak tree poking above the forest.

Beside him and a little behind, Hasselpatch followed suit, gliding effortlessly in his wake.

Both of them searched the forest, their silver eyes darting about, sharp vision piercing the forest ceiling to scan for signs of Sea Serpents. Not many hours before they had found Honer and Ganning leading a party of hunters.

Hasselpatch had spotted a Sea Serpent slipping through the trees toward the hunters. She angled her wings for a swift descent, reversing her direction and returning in time to warn Honer and Ganning.

Forewarned, the men spread out and surprised the serpent, falling upon it from all sides and efficiently dispatching it.

Since that incident neither of the birds had seen anything of consequence.

Seivar glanced back at his mate. "Master must have reached the coast by now." He noted with pride how the sunlight glinted off Hasselpatch's hooked beak. No Nuvitor rivaled his mate's graceful form and, though they had not spent much time in the company of their kind, he had noticed envy in the eyes of many Nuvitor males they'd encountered in the Hemmed Land forests.

Snapping her beak at him, Hasselpatch twisted in the air, unabashedly flirting with him. For that he admired her all the more.

But as he twisted in the air to return her play, a wedge-shaped, black-scaled head penetrated the forest's ceiling. A Sea Serpent closed its white eyes and opened its jaws to intercept Seivar's mate.

With a screech of terror and anger, Seivar pulled himself with natural fluidity through the air. He dove for the serpent's closed eyelids, ripped into them with his talons and pulled them apart. The big round, white eye of the serpent lay exposed for that moment. And he opened his silver beak as wide as possible, stabbing deep into the rubbery ball.

The Sea Serpent recoiled from his attack, dropping through the tree, uncoiling from its branches as it fell.

Tightening his bite, Seivar yanked out the apple-sized eyeball and flapped his wings, using them to carry himself back above the forest. After flying a victorious circle around his mate, making certain she saw the prize he'd obtained in her honor, he dropped it into the forest and dove back in.

It was his intention to take the serpent's remaining eye, but the serpent was thrashing about, knocking into tree trunks. The commotion had brought several men armed with spears and axes.

Seivar left them to attend to the creature, shooting through the forest canopy to join Hasselpatch. Her silvery eyes regarded him with soft affection, and he indulged in flying another circle around her before leading her eastward.

The forest passed easily beneath them. Not much farther and the birds saw the end of the forest. The harvested cornfields stretched to the white shore of the Sea of Serpents and the town lying in their midst. Smoke rose from the town, the buildings crumbling, burning.

Black, shiny forms slipped through the streets, crashing into the buildings with their tails. Other serpents slid from the forest, first a few, then more. They cornered a group of perhaps fifty people, huddled together in the fields.

The serpents in the town left their destructiveness in order to join the newcomers.

Seivar angled to the left, Hasselpatch flying above him. He watched the line of trees as the mighty sea creatures slithered out in great numbers. He stopped counting at sixty.

He had to find Ilfedo and warn him.

Sensing his urgency, Hasselpatch extended her wings with greater speed and followed him high above the gathering, coiling

mass of serpents. They cut through the air, their talons curled to
their bodies, their white feathers smoothed back.

In the distance, northward along the shore, six human figures approached. A tight cluster of smoking buildings lay behind
them.

&#x2672;  &#x2672;  &#x2672;

The line of white sand bordering the Sea of Serpents brought
Ilfedo and the sisters within sight of a walled town.

Evela stepped up beside Ilfedo as he surveyed the weathered,
wooden buildings and the fields surrounding them. "Is something wrong?"

He looked down into her dark eyes. She gazed back with
humble honesty, as if seeing through his flesh and into his soul.

"They're here, my sisters." He generalized his statement on
purpose, uncomfortable with Evela's proximity. There was something about her that most reminded him of Dantress.

"Good," Rose'el retorted, "it's about time. Now, this time,
you're not taking them on alone."

"Agreed." Caritha set a hand on her shoulder, but rebuked
her with a glance. She directed her attention to Ilfedo. "But we
will follow your lead, Ilfedo."

Laura and Levena nodded. Evela stepped back and stood
ready with her sword pointed at the ground.

Surveying the town up ahead, Ilfedo recognized the wall
surrounding it. No high buildings poked above the barrier. This
was the place where he first faced the Sea Serpents. Here, where
it began, he would end it. Smoke curled up from some place near
the wall. A dark mass appeared. *Serpents.*

"If you are coming with me, my sisters"—he drew the sword
of the dragon and let the living fire cover his body, clothing him

in the armor of fire that glowed with white light—"then stay close." He fastened his gaze on each of them in turn, raised his sword aloft. "As long as you stay with me you will be safe." He glanced at Evela. "I promise."

An eagle-like screech caught his ear. He looked up and smiled as his faithful Nuvitors dove from the sky, flapping their wings to slow their descent and land on his shoulders.

"Master," Seivar snapped his beak, "the serpents are gathering prisoners."

Hasselpatch fluffed her feathers. Her silvery eye regarded the sisters.

"How many?" Ilfedo asked.

Seivar cocked his head, his eye rolling as he considered. "Almost a hundred, Master. At least."

"You've done well, my friends," Ilfedo stroked Seivar's chest and then Hasselpatch's. "Now . . . I want both of you to go to the forest and wait until the fight is over."

"Master!" Seivar protested.

But Hasselpatch reacted by flying off of Ilfedo's shoulder and circling his head. "We will not leave you, Master." Then, in evident rebellion, she landed on a startled Rose'el's shoulder.

The tallest sister cautiously stroked the bird's chest.

Ilfedo knew the Nuvitor too well to try and change its mind. With a resigned sigh, he faced the town and walked toward it. The five sisters flanked him on both sides, their expressions hardened, their hands tightening around the leathern grips of their rusted swords.

Rose'el's mouth froze in a frown and she glanced at Hasselpatch. The Nuvitor remained perched on her shoulder.

Pushing the sisters and the birds from his mind and focusing on the fight ahead, Ilfedo put on a burst of speed to reach the serpents first. He could see their forty-foot lengths gathered a quarter of a mile from his position. The first of the serpents' prisoners was plucked from their midst as he approached, tossed into the air by one of the vile creatures. Ilfedo's heart flamed within his chest as the helpless individual was ripped in two by a pair of serpents that raised their heads, one grabbing the legs and the other taking the torso.

Like a living firebrand, Ilfedo rushed upon the Sea Serpents. Seivar launched from his shoulder, pecking out the eyes of the first serpent to turn and face him.

"Come on!" Ilfedo screamed, laying about him with the sword of the dragon. "Face a real challenge! Face me and die, you cowards!" His blade opened the blubbery forms with ease, spilling blue serpent blood on the ground.

Standing back as the serpents turned to face him, he pointed his sword's blade at them and willed destruction upon them. Five of the creatures fell immediately beneath a torrent of fire thrown from the sword's blade.

Uniting with his blade in a mental bond, he half-closed his eyes, sensing rather than seeing his opponents around him. The serpents lashed out with their fangs and swung with their tails, stabbing at him. But he evaded them, ducking under their blows.

Three of the creatures slithered around him, working together against him. Their numbers were overwhelming. A few of them would have been difficult enough; now he felt a hundred pairs of white eyes focusing on him.

The townspeople in the serpents' midst ran for freedom. Some were killed by the massive bodies thrashing around and over them.

Ilfedo's blade sank into the serpents' bodies again and again, ending their vile existences as fast as his sword arm could move.

A tail slapped into his back, throwing him to the ground. He rolled, landed kneeling, and pointed his weapon at the attacker. His fingers clamped harder around his sword handle as fire shot from its blade and raged through the air, felling the serpent into a crumpled heap.

Some of the serpents slithered after the fleeing people. Their fangs stabbed downward, impaling over half of the group's number. Men, women, and children screamed. They fell to the ground, twitching horribly as the serpents' venom spread through their bodies.

The five sisters screamed and one by one knelt on the ground. Tears poured down Evela's face and shone in Laura's and Levena's eyes. A dozen sea serpents rose around them with fangs exposed, drawing their heads back to strike.

Even Rose'el dropped her sword to hold a little girl who'd been poisoned. Her eyes brimmed with tears. Caritha's face riveted on the bodies before her.

"My sisters, what are you doing?" Ilfedo stabbed another serpent between its white eyes, swung the sword in a long arc, slitting open three more serpents' throats.

As the serpents' bodies slumped around him, he leaped over them and ran to the ring of serpents preparing to strike Dantress's sisters. He landed in the sisters' midst, loped off a nearby serpent's head and sent flames from the blade into several others.

"Seivar, Hasselpatch," he yelled at the top of his lungs as his faithful companions flew at the serpents, "go for help! There's nothing you can do here!"

Tearing out a serpent's eye, Seivar screamed into the air and shot away. His mate set off in the opposite direction. Ilfedo knew that the birds would split up to cover as much territory as possible and bring whatever aid they could. In the meantime? In the meantime he was alone with five weeping women whose help he had been counting on.

"My sisters, rise!" He glanced at Evela, her shoulders quaking.

In that instant one of the serpents lashed out with its tail. The blow took him by surprise, sprawling him on the ground. The sword fell from his grasp and the armor vanished, leaving him unprotected.

Hissing with new confidence, the Sea Serpents lashed out at him. One of their fangs reopened his old shoulder wound, and he felt the venom swell his limbs.

Looking around for his sword, he spotted it not a dozen feet from his position.

One serpent's eyes followed his gaze. It rested its tail over the sword and opened its mouth in what resembled a sneer. Its fangs glinted with venom as sunlight struck them.

"No you don't." Ilfedo rushed sluggishly forward, clasped his hands together and used them like a club, striking the serpent's nostrils.

The serpent snapped at him, but he dropped to the ground in a roll. He forced his arm under the serpent's tail, cutting his skin on the rough scales in the process. His fingers touched metal and closed around the vine-wrapped handle of his sword.

The metal blade rang as he drew it from under the serpent's scales. The flames leapt up, engulfed him, and clothed him in the armor of living fire. Immediately his wounds staunched. The poison seemed to surrender to the energy the sword sent through his body, warming him, renewing him.

He poised his blade point up, and drove it through the serpent's lower jaw, aiming for the creature's brain. It dropped to the ground. The blade of his sword slid from the serpent's head, dripping blue blood.

Flames roiled around the blade as he gripped it with both hands. The smell of death filled his nostrils.

The serpents pulled back, stunned by his sudden victory.

"My sisters," he said again, this time shaking Caritha's shoulder, "now is not the time for this! I need your help. Now rise and fight!"

# DEMISE OF THE
# SERPENT KING

Caritha heard Ilfedo pleading with her and her sisters to rise and aid him against the Sea Serpents, and she wanted to, but never had she been thus surrounded by death and suffering. If only Dantress were here, she would have known how to draw the venom from the victims' bodies. But Dantress was gone. Dead.

The strongest among the sisters had fallen prey to an early death. What was worse was the fact that Dantress had *allowed* it to happen.

*No.* Caritha stopped herself. Her younger sister had done the right thing. Just looking at the innocent child she'd brought into the world proved that. If Dantress were here, she would rise, the sword of Xavion in her hand, and fight alongside Ilfedo. If she were here, she would tell Caritha and the other sisters to do the same.

The time to mourn was not now.

Summoning all her strength, rising from among the dead and dying, Caritha raised her rusted sword. She deafened her ears to the pleas of those around her, turned her eyes away from the suffering, stepped over the bodies of the dead women, children, and men. And she drew upon the power in her dragon blood until she felt it turning her sorrow into anger to fuel her for the battle.

Around her rose her sisters. They stood with her and she felt their anger, their lust for justice, their cold determination as they turned their dark eyes to the serpents' white ones.

Ilfedo was having difficulty fending off all of the beasts on his own, despite his skillful maneuvering and use of the sword's flame-casting ability. He met two serpents head-on, grappling with them in a strange wrestling match. His blade stabbed through one side of a serpent's head and emerged out of the opposite eye. Fire shot from the exposed sword tip, turning the other serpent's neck into a pillar of flames.

Wordlessly, the sisters advanced toward the serpents, slowly, patiently biding their time. Caritha wiped fear from her mind, feeling the strength of her dragon blood combine with that of her sisters.

Five of the massive Sea Serpents moved against the sisters. Their jaws hissed open; their long fangs glistened in the sunlight as they raised their heads a dozen feet in the air.

The sisters formed a close-knit line as a gust of wind flung their long, dark hair across their faces. Caritha ignored the distraction and lowered her sword to point at the serpents. Her sisters copied her movement and touched their blades together with hers. Drops of blood fell from the weapons as blue energy sizzled along the rusted metal. A beam formed and shot toward the approaching serpents.

Severing the heads of the two nearest serpents, the beam continued on, leaving deep gashes in the necks of the other three.

Wide-eyed, a dozen of the creatures' companions slithered backward. But others attacked viciously. The sheer number of them overwhelmed the sisters. Caritha saw Rose'el, Laura, and Levena disappear down serpents' throats. She would have intervened, yet the other serpents crowded around her and Evela.

Without the other three sisters, Caritha and Evela had to fight an impossible battle. Ilfedo frowned as he caught sight of them, but he was too engaged in his own battle with a dozen more of the creatures and wasn't able to come to their aid. At least the creatures' carcasses were piling up around the man faster than they could replenish their numbers.

Not even half of the hundred or so serpents that had first met Ilfedo's attack were still alive. His feet stood in a river of blue blood, lit by the brilliance of his sword and armor.

Caritha stabbed the body of a nearby serpent, but the creature hardly twitched. The blade probably felt like nothing more than a nasty prick.

Its head swung around as if to move away. She lowered her sword, looking about for a next target. The options were vast, the serpents many.

But she had underestimated the wounded serpent. Its body had encircled her, separating her from Evela. She tried to jump as it tightened the coils around her. She was too late. Its body clutched her in a deadly embrace, squeezing until her breath was forced from her lungs in a burning gasp.

Her feet lifted off the ground as the serpent raised her into the air with its coiled tail. Several pairs of big, round white eyes feasted on her as other serpents raised their heads to witness her demise.

Her captor slipped its long, forked tongue out of its mouth. The twin tips of its tongue cooled her neck as they touched her.

She looked down the long, red tongue and found herself gazing with helpless fascination down the serpent's gaping throat.

Beside her, another serpent captured Evela and hung her upside down from its tail. The youngest sister struck at the creature with her sword until it managed to pin her arms to her sides. "Let go of me!" Evela yelled before the serpent tightened its grip.

Caritha struggled for air. If she didn't breathe she would black out.

One of the Sea Serpents rose beside her and opened its mouth as if to receive her. Suddenly the scales on the back of its neck rose as if pushed from inside its body, and the rusted point of a sword stabbed through.

The serpent's eyes seemed to pop out of its sockets; its jaw opened as if in pain. But the rusted blade divided the back of its neck with an incision several feet long that laid bare the white vertebrate of its spine.

Rose'el rose out of the serpent's body as it fell. She stood inside the incision and spat. "All right! All right," she growled. "Fine—humph! Take that, Ugly!" She glared at another serpent, lunged for it. "You want a chunk of me, too?"

Almost at the same moment that Rose'el's blade cut into another serpent, two more of the creatures fell dead. Caritha gasped for air. Her captor seemed frozen by Rose'el's actions. Its hold on her relaxed—though only by an inch—and its mouth opened and closed several times. But it was enough for her to catch the air she needed and to see that Laura and Levena had also killed their would-be-slayers.

The group of serpents surrounding them slithered away from the sisters. Caritha counted twenty of them racing for the sea. A mere twenty more now remained to contend with. And these looked at the sisters and tried to avoid Ilfedo's attacks.

He dispensed with two more of them, sent three more scrambling to the water, and launched himself onto Caritha's captor. The sword of the dragon in his hands made mincemeat of the creature, dividing it into several sections before it had time to react.

Caritha breathed deep. She held her sword with both hands and joined her sisters, cutting the serpents at every opportunity.

※　　※　　※

The waves that crashed onto the shore seemed to explode as a wedge-shaped head punched out of the Sea of Serpents. Ilfedo paused in the midst of his battle, catching his breath.

The seawater rolled off of a shiny black body sliding onto the shore, stretching to a length at least twice that of any sea serpent he'd encountered. Great bumps covered its face and its nostrils spouted water from its forehead as its white eyes bulged from the side of its head. The dent in the ground which the creature left behind was so deep a man could stand in it. Yimshi's rays played off the gigantic serpent's white, scaled chest as it forged ahead.

As if responding to their master's domineering entrance, the surviving Sea Serpents stopped their retreat and struck with new energy, trying to bring the sisters down.

Ilfedo was torn between facing the approaching menace and helping his sisters. But if the monster joined its companions, he could only imagine how short the battle would be.

Ilfedo raced across the field. Standing halfway between the sisters' battle and the monster, he quelled his trembling body.

With a head the size of a small house, the Sea Serpent rose before him, its head looking down upon him from the equivalent of a four-story building. Its lips curled up, and its jaws dropped open. Half-a-dozen fangs dripped thick black venom, spotting the ground with puddles of the sticky substance. Each of the monster's fangs was the length of a spear and the thickness of a small tree. Lesser teeth of shark-like quality filled the rest of its mouth.

Ilfedo felt light-headed just looking at the thing.

His fingers tightened around the sword of the dragon, and courage swelled his being. His armor flashed with light as if he were a miniature sun. Flames twisted around his sword's blade, rising to the tip and feeding into the air.

"Back!" he said to the monster. "Go back into the sea where you belong! And take your minions with you!"

The gargantuan serpent lashed out a purplish, forked tongue. It did not touch him or his sword. Its eyes turned lazily in the sisters' direction, and it spat a wad of venom from its mouth. The venom struck Evela's face and upper torso. Her hands clawed at the venom, trying to wipe it off in order to breathe.

With a snap of its massive jaws that sounded like a small clap of thunder, the monstrous serpent looked back at Ilfedo as if waiting to see how he would react to the unexpected assault.

Racing to Evela, Ilfedo touched his sword's blade to her face. Its flames baked the venom into a crust. He dug his fingers into it, breaking it from her mouth. She held onto his arm, coughing. Prying off what remained of the venom, he gently pulled her hands from his arm, noting that her lips bled where he'd torn away the dried venom.

Turning, he strode back to the enormous serpent. "You will return to the sea,"—he let flames shoot higher from his blade— "and there you will remain . . . or I *will* hunt your species to extinction."

"Hard words, thou brave warrior." The serpent ended with a hiss.

Ilfedo gazed into the malevolent white eyes. *It can talk?* He lowered his blade a few inches and took a step backward.

"Before thy kind roamed this land, warrior, *I* dwelt in this sea. Before thy ancestors laid claim to this soil, *I* ruled it." The serpent's tail lifted into the air and then smashed the ground. Ilfedo set his feet wide to maintain his balance. "Now I have returned and all that herein is, *I* claim to be mine. Even as all in the sea is mine, so is this land.

"Knowest thou not that *I* am King of the Sea Serpents?" Its fangs touched the ground as it lowered its head to gaze into his eyes. "*I* have battled the ancient dreads of Subterran, yes, even the Glorigathans and the Dudans . . . the Water Skeels, also.

"Thou presumest to stand before *me*, little warrior, to do battle with me. But *I* can crush thee as an insect. Go thy way, leave now, and *I* will let thee go. I admire thy initiative, little warrior, but to stand against *me* thou hast neither the strength nor the means."

"But I *am* standing in your way." Ilfedo poised his sword to aim its point at the monster's head. "And for the crimes your minions have committed against my people, *you* will pay with your blood and they with their lives."

"Thou art brave, little warrior, to speak thus against me and mine." The creature hissed, pulling back its head and opening wide its jaws. A blade-like fin unfolded from its head, rising from the tip of its snout and arching back to the base of its skull. It lowered its voice. "I do not leave brave enemies standing. I prefer thy death so that I may never confront thee again."

Ilfedo remained steady as the creature postured for attack. His life was on the line here and the odds seemed . . . towering. But when he considered the possibility of his own death, all he could see was the familiar face of she whom he loved. Death could only bring him back to her. It could only end his heart's ache and bring him to meet the Creator.

No, he had nothing to fear from death. He had nothing to fear from anything. And to die defending those who could not defend themselves was a far better way to leave this mortal existence than to die of old age.

He faced the King of the Sea Serpents and held forth the weapon given to him by the albino dragon. His eye blinked involuntarily as a sunbeam reflected off of the silver band on his finger. The Eternal Band, its flame extinguished. He'd kept it nevertheless. It displayed to the entire world that his heart belonged to someone special. In his eyes it also stated that he would never give his heart to another.

A swath of flames ignited from the blade as the enormous serpent's head rushed upon him. The serpent's white underbelly blackened as the flames struck, but the creature remained unfazed.

Its head burrowed into the ground under his feet, ripping it out from under him, throwing him yards away as the head came up through the soil. The forked, purplish tongue lashed at him, roping his legs together as he fell.

Before he could react, the serpent tossed him like a toy. It whipped him around, smashed him into the ground. He tensed his arms, swung the sword at the monster's tongue. But the purplish thing unwrapped itself from his legs and he sprawled on the ground.

The serpent's tongue returned into its mouth. Sucking in its cheeks, the serpent parted its lips just enough to spit a dark wad at his face.

Ilfedo held his blade in the venom's path. The black liquid fizzled harmlessly against the blade.

The enormous tail snaked toward him from behind. He dropped flat on the ground. The hard tip of the serpent's tail stabbed the air where he had been.

Thrusting his blade upward, he stabbed into the serpent's tail. Blue blood spurted from the wound. Ilfedo immediately sent flames shooting from the sword, burning into the flesh exposed beneath the scales.

A scream escaped the Serpent King. The creature recoiled from Ilfedo, its white eyes wide open. Its blade-fin altered from black to dark red.

"Thy skill *surprises* me, little warrior." The serpent hissed. "Thy manner is reminiscent of the ancient human kings, and the weapon thou bearest is no ordinary sword."

The serpent's tongue slipped from its mouth, wetting its lips. "Perhaps thou wilt prove a worthy challenge for me. Perhaps"— its eyes glinted with anticipation—"*I* will bury thee in a bed of coral beneath the sea instead of feasting upon thee along with the rest of thy people."

"*That* is—not—going—to—happen." Ilfedo dodged the serpent's swinging tail, jumped onto its back and drove his blade up to its hilt in the monster's body.

As blood flowed from the new wound, he grinned. Life was in the blood. His mind merged with the sword's powers, latching on to the life force of the Serpent King, drawing it into the sword. The weapon radiated white energy, burning deeper into the creature's body.

The serpent king screamed rage and fear. It slithered toward the sea as fast as it could move. Holding on to the sword with all his strength, Ilfedo concentrated on stealing the creature's life blood.

He glanced behind him. Several people ran to the sisters' aid, raising swords. Among them were Ombre, Honer, and Ganning. He only wished that someone could have come to *his* aid.

Quickly the others receded into the distance. The gargantuan Sea Serpent splashed into the sea, pulling him with it under the cold waves.

⚗   ⚗   ⚗

Ombre raised his eyebrows as he stood still and watched his friend ride the scaly serpent monster into the Sea of Serpents. The creature's seemingly unending length cut into the waves, immersing Ilfedo. He'd always thought Ilfedo was a bit on the reckless side—but *that* seemed a little carried away.

"What is he doing?" Honer's question came out as an angry yell, and his brow furrowed. "He must be mad!" The sword in his hand dripped blue blood from its blade.

Beside him, Ganning limped toward the sisters battling the remaining Sea Serpents. He didn't say a word, only ran.

Ombre shook his head as he took a final look at the sea into which Ilfedo had disappeared, then started running toward the nearby battle. Ilfedo was beyond his help but these women were not. He overtook Ganning and passed him, making for one of the dozen remaining serpents sneaking around to attack Caritha from behind.

The serpents swung their tails at the sisters. They opened their mouths wide to expose their fangs and attempted to stab each of the young women. The sisters evaded the attacks, and the creatures' fangs sank into the ground instead.

Ombre vaulted the bodies of several lifeless serpents before reaching his intended target. The Sea Serpent must have heard his approach. It snapped its head around to face him, forked tongue tasting the air between its fangs.

Taking it head-on, he whaled on it with his blade. The metal first bruised the serpent's snout and then broke through its scales, splitting its head apart. As it fell, he leapt another fallen serpent's body, taking position next to Caritha.

The sister looked at him, acknowledged him with a sober nod. Compared with her sisters, she had thinner eyebrows and longer lashes. Blue blood ran in rivulets down her purple dress. But her dark eyes shifted back to her blood-soaked blade as she brought it around, stepping forward to thrust it into a serpent's wedge-shaped head.

With a gesture, she summoned her sisters to her other side. Rose'el growled as she slit another serpent's throat, came to stand with the others. In unison they lowered their blades, closing their eyes.

Energy shot from the handles, up the blades, joining at the tips. A bolt of blue light streamed from the blades. Ripping through the air with a crack, the light struck three more serpents, burned through their bodies, leaving smoking holes. The serpents closed their white eyes and slumped to the earth.

Ombre looked at them, raising his eyebrows again. First Ilfedo rode a monster into the sea. Now the sisters threw deadly energy from their blades—what he and anyone else in the Hemmed Land would term magic. There was more to these beautiful women than met the eye.

As Ganning and Honer rushed a serpent to his right, the woods seemed to blossom with lines of men. First the rest of their hunting party joined in, then swarms of townsmen armed with whatever tool or weapon they'd been able to find. The people yelled, running forward with eager faces.

The few Sea Serpents that still lived now turned tail, too late.

The people cut them apart with knives and swords, stabbed them with spears and shovels, and pierced them with pitchforks. The battle was soon over.

Everyone gathered around the five sisters, their dark hair flaming red in the afternoon light and their swords glowing rusty-orange.

The weary farmers and townsfolk cheered, screaming out, begging to know who the sisters were. But the sisters ignored the questions and ran toward the sea. The townspeople hushed into stillness, standing and watching.

"Wait!" Ombre ran after them alone. He caught up with them as they reached the white sand, their feet leaving clear imprints. Grabbing Caritha by the arm, he jerked her to a halt.

"Sir, let go of me." Her eyes burned back at his.

The other sisters stopped, staring back at her.

"Okay, first of all," he stated matter of factly. "Don't call me 'sir.' My name is Ombre. Second of all, what in Subterran has gotten into your head?

"If you're thinking of doing what I think you are—"

"I am." She tugged at his arm, pulling from his grasp. "Now let me go."

He held her tighter. "Yeah right!" He forced a laugh. "And what do you think Ilfedo would say if he found I let you go?

"There's nothing you can do underwater. And if Ilfedo regains his senses, he will come back before he drowns. But I am *not* going to let you throw your lives away." He nodded his head at the other sisters, still looking into Caritha's eyes. "They follow you. That is admirable. But *this*—what you plan to do—is foolishness."

She looked at his arm. "Please, my Lord Ombre, let go of me."

Tightening his grip on her arm, he waited for her to return his gaze. When finally her dark eyes met his, she bit her lip. "I will gladly do so, my Lady," he said, "if and *only if* you give me your word that you will stay on dry ground."

She hesitated, glanced at the rolling sea. "We cannot let anything happen to him. We promised to protect him."

"And I am here to protect you." He sighed. "If there was anything that could be done, then I would be the first to go, believe me." He looked at the Sea of Serpents, the water that had swallowed his friend. "Ilfedo is on his own for now. All we can do is pray for his safe return."

Her dark eyes scanned his face, "Then I give you my word—we will stay."

"Thank you," he said in a voice too low for anyone else to hear.

She averted her eyes from his gaze and shifted her feet. "Please, let go of me."

Still holding onto the sword of the dragon, Ilfedo felt the slippery body under him losing energy as his blade leeched off its blood. The instant the monster pulled him under the waves, his head slapped against them as if striking a hammer. The cold Ilfedo could endure, but his head smacking the waves, he could not.

So hard was the blow that the world around him blurred and his conscious mind sank into blackness. He could feel the cold water filling his lungs, the saltiness of it covering his tongue.

Was he going to drown here in the sea with only his adversary privy to his death? Was this the end?

Ilfedo awoke with a green light glaring at him from high above. His chest felt heavy as he rolled onto his side to ease his aching back muscles from the rigidity of the flat stones on which he lay.

He might as well have had a sandbag weighing on his chest, and his body no longer glowed. Thus he deduced his armor was not on him. He could also feel that the sword was no longer in his hand. His fingers touched a moist and blubbery substance covering the right side of his chest.

Blinking to clear his vision, he focused on a tubule connected to his chest. Long and narrow, it compressed and expanded with the regularity of a heart beat.

His vision sharpened. He stood to his feet, or rather was pulled up by the tubule. Its end released its hold, popping off, sloshing liquids all over his chest. It retracted several feet over his head. He followed the movement and spotted a curious being towering above him.

It balanced on long, round legs that bent backward like a chicken's rather than bending forward like a human's. It slapped its frog feet on the circular stones and leaned over him. Its bulbous body was transparent and resembled a jellyfish's hood. But the upper half of its body melded with the chest, arms, and head of a man.

Its angled ears tapered to sharp points. The muscles along its jawbone twitched, strengthening its handsome face. A green light shining from high overhead made its eyes glimmer like smooth pearls. Not a single hair graced its head.

Crossing its arms over its chest, the being bowed its bald head. Its eyes seemed to roll back into its head and the large, white shells that padded its shoulders swayed forward as the tubule retracted into the being's side.

"*Sevat,*" it said through the gill slits covering its mouth. "*Sevat eb Crysallis!*" Spreading its arms wide, it clumsily spun, raising its pearl eyes to peer at the half-shell energy dome that held back the open sea surrounding it.

For the first time, Ilfedo took notice of the tableland on which he stood and the metal arch rising like a giant drafting compass from opposite sides of the circular floor of stones. The legs of the compass dropped over the edge of the round tableland, but from their junction a couple hundred feet above him, a green star burned blinding bright.

Shielding his eyes with his hand, he traced four arcs of green energy from the star to sheer cliffs rising into the darkness far above.

A sliver of light glowed in the darkness. It bent and stretched like a river into the distance. Turning, he watched the river of light as it vanished in the dark distance. It was as if a slice had been carved out of the sky. But it was a sky unfamiliar to him.

Ilfedo's eyes alighted on the ruins of a city rising from the bed of the sea. The buildings looked like grain silos, some larger than others, some low and others exceedingly high. The green light touched the ruins with faint fingertips, illuminating the seaweed filling its deserted streets.

He blinked again to be sure he was seeing things the way they actually were. This place was under the sea . . . at the bottom of it. That river of light must be the light of day—far above him. Somehow he must have fallen through a rift in the ocean floor.

How impossible it seemed. The energy from the star formed an enormous bubble around the tableland. The ocean currents washed against it, and it shimmered, holding them back.

"*Trispal sevat?*" the being spoke again. It let its arms swing at its sides.

"Sorry." Ilfedo gazed into the creature's pearl eyes. When it shuffled its flat feet and waggled its head at him, he breathed out deep. "I don't think we speak the same language."

Shuffling its feet, the being spread its arms wide.

Ilfedo stepped back, and his foot landed on metal. Looking down, he saw his sword. Flooded with relief, he picked it up. The living fire sprang from the blade, braided up his arms and covered his body, in a moment transforming him into a warrior garbed in armor of white light.

The being rising before him did not so much as twitch a muscle in response. It regarded him with its pearl eyes, arms still spread.

With his mind focused on finding a way back to the surface of the sea, Ilfedo hardly noticed that the edges of the tableland were filling with members of the tall being's race. They were swimming through the depths, penetrating the green energy barrier, climbing onto the flat circle of stone rising from the midst of the city ruins.

They had him closed in on all sides.

"Stay back."

"*Poonie*," the first being said through its gills, gently gesturing at its companions and then crossing its arms over its chest.

Ilfedo lowered his sword and pointed cautiously at the being. "Poonie . . . is that what you call yourselves?"

The being shuffled forward, holding out its hand. "*Alartis!*"

Bowing, Ilfedo shook hands with the Poonie. Its pearl eyes dropped gold tears.

"I do hope those are tears of relief." He released the Poonie's hand and gazed around at the other beings standing in silence.

Spreading their arms wide and moving forward on their ungainly legs, their frog-like feet slapping against the stones, their bulbous bodies dripping sea water from their recent swim, the Poonie said in unison: "*Sebat eb Crysallis!*"

*Sebat?* Was that their word for hello? He watched the congregation fix their pearl eyes on the green star hovering above the junction of the compass.

A hand touched his shoulder lightly. He jumped, spun around. But it was only the first Poonie, leaning over him.

It pointed at the city around the tableland, spread its arms wide. "Crysallis!"

"This city?" Ilfedo longed to break the language barrier and understand, but he thought he understood at least one thing. "Crysallis . . . it's the name of this place . . . this city. Your city?"

But the pearl eyes revealed nothing. Gold tears fell from the Poonie's eyes, filling the cracks between the stones on the tableland. Gazing around at the rest of the circular floor, Ilfedo caught his breath, seeing but hardly believing his eyes.

Gold tears flooded the cracks between the stones, falling from the pearl eyes of every Poonie present. The gold ran toward the center of the tableland, collecting around Ilfedo's feet. He felt the tears raise him off of the floor. First his head leveled with the Poonie's eyes, then he rose above them and faster and faster, higher and higher, gold tears surrounding him until he passed into the blinding brilliance of the green star.

The ocean fell upon him, roaring through a gap forming in the shield of energy that had kept it at bay. The sound of weeping filled his ears and he looked down to find the ocean crashing over the Poonie, whose gold tears continued to flow.

He pointed the blade given to him by the dragon, aiming for the ocean. Surely the powers in his sword could save these poor beings. But the star rose through the sea, carrying him with it, and he felt the surface of the Sea of Serpents break around him as he shot into the air, water pouring from his glowing armor.

Around him the green star vanished. Such was the force with which the star threw him that he almost flew through the air, over the water and toward the distant shore.

Before he splashed back into the water, he spotted the monstrous form of the Sea Serpent king, slicing through the waves, returning to land. His trajectory landed him with perfect balance on the creature's massive head.

With all his might he drove the sword of the dragon into the serpent's brain, spewing fire from the blade, cooking the creature from the inside out.

The serpent screamed a horrible sound that sent shock-waves through the water for a dozen yards around its head. It breached the water's surface within a hundred feet of the shore. Ilfedo saw lines of people building rank upon rank on the dry ground.

Ombre was standing closest to the water, his sword drawn, his face taut. Beside him the five sisters drew their swords and charged into the waves, soaking their purple dresses. A sea breeze wrapped their hair around their heads, wild, free.

Struggling to its last breath, the enormous creature shook Ilfedo off of its head. Blue blood dyed the sea.

Ilfedo stood in the shallow water, aimed his blade for the Sea Serpent's neck, and threw it like a spear. The weapon lodged in the targeted spot; the armor of light vanished from Ilfedo's body as soon as the sword left his hand; the monster screamed again.

It spat venom at the sisters. They ducked the flying poison, came within arm's reach of the creature's body, and sank their blades through its scales.

Taking advantage of the creature's divided attention, Ilfedo sloshed through the water. Grabbing hold of the hilt of his sword as it remained stuck in the serpent's neck, he waited for the living fire to garb him. Drawing with all his strength and summoning the powers in the sword, he ripped the blade up the serpent's gullet.

A shower of blue blood rained on him. The serpent's scream was cut short. Its house-sized head bombed into the sea.

Ilfedo held up his blade, and the water stormed past him without so much as touching him. When the sea calmed, he walked ashore. The five sisters stood there, sober despite the victory.

When Ilfedo reached the sand and sheathed his sword, he heard a low rumble of voices and looked up at the crowds of smiling townspeople. They sent up cheers that shivered up his spine. At the sound, the sisters standing beside him turned to look at the crowd.

Joining in with the masses, Ombre first, then Honer and Ganning, raised their voices. Ombre lifted his fists into the air and shook them.

Suddenly the people grew quiet. Whispers raced through their midst. A chant began.

"Hail! Hail Ilfedo, master of all swordsmen! Hail! Hail the women who stand with him! Hail the Lord Warrior and his Warrioresses!"

When the chant ceased the people grew quiet. Then, one by one, with solemn, eager faces, the men knelt on one knee and bowed their heads toward him. The women fell to both knees, heads lowered.

The sky paled to orange, and the dead serpent king washed onto the shore.

Ilfedo cringed as the people bowed to him. Obeisance—he did not want it.

His discomfort changed to horror when, beside him, the five sisters—his Warrioresses—started to bow. And Ombre, with a broad smile, knelt. Honer and Ganning also fell to their knees.

"No, my sisters!" He pulled them to their feet. "Never, I vow, will the blood-kin of my Love kneel before me."

Walking through the sand to his three childhood friends, he pulled them to their feet as well. "You will rise with me, my friends. Together we will build a great nation for our people. With you by my side, only with you by my side, can I do this. Do not kneel to me."

"As you wish," Honer and Ganning replied, standing.

Ombre rose too, dusted the sand from his pants. "Of course, *Lord* Ilfedo." There was no sarcasm in his statement, only a playful congratulation.

Turning to the people, Ilfedo bid them rise. He surveyed the sea of faces, knowing that this was a turning point for the Hemmed Land. Things would never be the same.

He would embrace his new role and use his influence as best he knew how. With a heavy sigh, he prayed to God for guidance, praying also that he would not let this newfound power lift him in pride's ugly hands.

He thought of his child and set his jaw firmly. The Hemmed Land must be made strong to protect Oganna. She was all he had left of Dantress. Her future was all that mattered to him now.

# 4

# AN EPOCH'S BEGINNINGS

The storms of Ilfedo's life had changed him. He felt different. As he marched through the streets of the various towns and settlements in the Hemmed Land, the people's faces brightened and they bowed. The parents whispered to their children, and the elderly nodded to one another in wordless communication.

"Look well at him," one father said to his son as Ilfedo marched by with Ombre and the Warrioresses in tow. "This man will lead our people into an era of prosperity."

"Did he really take on the king of serpents all by himself?" The son's eyes sparkled as he kept his ear inclined toward his father and his gaze upward to Ilfedo. He pointed with his small hand. "Is that the sword people say was given him by a dragon?"

"He is looking at you, my son! Stand straight and smile. One day you will tell your children that this hero noticed you in the crowd today."

The boy stood stiff and grinned.

The next several months mayors and other representatives from all over the Hemmed Land sought Ilfedo out, pledging their support. A few men of evil intent came to him as well, but he saw through their facades, found out their corrupt states, and replaced them with simpler, more honorable men.

By unanimous decision, the inhabitants of the Hemmed Land accepted Ilfedo as the Lord Warrior: a title that had belonged to only one other man in recorded memory.

Scrolls made of skins had been passed from generation to generation—scrolls that gave them precious insights into their heritage, though not enough to solve the mystery of their origins. One man was spoken of in the scrolls, a man who'd held the title of Lord Warrior.

The scrolls made it clear that this role not only carried with it the responsibility of safeguarding the people, but it also gave him who held the position final say in all matters of government. Pertaining to responsibility it did not match the position of a king, as it was commonly understood, for the Lord Warrior was *obligated* to put his life before those of his people. And it was known that he was a man of integrity who would not be swayed by bribes, nor live in the lap of luxury.

Most people considered the majority of the scrolls in which these things were written to be little more than fiction based on threads of fact that were so slight the truth could not be discerned from them. Compounding this belief was the fact that the scrolls had been scribed by a man known only as the Count. His writings were loved by all. However, the vast majority of the Hemmed Land's people laughed aside his fabled travels, in which he always happened to fill a central role in the saving of a civilization, or the mediation of some territorial dispute, or some other such fantastic event.

The Count claimed in his writings that there had been many Lord Warriors. Some, he declared, purportedly built themselves crafts to fly through the sky. At this juncture, people would smile and advise their children that this was nonsense. And they would point out that the Count, having exaggerated the legends of their ancestors to such a gross extent, could not be wholly believed to have been telling the truth.

But the people embraced the idea of having a Lord Warrior. Ilfedo fit the image that every child, parent, and grandparent had pictured a Lord Warrior to be. He was tall, strong, sober, and his battles with the Sea Serpents, his hunt for the man-killing bears, and his duel with the serpent king had made him a living legend.

In Ilfedo they saw hope for the future and a land freed from the fear of monstrous beasts roaming at will.

The Hemmed Land started to change under his leadership. Most thought it was for the better.

He ordered the building of roads to connect the towns and settlements along the shore of the Sea of Serpents. With travel quicker and easier between once-distanced centers of civilized living, the towns grew and the forest settlements cut down the trees in order to expand.

The five sisters had become legends in their own right. Wherever they went they were treated with admiration, honored, but too closely observed for their comfort. Keeping for the most part out of the public eye, they dwelt in the wilderness, caring for their deceased sister's daughter.

❀　❀　❀

The bearded old fisherman and his crew gathering their nets on the shore muttered to one another as impenetrable, misty rain seeped through their tunics. It seemed the gray sky thickened with each sopping minute.

The sky lightened for an instant, or rather it flashed. Young and old faces turned upward, blinking back the water that coursed down their skin. Chilled to the bone and weary after a most unprofitable day, they grunted and renewed their attention to their nets. As they stretched the nets on the shore and examined them for rips, a distant rumble made them stand upright.

He looked out to sea, that old Sea of Serpents, expecting lightning to flash. Instead a dull boom echoed from the east above the frothing waves, and a bright object hurtled through the clouds, large and pulsing.

The fisherman let the slimy net slide through his fingers and fall to the white sand. He narrowed his eyes, inquiring of his neighbors with a glance before looking seaward.

Pulsing white light burned a determined path toward the shore. It descended rapidly. The rain thickened and evaporated into steam around it. At last it touched the tumultuous waves, sending a fresh cloud of steam upward as it buried itself in the sea.

"Meteor," the grizzly-bearded fellow grunted to the others. He returned to his net and began mending a tear.

His friends joined him, picking up the work they'd neglected.

Absorbed in his task, the fisherman let time fly around him. The rain lessened, the clouds thinned, and thinned some more, until moderate sunlight warmed his shoulders. It had to be at least an hour later. "Yimshi's light is burning today," one of the fishermen admitted, glancing at his red shoulders. He rolled his net into his wood boat and jogged into the surf.

"Yeah, 'nuff work for now!" another man said, loosening his tunic and joining the first. "I can use a cool swim."

The remaining fishermen stampeded into the water, grins brightening their tanned faces. The grizzly-bearded fellow laughed as he watched them, but remained by his net. He finished mending the tear and slung one corner of the tri-sided net over the bow of his single-masted fishing vessel. The prow of his boat rested solidly on the white sand while the sea water lapped at the stern. He held the rail and let his knees buckle, hanging on as his weight stretched his stiff back muscles.

Something knocked into his knee, and he glanced down to find a ghostly-white face glaring up at him. "Shivering timbers!" He jumped back. The other fishermen sloshed out of the water and stood in a half-circle behind him. He knelt and waved his hand across the face of the individual before him. The new arrival's eyes seemed frozen open, and his shoulder-length white hair pulsed in sync with the incoming seawater.

"Who is he?"

"How should I know?"

"Would you look at those eyes! I thank God I don't have eyes like that."

"Yeah, would be a bit embarrassing—girlish, even."

"Big fellow, though. *I* wouldn't cross him."

The grizzly-bearded fellow flipped their white-haired guest onto his stomach and pounded his fists into the man's back.

Bile and water spewed from the new arrival's mouth, and he coughed. When he could breathe freely, he rose to his feet and faced the assemblage of humble laborers. His pink—almost white—eyes made him seem soft and childlike, that is, until he spoke in a voice deeper than any present. "My gratitude to you all. You have, perhaps, preserved my life. Tell me now: what part of the world is this?"

The grizzly-bearded fellow stood in front of him. He crossed his arms in front and eyed the white-haired man up and down.

No shirt, only loose-fitting blue-gray pants made of coarse fabric, but around his waist a belt of hammered steel. An assortment of heavy tools hung from it, including an anvil no bigger than a large man's fists, tongs, a long narrow file, and a curious hammer with a wooden handle and shiny silver head. It was a miracle the stranger had washed ashore with those heavy items attached; they should have drowned him in the depths of the sea.

"Before answering your questions"—the grizzly-bearded fisherman held up his forefinger—"how about answering a few of my own?"

For a moment the man's pink eyes flared, then he gently nodded his head.

"Good. What is your name and—"

"I am Linsair, a sword smith. My origin is harmless, though none of your affair, and I speak without guile. So you need not fear me."

The grizzly-bearded fellow unfolded his very large arms and leaned against his vessel. "Smoothly spoken, Linsair the sword smith, but we know not you nor *of* you. And whatever cause would make you hide your origin concerns me. Well, rather, it concerns us?" He paused.

"Yes," his fellow fishermen declared.

"So you see, Linsair, I do not desire to make an enemy of you, and I am not forbidding your entry onto our soil. Ilfedo the Lord Warrior himself welcomes travelers who bear us goodwill. It is part of this process of growing many settlements and towns into a strong nation." He cleared his throat as the other men lent him a short cheer, for he thought he'd handled that phraseology rather fine. Though there was a lack of truth in his statement concerning travelers, for the Hemmed Land, to his knowledge, had not been visited by a foreign human in his generation.

"I am not a suspicious old sea lubber," he said. "But I do find the timing of your arrival a bit strange. Never in our recorded history has a stranger come to us from the Sea of Serpents. Did you fall from the heavens by meteorite?"

"You have deduced correctly." Linsair bowed to the grizzly-bearded man and walked barefooted toward the coastal town with his head held high.

It was a strange encounter by all counts, the fisherman said to his neighbors. Some thought they should stop the stranger and moved as if to follow. The grizzly-bearded fisherman held them back. "Let him go where he will. He seemed to be an honest fellow, even if a bit water-logged—'fallen in a meteorite,' indeed preposterous! And yet he may prove useful to the Lord Warrior."

⚜   ⚜   ⚜

Linsair left the shore in peace and, arriving in town, found the sign of The Wooden Mug. He tried to blend in with the townsfolk. But two men who had too much to drink harassed the proprietor. Linsair bade them go home and consider God's ways. "Are they not the chief of all ways?" he asked them. "He gave you breath and life. Should we not honor such a glorious master?"

One of the men hiccupped. "Look, Smithy, you're in the wrong part of town." He took another swig from his mug and put it back on the table, gazing into Linsair's pinkish eyes. "Take your preaching to Brother Hersis where it'll be appreciated."

Linsair overturned the table and growled with such force that he might as well have been a creature, not a man. The inn quieted around him as he strode to the door and onto the cobble-stone street.

⊗   ⊗   ⊗

On the Hemmed Land's northern border, Ilfedo camped his makeshift army of five hundred men in the shade of the trees. He spread them thin so as to cover as much territory as possible. If the sorcerer and his minions returned through the desert tonight, the warriors would meet them.

As evening fell he stood between a pair of sturdy trees, stabbing his gaze northward into the stone-strewn desert. Some kind of creature had been reported to come from that desert. In three separate incidents, it had slain three men and two children dwelling along this stretch of the Hemmed Land's border. All attacks had reportedly occurred in the dead of night.

The wind howled over the desert and whistled into the forest. Ilfedo fingered the hilt of the sword of the dragon. People in his territory had taken to calling it the Sword of Ilfedo. But for him it remained the Sword of the Dragon.

He wondered how well his baby had fallen asleep tonight. So delicate, so precious; someday this land would fall to her as an inheritance. She was already commonly called Princess. He did not doubt that, with her mother's dragon blood flowing through her veins, his daughter could become a great ruler. But what of her character? Power should not be lightly handed to a youth. The Warrioresses would not spoil her. He felt certain of that. They would keep her safe, too.

"Dantress, why oh why? If you were here now our child would grow in your footsteps. Play with your skirt, learn from your voice, and smile at your love. Oh, I want that. I want that more than anything."

Someone's sword clinked against a nearby tree, and Ilfedo retreated into a deeper shadow. No one must see him like this. He would show himself strong at all times for his departed wife.

She had sacrificed herself so their child could grow. How could he let his people perceive his still-grieving heart and expect them to focus on a bright future?

A breeze bent the short stalks of grass on the forest floor. He could see for a couple of miles through the trees as long as he kept his gaze near the desert where the trees thinned. First one of his shadowed warriors stepped toward the dry, stone-strewn landscape then another beyond him and five a dozen yards farther. Soon a substantial force marched in a line from the forest. Even in the darkness Ilfedo could see that they all kept their faces toward the desert and their hands on the hilts of their swords.

None of this would be happening if his life had followed a different course. If Dantress were still alive . . . things would be different. He sighed and leaned his shoulder against a nearby oak tree. The hard bark released some of the tension in his muscles. Every day her death returned to his heart as potent as that fateful morning.

"Release me from this world, dear God," he whispered through the shadows. "I want my heavenly rest in her bosom."

"Your time is not yet, my love." Dantress's voice wafted so gently into his mind that he almost believed she was really there, standing beside him in the tree's deepening shadows. "You and you alone must protect our offspring. She is the hope of your people. Stay for the fruit of my womb to blossom." The voice faded.

"If only you were here, Dantress. If only." Ilfedo turned toward the heart of the forest and walked into the darkness. A fleeting shadow of a woman slipped deeper into the woods and vanished. He froze, wondering for a moment if somehow Dantress had really spoken to him. The darkened floor of the forest offered him no reply. A breeze rustled the leaves; an owl hooted above him. Ilfedo shook his head and skirted behind the treeline, checking on the warriors as they waited in the shadows.

A long while later, Ilfedo stood again looking out over the desert. A cloudless sky allowed the starlight to illuminate the rock-strewn sand. Nothing had come from the desert so far as he could tell . . . and nothing indicated anything would come. The sands remained settled on the cool desert floor. The rocks seemed frozen in its midst.

A swordsman crept toward him, twisting to glance at the desert. Another warrior knelt behind a bush and rested his longbow on the ground, peering through the trees at the barren landscape.

Slowly he walked to the edge of the forest. He stood gazing across the desert for a few minutes more, then he strode along the tree line.

Four of his armor-clad men emerged from the trees ahead of him and fell in alongside him. "My Lord, we have seen nothing."

"Remain at your posts until I give you leave." Ilfedo waved them back and issued the same command, as every fifty feet he came upon another group of men. He glanced over his shoulder as the soldiers obediently shrank back into the forest. They would await his command, as they always did.

Facing west, he made his way up a steep incline to a thick group of trees. Behind them the ground descended gradually into a large valley where a hundred canvas tents dotted the grass. Not a single tree grew in the valley, but a line of oaks ringed its rim, rising like mighty sentries.

From the midst of the camp a group of lightly-armed men rose from around their campfire and wove their way between the tents. As they approached, Ilfedo smiled at their commander. "Ombre."

"How's the first watch coming?" Ombre slapped him on the shoulder. "If you need a better set of eyes on the ground, I'll be more than happy to take your place!"

Ilfedo shook his head. "I want you to rouse Honer and Ganning." He stood at the valley's crest and pointed briefly out over the desert. "If something is out there, I want it found."

"We could continue waiting, Ilfedo. You haven't given it all that much time."

"We could, you're right. But I want whatever is out there, if it *is* out there, found. Rouse however many men you need and start search parties. Just make sure Honer and Ganning are in on it."

"Too bad you didn't bring Seivar." Ombre cleared his throat and grinned. "I told you that bird would be handy out here."

Too bad, indeed, Ilfedo acknowledged to himself. He left the valley, keeping inside the tree line as he made his way back to his post. Once again the men hiding in the shadows acknowledged him as he passed, and he beckoned them to remain in their positions.

He had laid the trap for whatever the inhabitants of this part of his country had encountered. Now, if it came at all, the creature would have to come to him. If not, perhaps the search party would find something.

The next morning, Honer and Ganning reported to Ilfedo that they had braved the desert cold with a hundred men. "There's nothing out there save for lizards and rodents' tracks," Ganning said.

The next evening Ilfedo commanded the watch to continue while he went in search of one of the recent victim's cabins. He found it tucked in the edge of a small meadow. The grass there was peculiar, for its blue stalks glowed. He paused at the meadow's edge to marvel. It was unlike anything he'd ever seen.

He ran his fingers along one of the stalks and found it soft . . . like rabbit fur.

At the far side of the clearing, a single lantern shone from one of five small windows. The place sported a second floor, but the lantern provided the only evidence of habitation.

The grass shimmered around him. It stood up to his waist, and when he looked down, deeper hues were rippling around him. He watched the ripples expand to the edge of the meadow and then headed for the cabin. The grass continued to shimmer in the starlight.

Despite the dampening air, he felt incredibly warm.

The cabin door eased open a crack, and a woman's sharp voice rang out. "Who's there? Tell me now or else I shoot!" A round woman of no mean size slammed the door open the rest of the way. She leveled a crossbow at him.

Ilfedo raised his arms. "There is no need for that, madam! It is your Lord Warrior."

The crossbow clicked as the woman locked her arrow in position. "If you really are who you claim to be, my lord. I need you to stand where you are so you can prove your identity to me."

"Very well, madam." Ilfedo stood still and crossed his arms. "How shall we proceed?"

"I . . . I . . . I hadn't thought about that, my lord." The woman shrugged her shoulders. Two children emerged from behind her, clinging with tiny fists to her skirt. She tightened her tone. "How do I know you are the Lord Warrior? You could be that *thing* come back to take another of my babies. I will not allow it! You will pay for that, you blood-thirsty coward. Murderer!"

Whether she had intended to or not, the woman released her projectile. Ilfedo heard the arrow whoosh through the air. It struck his right shoulder, spinning him around. He gritted his teeth as he fell.

"Curse you, woman," he muttered. "I have a child, too!"

She must have heard him, for as he looked at the shaft of the arrow sticking through his shoulder, she came running. Kneeling down she clasped her hands over her mouth. "I am so sorry! When you said that you, too, have a child, I knew it must be you. Oh, what have I done?"

A screech rent the air, like a woman's cry and an eagle's scream, blended in one. Ilfedo struggle to his feet as the woman barreled through the glowing grass back to her cabin. She screamed, "No!" and tackled a shadowy figure darting toward her door. The children froze as their mother fought the would-be kidnapper.

*The creature!*

Ilfedo's useless right arm hung at his side. When it came to sword play, his left hand was nearly as useless. He left the Sword of the Dragon in its sheath, ignored the pain stabbing across his chest, and ran to the cabin. The glowing grass illuminated the woman as she tangled with a humanoid with feathered wings.

He swung his boot into the side of its head with all his might. The creature screamed. Two more like it leapt from the roof. The impact twisted the arrow inside Ilfedo's shoulder. But hands raised, he faced the creatures, also fighting without weapons. He swung his fist at one creature, then another. Every blow he delivered seemed to bounce off a leather muscle in their bodies.

In a blur of movement, the thickest creature punched at him. He ducked, and his foot struck a rock. With his make-shift weapon, he battered the creatures mercilessly on each of their gaunt manly faces. They fled into the trees. The remaining creature turned from the frenzied mother. Dropping to its hands, it raised its legs and kicked the stone out of his hand. Then it stood and screeched birdlike at the trees.

Four other creatures glided from the branches and landed in the meadow behind Ilfedo. He regarded them wearily. He had lost a lot of blood in his wounded shoulder, and his arm had lost its strength again.

The big woman stumbled into her cabin and closed the door. Now the only light that remained for him to see by emanated from the blue grass.

His vision wavered in and out of darkness and then he collapsed. Again the grass seemed to warm him. The creatures cackled, and one of them walked up to the cabin and leapt through a window. Glass rained around Ilfedo. The woman and the children screamed.

"I won't let this happen!" Ilfedo's left hand found the hilt of his sword, and he struggled to draw his weapon. One of the creatures—men, it would seem—held him back and yanked the sword from his grasp.

It screeched and smiled at its fellows. They cackled and pinned Ilfedo to the ground.

Raising the sword, the creature stabbed it at Ilfedo's heart. Living fire sprouted from the blade. The hilt ripped itself out of the creature's hand, twisting as it did so to cut off a couple of fingers. The blade hovered in the air and angled at the creature, blazing with glorious light. Ilfedo felt a surge of victory.

The creature spread its wings and raced into the trees. Just as it seemed to have escaped, the Sword of the Dragon speared through the air and pierced its back. Its light illuminated the scene in the midst of the dark trees. The living fire engulfed the creature from head to toe, burning the body to ashes that rained on the dry leaves and formed a heap.

The sword floated over the remains and stabbed itself into the midst of the ashes. A voice spoke from its blade. "As spoken by his holy prophet, I am living fire. From the hand of God I came and if ever used for evil I will, of my own accord, turn upon the wicked one."

The remaining winged men stumbled over each other as they fled into the forest.

Ilfedo could hear the woman inside the cabin fighting for her life with the one who had crashed through the window. But he could not find the strength to move. "I am coming home to you, my love!" he cried to the starry sky.

"Not so soon, my friend!" Ombre crashed out of the woods and stood over him. A contingent of soldiers swept into the cabin.

The winged man stumbled out of the window. A couple of his fellows swooped in and carried him into the darkness.

Ilfedo lost consciousness.

Ombre darted to the heap of ashes, wrapped his fingers around the cold blade of the Sword of the Dragon and carefully pulled it out of the dirt. He waited, half-expecting the frightening weapon to blaze anew with fire. But it did not. He walked back to Ilfedo, knelt, and placed it in Ilfedo's hand. The Lord Warrior's wounds were beyond a quick fix. But Ombre had seen the sword destroy an enemy by its own power and of its own accord. Surely this mighty gift, if it truly came from a prophet of God, could help his friend.

Light radiated from the sword, and the grass in its immediate vicinity died. The arrow protruding from Ilfedo's shoulder burst into flames and vanished. Blinding light sprouted from the blade in tendrils that latched onto the man's wounds.

Ombre stepped back and closed his eyes. "God, let him live." Footsteps scuffled beside him. He opened his eyes to find the woman of the cabin with her two children kneeling beside his friend. His helmed men came out the cabin door, lowering their swords. More soldiers darted from the forest, all of them gazing upon the awesome sight as the sword continued to keep Ilfedo alive. They shook their heads and smiled, then fanned out to search the forest for the escapees. Some of them remained and faced the forest with drawn swords. They kept their wary eyes on the trees.

The woman gasped and Ombre followed her wide-eyes to the place where Ilfedo lay. A man stood over him in white robes. The man's countenance exuded purity, and his eyes shone like golden suns. He was fearful to behold, but Ombre could not tear his gaze away. An angel? It must be. But how was this possible?

As they stared at him, the angel smiled down at the woman's frizzy, red-headed children. The innocent creatures had their heads bowed in humble prayer and their tiny hands, though bruised and bloody, they had folded in prayer.

Ombre fell to his knees as the angel put a healing hand on Ilfedo's shoulder and held the Sword of the Dragon in the other. How quickly his quiet life had changed. His best friend had married a wonderful girl, and now it seemed that God himself would let nothing be simple again. First the sword with its tremendous powers arrived, along with the Warrioresses and their almost sad companionship, then the winged men appeared in the Hemmed Land, and now an angel intervened on Ilfedo's behalf. He closed his eyes and thanked the Creator for it all.

When he opened his eyes the angel had gone and the sword was sheathed at Ilfedo's side. Nothing remained of Ilfedo's near fatal encounter apart from his torn clothing. His chest heaved steady and strong.

Ombre stood and smiled down at the boy and girl. They returned his gaze with weary curiosity. "The faith of the young is strongest of all, apparently." He helped the woman to her feet. "You need not worry about those creatures. They will not return. Five hundred men are encamped two miles north of here and another five hundred are combing the woodland. They will be found.

"In the meantime, I suggest you get these little treasures to bed. They well deserve it." He patted the woman's shoulder and summoned four of his men. "You will keep watch here tonight. If the creatures return, sound the alarm. Reinforcements will not be long in coming."

"My Lord Ombre." One of the men cleared his throat. "Our original force is spread too thin to effectively cover the entire border—"

Ombre clapped him on the back. "Yes, but not for long. Lord Ilfedo already sent a courier requesting additional troops. We are going to thoroughly sweep the forests for these creatures until we find them. Also, a fort will be established in the valley along the border. When we are done, this area will be as secure as any in the Hemmed Land."

Ganning limped out of the trees over to Ombre and shook his hand. "I heard what happened. How is he?" He glanced at Ilfedo.

"Fortunate to be alive. You'll not believe it, Ganning, but an angel actually healed him."

Ganning grinned from ear to ear. "Was she a handsome brunette with long wavy hair and eyes the hue of summer clover?"

Ombre shook his head. No matter what he'd say to the contrary, Ganning would never believe him. Perhaps it was his fault for being a jokester in his youth and letting it carry over into adulthood. Why couldn't he always be sober like Ilfedo? People believed Ilfedo and always took him seriously.

"Angels indeed!" Ganning limped over to Ilfedo and shook him out of a deep slumber.

☙ ☙ ☙

Caritha turned her back to the fireplace's warmth and brushed back her hair, opening the door on Ilfedo's house. Cool, damp night air rushed from outside.

"Don't leave that *open*, Caritha!" Rose'el said rather sharply.

Caritha glanced over her shoulder with a knowing smile.

The tall sister pulled a blanket around her body and lowered herself into the hammock. "You . . . you'll wake the baby." She looked at the floor, then pointed at the crib on the hearth next to Evela.

"The baby is fine, Rose'el. And haven't you used that excuse a couple times too many by now." Laura put a dish under the pump, washed it, and handed it off. Leaning against the counter, Levena took the dish and dried it as she whistled a soft tune.

Evela was sitting on the hearth. A contented smile warmed her face as she peered into the short wooden crib. She sighed. "I don't think any baby could be more content or secure than this one feels right now, surrounded by all of us. Rain usually calls for gloominess, but look at her. She sleeps as if there is not a thing in all of Subterran for which she'd stir."

Rose'el rolled her eyes. She often treated these sentimental moments as trivialities. But Caritha laughed, for Rose'el's eyes hesitated upon seeing the head of the bear Ilfedo had killed, hung above the mantle. She humphed disapproval and shook her head.

Caritha slipped outside and eased the door closed. She walked along the stone patio to the newly constructed outdoor fireplace. A scrap of flint lay on top. After throwing in a few scraps of dry wood, she sparked a flame that soon crackled warmly across the logs. An overhang made of skins and canvas kept the rain running away from the patio. Ilfedo had made a few modifications to the house before his departure to the Hemmed Land's boundary with the northern desert.

For an hour or more the fire warmed her while she sat on a bench looking down the grassy clearing. A few bugs fought through the raindrops until the downpour lessened to a drizzle. A rabbit hopped out of the forest to nibble on the grass.

From the tallest tree in sight, Seivar glided to the patio and swooped under its roof, perching before the open fire. "Mistress, mind if I share the fire with you?"

"Of course not. I will be happy for the company. My sisters have been a little distracted of late. The young princess has won their attention more often than I."

Seivar fluffed his feathers and raked his silver talons through them.

Caritha gazed around the remainder of the clearing. "Where is Hasselpatch? I have not seen her today."

Seivar blinked his silvery eyes at her. "Does Mistress desire me to find her?"

"No. No, that will not be necessary." She petted the bird's wet back. "I only wondered."

The rain continued to fall. The clouds thickened, then thinned and thickened again. The rabbit hopped back into the forest.

As the two sat enjoying the warmth of the fire, a curious sound caught Caritha's ear—a distinct cough that could have belonged to a very small person. She glanced about the patio and there, on the lowest step, stood Miverē.

Seivar lunged toward him with beak open, but Caritha caught the bird's tail feathers. "No! This is a friend."

She knelt and held out her hand. Miverē used his silver wand as a cane and teetered into her palm. "Hi," he managed. But his voice sounded hoarse.

"You poor thing. Did you catch a cold?"

In answer the fairy sneezed and hoarsely replied, "Yes." He jabbed a slender finger at his throat. "Laryngitis."

She hurried him inside where all the sisters could help. They decided first to get him warm by the fire and then give him a bath. He didn't protest. Levena carried the hot water from the fireplace to the kitchen, and they filled a bowl for him.

He held on to Laura's pinky, and she lowered him toward the water. As soon as his miniature toes dipped in, he shot out as quick as an arrow from a taut bow. His little body turned red to match his hair. They added some cold water and convinced him to try again. This time the temperature suited him fine.

If allowed, he would have remained in the bath for a long while, but Caritha pulled him out and insisted he get good and dry. He wrapped himself in a dishcloth and tapped his head with his wand. Every hair hissed, steam rose until his head dried, and his tiny quill formed out of thin air and stuck itself behind his ear. Pulling it out he smoothed the feather with tender care, then tucked it in place atop his head.

That evening he said not a single word. He sat wrapped in the dishcloth on Evela's shoulder the whole time, coughing and gazing into the crib. Caritha could tell he wanted to say things, but his voice wouldn't allow it. So he stared and occasionally a silvery tear rolled down his cheek.

Clearly the fairy missed his beloved friend, Dantress. He missed her a very great deal. Caritha wondered if that was why he had come—to see the infant for whom Dantress sacrificed her life.

"Is anyone hungry?" Rose'el held her stomach and it growled. "I am—*very*."

Laura and Caritha prepared a soup. Dantress's former garden had yielded a generous variety of vegetables. They sliced potatoes, red onions, and mushrooms into the pot. Rose'el muttered to herself as she walked to the back of the kitchen and opened the trap door to the root cellar. She vanished into the darkness and returned with a jar filled with a brown liquid. "Here." She handed it to Caritha and shuffled back to the fireplace.

Caritha poured the broth in, and before long everyone enjoyed a bowl of steaming vegetable soup in front of the fireplace. For Miverē they filled a small measuring cup. He sipped the soup for a long while, still staring at the baby.

"It is good to be with you, daughters of the great dragon," he said at last.

"Your voice is back." Evela smiled down at him.

He sniffled and coughed but nodded.

The hour grew late. The sisters rose to go to their chambers. Caritha remained by the fireplace as goodnights were said. "I'll put the baby to bed." She stood and watched the bedroom doors at the other end of the house close.

The fairy slipped out of the dishcloth and flitted onto the baby's stomach. "'Twas your fate to die, fairest of the dragon's daughters, and now I have come to give what gift I can to preserve your child."

Caritha knelt beside the crib. "She really is beautiful, isn't she?"

"Yes, fair daughter of the dragon. But too young to play with me."

"Miverē, why have you come?"

The fairy glanced up at her with his green eyes.

"You would be welcome to stay here, but I don't think Ilfedo should see you. He doesn't need to know that fairies exist, too. And he'd want to know where you come from." She frowned. "Emperia must remain hidden from this world and unknown to its people. There is evil on the rise. I can feel it growing as the months pass. Something ancient is stirring malice in its heart. This place, this land, and this child's father are a beacon of hope."

Three tears rolled down the fairy's face. "Maybe I can give her little life a silvery lining, a gift from us fairy folk to honor the fairest of the dragon's daughters." Thus saying, he sniffed back a sob, drew his little wand, caught one of his silvery tears on its tip, and suspended it over Oganna's clenched baby fist. The tear fell from the wand and splattered against her skin.

Miverē opened the baby's hand and plucked a long red hair from his head. He used his wand for a needle, sewed the hair through her palm, and then did the same to her other hand. He hovered over Oganna's head and kissed her forehead. A warm glow briefly passed from the fairy's lips over the baby's skin. The fairy hairs in each of Oganna's small palms glowed for an instant beneath the skin.

Miverē stayed that night in Ilfedo's house. He slept in the upstairs bedroom with Caritha and Oganna while the Nuvitors watched over them. Caritha lay in Ilfedo's bed, rocking the cradle next to it, and the fairy lay on the pillow. In the morning he left just as unexpectedly as he'd arrived. Caritha said nothing to her sisters of the fairy's strange gift to Oganna. She turned over the baby's hands and could see no sign of the red hairs sewn beneath the skin.

She went about her morning as if nothing had happened. Breakfast was served, the baby fed. Later Honer's wife Eva arrived to care for Oganna. Her three children ran into the War-rioresses' arms, peppering them with kisses before darting into the house. Seivar made a discreet getaway out a window.

The sisters had dressed in their familiar purple garments. They tied white sashes around their waists and marched east-ward through the forest. A couple hours later they crested a hill and stood still. The trees here had been thinned, and a clearing half a mile wide and as great in length spread before them.

Caritha parted the fold in her skirt and drew her rusted sword from its sheath. Five hundred white tents had been pitched on the cleared ground and in the shelter of the bordering trees.

A horn sounded from the far side of the camp. The flaps of the arrayed tents flipped open and a thousand men marched forth. They filed into perfect lines and waited in disciplined silence as the Warrioresses descended the hill. Caritha could feel the anticipation rising in the men. Out of several thousand original volunteers to join the Lord Warrior's army, these men had been selected for their aptitude for sword fighting and put under the Warrioresses' supervision.

A heavy-set man barreled out of the largest tent. A breeze caught the bearskin cape on his back, and it billowed behind him as he stomped up to meet Caritha. With a quick bow and a smile, he chinked his sword against the chain mail covering his chest. "We are at your service, my lady!"

"Commander Veil, this armor." She stared at the intricate chain mail adorning his chest. Never had she seen anything like it in the Hemmed Land. Back home in Emperia yes, but not in the Hemmed Land.

"A masterful piece, don't you think?" Commander Veil again smote it with the pommel of his sword. "An enemy would need a spear to pierce that. I got it from this fellow down on the coast. He's a new arrival; strange looking fellow with white hair . . . calls himself Linsair the sword smith. And the best part is I didn't have to pay him anything for it. He just made me promise a donation to the monk's parish."

Caritha did not answer him. It seemed a strange thing for a craftsman to give such a beautiful gift in exchange for a charitable donation to a parish. She knew of only one parish on the coast. She'd visited it a couple times for prayer. The monk there was young but zealous. When first she'd met him, she had thought he could have passed for a jovial brother to Patient the shepherd. He was pious and wise despite his meager experience.

"I hope your donation was generous." Rose'el stepped forward, looking down at the man's mail. "It is a magnificent piece."

"Oh, I was generous. Always try to be. They do serve God after all!" Commander Veil laughed. "Enough about me, the men are eager to begin again. Yesterday's challenge is still ringing in their ears, I daresay."

He led them down the line of men to the arena at the center of the clearing. One by one the men came forward and mock-dueled with a Warrioress. Not a single blow could they land on the sisters. The Warrioresses evaded their attacks with the practiced ease of dancers and always touched their rusted blades lightly on some vital part of the warriors' bodies to end the duels.

This went on for several hours until Veil ordered the Warrioresses to stand aside and let him take a turn in the arena. He did not move with the swiftness or lightness of foot that the sisters had. Instead of avoiding the sword thrusts, he struck back with his own, laying metal against metal until he wore down his opponent. Several times he welcomed two men to combine in their efforts to defeat him. Eventually a couple of them succeeded.

Veil bowed to each of them and yielded the arena. The pair of victors now faced their fellow trainees by pairs. The afternoon wore on in this manner, and the sweating swordsmen became an unpleasant aroma. Swords met blow for blow as they honed their skills. They were the Elite Thousand and, when the Warrioresses declared them ready, these men would look for the approval of their Lord Warrior.

Caritha stepped back into the arena with her sisters. The men about them effected deep bows and then angled their swords defensively. The sisters darted into their midst, working as one unit. Their swords struck swifter than arrows against the fifty warriors assailing them.

⬡ ⬡ ⬡

As the shadows under the trees lengthened and the sky paled, Ilfedo leaned against a tree. He wiped his sleeve across his sweaty forehead and undid the sling supporting his arm. The soreness was tolerable enough now to do without it. Laughter rang from his home. The door slammed open and Honer's son ran outside and around the house, then reentered.

The sisters of his wife filed into the clearing. From their slow walk he knew they must be tired from a long day with the trainees.

"Ilfedo, is that you?" Evela stepped toward him and laid a hand on his arm. His skin tingled where she'd touched him, like it used to for Dantress, and he pulled back. "You are injured," she whispered.

"No. I *was*. It feels sore and a little stiff—but I have been healed. It's a strange story actually."

Rose'el grunted. "Strange?"

He looked into her eyes. "Ombre believes—that it was the hand of an angel."

Caritha, Rose'el, Laura, and Levena strolled back to the house. Evela delayed for a long moment. She glanced up at him and smiled softly. "Anything is possible, even an angel from heaven. I think Dantress would have taken Ombre at his word. Now come!" She guided him to the house. "You must be tired."

That evening his baby girl laughed in her crib, holding his pinky as he smiled down at her. The blackened wood in the fireplace crackled while the sisters sat around the hearth drinking tea. He ran his hand down the length of the Sword of the Dragon's scabbard which lay across his knees. Such a magnificent weapon.

"The swordsmen are becoming more skilled with each day under Commander Veil." Caritha sipped from a cup of tea and informed him what had happened in his absence.

"That is what I have been waiting to hear." He glanced into the crib. "Ah, she is asleep." He pulled his pinky out of the baby's fist and drew the sword a few inches out of its scabbard. Flames coiled beneath the glassy surface of the blade. It seemed he could look through it at another world—a world of silver and blue, deep and vast.

Glancing up at the sisters he told them what had transpired in the north. They listened with rapt attention as he described his fight with the winged men and then of his defeat. "I recall losing consciousness and waking to find Ganning staring down at me." He chuckled. "Ombre won't let up about the incident. He has told everyone that he saw an angel appear over me to heal my wounds. He makes it a fascinating tale, and he seems convinced of the truth of it."

He smiled. "Only God and Ombre know what really happened. I'm just fortunate to come back and see my child again."

Ilfedo slid the sword back into the scabbard. "So," he said, "what are your thoughts on this incident. I know that you have seen some stranger things than I have."

The sisters' mouths gaped and their eyes widened.

He held up his hand. "You are all a mystery to me; I am still in the dark about many things. But from time to time my wife did mention things from her past—a few strange things that did not make sense to me. Now if you know anything that might help in this strange situation I am asking you to share it."

Caritha glanced at her sisters, and they put their heads together in whispered conference. What things were they hiding from him, and why? Someday, perhaps, whatever prevented them from sharing everything with him would be removed.

Finally, Rose'el grunted and the sisters faced him.

"These creatures you spoke of." Caritha cleared her throat. "We have dealt with them before. They can be ruthless and vicious in an almost animal way. Our father told us that the winged men are called Art'en and the winged women are called It'ren."

Ilfedo frowned. "The white dragon told you this?"

"You must be very careful, brother. The Art'en have been known to ally themselves with the vilest of men." Laura folded her hands. "So long as their master is strong, they flock to him and do his bidding."

"Do you know of any tactics that might prove useful against them?"

The sisters shook their heads. Their dark eyes bored into his as Caritha spoke for them. "Only a warrior with superior hand-to-hand combat training would be a match. Go for the wings before using that." She pointed at his sword.

What memories or knowledge she had drawn on for this information, Ilfedo could not even guess. Nor did he ask her to explain. The sisters guarded their past with a veil of mystery impossibly thick. Perhaps someday he would discover their mysteries. But not tonight.

He thanked them for their insight and picked up the crib with Oganna nestled inside. It was just a little crib, small enough to set comfortably on the hearth stones.

Caritha grasped his shoulder. "One more thing, Ilfedo."

"Yes, Commander Veil has a new piece of armor," Laura said.

"Yeah," Rose'el interrupted. "Some stranger is working as a sword smith on the coast and asking nothing in return for his labor. Well, almost nothing. His customers have to make a donation to the local parish."

Caritha set down her tea. "I think it warrants investigating."

Ilfedo lowered his voice and pulled the crib closer to his face. "What sort of armor are we talking about?"

"Chain mail—very finely constructed chain mail. I haven't seen armor like that in a long while."

Laura sipped at her tea. "We could use a skilled craftsman to equip the Elite Thousand."

"I'll look into it the day after tomorrow. For now, I need a little rest." He wished them goodnight and climbed the stairs to his bedroom.

Gently he rested the cradle on the floor. Seivar and Hasselpatch flitted onto the bed and nuzzled him with their silver beaks. He kissed Hasselpatch on her soft head and stroked Seivar's chest. The Nuvitors cooed in response.

Undressing, he opened the roof panels and lay in his bed. Home again! He hated popping in and out as he had been doing for the past few months, but things needed his supervision and he felt that his daughter's future depended on his actions. He watched the stars twinkle for a long while, then closed his eyes and heaved a deep breath. The Nuvitors nestled under his arms and cooed him to sleep.

※ ※ ※

Three days later the coastal town that Ilfedo had first saved from the Sea Serpents welcomed him. He met with the mayor but when the opportunity presented itself, discreetly slipped into a black hooded cape and wandered through the town. No one recognized him.

He asked directions of a hulking fisherman at the market who reeked of the sea, and of several farmers carting heaps of corn through the town gates, but none could help him. Finally an elderly woman with a red shawl wrapped around her face stepped up with a grin that encompassed her entire face, and pointed him in the right direction. A fishing equipment shop stood to one side of the log chapel—Ilfedo's destination—and a blacksmith's shop on the other. He entered via a gate in the white-post fence and followed a long dirt path to the chapel's double doors.

He entered a long room with benches flanking a narrow aisle up to a wooden altar. The floor and the benches had been painted white. The walls and doors remained brown except for the back wall that matched the floors. A round stained-glass window had been inserted near the top.

What really caught Ilfedo's eye were the paintings. Colorful canvases hung from the high windowless walls—four on the left and four on the right. He stepped closer to the nearest one and studied the image of a dark-skinned woman in prayer, her eyes closed, a lifeless baby in her arms, and a tear rolling down her cheek. Above her, a white-robed man placed a baby full of life into an enormous hand reaching from a cloud.

"This is of a bereaved mother who lost her young child," a gentle manly voice said from behind him.

Ilfedo gazed at the enormous hand in the picture. Was it the hand of Creator God?

"The innocent child is given into the hand of its Maker while the mother grieves for her loss. All the woman can see is her dead child. God sees another life delivered into His hand."

"Are you Brother Hersis?" Ilfedo studied the white-robed monk.

The man nodded back up at him, then his beady eyes flicked to the next painting. Yimshi's rays poured through the colored window panes, playing on his shoulder-length black hair. His shoulders spread too broad for his height, and his fingers engulfed Ilfedo's hand when they shook.

"Blessings be given to you on this glorious morning, stranger. I am Brother Hersis. God is my witness, savior, and judge. Can you say the same?"

Ilfedo laughed. "Yes, I believe I can." He wrenched his hand from the shorter man's iron grip and turned back to the paintings. "Whose work is this?"

"Does the artist deserve the credit for the work he does? Or is the praise due to the Artist who designed the artist and gave him the inspiration to paint?"

"I'll take that to mean *you* painted them." Ilfedo strode to the next one. In this one an elderly couple smiled down at a man lying on his bed. In the background the Grim Reaper stood inside the doorway, but a man robed in white held him back. "What do these pictures portray?"

The monk followed him and waved his hand before explaining each of his pieces. "Sometimes God takes away, as you saw in the first painting. In this one he sends his angel and restores the sick man to his father and mother."

Ilfedo walked to the next one. Here a man in wealthy clothing stood in the midst of a street. Beggars reached out to him while he clung to his bag of gold. Lacerations scored the man's back, and behind him stood a fierce angel with a whip in its hand.

"Pity that soul," Brother Hersis said. "God gave him much, and he hoarded it. Now his end will be bitter; the scourge of the Lord will follow him to death and beyond."

"I don't need you to explain this next one." Ilfedo looked at the fourth painting. A man dressed in rags knelt on a cobblestone street to wrap a starving child in his only coat. He offered a slice of bread in his other. A great tear fell from an empty sky with an angel inside it. "This is the man with whom God is pleased."

"Indeed." Brother Hersis smiled and led him across the room. "These other paintings are not lessons, just reminders of what we who follow God should become."

Brother Hersis had painted a soldier on the field of battle, standing over his wounded king. Lightning zipped from black clouds overhead. A path of escape lay through the enemy, but he stood over the king, sword drawn, while blood ran down his armor.

The next painting depicted a woman washing the feet of her weary husband. Another showed a family on a woodland picnic. In the last painting, a beautiful young woman knelt in prayer, a serene smile on her face.

Putting an arm around Ilfedo's shoulders, the monk led him into an adjacent room. "Allow me to show you the painting I am currently working on." His white habit swept the floor as he moved an easel, rotating it toward Ilfedo. Two children knelt in prayer beside a fallen warrior while a glowing angel holding a partially-painted sword rose over him. "I have still to finish the sword. And, as you can see, I have not painted in the mother, yet."

After gazing upon the painting for a long, quiet moment, Ilfedo walked with the monk out of the room and into the parish.

Ilfedo lowered his hood and draped the cloak over a chair.

"Ah, so it is you! Word of God's intervention on your behalf spread quickly over the last couple days." Brother Hersis folded his hands and grinned. "We must offer praise to Him for your escape from death, my lord. Such an event has not happened in our recorded history. It will be remembered, embodied in the painting for everyone to consider."

Ilfedo raised his hand. "Just don't raise me on a pedestal in the eyes of your parishioners; be very careful that does not happen. Understood?"

The monk bowed. "Of course. Now, if it please you, tell me why you have come. I did not expect the Lord of the Hemmed Land to visit my humble parish."

"I need you to introduce me to someone who, as I understand it, you met recently." Ilfedo crossed his arms and gazed at the man. "I'm looking for the sword smith, Linsair."

"Ah! Linsair. Well, I cannot say as that surprises me. It has been an honor to host that stranger. But his skills qualify him for many other things." Brother Hersis heaved a sigh. "In times like these our nation needs men like him. Men who will proclaim truth unabashedly and without fear, even with boldness, and men working diligently with their hands in the cause of the innocent." The monk led him outside and around the back where a few shacks lined a vibrant green lawn. Monks walked to and fro between the cottages, tending small gardens and gathering carrots, lettuce, and potatoes from the ground.

One man loomed out of the monks' midst, hulking over them. He left a basket of carrots in the garden and met them.

"This is the sword smith you inquired of," Brother Hersis said.

Ilfedo looked up at the man and marveled at the broadness of his shoulders and the thickness of his arms. His legs were hidden beneath the white habit of a monk.

"It is an honor to welcome you to my humble abode, Lord Warrior." Linsair bowed and his white hair fell around his face. He straightened, unsmiling. "I assume that you have seen my handiwork and wish to enlist my aid in forging swords and more armor."

"Yes," Ilfedo admitted. He craned his neck to look deep into the man's pink eyes. It felt strange to gaze *up* instead of at eye level or below. He couldn't help but feel a bit threatened by the man's size and strength. Yet there was something in Linsair's eyes that conveyed honesty. Something about this man struck him as familiar.

Linsair rolled his shoulders and took off his habit. His every muscle stood out hard and strong. "I am a valuable addition to your forces, yet I sense that you desire to know more about me—my origin, perhaps?"

Ilfedo wanted to ask. He wanted to know. "You came from the Sea of Serpents."

"That is correct. I washed ashore and made my home among your people."

"Can you tell me anything about the strange coinciding of your arrival with that of the meteor that reportedly crashed into the sea just prior to your appearance on my shores?" Ilfedo studied the man for any wavering of eyes or body that would indicate deception.

Linsair's eyes flared. "No. I cannot."

Ilfedo narrowed his eyes. "Are you willing to tell me how you came here?"

"Know this, Lord Ilfedo." Linsair rolled his shoulders again, every muscle rippled. "I came not to harm thee or thy people. My service I now offer; my skills are at your disposal. If you fear or distrust me, then accept not my offer. However, if your heart tells you that I am to be trusted, accept me as a blessing from the hand of the Creator."

Ilfedo did trust Linsair. He shook the man's hand, cringing in the powerful grip. There was a sober honesty in his new ally's face.

"Brother Hersis, my thanks for the hospitality." Linsair embraced the monk. "God will bless thee for all you are doing."

"Farewell for now, Linsair." Brother Hersis slapped him on the chest. "When you return this way, pay me a visit."

Linsair heaved a sigh. "I'm afraid such will never be, my friend. Farewell." Then he fetched his tools from one of the shacks and followed Ilfedo into the street.

They made their way out of town. On every hand people whispered as Linsair passed but kept out of his path. They reached the forest and journeyed on until they came to Commander Veil's encampment.

At their hail, Veil barreled out of his tent, the noon sun glistening off his chain mail like millions of diamonds. "Form up!" he ordered, and the men marched into parallel lines straight as two arrows.

With a deep bow Commander Veil greeted Ilfedo and then grinned up at Linsair.

"Commander," Ilfedo said. "Give this man whatever he requires."

Linsair strode down the long lines of men. Every twenty feet he paused to stare into the soldiers' faces. The men held formation with rigid formality. The sword smith returned to Ilfedo, and his huge chest heaved as he drew in a mighty breath. "The construction of their weapons is inadequate."

"Inadequate?"

Linsair rumbled in his throat and, turning to one of the men, commanded. "Hand me thy blade!"

The soldier glanced at Ilfedo and rested his hand on the pommel of his sheathed weapon.

"What are you waiting for, soldier?" Ilfedo pointed at the man's weapon. "Do as he asks."

The man drew his sword with grace and speed. He laid it in Linsair's hands and stood at attention.

Facing Ilfedo, Linsair grasped the weapon by its handle and poised it above his head, its blade aimed at the sky. "Draw thy weapon, Lord of the Hemmed Land."

Commander Veil's eyes widened and he frowned. He stood in Linsair's path, his hand clawing at the pommel of his own sword.

The sword smith's shoulders relaxed. "I do not intend harm. But this weapon's blade must be tested against the best before it is committed to battle."

Ilfedo drew the Sword of the Dragon and widened his stance as flames covered his body. He laid a hand on Veil's shoulder, and the man looked back at him. "Step aside commander."

Veil nodded, still wearing a frown, and stepped out of his path.

The albino man came at Ilfedo like a bear, and their swords clashed with such force that sparks flew. Ilfedo grasped his sword with both hands. The impact of Linsair's attack left his hands stinging. Nevertheless he advanced. As the larger, more powerful man attacked, Ilfedo grimaced.

Linsair's blade struck with great force, but the metal cracked and the blade broke in half.

Sheathing the Sword of the Dragon, Ilfedo shook his head. The sword smith had made his point. The soldier's blade now lay in the dust divided in two.

Commander Veil stared aghast. "Oh my."

Ilfedo looked up at Linsair. Those pink eyes stared back. "Do what you must. I will see to it that you are well-paid for your work."

"Payment." The man growled. "Did I ask thee for that? My services are free. I do not want payment. Simply require your men to follow my instructions."

"So be it." Ilfedo summoned two men and placed them at the sword smith's disposal. Linsair led them to one of the tents and ordered them to pull it down.

Then he spun about and returned to Ilfedo. His hand clawed toward the Sword of the Dragon, and he drew it from the sheath.

"Step back! How dare you draw the Lord Warrior's blade without permission!" Veil drew his sword, charged the large man, and swung for Linsair's sword arm.

Living fire sprang from the Sword of the Dragon, enveloping Linsair instantly, and armor grew over his body like dragon scales. Yet the flames did not subside as they had on Ilfedo.

Commander Veil's blade struck the scale-armor. He struck again, but Linsair parried with the Sword of the Dragon. The man's pink eyes flared; the blade of Ilfedo's sword pulsed white light as it made contact with Veil's blade and cut through the metal.

Holding the short end of his blade in his hands, Veil stepped back, shaking his head as he gazed at it. "Well, I guess I can't use this one anymore." He picked up the severed blade.

The armor vanished from Linsair's body, and he held the flaming sword before his face.

Ilfedo held up a hand, staying Veil with a sober glance. The man dropped the hilt of his broken weapon, and his hands hung limply at his sides.

"Only dragon blood could create weapons suitable for the battles your men will face, Lord Ilfedo." Staring unblinking at the Sword of the Dragon, Linsair nodded. "A thousand swords I will make for thy men—a thousand blades to defend the helpless in a manner similar to this blade."

"Dragon blood?" Ilfedo frowned as a chill breeze struck his back. "What do you know about dragon blood?" He remembered Dantress and the passion with which she had loved and the joy she had been in his life. He remembered also that her veins had flowed, not with human blood, but that of her dragon father. Her life was in her blood, and she had given it to their daughter.

"It is ancient knowledge that the life of a dragon is, quite literally, in their blood." Linsair lowered his voice, drew near, and thrust the Sword of the Dragon back into Ilfedo's sheath. "If a dragon sacrificed a drop of blood—sacrificed willingly and knowingly—one drop for me to blend with each sword I forge for these, thy men, then would I create beautiful weapons of light. They would be superior to other blades, though not as magnificent as thy own."

Ilfedo gazed beyond the man to the trainees. Many of them were young, too young to die on the field of battle. But what battle? The Hemmed Land was at war with no one. Well, there were the Sea Serpents, and the Art'en creatures attacking the northern boundary. But were they a nuisance, or an indicator of a broader struggle to come?

"Darkness will come before the dawn, thou Lord of the Hemmed Land," Linsair said. "Do not permit it to linger through inaction."

"You speak as a prophet, sword smith."

"If you hear wisdom then pay heed to me. If I speak falsely, then reject my counsel. But dark days lie ahead. Of this I feel sure." Linsair stepped back and his eyes shifted to look past him. "Ah, so these are the famed Warrioresses."

Ilfedo turned to find the sisters in a half-circle behind him. They stared at Linsair, without speaking. "My sisters," Ilfedo said. "This is the sword smith, Linsair."

Still, the sisters said nothing.

"Commander Veil." Ilfedo waved his hand at the waiting soldiers. "They are dismissed."

The commander bowed and walked between the rows of warriors, sending them to various tasks. Most of the men trooped to the makeshift arenas, challenging one another to improve their swordsmanship.

"Forgive us, Linsair." Caritha curtsied and swept her hand toward her sisters. "You remind us of someone."

Linsair bowed. "Then I hope he is someone you respected and loved."

"He was." She introduced each of the Warrioresses by name and then greeted Ilfedo. "You are heading back north, aren't you?"

"Yes." He turned to Linsair and shook the man's massive hand.

Linsair made a slight bow.

Ilfedo nodded back. "When you have outfitted all these men, you will have my thanks and that of your adoptive homeland."

The albino man stepped back, and Veil walked up to him, tilting his head to look in his face.

Evela rushed forward and planted a kiss on Ilfedo's cheek. Stunned, he looked down at her and held her away from him. He could see embarrassment in her sisters' eyes, yet none said a word. Tears welled in Evela's eyes. She sniffled and said, "Don't stay away too long, my lord. Remember you have a child to raise."

Ilfedo left as quickly as possible. He stopped on the brow of a hill and looked back at the camp. Inside an open tent Linsair set down his anvil and shouted for someone to help him build a forge. A dozen men answered his call.

In the arenas, the sisters raised their swords and commenced combat with the warriors. He turned to the forest and set off to the north. Now to deal with the Art'en haunting the Hemmed Land's border.

# 5

# SWORDS OF LIGHT

Ombre ignored the sweat dripping down his face and gripped his sword with a vengeance. Moonlight filtered through the trees in front of him onto the winged man thrashing on the ground. "Why did you come here?" Ombre shouted.

The creature shrieked and rolled in the leaves.

"Tell me what I want to know. I *will* spare your life."

A laugh erupted from the creature, a laugh that turned into a cackle. It stumbled to its feet and grabbed at him.

He poised his sword at its chest, prepared to strike. Suddenly, the forest around and above him erupted as five more of the creatures sprang upon him. He was driven to the ground but fought back. "Help!"

Several soldiers appeared. They ran a couple of the winged men through with spears and assailed the others with swords. But a fresh group of the vile beings arrived. They fought like animals, using no weapons, and quickly overcame Ombre's men. Again they attacked him.

Ombre growled as he fell to his knees and received a kick in the side. "Get back!" They swung at him, and he impaled another on his sword.

As he drew the blade from his opponent, a whinny rang through the trees, and a white stallion burst into the fight. Its silvery mane flew behind it as it reared and kicked one of the creatures in the head. It landed on its forefeet and kicked its hind hooves into another's chest, crashing it against a tree. Silver flecks flew off its hooves. It moved with the speed of lightning.

"My champion." Ombre rose and smiled as the animal rampaged through the winged men.

It wheeled close to him, and he swung his leg over its back. The white, silver-maned stallion raced him to a hill and dumped him. Ombre sat on the ground, breathing in the free air. The stallion pranced around him, flaring its nostrils in the direction it had come. Its silver-blue eyes watched the shadows. Then it reared, thrashing its silver hooves at the moon and screamed with such force that the sound echoed in the forest.

"Whoa there, boy. Take it easy. They aren't even close to us anymore." Ombre stood and sheathed his sword. He approached and stroked the wild animal's moist neck. "I'm going to call your species Evenshadow, after the glorious twilight hours." He chuckled. "You are magnificent."

The stallion blew its nostrils, and suddenly Ombre knew they were not alone. He glanced over his shoulder and three white mares crested the hill, whinnying to the stallion. The moonbeams reflected in their silvery manes, tails, hooves, and eyes. The grass glowed blue around their feet.

Ombre walked to the mares and reached out his hands. "You are all Evenshadows." They nuzzled him as if he were an old friend. He stroked their velvety muzzles and glanced at the forest from which he'd come.

A winged man sprinted from the shadows at the base of the hill. Ombre slipped his hand to the hilt of his sword. The villain dropped to all fours and raced up the hill.

Suddenly the forest erupted with blinding white light, and a torrent of flames ripped through the trees behind the winged man. The Evenshadow stallion wheeled and fled into the forest with the mares racing after him; silver flakes glowed on the ground in their wake.

On the other side of the hill, Ombre watched half-a-dozen winged men fly from the trees. The moonlight revealed their startled faces. They screeched and their companion on the hill sprang into the air after them.

❈ ❈ ❈

The Sword of the Dragon blazed in Ilfedo's hands. His body shone in the darkness with blinding brilliance. He saw the Art'en creature on the hill. It had been running toward Ombre but had turned to flee. Ilfedo ran forward and pointed the blade at the Art'en. Flames leapt from the blade, wove through the air, and engulfed the creature. It screamed and crashed into the trees.

The others had flown beyond the sword's reach, but Ilfedo cupped his hands around his mouth and yelled into the forest. "Archers!"

Arrows broke through the trees. They soared like an avenging rain into the fleeing creatures' midst. The Art'en floundered, and the arrows peppered them until they too fell.

Ilfedo climbed the hill and sheathed his sword. The living fire pulled from his body, the armor vanished, and the flames withdrew into the magnificent blade.

"Are you all right, Ombre?" They grasped each other's arms and laughed.

Ombre shook his head. "Every time I think you've proven the limits of that weapon, I am overcome with amazement and humbled."

"It is the power in the sword. I cannot call it my own strength. The Creator has given me a great gift." Ilfedo grasped the sword's handle for an instant. The living fire sprang forth. He released it and the flames subsided. "But it *is* a magnificent weapon."

Together they returned to the valley by the desert, and the men celebrated the victory around roaring fires. But Ilfedo summoned a dozen of his choice men and rolled out a map. "My lords and captains," he said, standing before them. "Consider the future of our land as laid out on this skin. In ten years' time the Hemmed Land will become an effective nation with an organized military and government."

He waved his hand over the map. Laid out for all to see were the three known borders of the Hemmed Land. "To the south of our land is an uncharted desert, to the east lies the Sea of Serpents, and here in the north the way is again cut off by desert. To the west is the Western Wood and beyond that we know not what. Our recent clash with this race of winged men, called the Art'en, has made us all realize how vulnerable we are to the unknown territories beyond our borders.

"Therefore we will secure the exposed northern, southern and eastern borders with three forts. And within the Hemmed Land we will establish walled towns." He tapped his finger on the map. "Here, in this valley, the first fort must be built."

❈   ❈   ❈

"Peace! All I require is a place to work in peace!" Linsair loomed before Caritha while her sisters fidgeted behind her in the tent's shade.

The crowd of soldiers milling around outside the tent grew as the sword smith struck his hammer against the anvil.

Linsair spun and threw the hammer into a heap of unfinished swords at the tent's rear. The neatly stacked blades clattered to the bare damp ground, and the smith faced her again. "I cannot work under these conditions. Too many people are watching, and my forge is open to the elements. I would that this task was completed. Already a cycle of the moon has passed and not half of the swords I promised Ilfedo are forged.

"Therefore I have something to show thee." He crouched near the swords, fished out his hammer, and stuck it in his belt before rising. With long strides he led her out of the tent and into the forest toward Ilfedo's property. The rest of the sisters fell in line behind her, as did a few of the Elite. Linsair roared at them, "This business is between the Warrioresses and I. Do not follow us!" Stiffly bowing, the men returned to camp.

It took well over an hour before Linsair halted them in a stony place. Broad trees had grown between numerous boulders strewn over a small hill in the forest.

Rose'el leaned against a tree and crossed her arms. "We followed, sword smith. Now, pray tell us what in Subterran you've brought us here for."

"We are near Mathaliah Hollow." Evela pointed to the northwest. "Ilfedo's parents died not far from here when he was a younger man. I wonder how well the cabin is holding up. He's not been out here for a long time."

Linsair used his foot to clear fallen branches from a stone. Then he bent over the boulder and dug his arms around it, rolling it out of the ground. In the boulder's place a hole no more than two feet across stabbed deep into the earth. An iron grating spanned its mouth, alleviating Caritha's fears that a person or animal might break their leg falling inside.

"Follow me." The sword smith barreled downhill through thick bushes. Caritha and her sisters swept after him until he paused by another boulder and stepped behind it, out of sight.

Caritha stepped over a dead branch. Her skirt caught, and she knelt to free it.

"Caritha." Laura crouched next to her and whispered, "He reminds me of Father."

"You mean Linsair?"

Laura nodded vigorously.

"Yes," Caritha admitted. She freed her skirt and stood, placing a hand on her sister's arm with a smile. "But Father is a good deal larger than any man."

Everyone laughed except for Rose'el. She rolled her eyes and trudged around the boulder.

Caritha followed to the mouth of a deep cave. Large torches lined the long tunnel that descended under the hill. Their flames spread a warm orange glow down the passageway, and at their end stood Linsair, a blazing torch in his fist.

Rose'el trudged forward, neither glancing to the right nor to the left. She stood next to the sword smith, unsmiling.

"What delayed thee?" the man demanded of the lagging sisters.

Caritha gazed around the cave's interior, a circular chamber of considerable size. The walls of solid stone behind the sword smith arched to an orifice at its center some fifteen feet above her head. Directly beneath it on the floor an enormous forge stood on tri-sided legs of hammered iron. "Linsair, what is this place?"

The smith strode to the forge and ignited its wood with his torch. The flames ripped through the dry bark, chasing the shadows farther from the smith. Next to the forge sat an anvil much larger than the one Linsair kept in Commander Veil's camp.

"My work will continue in secret," Linsair said. "Here, away from the noise and disturbance, I will create weapons for your lord's army." He set his silver hammer on the anvil. "The people of this land will know misery before they know a time of peace. I would that their passage through misery be eased."

Laura frowned. "We don't understand. Is there something you need us to do?"

"I can fashion swords that are lightweight and strong, Warrioresses. Yet, if I had one—" He held up his index finger. "If I had only one drop of your dragon blood to use with each sword, I could create weapons that would array their bearers in light. On the field of battle, when darkness fell, the bearers of those swords would shine like stars on Subterran."

His pink eyes flared as if with fire. He pulled a sword out of a dark corner and buried its blade in the forge. When he withdrew it, the blade glowed white-hot. "Give me only one drop. Sacrifice it willingly for the soldier who will one day wield it."

Evela narrowed her eyes. "How does he know these things?"

"Yes. How does a sword smith know that we are of dragon blood?" Caritha drew her sword and Laura did the same. "Speak, Linsair. We want to know the truth."

He regarded them with steady eyes. "Put down your weapons."

"No." Evela drew her rusted blade. "Answer her question."

"So be it." Linsair heaved a sigh and shook his head. "As you may have guessed by now, I am also of dragon blood. Remember how Lord Ilfedo's sword responded to my touch. Unlike you, I know both the limits and the extent of my abilities. Therefore the Sword of the Dragon will not ignite if one of you were to use it."

"Ah," Evela said. "You are mistaken. Lord Ilfedo is not of dragon blood."

Caritha smiled. Surely the sword smith had cornered himself.

But the man laughed—long and loud. "Thou art so innocent of that weapon's true nature," he said. "It is a weapon of living fire, not of dragon blood. The difference is vast, yet you cannot begin to understand. I could not explain it to you, and if I tried, I would likely fail.

"For the time being it must be enough that I *do* understand, that the Sword of Ilfedo covered me in living fire, and that I have the knowledge to use your gift for the good of mankind."

He frowned and swung the white-hot blade to point at them. "Do you believe I am a deceiver? Or have you any cause to think that I mean harm to the people of this land? And what of my faith? Do you find it in thine hearts to condemn me?"

The sisters regarded him in silence. One by one they lowered their blades.

"Surely thou hast seen purity in my heart. Otherwise I would not still be standing." Linsair relaxed his frown. "Trust me, dragon daughters, I intend only good."

Caritha sheathed her sword and nodded for the others to follow her lead. "Forgive us, Linsair. It is only—that we have lost so much, and we are cautious."

"Thou art deceiving thyself, Warrioress. It is not caution which compels you." The smith lowered the sword, resting it on the anvil. "It is fear.

He glanced from one face to the next. "Now, who will sacrifice a drop to empower this weapon?"

For a long while no one answered his plea. Then Rose'el stepped forward, drew a dagger from her belt, and pricked her finger. A single crimson drop splashed onto the sword. The metal thrummed as if it were the bass string on a harp. The blade glowed pure white, and Linsair beat it with his silver hammer. Sparks flew in every direction, and he smiled down at Rose'el. Flipping the blade on his anvil, he beat it with such rapid strokes that Caritha could not distinguish one strike from another.

Linsair plunged the sword into a barrel. The metal sizzled; steam rose in billowing clouds. Linsair held forth the sword, and it radiated white light. "Now you see." He smiled again. "My promise is true."

Caritha took a step forward. "Very well, Linsair, your point is well made." She swallowed and glanced at her remaining sisters. "We will contribute a thousand drops of blood to be used in the creation of swords of light for the Elite."

He nodded and went back to work. She glanced at the floor and walked up to him, putting her mouth close to his ear. His arm froze in place as he listened. "Later I have a favor to ask of you, sword smith."

⁂ ⁂ ⁂

Six years later the final wall rose in Fort North. Two dozen men strained at the ropes, holding it in place as others pegged it to the adjacent walls. Ombre, Honer and Ganning mingled with the laborers. One man slipped and fell, letting loose his rope. The wall leaned toward him, threatening to fall.

"Ah no, it doesn't!" Ganning limped up to the wall and threw his weight against it. "You stay where you are."

The wall groaned, the full weight leaning on Ganning. Ombre and Honer ran up, whipping off their shirts and braced themselves alongside him.

Ilfedo stood nearby and glanced over his shoulder at his officers. "Lend them a hand."

"Aye, my lord." The officers stripped off their shirts and weapons and ran to the tilting wall. Soon the barrier stood straight and firm. Five hundred men cheered, clapped each other on the back, and marched onto the parade grounds.

Ilfedo's officers slipped out of the crowd, donned their shirts, and belted their swords to their sides. They lined up behind him, and he led them between the ranks of smiling faces to the fort's central structure made of sizeable logs. He climbed a short flight of stairs and stood on the porch.

Down on the parade ground the men gazed back at him. Honer strode through the ranks and up the stairs until he stood beside him. Ganning limped up after, leaning on the porch rail. Ombre walked through the crowd. The men stepped out of his path, acknowledging his passage with slight, respectful bows. At last he too made his way up the steps and smiled at Ilfedo.

Ilfedo smiled back and faced his soldiers. Six years of hard labor had paid off. The fort filled the valley where once his men had encamped to hunt Art'en. Today log walls encircled the valley at its crest, and the trees camouflaged them from prying eyes.

"Today," he shouted, "thanks to your hard work, the citizens of the Hemmed Land know peace. Peace from the strange creatures that would hunt us from without and within our borders. The land has been tamed, and the towns are growing into cities."

He frowned. "Where once a young man could lose his father and mother in a single night to a wilderness beast, today those beasts have been hunted down. Where once the Sea Serpents haunted our shores, now coastal towns prosper. And where the Art'en flew into our northern forests, we have erected a fort."

The men cheered long and then feasted that night. Ilfedo slipped away from the milling crowd with Ombre. "I'm going home to see my little girl. It has been too long."

Ombre raised a mug of juice and smiled. "Safe journey, Lord of the Hemmed Land!" Ilfedo turned to go, but Ombre laid a hand on his shoulder. "I almost forgot." He set his mug on the ground and dug into his pocket before putting something small into Ilfedo's hand. "Please give this to her." Picking up the mug he walked off, eyes fastened on his cup.

Ilfedo watched him go, watched him mingle with the crowd. He shook his head. Ombre wanted a family badly, and he probably would have had one by now if he didn't have his eye on a certain woman. Caritha rarely let down her guard in Ombre's presence. And so Oganna had filled the gap. "Someday, Ilfedo. Someday I'll have a little angel of my own," his friend would often say.

Ilfedo tucked the gift into his pocket and tightened his backpack's straps. A long hike lay ahead of him, and Linsair had sent word that he'd completed the swords for the Elite Thousand.

The forest swallowed Ilfedo in its lonely embrace. He left the sword of the dragon in its scabbard, preferring a slow pace over bright light. Owls swooped from the trees, catching mice. A vixen raced through the bushes, barking at her three pups as they stopped to stare curiously up at him. They nipped at one another's ears, played with each other's tails, and rolled in the leaves.

He skirted the area and continued south toward home. It was a moonless night, and soon the depths of the forest grew too dark for him to see his path. Drawing the sword of the dragon from its sheath, he let the living fire clothe him in armor of light. The brightness obscured his surroundings, and he closed his eyes, hoping to somehow dim the light through will-power. When he looked, the blade no longer sprayed harsh light into the forest but glowed instead, gently illuminating every stone, tree, and creature in his path.

Until early morning he journeyed without stopping to rest. A few hours later he pressed on as Yimshi's rays split the sky. A rooster crowed in the distance, a reminder that the wilderness had been tamed. He shook his head. If only it had never been tamed. He preferred the wild, untamed land of his childhood. But that sort of land was not a place to raise his only child.

When he finally arrived home, the smell of onion soup greeted him. He opened the door.

"Father!" Oganna was six now. He spread his arms wide and dropped to his knees, letting a relieved smile play across his face. She raced from the kitchen, radiant with childish joy. Her blond tresses were so fair that they could have been woven gold. Her gold-blue eyes sparkled, and she giggled before throwing herself into his arms, pressing her cheek against his, and grabbing his hair in her small hands.

Evela stood up by the fireplace, resting her hand on the mantel. Her eyes shone almost as brightly as his daughter's.

"How is my little angel?" He kissed his child's forehead and lifted her off the floor, holding her at arms' length. "My goodness, have you grown in this past month?"

She laughed as he set her down. "Look what Rose'el made for me." She twirled, permitting him a full evaluation of the purple dress fashioned in the manner of the Warrioresses—and of Dantress's.

"It is beautiful." He kissed her forehead again and strode to the fireplace.

With a long wooden spoon Evela stirred the contents of the pot hanging over the flames. "Are you hungry, my lord?"

"Truly starved." He kissed her hand, immediately regretting it as her cheeks flushed. Over the past years her actions had told him that she held a romantic place for him in her heart. He sighed and turned to Oganna. "How would you like to take a walk after breakfast? Just the two of us."

She jumped up and down. "Oh yes! I would, I would!" Then she stopped and curtsied, glancing up at Evela. "I mean, of course I would *love* to, Father."

"Then we shall." He glanced around the room. "Is anyone else home?"

"Aunt Caritha was gone when I woke up. I know Rose'el and Aunt Levena went berry-picking." The child stuck her finger between her teeth and looked at the ceiling. "I don't know what happened to Aunt Laura."

Evela stopped stirring and pulled the spoon out of the soup. She dabbed her finger in the pot and licked it. "Laura will be back soon. She's checking the garden for tomatoes." She ran her tongue over her lips. "Perfect."

"Oganna." Ilfedo dug into his pocket and lowered his voice. "I need a few minutes alone with your aunt, so I'd like you to go outside. Can you do that for me?"

Her smile melted, and she turned away. He grabbed her shoulder. "Hold a second, my little one. Ombre gave me—well, I'm not sure what it is—but I have something here for you." Pulling it from his pocket, he placed it in her outstretched hands. The firelight revealed a wooden wolf, finely carved.

Oganna's face lit up, and she bounded to her bedroom at the opposite side of the house, closing the door after her.

"That was nice of him," Evela said. She stopped stirring and sat on the hearth, gazing up at Ilfedo.

Clearing his throat he sat next to her. How should he do this? He didn't want to hurt her feelings.

"Ilfedo, what's wrong?" She slipped her hand into his, her dark eyes earnestly searching his.

He felt awful, yet he had to do it. He pulled his hand away from hers. "I can see you have feelings for me," he said at last. "These past few years it has become more and more apparent to me *and* to those around me."

"Ilfedo, what are you saying?"

"Please, please let me finish." He swallowed. "It has taken me a long time to work up the nerve to approach you about this."

He hesitated, and in that moment she smiled shyly, lowering her gaze. "Then you feel something for me?"

"No." He watched her eyes well with tears. How heavy his heart felt. But the truth had to be told. "I'm so very, very sorry." He touched her hand, and she glanced down at it. A few of her tears splashed onto his skin. "Please understand. It is not you. In fact, if I were inclined to remarry, you would make a wonderful wife. And I've seen how my little girl looks up to you.

"But for me . . . for me there was and always will be only one woman. I loved her with all that I had. My heart is and always will remain empty where Dantress once filled it.

"I don't want to deny you happiness, but neither will I deceive you. I am still grieving for your sister. And my grief is as fresh—as painful—as the day she died." Suddenly the memories of Dantress flooded his mind, and his heart ached. He bent over in pain, weeping as he clutched his chest. Tears spilled from his eyes, and every tear spawned a new pain in his body until he felt small and childlike.

Evela stood, tears running down her own face. "Y . . . yes," she sobbed. "I do l . . . love you. But you have hardened your heart to the world. You cannot see and cannot allow me to love you because you are unwilling to let go of your pain. You are unwilling to heal. I pity us the joy we will never know because of your scars." With that she kissed his cheek and ran her soft hand down his face.

He instinctively closed his eyes. Her hand comforted him.

She withdrew it, cupping her hands over her face, and fled out the door sobbing.

As he sat there, miserable and heartbroken, Oganna opened her door and came to him. "Father? You are crying." She hugged him, burying her head in his chest. Such tenderness washed over him. He clutched her to himself, wishing that somehow the pain would vanish.

When he thought his sobbing had ended, he released her. But looking upon her, little beauty that she was, his heart pained him again. Tears flowed down his cheeks.

"Father, don't cry!" She gazed back into his eyes and clutched his shirt with her hands. As he sobbed, he saw her chest heave, too. His tears slowed, but they rained from her eyes. Oganna clutched at her own chest, and his pain vanished. With a startled cry, she fainted in his arms.

"Help! Someone help me!" His pain had disappeared and his tears had stopped flowing, but he could not rouse his daughter. "No! I will not lose you, too."

❈   ❈   ❈

Caritha watched Linsair drop his hammer on the broad side of the blade of a long sword. White-hot sparks splintered from the metal, and a wave of heat washed over him. Whereas sweat dripped down her face, the large man before her did not show a hint of moisture.

The walls of the deep underground cave where the smith worked had been hardened and singed by his tireless forging. He'd forbidden anyone else to enter the cave save for she, Ilfedo, and her sisters.

She gazed into the dark recesses of the cave. The firelight flared, revealing a portion of the one thousand identical swords leaned against the stone walls. She held her skirt off the dirt floor and moved toward the weapons, bending to keep from hitting her head on the sloping ceiling. Reaching out, she traced her finger along the engraved flame in the hilt of one of them, then followed the thin metal vine that wove down its hilt and around the arms of its guard. The three-foot-long blade extended to the floor. Its broad side mirrored her surroundings on either side of a thin fuller.

To each of these swords she or one of her sisters had sacrificed a drop of their dragon blood.

The hammer rang against the sword again, and she retreated to the smith's forge. She pulled out a handkerchief and wiped her face.

Linsair's biceps rippled under his rolled up sleeves as he clanged the hammer against the flat of the sword's blade. The blade bent, and he flipped it, struck the other side, and flipped it again. The man cleared his throat, though she thought it sounded more like a growl. She fastened her eyes on his face.

"It is time, young one." His pink eyes gazed back without blinking, and his chest heaved a deep breath.

She stepped deeper into the scalding air. The forge burned hotter. She wondered that the smith did not flinch in its heat. To her it was tortuous. But she had come to deliver a gift—one final gift.

Extending her arm, she hovered her wrist over the sword. Linsair's last creation. "Do I proceed in the same manner as with the other swords?"

Linsair nodded.

"But I want this weapon to be special." She pulled back her hand to wipe the sweat from her eyes. "I want Ombre to have a superior sword, something that will preserve his life as the sword of living fire has preserved Ilfedo."

"Thou art certain of thy decision then?" He furrowed his brow. "In order for this to be done, thou must be willing to give up part of thy gift, part of the life that is in thy blood."

Her mind flashed back to a moment not long ago when Ombre happened upon her alone in the forest. She'd tripped and he had caught her. Her cheeks flushed at the memory. "Linsair, I do know what it is I am asking you to do."

"Then so shall it be." Linsair grabbed her hand in his enormous one and forced her wrist against the searing metal.

She screamed in pain and tears streamed down her face, but through her tears she saw the smith raise her skin away from the blade. Large drops of her dragon blood remained on the blade and the sword began to glow with pure white light. Linsair released his hold, took up his hammer, and beat the blade with new vigor. A smile spread across his face and his pink eyes sparkled.

Caritha wept in the agony of her wound. She felt weak—too weak to use the power in her blood to attempt a healing. Instead she drowned her arm in the smith's barrel of water. When the pain eased and she drew out her arm, she regarded the crisscrossing scars which remained. As she twisted her wrist, pain knifed up her arm.

The smith plunged the sword into the water. Steam rose in clouds around him. He reached out and caressed her wound. From his touch, a sensation of coolness spread through her arm. The scars vanished, and she looked into his eyes with sudden recognition. "It is you!"

Footfalls sounded in the cave. Though she peered into every corner she saw no one. Then a voice spoke from the cave entrance. "Hurry, my master, the child has collapsed."

Linsair dropped his work. "Did you not watch over her as I instructed?"

"Indeed. It was not my doing. Her father returned home and Evela—"

"Say no more, Specter. Return to the hollow and wait for me there."

In the dimness a gray-robed figure congealed and bowed in Linsair's direction. Caritha thought her eyes were deceiving her, for the figure held a scythe blade in his hand.

The figure vanished, and Linsair rushed from the cave.

"Wait! Where are you going?" Caritha raced after him and up the slope, through the forest in the direction of home. She stumbled on a stone, but he raced ahead of her, flitting over bushes and around trees.

Not wishing to lose him now and eager to know what caused him to act this way, she picked up her skirt and ran with all her strength. Before long her breaths came with difficulty, yet she kept him in sight.

He slipped into the clearing before Ilfedo's house and ran to the door.

※　※　※

As the door crashed open, Ilfedo looked up. Linsair stood on the threshold. The sword smith glanced around the house, then his eyes rested on Oganna. He ripped the hammock off the post, making a direct path to her.

"What hast thou done?" Linsair's pink eyes flared as he pulled the child from Ilfedo's grasp and tenderly laid her on the hearth. "Tell me now, thou Lord of the Hemmed Land. What hast thou done?"

Such fury burned in the smith's eyes that Ilfedo shrank back. "I . . . I was distraught, and she came to me." He strengthened his voice. "The next moment she collapsed, and I no longer had any tears."

"Fool! Thy daughter's veins are mixed with the blood of humanity and dragonkind. Thy need called out to her, and her dragon side answered." Linsair rubbed Oganna's chest and closed his eyes, whispering a prayer as he did so:

"Father, holy Father, tend now this child I pray.

Father, heavenly Father, now our fears allay."

At that moment, Caritha burst into the room, her hair askew. Uttering a startled cry, she knelt next to Oganna. "Ilfedo, what has happened to her? Did she fall?" Linsair glanced at her with sharp eyes, silencing her.

"Too young, she is too young to manifest these abilities." Linsair's lips moved in prayer.

Ilfedo closed his eyes and sent up his own plea for his daughter's life. Had he broken Evela's heart and slain his own child in the process? He opened his eyes and found Linsair gazing back at him. "What did I do?"

"Nothing except plead for an easement of thine own suffering, Lord Ilfedo," the sword smith said. "The power in thy child's blood is beginning to manifest itself. I believe that when she touched you, she took on your pain; your sorrow, your grief, your tears all became hers. But it was too great for her tiny body to handle. And now I must take the portion of thy suffering or risk losing her."

The man's pink eyes brimmed with tears, and his chest quaked. He sobbed and wept until his tears sizzled on the hearth. Oganna sat up, her face red, yet a smile appeared on her face as she watched her rescuer. Linsair continued to weep. He caressed Oganna's face and smiled through his tears, then glanced at Ilfedo. "How truly deep, how truly vast is thy love for both the dead and the living." Then he rose and looked down at Caritha. Tears had formed in her eyes as well, and her lips started to form a word.

Linsair touched the side of her head. "Remember no more what thou sawest in me. Remember only my craftsmanship and this deed of healing. Pass this to thy sisters for me so that they will remember no more." He withdrew his hand. "Farewell, child."

Without another word Linsair fled the house.

⚙ ⚙ ⚙

Ilfedo didn't know what to think of the man's charge to Caritha. He clutched his child to his chest and laid kisses all over her head until she giggled and begged him to stop.

"Caritha, are you all right?" He watched the eldest sister rise to her feet.

"I think so."

He frowned. "What did Linsair mean by all that?"

"What are you talking about?" She wiped her forehead with a cloth.

"He told you to 'remember no more.'"

She sat on the floor, shaking her head. "Honestly, brother, I have no idea."

# 6

# THE GHOST OF
# MATHALIAH HOLLOW

The shadows deepened under the tall trees, and a gentle, warm breeze rustled the leaves. Dry leaves of red and brown crunched under the feet of a young girl as she skipped through the forest. An owl hooted in the darkness. The breeze strengthened, swirling the leaves around her legs, then weakened, allowing them to settle back on the ground.

Oganna glanced over her shoulder, watching the glowing windows of her father's house. She was ten years old now. Old enough to let her curiosity pull her outside while causing her to dismiss her fear. No one knew she'd snuck away. Aunt Caritha had been the last one awake, cleaning the kitchen. Her father was taking a deserved nap by the fireplace, swinging in his hammock with Seivar nestled under his arm.

She looked into the darkening woods. For the past several months something had felt amiss. Even when the house should have been empty, someone else seemed to be nearby. When she shared her feelings with her Nuvitor companions, Seivar and Hasselpatch, both agreed that sometimes, when only they and Oganna remained at home, something felt downright spooky. As if an extra set of eyes gazed upon them at all hours.

This evening she had been standing by the window, watching darkness fall beneath the forest branches. A chill had coursed through her body. She hadn't known why—until a cloaked human figure coalesced in the trees and then vanished.

Now she turned away from the house and stretched her hand toward the forest, feeling for . . . she knew not what. Suddenly her hand glowed, and she let out a little cry, quickly clapping her hands over her mouth and glancing back at the house. The door remained closed and the house silent.

Breathing a sigh of relief, she bit her lip and stretched out her hand again. It did not glow. Once more she felt drawn into the forest toward Mathaliah Hollow.

For years now, childish superstition had maintained that Mathaliah Hollow was haunted. The isolated narrow valley was part of Ilfedo's generous property. Actually it bordered the old cabin site where his parents had been killed. In recent months long blue stalks had grown in Mathaliah Hollow, stalks that glowed at night. People called it Night Grass, but its appearance in the hollow only seemed to confirm the local children's suspicions.

It took Oganna a long while to reach the hollow, but when she stood at the forest's edge, looking down into the meadow with its patches of glowing blue grass, she saw a shadow race to the opposite side and halt. Total darkness fell. She glanced up at the clouds covering most of the stars. The moon rose as a bright glow behind the trees. The shadow, if she had really seen one, blended into the larger, darker shadows.

She hesitated. Fear should give her caution, shouldn't it? There was no such thing as a haunted hollow, was there? Suddenly a hooded figure glowed into existence in front of her, as if waiting for her. A scythe rested in the figure's hands. No, that could not be. The Grim Reaper was only a myth—but there he stood in glowing gray garb—unless she was experiencing a dream.

Pinching her face confirmed that she was awake. She turned, prepared to run, but struck her forehead on someone's belly.

"Slow down, child," a familiar voice rumbled. "There is nothing to fear."

She craned her neck to see into the pink eyes of a man who, for the life of her, she could not name. Yet somehow, he was a friend—a long lost friend. "Sir, I . . . I think I should go home now."

The man knelt in front of her and smiled gently. He looked like a ghost, too—his skin so pale and his hair so white. "Do you not remember me, my dear child?"

Her eyes felt like they were going to pop out. "Linsair!" She leaped into his arms and giggled as he laughed with her. The memory of him, which had seemed buried, came back in a blizzard of knowledge awakened. He had worked for so long for her father and then, after saving her life, he'd left. No one had been able to venture a guess where he'd gone.

She'd always felt he was the grandfather she wanted to know. The dragon father of her mother—her real grandfather—no one interacted with him, they only knew of him or had met him. Every memory involving Linsair spoke of kindness to her; sometimes a coldness toward others, an austerity, but a decided softness to her.

Linsair stood, raising her off the ground, holding her away from him. His grin encompassed every corner of his face. "How you have grown, my child! God has been good to you. Oh, and I have missed you."

"Linsair, where have you been? Father and Aunt Caritha and Rose'el—they wanted to know why you left—"

"My task for your father was done," he interjected. "And, child, I had other things to attend to. But," he carried her down into the hollow and nodded at the Grim Reaper, "I always kept a watchful eye on you through my friend."

She shook with fear, seeing the scythe blade with greater clarity. The long shiny blade seemed poised to slit someone's throat. Thankfully the cavernous hood hid the immortal face of Death from sight. She clung to Linsair, wishing he would turn her away from the horrible scene.

*Oganna, do not fear him. It is not the Reaper.*

She glanced up into Linsair's soft face, startled. Had he spoken to her mind?

He looked at the cloaked figure and growled like a lion. "Specter, cannot you see that the child is afraid of thee?" He set her on the ground and crossed his arms, looming beside her. "Remove your hood and set aside your weapon!"

"Of course, my master. Forgive me; I had not realized." The hood slipped off the man's head, revealing his handsome features, albeit his sober face.

"Specter." Oganna bit her lower lip and then took a step forward, dipping a curtsy with her nightgown. If Linsair said this was not the Reaper, then she would trust him.

The man leaned his scythe against a nearby rock face and bowed to her. "At your service, princess. I have watched you all your life, and I continue to do so. Today, I'm afraid, you discovered me against my strongest attempts to hide myself."

"I do not think"—she cleared her throat and held her head high—"I do not think I understand."

The sword smith's pink eyes mirrored the moonlight, sparkling. "My child, you are special to me, and so I have given you into Specter's charge until the day that you are able to stand on your own. Until the day you surpass your aunts in mastering the power in your dragon blood and your father's skill with a sword."

"Does father know?" She pointed a finger at Specter.

"No. And you must not tell him."

She frowned. Linsair would have to give an awfully good reason if he wanted her to keep this from her father.

"Listen to me, my child." Linsair knelt in the wet grass. "The death of your mother broke your father's heart, resulting in a fear that threatens thy future. You must be safeguarded from all that would harm thee, but not sheltered from the storms that will come against you. Specter is my loyal and trustworthy friend. He once saved your life, and he may yet do so again."

She shook her head. "I know he trusted you, Linsair, but that is not a good reason for me to keep this secret. I have to tell him."

Linsair growled and stood back. "You are strong like your mother, little one. I shall have to convince you in another manner." Then his skin glowed pure white and transformed into scales. His arms and legs thickened and he grew. His head elongated, his neck lengthened, and a fin cut through the clothing on his neck while horns grew from his head. Suddenly there he stood in full majestic power, and she knew him for what and who he was.

Her father had told her the story of Albino: "A magnificent creature and the father of your mother." Oganna clapped her hands and laughed as the creature towered above her.

"Now you know me, child. The command that I now give you I charge thee to keep: Specter is a friend to you and me. I appeared to your father and to his people in human form to prepare them for things that will come. Tell no one of Linsair's true identity and keep thy hidden guardian a secret. Both of these things are for thy benefit and safety."

Soberly she nodded and, just as she thought of hugging the dragon's leg, he sprang into the air, his wings beating wind into her face. She fell against Specter, and he held her steady until Albino shot westward into the night sky.

Cold air filled the hollow, and the clouds thinned. Stars multiplied in the heavens. "Come, princess." Specter took her hand and led her to the rock face close by. He held aside some wet vines and waved her into a dark chamber.

"I . . . I can't see." Her hands glowed momentarily, but the light lasted only an instant.

A torch blazed from the darkness, and she looked up at Specter. His face was less sober now. More relaxed.

Down into the cave he slowly led her until it opened into a chamber some thirty feet wide. He stooped where the portions of ceiling dipped and let go of her hand when they reached a dry section of stone. A heap of sand formed an upgrade in the floor.

He stood to the side and motioned her to step up. As she did, a shaft of moonlight blazed through a hole in the ceiling and spotlighted a sword leaning against the stone in front of her. She caught her breath. The blade had rusted, perhaps from sitting in the moist cave, and the leather along the handle appeared to be peeling. She reached out and touched the blade. It glowed rusty-orange for as long as her skin made connection with it.

Something else lay half-buried in the dirt next to the sword, and she dusted away the dirt with her hand, uncovering a boomerang made of some sort of crystal. The elbow had been fashioned like a handle, yet the wings had been honed to cutting edges.

"Whoa there," Specter said, placing his hand gently on her shoulder. "Be careful now." He sighed and his eyes filled with tears that would not spill.

"Are they yours?" She gazed into his face, wondering what brought about such sorrow in this man.

"The sword was. A very, very long time ago." He stood and forced a smile. "But now it will belong to you."

She jumped up and down. What a gift! But the man laid a hand on her shoulder and guided her toward the cave's exit point. "The dragon said that one day you will have need of a sword, and when that day comes, you may return to this place and claim it."

"I want to show it to everyone!"

"Now, now." He raised his pointer finger. "Tonight's events are a secret between you and me. No one, and I mean no one, must know of my presence here. Understand?"

She nodded, though it would be hard to keep such a thing from her father and aunts. It would be hard to keep this a secret, yet the dragon had said it must be kept. She would not let him down.

"Come." Specter walked her out of the cave and retrieved his scythe. "I will escort you home. And please, Oganna, don't try to find me again. After tonight I believe you have the ability to render me visible. I won't pretend to know how. I only ask that you never do so again."

She hung her head, unsure if guilt or elation was the proper emotion at the moment. "I promise," she said.

With Specter at her side, she trod the leaf-strewn floor of the dark forest until they reached the trees bordering her father's clearing. Then she turned away, determined to forget her adventure, and slipped unnoticed into the house.

❈   ❈   ❈

Specter watched the dragon's offspring close the door to Ilfedo's house. An otherworldly cold seized his body, and he fell to his knees. A force seized his chest, constricting him until he could not breathe. He gasped, praying to God for instant help. He could not move.

Voices whispered in evil undertones from the darkened forest. Voices that sounded all too familiar. He remembered the battle in Al'un Dai and the demonic hands that had clawed at him, as if dragging him into their abode.

But why and how had those haunting spirits found him here? This place was so very far from the Eiderveis River, and no one in the Hemmed Land worshipped the evil spirits—at least not to his knowledge. So who had called them to this place?

Humanoid figures dropped from the trees and spread their feathered wings. Art'en! Eight of them! They chortled like birds and crouched, ready to spring on him.

Wisps of thick blackness rose from the grass in the clearing before him. They curved swiftly upward, and a skeletal hand coalesced, reaching toward him. The Grim Reaper congealed in all his awful potency, his deadly fingers clattering against the handle of his scythe, as if anticipating death. The serrated blade drew back and then swung toward Specter's head.

Unable to move, unable to scream, Specter closed his eyes. The Creator's will be done.

One of the Art'en shook its wild, lengthy hair and screamed long and loud into the darkness. The other creatures bounded to their fellow and covered his mouth. Apparently they did not want their presence revealed. The Grim Reaper turned toward Ilfedo's house, and his cloaked form began dissolving into smoke.

In the doorway stood the Lord Warrior—a flaming sword in his hand. Someone had heard the Art'en's cry.

❃  ❃  ❃

Ilfedo rushed toward the smoking figure in the clearing. The living fire enveloped his body. The darkness raced away from him, and over a dozen winged men became visible. They appeared to be standing in a circle, though he could see nothing in the center.

The Grim Reaper floated there in dreadful clarity. His body kept turning into smoke and solidifying as if something prevented him from escaping. Ilfedo tried to breathe slowly, but every moment he gazed upon Death, fear drove deeper into his body, making him shake as never before. The Reaper turned to face him with eyeless sockets and a blackened skull. The jaws moved yet uttered no words. Instead the teeth clacked against each other in a hollow sort of way.

May God help him, what horror was this? Had Death come to his lands? Even so, he would drive this creature out of this land, and forever the Art'en would fear Ilfedo and the sword he bore.

Suddenly invisible bands forced his arms to his sides. Darkness swirled from the Reaper's hand, tornadoing around his feet. He could not move. Death floated closer to him and pointed to the ground with a finger of blackened bone. Every muscle in Ilfedo's body fought to keep him standing, yet inch by inch he fell to his knees. His hand still held the sword, but its flames sputtered.

The door of his home flew open, and a small figure stepped into the moist night. "Father!"

Several Art'en bounded toward her, shrieking with freakish fury. Two of them brought her to the ground as she screamed and cried. "Father!" It seemed to be the only word she was capable of uttering.

"Let—her—go!" Ilfedo drew upon his rage and felt his connection to the sword reestablish. Voices whispered in the trees, and the screams of men and women echoed all around him. Darkness crept toward him, constricting the sword's circle of light.

The Grim Reaper approached him, but the living fire poured strength into Ilfedo's muscles. He laughed and rose, snapping the invisible band that held him in place. He raised the sword of the dragon, stepped forward, and drove the flaming blade into the Reaper's skull.

Death fell back but slashed back with its scythe.

Ilfedo brought the sword down upon the scythe's broad side, forcing it to the ground. The curved blade bent. With a yell of victory, he reached under the Reaper's tattered hood. His fingers found a vertebrate in Death's neck. Raising the sword, he smashed its pommel into the Reaper's forehead.

The Grim Reaper fell to the ground, its jaw opening in a soundless cry.

Oganna screamed. She collapsed, eyes closed. An Art'en scooped her up, turned toward the trees with her in its arms. Caritha charged out the door and jumped on its back, driving her rusted blade into its neck. Rose'el followed, driving her sword into the Art'en's head. Evela joined them and snatched the child from its arms, ducking to avoid another of the creatures.

Levena and Laura darted outside and wrestled the Art'en nearest the house to the ground before slaying it. Seivar and Hasselpatch streaked into the fray, digging their silver talons into the assailants' backs, ripping at their wings, and viciously stabbing their beaks into the Art'en's bodies.

Swaying to its feet, the Grim Reaper evaporated in a cloud of dark smoke that shot toward the sky. Ilfedo gritted his teeth. He needed to keep it from getting away. Holding his sword with all his strength and pointing its blade at the ground, he willed it to flame. The sword blasted fire at the ground, launching him into the air. He reached into the Reaper's smoky essence, hoping that the sword would force the being back into skeletal human form.

The Reaper's body begin to take shape again. His hand closed on one skeletal arm. He slowed. His fingers slipped. As he fell away from the Reaper, he cried out, "I'm taking payment, you foul creature. Remember me when you think of returning to this land!" As he fell, the sword of the dragon sailed out of his hand end over end, severing one of the Reaper's arms.

As Ilfedo crashed to the ground, he stared at the Reaper's startled face. The Reaper wisped from its bodily form into black smoke. Ilfedo looked down at Death's severed arm imprisoned in his fist. As he struggled to his feet, he dropped it, then raced into the forest after the Art'en.

Every sense seemed enhanced. He hunted the winged men with ease, finding several hiding in the trees. Inflamed by the sword's strength, he climbed the trees faster than the creatures could escape. None of the Art'en survived the night. The Warrioresses combed the forest floor, and the Nuvitors soared overhead.

A couple hours later Ilfedo counted twenty-three dead Art'en. Oganna woke with a headache and said that she'd been knocked in the head by one of the creatures. At first he thought she was trying to show that she did not fear the creatures. He shook his head and told Evela to put her to bed. But the child walked to the midst of the clearing, bent down, and picked up the skeletal arm.

With a smile on her face, she handed it to her father and kissed him. "I love you, Father." There was no fear in her blue-gold eyes, only gratitude.

He felt her head but found only a bruise, so he put her into Caritha's bed that night, more for his own peace of mind than for hers. "This attack," he said in a hushed voice, sitting on the edge of the bed and gazing into Caritha's sober face, "did you sense where it was directed?"

"How do you mean, brother?" she whispered.

The other sisters filtered into the little room, standing against the walls. Laura, Evela, and Levena brushed their long, thick hair. Caritha had already cleaned up. Rose'el's hair remained askew, and her eyes refused to leave Oganna. Evela offered her brush to Rose'el. "You need it."

"Keep it for yourself!" Rose'el said. Evela's eyes widened, and she stepped back. Rose'el offered no apology. Her gaze remained on the sleeping child.

Ilfedo half-smiled, then said, "I sensed the Reaper's focus. All it wanted during the struggle was my child. It wanted Oganna."

"But why?" Caritha looked at Oganna and lightly stroked the girl's blond locks.

Ilfedo shook his head. That he did not know.

For a long while everyone was silent. Then Caritha, gazing into each of her sisters' dark eyes, said, "The dragon promised you that dark times lie ahead. Perhaps it is time to begin teaching Oganna what we know. We can teach her how to fight and how to exercise the power in her dragon blood."

"She is my baby girl—"

"A dragon's offspring, nevertheless, brother. It is time you see that for what it is." Caritha frowned. "Untrained, she is helpless, but with our instruction she can be as strong as any of us."

Ilfedo paced to the door and back. Oganna was so young, so innocent. Must she be condemned to endure horrors in her youth, as he had? As hard as it was to admit, though, Caritha was right about her dragon blood. The dragon's sword afforded him great power in battle, but he knew nothing of the mysterious power inside his daughter. If only the sword smith had remained with them, Ilfedo would have gladly given Oganna into his tutelage. Without Linsair, he'd need to rely on the sisters.

"You may train her," he said at last.

Caritha smiled and nodded.

"However, you must not bring her with you on any mission. Perform what training exercises you must, but perform them here." As the sister started to object, he raised his hand to silence her. "These are my terms. My child's safety is my first concern, and if it is not yours also, then I cannot give her into your instruction. I lost her mother. I will not lose her."

"And if your fear leaves her less capable of defending herself in a desperate moment?"

"I will protect her, my sister." He stood, bent, and kissed his child's cheek. "Goodnight." With that he trudged upstairs and lay in his bed. Seivar and Hasselpatch flew to him. "My dear, trusted companions." They cooed, rubbing against him. He brought them downstairs and washed them in the sink. Then he trundled them into bed, leaned the sword of the dragon against the wall nearby, and fell into deep sleep.

⁂   ⁂   ⁂

Sitting against a tree, Specter spat blood and laughed. He looked at the sky. The Grim Reaper had shot like a black comet into the east. "You fled like the snake you are!" And he laughed again.

He still felt weak. The thrill of seeing the man defend his child, though, and the ferocity of Ilfedo's attack, made the dark being's defeat sweet as honey in his stomach.

How swift and sudden was the Reaper's humiliation. How unexpected and glorious! The evil spirits had fled as well. Peace reigned where terror intended to take root. A moist cold wind tossed the hood off his head and forced tears from his eyes.

Specter stood and smiled. He could sense the strength emanating from Ilfedo's house, and it had been a long time since he'd felt such security. In truth, he had not felt such strength in a very long time. Carrying his scythe on his shoulders, he strode into the depths of the forest. Hope seemed to shine from heaven, the favor of God upon Specter's young ward.

# 7

# LORD AND PRINCESS

Holding his ten-year-old daughter's hand firmly in his own, Ilfedo led her through the crowd thronging the streets. Stirred dust tickled his nostrils and clouded his path. He wrinkled his nose at the strong odor of lye coming from the wash hung between the small houses on either side of the street. Ignoring the stares and hushed voices that followed him, he made his way to the stockade fort at the street's end.

It was regrettable that its demand for wood had thinned out much of the forests, but he considered it a small price to pay for a secure nation, and he did not wish to stop cultural change. In this case, he believed, it was for the betterment of all mankind.

"Father." Oganna tugged his sleeve with her free hand. "Why is everyone staring at us?"

He'd found himself wondering of late when she would ask a question he could not answer. As with most children, she was full of questions. Crouching, he brushed a strand of loose hair from her forehead. "You and I are important to these people."

The child frowned, then turned to point behind them at Ombre. "They do not stare at him."

"I think they do. It's just that they have seen him before. We, on the other hand . . ." He smiled. "I've never brought you here before."

A breeze caught her golden hair and flung it across her face. She brushed it aside and returned the crowd's gaze. Her eyes bore a startling severity, and Ilfedo observed that many of the bystanders were more than a little taken with her.

He let out a long, slow breath, remembering how the people of the Hemmed Land had wanted him to become their Lord Warrior. That mantle of authority would pass, upon his death, to his daughter—the princess, as people called her. His position had enabled him to work for the greater good.

The past six months had seen no more Art'en appearances. The latest incident had inspired a thorough combing of the nation's forests. No more of the creatures had been found. He had chosen to keep the Reaper's involvement a secret. Some would have called him a fool for claiming the Specter of Death really existed. Some would have called him proud for assuming it would be interested in visiting death particularly upon him and his household.

Come what may, he was confident of the future—and he had reason to be. Ombre had taken charge of forming the military with a zeal equaled by none. Honer was organizing centers of learning and overseeing the building of a national archive to preserve the ancient scrolls and texts passed on from their forefathers. Besides this, Ganning oversaw the local governments and ensured that they executed justice with mercy.

In the past many people had been executed after controversial verdicts in cases of theft and bigotry. With his three friends aiding him, Ilfedo had strengthened the trust and loyalty of the people.

The fort's sentries acknowledged him with salutes from the guard towers. He approached and commanded them to open the gate. Wood creaked and an out-of-sight latch was lifted. The oversized double doorway opened outward, and he slipped inside, pulling Oganna with him. As the gates closed behind him, the sounds from the noisy streets without were cut off. He relaxed his stance.

A fist pounded on the gates, and they reopened. "Thanks for shutting the door in my face!" Ombre shook his fist at the guards, and they cowered out of sight.

"Sorry, Ombre." Ilfedo laughed as his friend dusted his clothes.

His friend shook his head and waved his hand, indicating the interior of the structure. "What do you think?"

"It's very nice. The walls look sturdy, the parade grounds—" Ilfedo lifted his eyebrows as he realized how roomy the fort was. "More than adequate."

To his left stood a long, low building with barred windows. The musty smell of hay affirmed his assumption. "The stables?"

"Yes."

On the right was a two-story barracks. The command center rose directly ahead of him. Stilts elevated it about eight feet off the ground, and a narrow ramp zigzagged from the ground to the door.

A rather plump man—but not a very short one—walked out of the command center and saluted before descending the ramp to address Ilfedo. "Commander Veil, at your service, my Lord."

"Commander Veil is living up to his reputation as one of our best officers." Ombre stepped next to the broad man and grasped his shoulder. "There is hardly another man in our army whom I would trust as much to safeguard our interests."

"You flatter me, my lord," Commander Veil said with a bow in Ombre's direction. The fine chain mail he wore glittered in the warm sunlight. "I simply follow the orders of my lords, trusting them to do what is best for our people."

Ombre slapped the man congenially then directed his attention to Ilfedo. "Veil has been assisting me with a personal endeavor."

He led Ilfedo to the stable, opening the wide doors to permit Yimshi's light inside. Fifty stalls flanked a broad aisle down the center. At least half the stalls appeared occupied. Whinnies filled the air, mingled with a few snorts.

Ombre proceeded half-way down the aisle and opened the door. Ilfedo peered in. The dark interior made it necessary to wait for his eyes to adjust to the light. A white stallion pawed the straw floor, spraying silver flakes from its hoof. Its mane appeared equally silver, glittering even.

"You caught him?" Ilfedo had heard Ombre tell again and again of the stallion that had saved his life and the unusual mares that had followed the stallion the night the Art'en attacked Ombre in the northward forest.

Ombre stepped into the stall and stroked the animal's neck. It flared its nostrils at Ilfedo but nuzzled Ombre. "I didn't really catch him. You could say he caught me. A most unusual animal, wouldn't you say?"

Ilfedo noticed Oganna take an eager step toward the horse. He held her back. "You were saying, Ombre, something about an endeavor?"

"Yes." Ombre patted the stallion's neck and backed into the aisle, closing the stall door. He strolled to the next stall and rested his hand on the half-door. A white horse poked its head through, and Ombre ran his fingers through its silvery mane.

"Two of the same?" Ilfedo reached out, expecting the wild animal to pull back.

"Actually," Ombre said with a chuckle, "this is the same breed. Only difference is, she's a mare. You remember the night these animals protected me from the Art'en?"

"It is impossible for me to forget. They were magnificent in the wild."

Ombre stroked the mare's muzzle. She snorted and turned away. "Veil and I searched out these creatures and brought them here. It wasn't exactly easy, but they are strong and more intelligent than ordinary horses."

He led the way out of the stable and dropped to one knee in front of Oganna. "How's my favorite little lady?"

"Can I ride one of those horses, Uncle Ombre? Please."

"That would be up to your father."

A fly buzzed in Ilfedo's face, and he swatted it away. "Are they tame?"

"The mares? No. But the stallion rides gentler than a Nuvitor in flight. I'm breeding them. The mares seem more free-spirited than the stallion, surprisingly." He patted Oganna's back. "She'd be safe with me."

"You said you are breeding them?"

"Evenshadow stallions would make invaluable mounts for the army officers, Ilfedo. I've tested these animals, and their strength and stamina is superior to ordinary horses."

Ilfedo nodded. He'd heard that Commander Veil had an affinity for horses. "So you and Veil are looking to train young stallions for battle."

"Precisely!" Ombre stood and tousled Oganna's blond hair. "What do you say I take her for a ride?"

At that moment Caritha entered the fort. As the great doors shut behind her, she strode toward Ilfedo. He kissed Oganna's forehead and shooed her toward Ombre. "Have fun but be careful, my daughter. And, Ombre, take care of her."

Then he turned to greet Caritha.

"The Elite Thousand are ready," she said to him, while casting a subtle glance in Ombre's direction. "My sisters and I have taught them everything they are capable of learning. It is time to begin instructing our new pupil."

He steered her toward the gates. "First, I want to see what the Elite are capable of."

Commander Veil joined them at Ilfedo's request. They left the fort and the town, making their way through the forest to the encampment of the Elite. Veil entered ahead of them. His orders rang from one tent to the next. "Lord Ilfedo wishes to test the soldiers. Every man, fall into line!"

The lines hastily formed with a precision Veil could be proud of. The afternoon sun left few shadows, and the dirt crunched dryly under Ilfedo's boots. He drew the sword of the dragon from his side. Every soldier gazed upon him, emotionless.

As the flames sprang from the blade, Ilfedo fondled the crystalline handle. It felt incredibly smooth, even soft. "One by one Commander Veil will call you forward," he said. The armor solidified on his body, rippling light that challenged the day. "Those of you who are called will individually step forward and demonstrate to me that you are capable of not only wielding your weapon but that you know how to defend yourself from fire by using its power."

Unrolling a scroll and holding it before his face, Commander Veil called out the first name. "Ezekiel Madon!"

A burly, short fellow stepped from the ranks and marched between them to face Ilfedo. He was garbed in nothing more than a long-sleeved black shirt, gray pants, and leather shoes. But he drew his blade from its sheath with great speed. Light flashed from his sword, and his body glowed a moment, decking him in white armor—a metallic breastplate and greaves and white-leather garments underneath. A white helm adorned his head. His sword never ceased to glow with white light.

Ilfedo took aim with his weapon and sent flames from its blade. The fire raged toward Ezekiel Madon but funneled into his blade, leaving him unburned.

Running forward, Ilfedo struck Ezekiel's blade with his own. The Elite warrior struck back, held his own. For several long minutes Ilfedo beat on the man's sword until, satisfied it would not break and the man could hold his own, he stepped back and bowed. "Return to your place in line, Ezekiel Madon. You have passed the final test."

Striking his chest with the pommel of his sword, the man sheathed his weapon, the armor vanished, and he marched back into line.

"Benediah Hilthan!" Commander Veil called out.

And so the afternoon progressed. Every man merited Ilfedo's sincerest respect. When evening came and Yimshi settled behind the hills, the Elite Thousand drew their swords, and the plain in which they stood radiated with beautiful light.

Ilfedo stood apart from them and exhaled slowly. "Magnificent."

❧   ❧   ❧

Oganna grinned at Uncle Ombre, and his eyes twinkled.

"Are you ready, little one?" He knelt in front of her, poked her stomach, and hopped to his feet again. "Someday I want to have a little girl just like you—"

"You do?"

His gaze wandered after Caritha as she walked alongside Ilfedo. "Unless your aunt softens toward me it will never happen." He sighed.

"I like you, Uncle Ombre."

"And I like you, little one." He bobbed his head toward the stable. "Want to go riding?"

She jumped, and he caught her, swinging her legs over his strong shoulders. He glided into the stable, ducking once to keep her from hitting her head on the doorframe. The Evenshadow stallion whinnied and kicked the stall door.

"Anxious, aren't you Midnight?"

"Is that his name?" she asked.

He chuckled as he opened the stall door and lifted her off his shoulders onto the magnificent creature. "Yes, my little princess. Midnight is his name." Her legs barely held on to the animal's shoulders.

Ombre patted the Evenshadow's shoulder and stroked its neck before slipping the bridle over its ears. He swung up behind her, his knees gripping Midnight's sides. The stallion's body quivered, and its muscles rippled beneath them. Ombre held her firmly with one arm while managing the reins of their mount with the other.

He leaned forward. "Fill your hands with his mane, Oganna." She grabbed handfuls of the long silvery hairs and tightened her fists.

Midnight lunged out the door, and she felt as if she'd left her breath in his stall as he raced through the courtyard.

"Open the gates!" Ombre called.

Four swordsmen put their bodies against the doors, forcing them open ever so slowly. Midnight screamed. He darted through the narrow opening between the gates. The people in the streets divided before them. At last they left civilization and raced through the fields. The rush of air cooled her face, startled birds flew past her head, and Yimshi's rays turned the greenery into gold.

Midnight's hooves beat methodically, pulling and driving him forward until he came to the forest's edge. The horse did not slow its pace. Reaching the tree line, it slipped between the trunks and fled over the forest floor.

Ombre leaned over Oganna, and his body pressed her against the stallion's neck until silvery hairs whipped around her head. He guided the stallion left, avoiding a large tree. A fallen tree lay across their path at eye-level, and she ducked her head until they passed beneath it. She raised her head.

The underbrush a dozen yards ahead of them appeared too thick to let them pass, but Ombre steered Midnight through at breakneck speed. She buried her nose in the flailing strands of mane—not harsh, but soft and comforting—and leaned forward.

Ombre wheeled the stallion around another tree and brought it to a halt. Golden beams streamed through the branches above, and vibrant green grass shivered in the meadow before them. Blue grass grew in small patches all about.

He kicked off the horse, then helped her to the soft ground. As her feet landed, they stirred pollen into the air. The fragrance of flowers filled her nostrils. She bent down, pulled a clump of blue grass by the roots, and ran her fingertips over the fuzzy blades. At night the blades would glow. She had seen it happen.

"Beautiful, is it not?"

She nodded and swatted a mosquito with her free hand.

"That stuff used to be a rarity. However, it seems to be spreading as time goes on."

Placing the grass in the dirt, Oganna nodded vigorously. "Father told me that some people are purposefully transplanting it. He said they want it to spread because it is so pretty."

"Like a beacon of hope after our clouded history." He smiled and patted Midnight's glistening coat. The stallion blew through its nostrils and galloped into the forest. "He'll be back after he finds a cold stream." Ombre gazed after his mount. Then he waved his hand toward the curious patch of plucked grass. "People want to spread this stuff for two reasons, not just for its visual appeal. They are anxious about the Art'en. They think that by spreading this around the floors of our forests they can illuminate the shadows of night, thus keeping those winged men from sneaking upon them."

She sat in the grass. Across the clearing a rabbit dove under a bush. "Yipe!" She could have sworn it had said, "Yipe!" She shook her head and looked up at him. "Uncle Ombre, do you think the winged men are gone forever?"

"Now that is impossible to say." He sat beside her and crossed his legs, patting her head. "Did they frighten you the other night?"

With a nod, she glanced at a finch perched at the meadow's edge. It shook its tiny head and sneezed—she was sure she had seen it sneeze. But that was impossible. "Achoo!" Again she shook her head, trying to clear the sound from her mind.

"Are you all right?" Ombre frowned down at her and felt her forehead. "You haven't been having bad dreams or anything like that, have you?"

"Oh no, Uncle Ombre, I never have bad dreams."

He chuckled and shook his head. "You can't fool me. Even I had my share of nightmares as a child. Used to be bears as big as a house—"

"Uncle Ombre?"

"Mmm?" He twirled a lock of her hair around his finger and glanced at the sky, shading his eyes with his hand.

She sighed and gazed up at him. "I *really* never have a bad dream—believe me. I'm not lying."

Returning her gaze he seemed to search her heart for a moment. His eyes widened and his brow rose. "That is not—natural." He stroked his jaw with his thumb. "You always have good dreams?"

Soberly, she fingered the clump of night grass. Should she tell him what was on her mind? He wouldn't believe her. Of that she was certain. But what if she could share the experience with him?

Ombre stood and took her hand in his. He walked her into the forest where bees buzzed past their heads and clamored over the blue and yellow flowers carpeting the ground. Butterflies of extraordinary variety flitted to more distant purple and white petals, keeping just out of reach. Yimshi's rays pierced the woods, spotlighting a pool of water surrounded by bright moss. A small rainbow graced it where a light mist rose from the water's surface.

They sat cross-legged on a moss-covered stone. Oganna watched the scenery for a long while, drinking in creation's glory. Then a strange voice entered her mind. "Fat, lazy humans—blurp! I wish they'd just leave." The only things in sight were the butterflies and bees. Oh, and one bullfrog spying from the opposite side of the pool, only its head visible in the mud.

"Uncle Ombre," she said, turning to him and frowning. "Would you think me silly if I told you a strange secret?"

"A strange secret?"

"Yes. It is something I have not told anyone else. I know that people would laugh at me for saying it." She suddenly jerked her head as another sound caught her ear. "I think I can hear the frogs talking."

He knit his brow, skepticism filling his eyes. "Talking frogs?"

"Never mind." She turned away, wishing she hadn't told him. And why should he believe her? It sounded very silly, even to her. Then his hand grasped her shoulder.

"Forgive me, little one. I should not doubt you." He sighed. "Please, go on. Tell me everything."

A second bullfrog joined the first, and they hopped onto lily pads. One croaked, and she again heard something, though this time she could not discern what had been said. She waited a moment, and the croaking resumed. An entire conversation entered her mind. Not understanding why, she reached up, touched Ombre's forehead, and listened to the bullfrogs. Their words formed in her mind, and she felt that he could now hear them too. His eyes grew big, and his jaw dropped in astonishment.

"Do you hear them, Uncle Ombre?"

In hushed tones he replied, "I do. I hear the bullfrogs talking!"

For several minutes they listened together. Oganna maintained her touch on his forehead. The bullfrogs boasted to one another of their underwater homes and of how many tadpoles they had raised. They talked about the weather and complained about their neighbors. All in all, it sounded very much like a conversation between two people—except of course that they spoke of the most distasteful things for supper and of mannerisms that, to a human, were very strange.

Oganna dropped her hand from his forehead. "Sometimes," she said, "I can hear other creatures talking too, and I—"

"Go on, little one. Tell me what's on your mind."

"Some of the wild animals come when I think of them." Silence followed her claim. She rose and closed her eyes to focus her thoughts on a buck, nearby in the forest's undergrowth. She could feel it respond to her call, and she heard it walk up behind her. A cool breeze rustled the leaves as the buck nuzzled her neck, then plucked a flower with its teeth and set it in her hand.

Ombre looked up at her with mouth agape and eyes shining. "I never . . ."

She petted the buck until it meandered back into the forest.

"Little one." Ombre gazed into her eyes. "I won't pretend to know how you do these things, but from now on I promise you can tell me anything, and I will believe you. You are special, Oganna. Like your mother, you are unique."

They remained by the pool a little longer, but daylight was fleeting.

"Are you ready to go?" Uncle Ombre threw her over his shoulder and returned to the clearing. She laughed the whole way until he set her in the grass.

Midnight lifted his head from his grazing, whinnied, and trotted up to them. Silver flaked off his hoofs as he moved, leaving glowing chips on the ground.

"Up we go." Ombre set her in front of him on the Evenshadow, and they rode back to the fort.

As Ombre put Midnight in his stall and removed the bridle, Commander Veil barreled into the stable. "Princess," he asked, "how would you like a tour of our little town?" He looked to Ombre for permission.

"If you promise to keep an eye on her at all times—"

"Of course I will!" Veil leaned down and grinned. "What do you say, Princess?"

She smiled back and gave him her hand. "I've always wanted to see the market."

"As you wish." He bowed. She giggled.

Ombre chuckled. "Beat it, you two! And have a good time."

When Veil and Oganna made their way to the market, a crowd followed them through the streets. The people pressed in and stared. They were not unfriendly, yet she found it discomfiting to be the center of attention.

When they reached the market, everyone finally turned their attention away from her to the farmers behind their carts and the merchants tending their stands.

"Come and see rubies, gold, even diamonds," called a round man with a bald head. He ran his hand over his display of glistening gems. Two men stood by him, each of them with a hand inserted beneath his cape. Likely they concealed weapons.

She peered through a white fence penning in a flock of sheep, at the young shepherd boy standing in the corner keeping an eye on them. Several passersby stopped, and a deeply tanned farmer stepped around the pen, grinning as he let them touch the wool draped over his arms.

Nearby, a hunter held up raccoon pelts. A deer hung behind him on a rack.

Occasionally a farmer's crops produced insufficient return, and he would find himself without the means to provide for his family. Sometimes a hunter would have an off-season and would find himself without the means to trade for that which he needed. These people came to the market as well and tried to barter as best they could for what they needed.

She saw one such man that evening. He was speaking with a merchant as she passed by. "I don't have anything to trade, good sir," she overheard him say. "But I am an honest man. I will pay you back double—soon as I am able."

"Sorry, mister." The merchant held up his hand as if to protect his produce. "I can't be giving handouts, or I'll end up in the ruts too. Now get lost! Come back when you have something substantial to offer."

The farmer hung his head as he turned away.

"Stop!" Oganna broke free of Veil's grip. She ran to the man and gazed up at him. As everyone watched, she reached into her dress pocket and drew out a beautiful gold chain. It had been a gift from a mayor's wife on her last birthday. "Use this!"

The man's eyes widened. He looked at her offering, then at her. "My child, you are too kind. But I cannot take it. Times will favor me again."

Confused by his refusal, she backed away. Then, seeing he was embarrassed, she spoke again. "The gold is nothing to me. Take it."

Commander Veil lumbered up from behind her and put both hands on Oganna's shoulders. "Do not refuse the future queen's gift."

"Princess!" The farmer fell to his knees. "Forgive me. I did not realize. Certainly I will not accept—"

Another voice interrupted him. "You most certainly can, and will." The crowd parted. Ilfedo stepped through with Ombre following. The people bowed and made room for him. "Oganna will one day rule over your children. Do not deny her this simple deed, for in the performance of such things her heart will be encouraged to do good rather than evil."

He addressed Veil. "See to it that this man and his family are given what they need." He picked up Oganna and she rode on his back.

Holding on to her father with one hand, she held out the gold chain and smiled at the farmer. "Hold out your hand."

The farmer's eyes sparkled as she dropped the chain in his open palm.

"Thank you, sweet child."

Oganna nodded her head slightly, Ilfedo turned away, and they returned to the fort. Once inside, her father set her at a wooden table in the command center. An array of weapons decorated the walls. There was a wide variety of swords, as well as some spears and a few shields.

"The Elite are prepared," Ilfedo said as Ombre and Commander Veil took seats. A fly buzzed by and landed on the table before him. With a deft motion he brought his hand down and squashed it. "Little is left to do as far as building the army is concerned and, thankfully, no military challenges have presented themselves. I suggest that, for the time being, we keep the army busy by using it to construct roads and bridges."

"We should consider forming a few more patrols for the northern border." Ombre leaned back in his chair, crossed his arms behind his head. He glanced sideways at Oganna. "I'd hate to see any more Art'en sneak across the border."

At that moment Caritha walked in. "Now the first task is complete. The Elite Thousand are ready to be incorporated into the army." Her eyes focused on Oganna. "With your permission, my brother, my sisters and I are ready to begin the training."

Ilfedo closed his eyes for a moment. When he opened them, he came to his daughter and stroked her blond hair. "Very well. When do you wish to begin?"

# A SWORD CALLED
# AVENGER

Oganna parried her opponent's thrust with ease, rolled on the ground, and came up behind. The strength of her youth was reaching its peak now, for she had passed her seventeenth birthday. She slipped her blade around the woman's neck and held it gently against the jugular. "Surrender?"

"Most definitely." Laura bowed and backed away.

"Well done." Caritha stepped from the ring of trees that formed the natural arena. "Not meaning you, of course." She shook her head at Laura and quietly laughed.

"Oh?" Laura asked with a note of challenge in her voice. "Why don't you try to best her?"

Oganna smiled and ran the flat of her sword's blade along her white glove. The metal zinged as she did so, and Yimshi's light caught its shining edge, casting rivulets of metallic radiance. "Aunt Caritha, you aren't afraid I'll win, are you?"

"How long have you trained with us?" Caritha crossed her arms.

Oganna knew that Caritha did not need to be answered—her training had taken seven years. In all that time she had exhibited an affinity for swordplay. No other woman in the Hemmed Land could match her now. In fact she was able to hold her own for some time in bouts with her father—though he won eventually. Of the Warrioresses, only Caritha had never tested herself against Oganna in one-on-one sword fighting, and some people had expressed the opinion that she was as good, if not better, than Oganna.

Caritha pointed at her. "You have trained with us for seven years. Now—at seventeen—you wish to challenge me?"

"Why not? Father and I have challenged each other on numerous occasions."

"Oganna, I do not fight in the manner of your father. He has strength on his side and size. Whereas he drives his blade like a hammer into his opponent, I rely on my speed and accuracy. Beyond that, I rely a good deal on the power in my dragon blood. To challenge me, you would need to first master your dragon half."

Levena and Evela emerged from the encircling trees and sat on a log. Rose'el followed them but leaned against a tree instead of sitting. She crossed her arms and rolled her eyes. "Humph! Caritha, stop this foolishness. You have put off Oganna's challenges for too long. I for one would like to see her prove herself. Her father does not utilize all his skills against her and among us *you* are the quickest with a blade. Give Oganna a challenge."

"Yes." Laura, Levena, and Evela raised their eyebrows. "Let's see teacher and student test themselves against one another."

Caritha shook her head and faced Oganna. "Stay clear of the ring everyone." She leaned down to part the fold in her garment wherein the rusted sword was concealed. "What conditions would you like to lay down with regard to this match?" Caritha asked.

"No conditions," a male voice said from the trees. Ombre stepped out, grinning from ear to ear. "Let's see Caritha use everything available to her!"

Caritha looked at him out of the corner of her eye and picked at the ground with her blade. "Everything?"

"Yes." Oganna grinned. "Use everything you can."

"Oganna, you have not yet learned anything about the true power of dragon blood. But that is my greatest defense. Without it you haven't a chance in this world of beating me."

There was a thick chuckle from Ombre when he heard that, and Oganna glanced at him. Would he be able to keep secret the reason for his confidence in her long enough to let her surprise the Warrioress? She watched him move to Caritha's side.

"How about a little bet?" He brushed his nose against her cheek, and she flushed. "You say that Oganna has no chance against you, but I think you are wrong. Dead, dead, dead wrong." He took a step back.

Caritha cleared her throat. "Oh, and what stakes did you have in mind?"

He leaned over and whispered something in her ear. Color mounted to her cheeks again. When he backed away, she glanced about the clearing into everyone's faces. "Well, Caritha?" Ombre chuckled, and Oganna thought he sounded hopeful.

Slowly, Caritha nodded her head. Whatever the wager, Ombre seemed happy about it. He walked away, sat on a tree stump, and waited for the match to commence.

Many opponents Oganna had observed tended to circle each other, evaluating before joining in combat. She preferred a different approach; she preferred to strike immediately and thus force her opponents to respond on the defensive.

She stood straight, letting her blue-gold eyes stare blankly ahead as she relied on another sense. Deep within her being she had long ago discovered a source of inhuman strength and drive that she could explain only as dragon power. There were things she could do that were not possible unless she searched for that something within her—things she could feel and things she knew that no one suspected she could do.

Even now she felt the power growing inside her, filling her, and branching out. But she held it back, only using it to block Caritha's attack. The first strikes, she was determined, would not be won by magic. No, they would depend on her skill with a blade.

Flipping forward, she landed in front of her aunt, and they both swung their blades simultaneously. Metal clashed with metal, and such was the force of their attack that they both reeled backward.

The observing Warrioresses gasped. Even Ombre with his tendency to treat events lightly, narrowed his eyes. Perhaps he'd assumed a 'friendly' bout would mean an easy one. But this was her chance to prove her worth in battle.

Caritha swung her rusted blade, and Oganna blocked with her own sword. The force of the rusted weapon buffeted her. It might as well have been her father wielding the sword of the dragon against her. She fell to the ground and rolled to the side, rising again to her feet.

Once more Caritha struck, and once more Oganna fell. Caritha struck at her with rapid strokes, ringing metal against metal until Oganna's wrists ached. She closed her eyes and let her senses dig deep into that reservoir of energy she'd discovered in her blood. Strength flowed into her arms and her wrists. She opened her eyes and smiled up as her aunt darted to the side and swung her sword for another strike.

This time Oganna had no difficulty absorbing the impact. She swung her weapon up and stood. Their blades clashed, and this time Oganna sensed an extra force behind her aunt's blade, something strengthening the older woman's arms and steadying her weapon. But now Oganna's power matched her aunt's. Their blades locked against one another, neither giving way.

Gazing between the swords, Oganna met the woman's eye and laughed. Caritha's eyes widened, and she gritted her teeth.

Oganna spun to free her blade from the stalemate. She came around and rained blows like hail against the rusty sword. Her breaths came easily, yet she maintained a speed to her movement that was unrivaled by either the Warrioresses or her father. She knew it. She could feel it.

Soon Caritha's hand no longer held the rusted sword as tightly as it should. Oganna charged, but Caritha rolled out of her path. Turning, Oganna saw her aunt facing her with her outstretched hands, palms up. Suddenly the tree branches grew. From over Caritha's head they extended to the ground before her.

The branches left no room for Oganna to slip through. She could hack the branches and waste precious time as Caritha recouped her energy. She bit her upper lip. The barrier presented a new challenge of a sort she'd secretly played with on numerous occasions.

She reached out with her mind until the trees' essence reached her subconscious. Her vision darkened, and in place of the normal world she saw the root systems of every tree and the skeletal forms of her aunts and Ombre. For a moment the comical appearance of things made her want to laugh. Then she reached out with her hand and pulled at the tree roots with her mind.

The roots stabbed out of the ground, wrapped around Caritha's feet, and grew six feet high. She held her palm toward the branches, willing them to return to their lofty abodes. The branches shrank away from the ground. Oganna closed her eyes and held the back of her neck. A feeling of weightlessness washed over her for an instant. When it passed she blinked open her eyes to find Caritha suspended in the air by her feet.

"You were harder than I thought you would be." Oganna curtsied to the disheveled woman. "Are you ready for me to let you down?"

For a moment it seemed Caritha would admit defeat. Then Ombre stepped closer with a smug grin on his face. "Well, my lady, it looks like you will have to live up to your end of our bargain!"

Caritha grunted, struggling to free her feet. She shook her head. "Not yet, Oganna. I'm not finished yet."

Oganna's strange perception faded. People were no longer skeletons. Sizzling purple energy appeared on Caritha's body. It wove around her in a web of sparkling light, and the tree roots started to recede.

Oganna walked up to the roots. Her hand glowed blue as she touched the forest growth. Her soft light spread up the roots. Her vision returned to that of an ordinary person. The tree roots spread around Caritha's ankles, then her legs.

Caritha's struggle resulted in a partial release from the branches. One of her feet fell loose and dangled in a most undignified position.

The woman was strong, Oganna was forced to admit. She could feel Caritha's resistance through the roots. She held one of the roots, reaching deeper, manipulating the trees and using their direct contact with her aunt to read her intentions.

Shocks of energy coursed from Caritha into the roots. But Oganna cancelled the attacks with her own power. The trees shook violently as if unable to contain the powers struggling within. Cracks appeared in the bark. Water failed to feed the leaves. No longer could the plants function as a whole—the pressure was too great. The green leaves browned, the bark burned, and large sections splintered.

Her powers were coursing through them. Oganna could feel it happening. It coursed through them, over them, and at last her powers overwhelmed Caritha's resistance. The branches exploded, and the woman dropped to the earth.

The alarmed observers hastened to remove the debris. "Caritha, are you all right?" Laura felt for a pulse and heaved a sigh of relief. "Thank goodness! I thought you'd killed yourself with that display."

Dirty and sputtering, Caritha sat up. Turning her sword, she held it pommel-first toward Oganna. "I give up."

Oganna sat in the grass. All around them lay splintered and smoking wood. "I must admit you put up quite a fight. I had no idea you knew how to manipulate trees."

"And I had no idea you could use your powers, at least not with such control. Oganna, we did not teach you. Who did?"

"No one."

This reply did not appear to satisfy the woman. Standing, she glanced doubtfully at her and said, "It is impossible to learn how to use the power in dragon blood without an instructor. Responsibly, that is."

Oganna did not know how to reply. How could she deny the woman's wisdom and yet maintain the truth of what she said? Albino had taught them the use of their powers. "I've been tinkering with my 'abilities' ever since I discovered that some creatures talk."

Evela gasped and covered her mouth with her hand. She glanced at Caritha. "Just like Dantress!"

"Oganna is only half-dragon, Evela. The rest of her blood is human. I'm only assuming, but doesn't that mean she does not have the same potential? Dantress caught on more quickly than the rest of us. Her ability to manipulate her dragon powers was beyond anything we are able to do, so I suppose that is in Oganna's favor. Yet the limit of her power cannot be any more than ours. It may be less, but not more."

"Humph! You say that after she soundly thrashed you in fair combat." Rose'el waved her hand in dismissal and walked off. "Don't feel so certain of yourself, Caritha. I for one think my niece has great potential." She looked over her shoulder and winked at Oganna.

Oganna smiled back. "Thank you, Rose'el."

Ombre grasped Caritha's shoulders and gently turned her to face him. "I do believe this settles our little wager, my lady. Are you going to honor our agreement?"

"Rose'el, where are you going?" Laura called after her.

"Humph! Where do you think?"

"Oh! I almost forgot. Come along everyone," Laura said. "We should return to town and get these two cleaned up before dinner."

Oganna grimaced. "Ugh! I hate state banquets."

"No, you don't," Ombre said.

The tallest sister laughed as she stopped in mid-stride. She spun to glance at him. "Oh yes, she does."

He furrowed his brow. "What makes you say that?"

She raised her eyebrows knowingly. "One word of explanation, my dear friend."

Oganna watched Rose'el's amused expression, for Ombre was twiddling his thumbs as he waited for her to finish. "And, and—" he demanded. "What word?"

"Men."

"Men?" He looked confused. "Men aren't a problem. They love her."

Rose'el nodded. "Let me be more precise. *Young* men."

"Nonsense!" He rested a hand on Oganna's shoulder. "Oganna, if any of the young men behave improperly, just slap them in the face!" He raised his eyebrows. "But if you find one of them appealing—treat him nicely and just flash your eyes in his direction from time to time."

"Ombre!" Caritha scolded. "That would be no way for the future queen to behave."

But Oganna smiled to herself, amused. She mulled it over and pictured the consequence of such an action. Ombre winked at her, and she winked back. Though she loved her aunts, Uncle Ombre was closer to her than they. Even though she was not his blood relative, she knew that she had adopted a few of his mannerisms.

"Come now, everyone," Evela said. "The mayor of Gwensin will be looking for us at the table, and we mustn't keep Ilfedo waiting."

※　※　※

Emerging from the trees, Oganna sighted the city of Gwensin. It was now the fastest growing town in the Hemmed Land. Centrally located, it had been designated the national capital. She followed Ombre and her aunts along one of the broad dirt roads that led past prospering farms to the city itself. Rows of corn stood guard on either side, waving their long leaves in the wind as if in respectful acknowledgement of her passage.

Ahead rose the tall stone structures of Gwensin—spacious homes and businesses painted shades of blue and some of white. At the city's center lay the castle-like residence of the mayor. She turned a corner into the main street. Cheering people lined the way, waving streamers and shouting to her and her companions. She quickened her pace and hid between Evela and Levena.

They turned to her quizzically, and she put a finger to her lips. "A princess must never appear in public when she is filthy!" They understood and kept pace, shielding her from the crowds' stares.

The roadway was cobbled up to the open iron gates of the mayor's residence. Passing through, Oganna was struck by the manicured flower gardens. They were beautiful, broad, and disappeared around the building's solid corners as if they circled the entire mansion. Stone pathways formed a maze through them, with intermittent fountains and park benches placed along the way.

"Welcome to the State House." She acknowledged the butler, noting his yellow and black suit as well as his tall black hat.

"If you will follow me, Princess?" He led her away from her companions up one of the wooden stairways flanking the foyer. He took her to a large bedroom where he introduced her to three maids. "These girls will tend to your needs," he said.

She thanked him, then greeted her assigned helpers as he departed. "You work for the mayor and his wife?"

"Yes, my lady. We serve Master Vortain and his lady," one of them replied, dipping in a low curtsy. The other girls followed her example.

"Um, no. I will have none of that," Oganna said. "I do not keep servants."

"But, my lady, that is what we are—"

She chuckled. "Maybe you were, but you *are* no longer. The mayor knows I do not approve—of servitude, that is. I will see to it that you are given wages for your services. Understood?" They nodded, but they still looked confused. She opened a nearby closet and surveyed the elaborate dresses. A delightful idea popped into her brain, and she stifled a laugh.

"Please," she said to the girls, "go tell the staff to set three more places at the table for this evening." They left to carry out her instructions.

"Now let me see," she said when they'd gone. She laid the elaborate dresses on the bed. "Which four shall I choose?"

At the sound of a knock on her open door, she turned.

"May I enter?" Ilfedo stepped in, dressed smartly, with the mighty sword swinging from his belt. His creased, white pants were tucked into his freshly shined black boots. He wore a black shirt embroidered with gold, and long white gloves were on his hands.

After an affectionate embrace, he pointed to the bed. "Having trouble deciding which one to wear?"

"Not at all, Father. I think I'll use the crimson-and-white one."

"Then why the mess?"

She rolled her eyes. "The mayor assigned three maids to me—"

Ilfedo put a hand on her shoulder. "Do not do anything to embarrass our host. You may not agree with Vortain keeping servants, but he does them no wrong and they remain here of their own free will."

"Father, you have told me time and time again not to worry what other people think but to do what I think is right." She flashed him a smile. "Don't worry, I won't embarrass him. I'll just make him rethink his practices—and let him know I do not approve of keeping servants!"

"Very well." He pecked her on the cheek. "I'll see you at dinner."

As he left the room, the maids came back. "We did as you told us," they said.

One of them came close. She had a pretty, dimpled face, and long red hair. "We'd heard rumors, my lady, that you also disapprove of *other* people keeping servants. Is it true?"

She laughed and ran her fingers like a spider down a strip of lace. "It most certainly is."

"But this is how we earn our livings. We're indentured. There is nothing we can do about it."

Oganna held one of the dresses she'd chosen up to the girl's shoulders. "Mm hmm . . . now, take this into the washroom and put it on."

"My lady, I dare not!"

"Oh yes you do." She gave the girl a gentle push and looked at the other two. "Don't think you are getting out of this. I have dresses for you as well."

They opened their mouths to protest, and she shook her head. "It would be indiscreet for you to challenge me on this matter. My father may tolerate some things that his men of state do, even if he questions it. However, one day *I* will be queen." The warning seemed to drown out their protests. She saw to it that they changed, then slipped into her crimson dress. It fitted her perfectly.

When the maids finished dressing, they returned to the room and fought over the mirrors. When Oganna put on her dress, they put their hands over their mouths and squealed with delight. "You will drive the lads crazy with that!"

"I hope not." She eyed the others and whistled. "You girls *will* be driving the lads crazy."

They looked horrified. "Our lady, we cannot go to the banquet."

She listened for a time as they raised objections, but in the end waved them aside and shooed them ahead of her through the door. "There will be many eligible young bachelors at this party, and they will have to be fools to pass up you three."

"No one will have us," one protested. "We are mere maids."

"Nonsense! The honorable young men may be fewer than the fools, but the honorable ones will not care about your social standing. And those who do, cannot help noticing that you enter with the Lord Warrior's daughter."

"But we don't know anyone—"

She sped toward the dining hall. "Don't worry, I'll introduce you."

Under the vaulted ceiling of the dining hall stood a hefty, carved table of mahogany. Its eight thick legs curled up from the floor, shaped to spiral to the tabletop. Oganna guessed it was just over forty feet long. Finely dressed gentlemen and ladies rose from their chairs as she entered, and she spotted her father at the table's far end.

The mayor's wife frowned at the maids, and Vortain himself followed her example. He ran his fingers through his long blond hair until she caught his eye and nodded. He relaxed his shoulders and bowed as she sidled up to him.

"I do not need servants, Vortain," she whispered in his ear.

When his gaze returned to the maids and their fiddling fingers, she smiled. "What sort of a queen do you desire? I could have a retinue; indeed your own daughter might be my servant. Or shall I make peace with all that I meet and treat them as my equals?"

"If I may speak with all honesty, Princess." He folded his hands behind his back and scowled. "To build a kingdom requires strength of arm. Your diplomacy endears you to all you meet. But when you are queen, no one will be your true equal. If you lead this nation into a glorious future it will be *your* name that is remembered, and none other."

She bowed and gazed up into his eyes. "Without the hearts and minds of the people, Vortain, where is our strength?"

His face relaxed, and the hint of a smile touched his mouth as he dipped and kissed her hand. "Truly you will make a great and memorable queen, my lady. Shall we continue this debate at another time?"

She pulled back her hand with a nod and gestured to the maids. "These are lovely young ladies, and I hope you will extend to them the same courtesy that you have to me and the rest of my father's guests."

"As you wish, Princess." He managed a smile in the direction of the maids. "Your word, as it always shall be, is my command."

Nodding gracefully to the other guests, she bid them, "Good evening," and sat beside her father, indicating that the three girls were to sit on her other side.

Ilfedo put his arm around her shoulder, pulled her close, and whispered in her ear. "There's a rumor circulating that you bested Caritha in a sword match."

Catching the praise in his voice, she kissed his cheek.

He chuckled. "Well done, my daughter. Well done."

They greeted Laura, Evela, Levena, and Rose'el as they arrived. Honer and his wife Eva came next. The woman paused by Oganna's seat. Oganna took her hand, and Eva returned a squeeze. Shortly thereafter Ganning limped in with his wife on his arm. Now only two seats remained empty, one for Ombre and one for Caritha.

As the moments passed and neither showed, Oganna wondered where they had gone. "Father, do you know if Uncle Ombre and—" She hushed as his eyes looked past her to the entry doors. Ombre marched across the polished floorboards in a green dress coat and white trousers. His black boots shone, and his sword swung in its sheath by his side.

Caritha, her face slightly flushed, was holding his arm. She was arrayed in a fine dress of lavender, and her hair had been brushed until it shone like the still surface of a lake. Twin ruby earrings glinted in the lamplight, and a necklace of miniscule jewels adorned her neck. Her feet were bare. As she followed her escort to her seat, she allowed him to seat her before he settled beside her.

Their entrance created no small stir. Oganna saw people whispering to each other and could well imagine the questions they were asking. She couldn't help wondering herself: Was this the beginning of a permanent relationship? The answers were nobody's business—not even hers. She would have to wait to see how events unfolded.

Later that evening, as the guests filtered into the flower gardens, Oganna followed, stopping on one of the porches. The cool night air smelled of perfume and a lone cloud drifted across the sky. Ombre and Caritha walked along a path toward one of the fountains.

"Keeping an eye on our lovebirds?" Laura came up behind her.

Oganna had been resting her hands on the deck railing. Now she turned to reply. "If I hadn't seen it, I wouldn't have believed it."

"Don't get your hopes up that it is permanent." Laura nodded toward the couple. "Caritha is probably just fulfilling her end of that little bet she made with him earlier today. Still—I suppose if she didn't like him, she wouldn't be with him."

Oganna crossed her arms. "I hope there is more to it than simply keeping her word. They are two of a kind."

A moment's silence passed before Laura spoke. "Don't rest hope on it, for a union between them could never be. That would result in a child . . . and that would be the end of her."

At first Oganna felt like laughing her aunt's statement aside, but there was something cold about the way Laura had said it, as if she spoke from a deeply rooted conviction. "Why? Why would you say that?"

Laura shook her head and sighed.

"Does this have something to do with what happened to my mother? Are you saying she would have lived had I not been born?" A tear fled her eye, running down her cheek.

"I'm sorry." Laura wiped away the tear with her sleeve, then she sighed again and gazed after the couple. "Your father never told you how and why your mother died, did he?"

"No. He hasn't."

"Have you asked him about it?"

"She died giving birth to me. What more is there to know?"

Laura gazed back at her and tears formed in her eyes until they shone. "Giving birth, for a dragon's daughter, is always her last deed in the land of the living. Your mother knew she would die the day she found out she was pregnant. She fought to live, but ultimately the power in her blood had to be given to you—otherwise *you* would have died. So, you see, it was and was not by her choice." She swept her hand in a circle. "And the same is true of Levena, Rose'el, Evela, myself, and—yes—even Caritha. Ombre may want her fiercely and she may want him, but they could never be together."

Their conversation was interrupted as Rose'el joined them. She was frowning down at her dress. "Tore the fabric on that wicked chair," she muttered.

A young man in a long suit jacket swaggered toward them. His eyes fixated on Oganna. "Hi there," he said to her. He excused his way between Laura and Rose'el to her side. "I am Faynor."

After Laura's revelation, Oganna was not feeling social, and Faynor's manners lacked discretion, so she excused herself and moved toward the garden. The young man followed several paces behind. Perhaps he had mistaken her departure for an invitation.

"Faynor," she said, turning to face him, "I am not interested in your advances. If you wish to be a gentleman, you will leave me be."

He smiled in a foolish way and proffered his arm. "Later there will be dancing—"

"Thank you for your offer, but I am not interested." She left him and wandered alone through the gardens.

To her delight she stumbled upon the maids who'd been assigned to her. A dark-haired young man accompanied each of them. Each of the youths bowed to Oganna and politely moved aside. The girls' faces were no less than radiant. Oganna slipped past them, smiling encouragement and nodding as each girl lipped a "thank you."

Finding a quiet spot on a bench surrounded by petunias, she settled back. Nearby, hidden somewhere behind a shrub, she could just make out Ombre talking with Caritha. His words were too soft for her to pick out, and she was glad, for if he wanted her to know of what he spoke, he would tell her later. She was content to sit on the bench where her presence would not disturb them while she listened to the rhythm of their conversation.

Laura's words rang in her mind, but her aunt's fears seemed misplaced. Better to fear that Caritha would judge her own life more valuable than Ombre's love. She smiled to herself. Yes, and that is what her mother would have taught her, or had taught her by making such a sacrifice on her behalf. True love had no price.

Above her the sky filled with stars. Tonight was the time of new moon, the darkest night of the month. The constellations decorated the heavens. She picked out her favorite: the Fire Tree. It lay near the celestial pole, its imaginary branches marked by a plethora of bright star clusters and gas clouds.

Below the Fire Tree stretched the Blood Sword. Eight emerald stars formed its handle, six gold stars represented the sword's guard, and twenty brilliant ruby stars made up the blade. To the west a tiny comet blazed its steady trail of white across the heavens, and overhead a great fireball suddenly burst, lighting the ground in one flash as it burned through the atmosphere and burst apart without a sound.

She recalled speaking with an astronomer on the coast—an astronomer who also wore a monk's habit. He spent many evenings studying the heavens, and her father had once brought the man home for a visit to share his knowledge with Oganna. That night had been similar to this one—moonless and clear skies. A fireball had burst in the heavens, and she had gasped at the beautiful display.

But the monk frowned. "It is odd."

She turned to gaze at his face. "What is?"

"Child," he said, "if something as large as that apparently is exploded in the sky, you would expect to hear an explosion, even if it were only a faint one. Would you not?" He had shaken his head, still staring skyward. "It is as if something keeps the sound from reaching our ears. I wonder—I wonder if the Creator means for us to find out why."

Oganna sighed at the recollection. The world was beautiful, life was good, and she was content. Beside her an invisible foot left an imprint in the ground, and she slid to the opposite end of the bench. The seat creaked as someone unseen sat down.

"I was impressed with your duel today. It is most incredible how quickly your powers are manifesting themselves."

"No one is around," she said at the empty seat. She pleaded with her eyes. "Can you simply talk with me face to face?"

Specter's hood fell away from his smiling face. He looked down at her and rendered his whole body visible, then stretched his arm along the backside of the bench. "I overheard your conversation with Laura." His face sobered. "Are you all right?"

With a sigh that told him she was content, she slid next to him and let him put his arm around her shoulders. "Specter— my dear, silent guardian—my mother was blessed to have you watching over her. And now I am as well."

"Ah, your mother was a wonderful young woman." He exhaled slowly and gazed at the stars. "Your father was, I truly believe, the luckiest man on Subterran when it came to his wife. She was strong and beautiful—and you are like her."

"Don't disappear again for a little while. Please stay with me. You know you are like a second father to me."

A soft laugh escaped him, and he leaned his scythe over the back of the bench. "More like a long-lost great, great grandfather?"

She smiled up at him and warmth spread through her body upon seeing the softness of his gaze. "Tell me more about my mother. Please?"

# 9

# INCURSIONS

Each plod of the creature's feet sent shivers running down the observer's spine. His ruined town on the Hemmed Land's southern border with the desert shook. It was too dark for him to see clearly, but he peeked from concealment. In the middle of the road lined with rubble, he spotted the creature's enormous form outlined against the horizon stars. As glowing yellow vapors emanated from its nostrils, he trembled.

Sweat built on his forehead. He reached up to wipe it away, but a woman's scream stopped him. It had been impossible for the people to defend themselves, but apparently the creature hadn't found everyone. The frantic cry had come from a house by the bridge. Casting off consideration for his own safety, he darted across the bridge and entered the front door. A roar sounded, and in that instant the creature smashed its tail through the wall, turning the house into an impossible maze of fallen beams and broken glass.

Not daring to look through the gaping hole at the creature, he clambered over a broken couch and looked about. The woman was pinned to the floor by a beam. Again the creature roared and spurted flames, setting what remained of the roof ablaze. The woman's leg, glistening red with blood, protruded from under the wooden rafter. Her face was turning white.

The creature's hand smashed into the wreckage, sending rubble flying in all directions. The would-be-rescuer moved to cover his face with his arms, but a beam struck him and threw him from the building onto the bridge. Pain shot through his leg. He looked down. A large piece of glass had lodged in his calf, and his blood was pooling on the bridge. He grasped his leg with both hands. Ripping his belt off, he tied it just below his knee. The bleeding slowed, but he knew that unless he received medical attention soon, he would die.

The house walls had fallen outward, as if the creature had pulled them down, and a long, tooth-ridden snout poked over them. The woman screamed again. This time the creature blew a stream of vapors into the house. Its victim's cries broke off into a spasm of coughing, then ceased. Clenching his fists, the man ground his teeth. The tears streamed down his face. That woman was one of his neighbors, a good friend, and a good soul. Was there no pity in this creature's heart? Was there no shred of remorse for this senseless murder?

Several enraged townsfolk ran from their hiding places. Unheeding of their own peril, they stabbed pitchforks into the creature's thick hide. As it continued to pour vapors from its nostrils, their attack faltered. The townsfolk stumbled and fell, and the creature tossed their bodies into the town well.

Remaining out of sight, the man scrambled out of town. Reaching the shelter of the forest, he grasped a tree trunk for support before glancing back to let another tear hide the carnage from his eye.

Through the darkness he stumbled northward until he came to a woodcutter's secluded home. He beat on the door until it opened. Weakened from loss of blood, he fell forward on the floor. Excruciating pain shot through his body, and he cried out. "Please, send for help." He could not go on.

The woodcutter and another man came into the room, cleared the table, and lifted him onto it. They tended to his leg and gave him liquor to numb the pain. "That's the limit of my knowledge," the woodcutter said. "This man needs a doctor." He grabbed a lantern and barreled outside.

The man felt weak. He *was* weak. As the door closed, he blacked out. When he awoke, light was coming through a window to his right. He was lying in a comfortable, clean bed, and a woman was dressing his leg.

"You've been out for a while," she said, putting a hand to his forehead. "How do you feel?"

He breathed deeply. "Much better."

"Good." She turned away, but he caught her sleeve.

"Must not let that creature get away!" He spoke through clenched teeth. "Send help to my town. People are dead—some might still be alive."

"Your town?"

"Town of Bordelin." A wave of exhaustion swept over him, his vision blurred, and he lost consciousness.

⁜    ⁜    ⁜

Ilfedo was at his home enjoying a quiet afternoon when a messenger arrived. "My Lord, I have troubling news from the southern border." He proceeded to tell of the unidentified creature's attack on the town of Bordelin. "Several smaller settlements along that stretch of territory were also decimated." He extended the message toward Ilfedo. "People are panicking. Some have fled the border towns."

After the courier delivered the sealed dispatch, he left.

Going indoors, Ilfedo sat at the table and opened the letter written on animal skin. Laura and Caritha had been cooking dinner, but they paused and looked at the letter.

"What do you have there?" Laura asked.

"Trouble, likely." He laid out the skin and read aloud:

> To the Lord Warrior:
>
> Greetings from your faithful subjects. To you be health and prosperity all of your days. May Yimshi shine down with favor on you.
>
> With high consideration to your many duties, we request your attention to a matter that has presented itself in our midst: A creature of formidable strength has, in a single night, destroyed the town of Bordelin. Many of the town's inhabitants were slain, but a privileged few escaped the monster's clutches to tell us their tale.
>
> All the reports gathered from survivors were consistent, so we sent warriors and hunters to find the creature. They followed its tracks into the southern desert, but none of them has returned, and no word of their whereabouts has been received. We fear that the worst has befallen them and that our lives may also be in danger.
>
> The survivors have stated that the creature stands on six legs and exhales poisonous vapors from its nostrils. Some say that it breathes fire as well. Reports indicate that the creature's hide is too thick to be penetrated

by a spear and that it stands about ten feet high at the shoulders.

We are at a loss what to do unless a champion is sent to our aid. Please help us and avenge the innocents whose lives were so brutally taken.

We are respectfully,

Your humble subjects of the Hemmed Land's Southern Border

Ilfedo set the letter down, rose, and walked to the fireplace. This was supposed to be his vacation, yet this report was the second he had received today. Earlier he'd read a note given to him by another messenger, that one sent by Ombre.

For the last couple months Ilfedo had received disturbing news of vipers coming out of the northern desert under cover of darkness and poisoning people along the Hemmed Land's border whilst they slept. A dozen people had died, and he had sent Ombre to assess the situation from the safety of Fort North.

Caritha interrupted his thoughts. "You look perplexed."

"You might say that. This problem is along the *southern* border, and I already sent word to Ombre that I will meet him at Fort North within the next few days. I need to make certain the Art'en are not behind the viper problem. My previous struggles with them focused on the northern border. If the Art'en have returned, then Ombre will need my help in dealing with them."

Footsteps alerted him to the other sisters' presence. Rose'el, Evela, and Levena came from their bedrooms.

"Well, that cuts our vacation short," Caritha said with a sigh. "Say no more, Ilfedo. We will deal with this situation."

Rose'el huffed in a very loud manner and placed her hands on her hips. "Like he didn't know that you would volunteer our services."

He returned her accusation with a smile. "Whom else can I rely on to truly get the job done? I could send soldiers, but they would not be as efficient. I can't send the Elite Thousand because they are deployed along the northern border. I can't send Ombre because he is engaged at Fort North." He shook his head. "Of course—you don't have to go."

Drawing her rusty sword from the fold in her garment, Caritha sobered. "We will reap vengeance on the creature. Its blood will be spilled in payment for the blood it shed." Her hands glowed, and her sword's blade gave out a steady reddish light as she spoke.

The others followed her lead. Raising their swords, they formed a circle and touched their blades together in the center before pulling them back with lightning speed. "The five who are one," Ilfedo murmured. "May your swords execute justice in the Hemmed Land."

Putting away her sword, Evela cleared her throat then looked at him. "Actually, there is one more whom we would like to add to our party."

He narrowed his eyes. "Oh?"

"Oganna is ready, Ilfedo. In fact, she can stand among us as an equal."

The others nodded their approval. Caritha spoke up. "She has the makings of greatness, Ilfedo. Let her come with us."

"No. To that I will not consent. She is too young."

"Only in your mind, my brother." Caritha laid her hand on the table. "Did she not prove herself capable when she bested me?"

He shook his head, determined not to concede the issue. "Continue to train her in your ways, if you must. But do not permit her involvement in potentially lethal situations. When I feel she is ready, I will let you know."

"You send us into 'potentially lethal' situations quite often," Laura said. He could tell she regretted saying it as soon as the words left her mouth. She apologized and asked his forgiveness.

He waved it aside and put a hand on her shoulder. "I will think on the things you have said, and I am pleased that you hold Oganna in such high esteem. However, I do not believe she is ready. She is too young."

※　※　※

Standing outside, Oganna had heard the majority of the conversation through the skin that hung in the doorway. She was both saddened and hurt by her father's apparent lack of confidence in her. Evela was right. She *was* ready. Why could he not see that? Was he letting his fears interfere with his judgment in this matter? Regardless of the reason, she reached a decision of her own, but she went indoors and made no indication of what she'd heard.

Later when night had fallen and everyone slept soundly, Oganna slipped a robe over her silky nightgown and put on wool slippers, quietly opened her bedroom door, and peered around the kitchen and living room area. Embers glowed in the fireplace, casting flickering light around the room.

She tiptoed into the kitchen and opened an upper cabinet. It was too dark to see what lay on the top shelf, but she knew what she was looking for. Her fingers found a large iron lantern. She pulled it down and set it on the counter. Then she slid open one of the drawers by the sink and plucked out a small can of matches. Closing the drawer and the cabinet door, she tightened the cord around her robe and opened the house door.

Chill air blasted her, and the coals in the fireplace flared. After closing the door, she lit the lantern. Overhead a blanket of clouds blocked most of the stars, and no moonlight warmed the forest. She ran into the woods, following a familiar, albeit unmarked, trail beneath the high trees.

Owls hooted from every direction, and a possum skittered out of her path. At last she stopped at the crest of Mathaliah Hollow and gazed down, reaching out her senses to determine if Specter was nearby. Blue grass pretty much filled the hollow and outlined the cave entrance.

"Specter!" A gust of wind stole her voice, and she ran to the cave entrance, shivering. If he was there, she could not sense him. "Are you here?" She walked into the cave's main chamber and found it empty except for the old sword and crystalline boomerang. She drew in her breath slowly, then knelt in front of the weapons and reached out to at last take her sword.

"Oganna, why have you come to me at this hour?" Specter coalesced beside her, his face buried in the depths of his hood. His hand held the black-handled scythe. Its blade glistened as she set her lantern on the ground.

Craning her neck to look up at him, she smiled. "The time has come for me to take my place among the dragon's daughters. Father is sending the Warrioresses into the southern desert to find a creature that raided our border towns. It is the mission that I was born to begin, Specter. I know it in the deepest reaches of my soul."

"Does your father know of this?"

"No. And for the time being I do not wish him to. His grieving is an obstacle that he must be forced to surmount; otherwise I will forever be a prisoner of his fear."

The man reached for his hood with his free hand and slipped it off his head. As his hand dropped back to his side, she noticed for the first time the extent of his old burns. Without thinking she reached out and touched his injuries. Immediately the power in her dragon blood boiled forth, her hand glowed blue, and when she withdrew it, Specter's hand had been healed.

His mouth startled open. He brought his hand up and examined it for several long moments. "Strange, someone else tried to heal those wounds when you were very young, and I objected. I told him that I was proud to bear those scars because they had been inflicted while saving an innocent life. You have a strange effect on me, child. I feel—grateful—and I thought I would resent it."

"I . . . I don't know how or why." She looked down at her hand, turning it over. "I just reached out, and it happened."

"You are growing very strong, child. I think even the dragon's daughters underestimate your potential. You have the strength of your father and the compassion and purity of your mother—a potent mix." He laughed and held up his once-burned hand. "The innocent life I once saved when I received this injury was your life."

"Mine?" She frowned. Why would he have received an injury saving her life before she could remember? "How did it happen?"

He let her words hang in the air and merely smiled. She sighed, knowing that the secrets this man harbored would take a lifetime to dredge up. Facing the sword and the boomerang, she sighed again. "Now that I am here, I'm not sure what to do with them."

Specter stood still as a statue.

"This sword looks similar to those my aunts are carrying. And its blade is rusted also, yet not so extensively, and the blade is longer than theirs." She reached out, grasping the handle that she'd been forbidden to take and that she had not touched in all these years. The blade glowed ruby red and the crystalline handle shone white, then dimmed.

She released her hold and pulled Specter out of the cave. He appeared confused, as she expected him to be. She took his scythe from his hand and began cutting the glowing blades of grass and kicking them into heaps. Before long she had mowed down the majority of the beautiful growth. She smiled however, for the blades that she had severed continued to glow.

After dropping the scythe, she filled her arms with the glowing grass and grinned at Specter as she reentered the cave. "Do not come in. Whatever you do, stay out there."

"W . . . what? But why?"

"Just do as I say. Please." Again and again she filled her arms, then heaped the grass inside the cave. Its glow, as that of many flickering candles, dimly illuminated the cave's interior. When she finished, she sat on the moist floor and centered herself, meditating. Yes, there it was! Energy, a source of fresh power, radiated from the blue blades. It was a power source she could draw on. Just as her father had drawn it with his sword, she fed on it with the power in her dragon blood.

Rising, she found Specter's stash of dry kindling and dead logs. Although she doubted he'd ever lived in this cave, she knew he frequented it, and the dampness was enough to make anyone desire a fire's warmth. She tossed the wood onto the glowing grass and then dropped to her hands and knees. Carefully she arranged some wood on a dryer section of the cave floor. Then she used a match to start a blaze.

When the little fire ran its course the dirt beneath it had dried somewhat. She stood back several feet, held her hand palm toward the ashes, and squinted her eyes. If only she could clear the dirt away from the stone beneath. As the thought passed through her mind, her hand glowed. White energy blasted from her hand, and she gasped. The energy impacted the dirt, sending it flying in all directions, including her face.

She wiped the dirt off and smiled to herself. The floor ahead had been cleared of all dirt. Only flat, shining stone remained.

Kneeling, Oganna ran her hand over the stone, feeling every imperfection. Then she folded her hands and pictured God on his throne. "God, you know what is in my heart. You know how many people have suffered and how some have even died for my sake. I have an opportunity now to use my unique heritage to help others. Now, in my time of need, grant me a weapon that my dragon powers will feed. Grant me a weapon to defend my people. And please give me wisdom to exercise strength with humility."

So saying she rose and, stretching forth her hands with palms facing one another, waited as crackling energy spiked from one hand to the other. A ball of light spun into existence, pulsating blinding white light that forced her to avert her gaze. Then she threw the energy with great force into the pile of night grass and sticks, engulfing it in flames.

The heat of the fire built until steam rose along the cave walls. Specter raced in and opened his mouth in horror. "What are you doing? Get out of there!" He raised his arm, shielding his face from the waves of heat rolling toward the cave entrance. "Oganna, get out of there before you kill yourself!"

But she formed another ball of light and threw it into the blaze. The flames rose to the ceiling, sweeping toward the exit. "I told you to stay outside!" She spun on Specter and held out her hand, sending a wave of energy that pushed him out of the cave. A second later flames roiled into the space he had filled.

For some reason she could not explain, the heat did not affect her. The flames filled the cave, and she fed the inferno repeatedly with blasts of white energy until the stone walls arching above her began to melt and fall apart.

Fire consumed the pile in its entirety, leaving a seething mass of liquid on the cave floor. While the cave continued to burn, she knelt and held one finger in the molten mass. A thrill passed through her when she pulled it out, white-hot like an iron poker! With this finger she carved two impressions in the stone floor— that of a sword and the form also of a boomerang. She took great care in designing the sword as she envisioned it should be and not as it currently was.

When the impressions were complete, she grabbed the sword and the boomerang from their places. First she laid the boomerang in the impression. It fit perfectly. Then she balanced the sword in both hands and sadness filled her for a moment. A tear fell onto the old rusted blade and, as it ran down the blade, crimson rivulets ran out of the metal. Was that blood?

Stunned, she dropped the weapon and watched. The blood ran off the blade's tip and pooled in the impression she had carved for the sword. It formed into a sphere and held its place at the end of the handle, like a liquid jewel ready for placement.

The heat intensified again, and now sweat poured from her body. The sweltering air drove the oxygen from her lungs. She had remained too long. Grabbing the sword, she positioned it in its mold and raced from the cave.

On her way out she ran into Specter. In the light of the star-studded sky now visible through the thinned clouds, his face appeared fearful. He narrowed his eyes. "You have done enough for tonight. Come!" He caught her arm. "I'm taking you home."

"The thing that I am doing I cannot stop!" She desperately tried to shake him off, but his arms felt solid as iron. "Let me go. I will free myself by other means if you do not."

He dragged her toward the edge of the clearing.

With her free hand she reached up and touched the side of his face. "I'm sorry, my dear guardian. But this task I have set myself to complete." His eyes closed, and he collapsed to the ground.

She covered him with his hooded cloak and then touched it. The fabric rendered him invisible, and she sped northward deeper into the hollow. There she found the dilapidated ruin of the cabin her grandparents had died in. And near the cabin she spotted the old well.

Leaning over the lip, she drew up the old bucket by its chain. The water felt cold as ice. She ran it back to the cave, sped inside, and cast the water over the molten forms of the sword and boomerang. A blast of steam flooded her nostrils and stung her face. She ran outside, not stopping until she was a safe distance from the cave's entrance.

Daring to look back, she saw beams of light radiate from inside. Grazing deer scurried away, their white tails flashing as warning flags in the darkness. The cave blew up, and the ground shook beneath her feet. She raised her hand to shield her eyes from the blinding flashes.

There was another explosion, dazzling and more forceful than the previous eruptions. A beam of light blasted from the roof of the cave and shot into the sky. It traveled unhindered, thundering through the air, and then it lost momentum and fell back to the cave with a resounding *crack*. Its impact knocked her legs from under her, and she fell.

She could feel the power within her growing in magnitude until she feared she would burst. Her hands glowed, and the grass around her fingers steamed as though it would catch fire. The energy surged through her one final time from her feet, ending at her finger tips. She shook her head to clear it and looked toward the cave.

A woman, body blazing with fire, blocked her way. "Steady yourself, my child," the woman said. "You have had a busy night." She extended her arm and pulled Oganna to her feet. The stranger's clothes were blazing fiercely with red and orange flames, yet they were not consumed. Her dress was crimson, and she wore a belt of silver and gold. Her hands were gloved, and the material appeared to be woven of silver. Her long, dark, wavy hair was held back with a silver strand. Flames obscured her face.

The woman rested a hand on Oganna's shoulder. "Use your powers for good, Oganna, and do not be corrupted by the lust for control." She dropped her hand and walked away.

"Wait!" Oganna held up a hand. "Who are you?" The woman retreated, wrapped herself in flames, and vanished.

A tornado of air whipped the clearing, and a shadow obscured the stars. Leathern wings snapped against the wind, and great claws dug into the ground before her. Towering through the night was the great white dragon. Oganna caught her breath and eyed his tremendous form, strong yet agile.

Bowing low, she spoke in near reverence. "To what do I owe this honor?"

His elegant head dipped lower as he replied. "I have watched you from afar, Oganna. You are still young and somewhat impulsive. However, thy heart is full of compassion, and you hate evil as do I." He paused and held out one of his hands. A sphere of white light formed and hovered above his claw tips. "There are precious few in this world who wield power with wisdom—I pray you will be one of them."

She gazed up at him in all his potency. That time as a little girl when he had first revealed himself to her, she had wanted to embrace him as the grandfather she never knew. But at the moment fear of him felt more appropriate. He was capable of terrible things, yet he seemed concerned for the good of all. He was such a noble creature. How could she deny this dragon? "I will do my best."

A smile creased his scaly face. "That is all I ask of you. Remember Starfire's words: 'Use your powers for good and do not be corrupted.' There will come a time when you will be tempted to turn against the good and follow the easier path. Evil men will seek to corrupt you and use you for their own purposes. Oganna, you must not let them!"

"Starfire? Is she the woman that I just met?"

"Yes. Listen to what she told you. Always use the weapons you have created for good. Defend the helpless and exercise judgment with wisdom."

She nodded her head.

The dragon shook his body, twisted his neck to look at the sky, and spoke in a low rumble. "I do believe that *you* will not fail me." Then he spread his wings and flew into the night sky.

The wind buffeted her for a moment after he'd gone. She braced herself until it had passed and then looked to the cave. She neared it, wondering if her labors had been fruitful. The explosion had more or less split it apart, spraying dirt and stones in a circular pattern and leaving the cave floor exposed. A thick, transparent, crystal-like substance covered it. She chipped away the cooled crystal from her molds and examined the results.

Her hands trembled with excitement as she lifted the sword and the boomerang from the floor. They were both composed of identical transparent crystal, and the slightest flicker of light danced on them like stardust. The top of the sword's handle, where the blood had collected, now held a transparent ruby of enormous size.

She stood to her feet and held the sword in one hand and the boomerang in her other. A feeling of satisfaction welled up inside her like warm water filling her soul, coursing through her, and driving all doubt in her abilities from her mind. She laughed to the sky and threw out the boomerang in a long arc. Its transparency was so absolute that it was rendered invisible. Gentle as a feather, it returned to her hand. She raised her sword. Its blade turned crimson, and the crystal handle pulsed with light. Luminescent silver spread from the sword over her arm, coating her body and leaving her covered in a dress of woven silver. The stars reflected on her garment as if in a mirror, causing it to shimmer in the darkness.

"Now," she said, "I am ready!" She slid the sword under her belt, and the silver garments disappeared. Its unguarded blade rested against her side, and so perfect was its crystal that it was hardly visible. She tucked the boomerang under the belt's other end, over her right hip.

Invisible weapons—ingenious! She whistled a soft, cheerful tune as a wind kicked up, and she turned toward the home. Specter stood before her.

At first she feared him, then she saw the spark of hope in his eyes, and when she smiled he returned it with one of his own. "Go, dragon's offspring! God speed you on your journey, and I will follow, always, to watch over and protect you as I did for your mother."

She flung her straying hair over her shoulders, left the area, and passed swiftly through the forest toward home. Cool moisture was settling in the air, testament to the late hour. A mouse darted past, stirring the leaves at her feet. She heard the beat of an owl's wings as it dropped from its perch and caught the protesting rodent in its talons.

Oganna felt for her sword's pommel. The sword was a weapon to defend the innocent and to destroy the wicked, a saver of lives, a destroyer of lives. "All things that begin must someday end, little mouse," she whispered into the night. "*All* things eventually end."

❈   ❈   ❈

The soft patter of rain on the roof greeted Oganna the morning after her encounter with Albino. In order to avoid questions, she hid her weapons under her bed and joined her father and aunts for breakfast.

Ilfedo stirred his porridge for a couple minutes, glancing from time to time at the sisters. "Oganna," he said, "an urgent matter has come up, and I must leave again."

She dabbed at the corner of her mouth with a napkin. "When do you leave?"

"This morning." He stared at her. She knew he was waiting for her to ask if she could go with him.

She nodded to her aunts as if in resignation. "Are you going with him?"

"No. There is another matter that requires our immediate attention." They told her of the reported creature, and then Ilfedo related Ombre's report.

Oganna momentarily nodded again. "That's nice."

Ilfedo raised his eyebrows. Either he was relieved that she wasn't pestering him, or he was confused by her detached attitude. Maybe it was a little of both. She laughed inwardly, amused by their confusion and enjoying every minute of it. If only they knew what she had been up to whilst they slept last night, then they would have guessed her intentions.

About mid-morning, Ilfedo bade everyone farewell and left for the northern border. A little later her aunts set out to the south, waving goodbye as she wished them God speed. As soon as they were out of sight, she raced indoors, grabbed her weapons and one of her father's hunting packs, filled it with food and clothes, and set out with determination to track her aunts. She hiked the pack higher on her shoulders. "Path into the unknown—here I come!"

# 10

# TOKEN OF A PROMISE

Caritha stretched her hands toward the blazing fire and craned her neck to look at the night sky. The air felt cool and damp, reminiscent of her days in the cave when she and her sisters had resided in the forests west of the Hemmed Land. She threw another log on the fire. The flames licked around it, curling yellow and orange fingers along the bark.

"Just about done," Evela said from the opposite side of the blaze.

"Good." Caritha rose to watch her sisters finish setting up the tent.

Rose'el, wielding a wooden hammer in one hand and holding a stubborn stake in her other, harrumphed. Her blows stabbed it into the ground at last. "Now stay put you stupid thing!" She straightened and kicked at the stake before wrapping a tent rope around it. She wrapped the rope tighter and pulled, stretching the tent over its frame, and then stabbed the stake into the ground. Caritha smirked. "Having trouble with that?"

"Some sisters don't know when to hold their tongues and when to pitch in," Rose'el muttered under her breath. She pounded the stake's head with the hammer, driving it farther into the ground. This time she applied too much force. The stake split and the near corner of the tent collapsed. "That's it! I'm not wasting any more time on this nonsense." She dropped the hammer, stormed off several steps, and pointed at Caritha. "I've been at this for almost half an hour. If you feel so smart—then why don't you try it?"

"Take it easy, Rose'el." Caritha picked up the hammer and chose a new stake. "Patience is required when setting up one of these contraptions."

Standing near her shoulder with arms crossed, Rose'el huffed. "I still don't see why we couldn't just lay out our mats and sleep under the stars."

Caritha wrapped the rope around the stake, pulled it taut, and drove the stake into the ground. It held firm, and the tent walls straightened. "See? With a little patience the task is done."

"You want to know something, sister?" Rose'el placed her hands on her hips. "Sometimes you can be the cockiest, most arrogant—"

Laura, Evela, and Levena threw their bedrolls into the open end of the tent and lay down. "Come on." Levena crossed her arms and rested her chin on them. "We all need our rest." Rose'el relaxed her arms and went inside.

As Caritha entered the tent, her ear caught the faint snap of a stick. She stopped and looked outside at the dark trees.

"Anything wrong?" Evela raised her head.

"I thought I heard a twig snap—like someone stepped on it." Her eyes roved the forest. Nobody was in sight, so she shook her head. "I must be more tired than I realized." She rolled out her bedding and lay down.

The wind outside their shelter howled through the trees and the light of their fire flickered. Laura fell asleep, as did Evela and Levena. Rose'el's soft snoring followed.

With a last glance at her sisters, Caritha made certain they were really asleep before pulling a small object out of her pocket. She held it up and looked at it in the shielding dimness. If her sisters knew what she was considering, they would most likely try to dissuade her. She felt the smooth gold band in her fingers. The small diamond cradling its surface sparkled.

She sighed and closed her hands over it. "I don't know what holds you back," Ombre had said. "But I do know that I will never love another as I love you." He had pressed the ring into her hand. "I had hoped you would accept this tonight, but I want you to do what is best for you." He had stroked her hair and looked fondly into her eyes. "Keep this, and when you are ready to be mine, put it on. I will wait until my eyes can no longer see, and the hairs on my head have turned gray."

Oh, how she had longed to say yes, right there, right then. But for all his love, Ombre could not understand what held her back. She had seen what had happened to Dantress, and she knew that as the daughter of the dragon, she too bore the gifts and the curse. Was a year of love worth the sacrifice of a life-time? She envied Dantress. Envied her certainty, her courage, and the life she'd brought into the world. But she had also seen what Dantress's death had done to Ilfedo. She had seen how it hurt him, and she could not bear to leave Ombre in the same way. Something deep inside told her not to worry about it, that Ombre was cut from a different mold and his life would go on.

Feeling sorrowful, she shook her head. No, she could not bear to wound Ombre. She put the ring back in her pocket, rolled on her side, saw his caring face in her mind, and silently wept. She craved his love, craved his embrace, and yet feared the consequences. With a full heart she closed her eyes. Morning would bring a string of activities to keep her busy.

#### ⸙ ⸙ ⸙

The next morning the Warrioresses traveled to the village of Harpen. The sunlit streets were thronged with people. Some refugees from other southern towns trudged through town, carrying their possessions on their backs or in carts. Caritha led the way to a large inn and inquired as to the whereabouts of the doctor who had cared for the survivor from Bordelin.

"Follow the main road west," a burly man said. "The doctor lives at the very edge of town in a fine, two-story brick house. It's the last on the right. You will have no trouble finding it."

She thanked him for his help, then turned to her sisters. "Did you—"

"Wait a minute." The blond, curly-haired innkeeper stepped closer. "Aren't you the Warrioresses?"

A small crowd of mug-holding men gathered around them.

Dropping her voice, Caritha whispered in Levena's ear. "Get out of here and meet me at the doctor's house. I'll keep these people distracted long enough to keep them out of our way." Her sisters filtered out of the door, and Caritha faced the friendly faces with a charming smile. "Yes, I am a Warrioress."

The men came in closer, some shaking her hand, some trying to kiss it. She turned to the man who'd given her directions and played at being shy. "I need to find a ladies' room," she whispered.

He puffed out his chest and boomed orders to the crowd. "Make way for the lady!"

She strode into the restroom at the back of the inn and locked the door behind her. A couple of windows, built high in the wall to let in fresh air, offered her the perfect escape route. She sprang up, grasped one of the sills, vaulted through the window, and landed in a crouch on the dirt in a back alley. Keeping to back streets, she made her way to the western side of town.

The last building on the right hand side of the main road was a two-story brick house. Her sisters were waiting for her in the front. "Caritha, come!" Laura beckoned with her hand. "We were considering going back to make sure you were all right."

"Well, I got away rather quickly, but I wanted to make sure I wasn't seen." She ran her hand through her hair and dusted off her skirt.

Laura went up to the front door and knocked. A tall, tanned woman wearing a bright yellow dress opened the door.

Caritha stepped forward. "Ma'am, we seek information—"

"Are you the Warrioresses?"

"Yes. Lord Ilfedo sent us to—"

The woman nearly tripped over her threshold as she stepped out and held the door wide open. "Please, please. Do come in. I am Doctor Malinda."

"Thank you."

The lady doctor was all smiles as she showed them into her cozy parlor. Long, lace curtains covered the high windows. Plush, green carpeting covered the floor. Three portraits adorned one wall, a grandfather clock chimed in the corner of another, and two couches layered with animal furs formed an L around an oval, knee-high table in the room's center.

"My husband is gone for the week. Oh, he'll wish he hadn't been! If we had known that the Lord Warrior would send *you*, we could have arranged a more fitting welcome." She invited them to sit, then served them tea and joined them.

"You will understand, ma'am," Caritha said, "that we cannot stay. We are on a mission to find the creature reported south of here."

Laura smiled at the doctor and held her gaze. "We were told that you cared for a survivor from Bordelin, and we were hoping you could tell us where to find him."

"Well, I can't say for certain." The doctor combed her fingers through her long blond hair. "However, the last time I saw him, he had decided to stay for a while at the house of the woodcutter that saved his life." She leaned back. "Their house is southwest of here in the forest."

Caritha stood. "Can you show us?"

"Oh, I had hoped you'd stay a while." Malinda rose, wrapping a white shawl around her shoulders. "But I understand. The creature needs to be found before it can return. Come, I will take you there." Malinda led them out her door and escorted them out of town and down a forest trail. About mid-afternoon, after trekking a few miles through the woods, they came to a little house set by itself in a small clearing. Beds of flowers were on either side of the front door. "That is the place," Malinda said, grasping each of them by the hand. "I will say good day to you now. But if you come my way again, please stop in."

As the doctor disappeared back down the trail, Caritha approached the house and knocked. A pale man with splints on his legs and bandages on his arms and neck opened the door. Hobbling on crutches, he brought them inside where he could answer their questions. He sat at the dining room table and invited them to do the same. "Thank you so much for coming."

Leaning forward, Caritha folded her hands. "We have a few questions for you, sir. Then we must be on our way."

"I will answer what I can."

She and the other sisters questioned him for at least an hour. For the most part, their questions revolved around what little he had been able to see of the creature. What he reported disturbed her. Never before had they heard of a creature that could exhale poisonous vapors from its nostrils. The survivor recollected how he'd tried to save the injured woman and how she'd choked and coughed in the foul air until she died. His eyes moistened at the telling of it.

"Thank you. You have been most helpful." Caritha grasped his shoulder gently and held his gaze. "We will deal with the creature. Your loss will be avenged. *We* will see to it."

As they rose to go, Laura asked him to point them in the direction of Bordelin.

He pulled himself to a standing position and flinched. "Go due south through the forest, and you will find it on the edge of the desert."

"We will find the creature. You get your rest." Evela smiled at him, and he beamed back.

He cleared his throat, and his eyes wandered down and up. "I'll be here if you have any more questions."

Evela's face flushed. She slapped his cheek, looked at the floor and walked outside.

"Wow. I meant that in a kind way." He swallowed and gazed after her before glancing at Caritha. "Let her know that I think she is beautiful and spirited. She is welcome to visit me any time."

"Goodness. Give me a break!" Rose'el rolled her eyes, and followed Evela outside.

As Caritha, bringing up the rear, closed the door behind her, Evela walked up. "I am so ashamed."

"Don't tell him that, not at the moment anyway." Caritha chuckled and walked into the forest. "That man seemed taken with you, Evela."

"Him? I doubt it." They marched for several hundred feet more. Evela kicked a stone. "Did he say something about me? To you, I mean."

Caritha laughed and shook her head. "You are a hopeless case. Yes, he thinks you are beautiful and spirited, and he'd love to see you again."

"He would?"

The other sisters joined Caritha in a hearty laugh, and Evela even giggled.

Soon after they emerged from the forest and stood at the edge of an expanse of open grassland. Smoke rose from blackened buildings. A few dozen men and women wandered through a maze of structural beams, broken furniture, and upturned boulders. Some of the people wore bandages around their heads; others had their arms supported in slings.

Wandering around the town, Caritha found the graveyard. A few men kicked spades into the earth, digging graves while others took linen-wrapped bodies to the holes and lowered them in. Flowers had been strewn on the ground, probably in an attempt to subdue the stench of death in the air. New stones lay on the ground next to unfilled holes, some with half-completed epitaphs chiseled on their faces.

"One creature did all of this?" Rose'el growled. "Just wait until I get my sword in range of its throat. If it is an intelligent beast, it will wish it had never touched this place."

Deeply imprinted clawed footprints led from the town through a large, flat field into the southern desert. Bordelin—what was left of it—nestled into the very edge of the Hemmed Land's forests.

Caritha pointed to the desert. "*That* is where we must go."

"We should take stock of our supplies," Levena said. "It may be a long trip, and we don't want to run out of food and water—or shelter. We should return to Harpen for supplies, then come back here tomorrow morning."

On the way back to town they happened upon Doctor Malinda as she returned home through the forest. "I was almost home when I realized I should have accompanied you to the house in the forest. So I went back and checked on him. Did you find the border town?"

"We did," Caritha said.

Rose'el laughed harshly. "And it is a disaster."

"We will be making a trip through the desert tomorrow, but first we'll need to rest," Caritha continued.

They emerged from the forest and into an open field leading up to the town. Malinda pointed out her house on the edge of the rows of homes and businesses. "I have several guest rooms upstairs that you are more than welcome to use. I insist, you must spend the night in my home. And tomorrow morning I will have breakfast ready bright and early so that you can be on your way."

Nodding a thank you, Caritha instructed her sisters. "As soon as we get into town, buy the things we need, for we leave on the morrow."

Much to Caritha's relief, the doctor accompanied them into the stores. The woman was very friendly but had a forceful nature that seemed to drive away the crowds of onlookers. "Quit staring," she would yell. "You are making our guests uncomfortable!"

That night the doctor cooked them a nice meal, then showed them to their quarters. "If you need anything," she said, "just knock on my door. It's the one at the end of the hall."

Caritha plopped into the bed, felt in her pocket for the ring, and fell asleep clutching it to her breast.

The next morning dawned humid. A thick fog rolled through the forest before Yimshi's rays dispersed it. Caritha brushed her hair, then pulled out her rusted sword. Its blade had killed before, and if they found the creature, she suspected her weapon would have to do so again. Her hand trembled as she remembered the purported size of the creature. If they found it and engaged it in combat, she did not know what she would do. What if the beast's hide proved too thick for her sword to penetrate? She put the blade back in the fold of her skirt and closed the fabric over it.

Opening the bedroom door, she followed the greasy scent of frying bacon downstairs to the dining room. In keeping with the doctor's expensive taste, the table was set with silverware and wooden plates carved in the likeness of flowers and butterflies. She picked up one of the napkins. Silk.

Laura and Levena swept in and raised their eyebrows at the arrangement. They took their seats, and soon Rose'el and Evela came in too. Rose'el stopped, shook her head, and spoke only loudly enough for them to hear her. "What foolishness to waste one's time on such frivolities. A plain and simple table is more than adequate."

Evela elbowed her. "Exercise some of those manners Elsie *tried* to burn into you as a little girl. I, for one, enjoy eating in a more formal manner." She neatly unfolded her napkin, laid it in her lap, and sat ramrod straight. "Setting a table like this requires thought and preparation, which *I* appreciate."

"Oh well, la-de-da!" Rose'el scowled.

"I hope you all slept well?" The doctor emerged from the kitchen balancing a silver tray loaded with bacon in one hand and a large bowl of scrambled eggs in her other. Rose'el forced a smile.

The doctor was beaming, and Caritha made sure to compliment her on her beautiful table and the tempting smells that had drawn them downstairs. She chuckled to herself when Rose'el went to greater lengths of eloquent praise.

"I get company so infrequently," the doctor said as she set down the food and turned to go back to her kitchen, "that I decided to go all out for you. After all, it isn't every woman that gets to entertain the Warrioresses." She disappeared into the other room and returned with a bowl generously heaped with freshly cut fruit.

Caritha ate until her stomach couldn't fit any more. Each of her sisters had pushed aside their plates, mostly scraped clean. Feeling the need to be on their way, they thanked their new friend, gathered their things, and left the house. "Come back any time," the doctor said. "I have enjoyed your visit."

"As have we." Caritha stepped into the street. "Thank you again—for everything." Many townspeople were already up and about, though the sun had risen not an hour before. Laura stopped and searched the milling people with her gaze. Her gaze sharpened.

Caritha eased up next to her. "Is something wrong?"

"I thought . . ." Laura shook her head. "I thought I saw Oganna."

"Oganna?" Caritha let her eyes roam the faces of the towns-folk. No one even resembling Oganna caught her eye. She shrugged and turned to go. Her hand slipped into her pocket, and she reached for the ring. It was gone! Frantic, she looked at the ground, trying not to let her sisters see the fear in her eyes.

"Go on ahead," she said. "I forgot something in the house."

"You forgot what?" Rose'el crossed her arms. "Come on, Caritha, I want to get this hunt over with."

Caritha waved a hand at them and ran to the house, shout-ing, "I'll catch up with you!"

As she raised her hand to knock on the front door, the doctor opened it.

"Thank goodness you haven't gone yet." There was a twinkle in the doctor's eye. "Did you drop this?" She held out a hand, and the light danced off the diamond.

Caritha took it, trying not to let the tears of relief show. "You have no idea how much this means to me." She put it back in her pocket and tied it securely in place. "Thank you."

With a departing wave, Caritha raced after her sisters. It was all she could do to keep her joy to herself as she joined them.

Laura turned to her with a curious expression. "Find what you were looking for?"

"Yes. Yes, I found it."

# 11

# ADVENT OF THE MEGATRATHS

Wasteland, that's all the southern desert was—a barren stretch of white sand extending to the horizon. Ilfedo had told Caritha that the Hemmed Land had been designated "hemmed" because of its geographical isolation. Its eastern border ended at the Sea of Serpents. According to a couple of adventurers, a vast swamp cut between the western forests and an active volcano. And both the southern and northern forests bordered vast, uncharted deserts. In a manner of speaking, the Hemmed Land was an oasis.

Ilfedo said his ancestors came from an ancient civilization in the distant southwest that, for some unknown reason, fell apart. According to legend, these ancestors harnessed the power of sunlight and made machines to carry them into the sky. But that was so long ago, no one could be certain the stories were true.

And Caritha knew that many people considered such claims to be myth.

She squared her shoulders, breathing deeply the forest air before heading into the hot, dry desert. The stinging wind threw salty sand in her face as if forbidding her passage. She spun around. "Are you ready, my sisters?"

Rose'el grimaced. "Ready."

Bending down, Laura picked at the large footprint of the creature with a twig. She could have curled up in the impression. Her blade sifted the dirt and sand. She held up her sword, flipped it in the air, and raised it level in both hands. Her eyes scanned the blade.

"What are you doing?" Caritha asked.

"I was thinking that the creature, especially being so large, must leave skin samples wherever it steps." She pointed into the desert. "The wind will obscure the creature's tracks, but I think I can tune my sword to detect the residue in the sand so that we won't lose the trail."

It sounded logical enough, so Caritha voiced her approval. Then she led her sisters into the desert. The creature's tracks followed a straight line, leading to the south, though at a decidedly western vector.

That night they set up their tent and tried to sleep. Their canvas walls protested, and the finer sand sifted through the seams. When Caritha at last dozed off, her slumber was restless.

In her dreams she saw herself and her sisters standing on the strange shore of an inlet, surrounded by mountains of ice. Clouds overshadowed the sky, and the air was frigid. Beyond the inlet lay a deep blue sea stretching to the horizon.

The sandy ground trembled, and a long-necked creature rose before them. She gaze up and quailed, for the creature's size dwarfed any dragon. He smashed his fore-flippers together and addressed them in a voice that rang around them. "You have fought worthy of a Water Skeel." The creature lowered its neck so that it was only ten feet above their heads. Needle-like teeth filled its enormous mouth. "But you are no match for me!"

Caritha felt exhausted. She tried to summon her powers but found only hints of strength. Her reservoirs had been depleted. She looked to her sisters for help, but their faces froze in terror. The creature pulled back his head, and a geyser of water issued from his nostrils. It slammed into her chest, drove the oxygen from her lungs, and threw her against a large boulder on the shore. She felt as if every bone in her body was bending and every organ had been bruised.

On either side, her sisters were trying to rise from beneath the deluge of water. She raised her sword. "Join with me, my sisters!" Their blades met, and a wall of energy surged against the water, turning it away before it could do further harm.

The creature laughed and bore down upon them. His gargantuan body slammed into the beach and his flippers smote them. "Your puny powers cannot compare to the might I wield!" He dug his flippers into the inlet and plucked, as it were, large cubes of ice from the water. These he chucked effortlessly in the sisters' direction. Caritha felt a stabbing pain as the cubes neared, and the magic within her was stifled and confined. Her body temperature dropped—she was freezing though she remained alive!

Suddenly she sat bolt upright in the tent. Sweat had soaked her clothes, and her breathing was irregular. Laura woke up with a scream, and the others started from their sleep. They looked at one another, then at Caritha.

"I was dreaming . . . a nightmare of ice and an enormous white monster." Rose'el breathed fast.

The others glanced at her, then at Caritha. As they chattered about the dream, sharing the same details she knew, she realized that her dream had also been theirs. But how could this happen? Had they received a warning of some kind? Or was it a mere coincidence?

She raised her hand, silencing her sisters' chatter. "We are the daughters of the dragon. We do not fear fate, and we will not let doubt cloud our way. If this was a shadow of something to come, then we will face it as we face everything else—with vigilance and determination."

Evela swallowed hard, then forced a smile. "You are right, Caritha. We must not let this overshadow the task at hand."

Everyone else lay back down. Their eyes, however, remained open. Caritha lay down too, forbidding the fear to get a hold on her heart. She felt inside her pocket for the ring. In this mindset she closed her eyes, letting her body rest for the day ahead.

&#9934;   &#9934;   &#9934;

The following morning the desert wind fanned them like a hot breath and drove them to continue their journey with haste. As the day progressed, the wind grew in intensity. Small whirlwinds wavered between dunes, throwing clouds of sand in all directions.

Shielding her face with her arm, Caritha spread her legs to steady herself. "We need to find shelter."

Laura laughed sardonically. "Oh, sure. As soon as you see a tree or a house, just let me know."

Visibility decreased with alarming swiftness. Though Caritha knew Yimshi was shining, she found it difficult to see more than a few feet in any direction because clouds of sand wound through the air. She was about to call a halt when her foot caught on a buried stone and she tumbled forward. Cringing, she waited to hit her head on some unseen protrusion. Instead she felt herself falling farther, as if the ground before her had given way. When she landed it was rather softer than she'd expected.

She rolled to the side just as Laura, Evela, Rose'el, and Levena all fell in behind her. She looked around at the subterranean cavern. About ten feet above her head the desert sand swirled over the hole through which they'd fallen.

"Oh this is much better." Rose'el punched the ground with her fist. "Now how are we going to find that creature? Its tracks will certainly be buried by the time this storm stops."

"I don't think we'll have to follow the tracks," Evela said. The others looked puzzled. "Desert inhabitants tend to travel the most direct route possible in order to conserve water and strength. If we continue in the direction we know it took, we should eventually stumble upon its destination."

Laura lowered her eyes. "You're right, and we don't really have another choice because I tested my sword earlier today, and it won't find the creature's footprints."

The storm abated a few hours later, and the sisters looked for a way to get out of their hole. Above them the ceiling was a mixture of sand, dirt, and stone.

"Why don't we just blow up the ceiling of this chamber?" Rose'el asked. "If we take out one corner, the material above should be enough to raise the floor so that we can climb out."

The sisters touched their sword blades together. A blue flame ignited between the tips, then shot upward and struck the stone ceiling. The hole through which they had fallen widened. The stones shattered, then fell in a heap tall enough for them to climb up to the desert floor.

Over the desert an unearthly calm reigned. Not even the slightest breeze troubled the sand, and the sunlight fell oppressively on their skin. "Come on." Caritha walked a few hundred feet more. The ground gave way, and she fell into another subterranean cavern, her sisters following after.

"I don't know about the rest of you." Rose'el clambered back up and grabbed Caritha's arm. "But I think we should take greater care where we are stepping."

"Agreed." Caritha took off her shoe and held it upside down, draining it of sand.

The others clambered up behind her. She set out again, this time stabbing the ground ahead with her blade before proceeding. It was a good thing she did, for she discovered that the region was pocketed with numerous caverns just waiting for the unwitting traveler to step into them. Night fell, and the moonless sky made progress even slower.

"Maybe we should camp in one of the caverns," Laura suggested. "It would offer us shelter from any more sandstorms."

Everyone nodded, and Caritha peered into a nearby hole. "This looks suitable *and* a lot easier to exit." She descended first.

"Yep, this is much better." Rose'el arrived beside her and laid out a bedroll.

"Better, yes." Levena looked around at the strange formations on the walls. "It's still not to my liking."

Rose'el scratched her head. "What *would* be to your liking? An inn out here in the desert?"

"Home would be preferable," Levena said.

Rose'el clacked her tongue. "Tut tut, living at Ilfedo's house has made you soft!"

At last the sisters settled in, and the night passed without incident. In the morning everyone confirmed that their dreams had been pleasant—no more massive swimming creatures pummeling them with ice.

They ate biscuits for breakfast and pulled themselves out of the cavern. There was no breeze, thankfully, so no sand whipping about. Once on the desert floor, they used Yimshi's rising disc as a frame of reference and continued their pursuit of the creature.

Several days passed, and they had about given up hope of ever finding the beast. But a wind kicked up, and when it stopped, they saw the creature's tracks clearly imprinted straight ahead of them and continuing on to the horizon.

They followed the tracks for an hour or so and then stopped. As far as Caritha could see, a vertical wall of solid yellow stone rose from the desert floor.

The barrier stood over two hundred feet high, and its smooth face was unbroken except in one place. About two thirds of the way up a large opening cut into the rock, most likely a cave. Deep claw marks marred the rock face beneath the opening. Caritha bit her lip.

Rose'el let out a long whistle. "Now that is something incredible. How can a creature that *large* climb that? Why, it is almost vertical. Do you realize what it would take to pull that much bulk up *that*? I don't know about the rest of you, but I'm duly impressed."

Gritting her teeth, Caritha tied back her hair and stepped up to the wall. Gazing up made her a bit dizzy. Rose'el was right. The rock rose from the desert floor at a near-vertical angle. Grabbing hold of a crevice in the rock face, she pulled herself up and set her foot on the slightest excuse for a ledge.

Repeating these steps, she soon reached a place some twenty feet above. Careful not to offset her balance, she glanced under her arm. "What are you all doing standing there? Climb, ladies. Climb!"

The stone under her hand crumbled, forcing her to grab another handhold. The climb demanded all her attention. She lost track of time. When she was within ten feet of the cave opening, she dared to look down. First she noticed her sisters making their way up the rock face behind her, then her gaze wandered out to the desert and, for an instant, she thought she saw a human figure on the horizon.

"Is someone following us?"

Rose'el closed the distance between them.

"For all that is holy! Move along Caritha. I can't climb over you, you know." She grunted, pulling herself higher. "This isn't so easy in a dress. Now quit staring out there—it's probably a mirage."

Taking one last look into the desert, Caritha had to admit a mirage sounded plausible. Heat waves created several images of people in pursuit, but one by one they vanished. She put her attention back where it should be and led her sisters the rest of the way up the daunting rock face. Upon reaching the ledge of the cave, she pulled herself in, sat near the opening, and breathed a deep sigh of relief.

She leaned over the edge. Rose'el extended an arm, and Caritha helped her into the cave. Then she reached down to help Laura up. "Here give me your hand."

"No thank you!" Laura pulled herself up, and the others soon followed.

They gathered on the ledge, looking at the desert below. At last Caritha drew her sword and scraped it along a claw mark in the floor. Grimly she faced the cave's dark interior.

Caritha moved her finger to her lips. "From here on we should keep quiet." She pointed to her sword, signifying that her sisters should produce their weapons. From their robes they drew their rusted blades and held them at arm's length as they followed her into the darkness.

"Shine, oh my sword," she whispered. Her command could not affect the weapon, but saying it aloud and willing it in her mind somehow steadied her, and immediately her blade glowed with a brownish-red color.

The others followed, murmuring, "Shine." One after the other their blades illuminated the area, albeit dimly. Caritha moved ahead into the pitch-black chamber. So dim was the light from the swords that she halted until her eyes adjusted to the darkness. Gradually the floor and walls became distinguishable, and she walked on.

At the rear of the chamber, Caritha found a tunnel of great size that led downward at a steep angle. The tunnel floor and walls bore numerous deep, long gashes suggesting claw marks— ones the formidable creature might have made. She planted her feet in the grooves, and the descent progressed smoothly.

The tunnel leveled, and the ceiling rose out of sight. The walls curved into shadows too deep to see through. Caritha strained to see into the darkness. The light of the swords revealed a flat floor of stone, worn and polished by usage. Whichever direction she walked there was no end in sight.

Laura lay a hand on her shoulder and whispered, "I hope you are thinking caution is in order, Caritha. You do realize this could be the creature's lair." Something thumped somewhere ahead of them. They stopped, though Caritha's heart thumped almost as loudly as the sound she'd just heard.

A rumbling voice penetrated the stillness. "Who art thou that dares enter this dark dwelling, and what right have ye to disturb Vectra?"

"We come on an errand from the north in search of the beast that has murdered the inhabitants of our land. We come at the request of that land's lord, whom we serve." She grasped her sword with both hands and waved it from side to side, searching the darkness for the beast. "Are you the party guilty of this deed?"

A mocking laugh preceded the creature's retort. "You actually camest all this way. Flattered I am and, if you wantest to fight me, come to me."

Cautiously, she led her sisters in the voice's direction. The light of their swords revealed a small area around them, but nothing more. An enormous, clawed hand slashed at them, nicking Caritha on the neck. She rolled to the side as another hand came from the other direction. She stabbed at it. The creature pulled back. She could hear it lick its hand as it stood back a safe distance.

Another voice rumbled out of the darkness, this time from above them. "Loos, stop immediately!" The creature grumbled assent and remained out of sight. The new voice spoke again. "Loos, what have you there?" There was agitation in the tone and sharpness to the question.

The aggressor was quick to respond. "Intruders, Vectra! They were going to kill us in our sleep."

A long silence ensued before the creature above continued. "Harm them no further. Start the firelights."

Their attacker grumbled as he moved farther into the cavern. Behind Caritha her sisters whispered to one another; doubtless their minds were filling with as many questions as her own. What kind of creature were they dealing with? Obviously not some brute beast, but something intelligent. Did this other voice belong to another member of the same species?

A flame broke the surrounding darkness and sparked a channel in the rock. The strong smell of burning oil filled the stagnant air. The flame spread, blazing brightly as each succeeding channel fed the next. Soon the cavern glowed with firelight.

Chiseled designs—and rather ornate ones at that—decorated the walls. The sisters were standing in what appeared to be the main chamber. Its height was undeterminable because the firelights did not reach high enough. Hundreds of tunnels branched off from the chamber, some gargantuan and others not so large.

Deep cuts crisscrossed the cavern's rock walls, leading to count-less caves above their heads.

The creature that had attacked them stood near the far wall. Caritha felt a lump build in her throat; Loos was truly a monster! He took a few steps in their direction, his muscular body sup-ported on four tree-size legs only slightly smaller than his two forearms. A layer of dark gray scales covered his back and all six of his limbs. His underbelly was armor-plated too, though with creamy white scales instead of gray. He swung a heavy reptilian tail, not as long as a dragon's, tapered to a bony point.

At sight of his crocodilian head riddled with sharp teeth, Caritha shivered. The creature's forearms had five fingers, and as he flexed them, long claws slid out. A cold sweat broke out on Caritha's forehead, for she could now see several dozen heads peering down from the cave dwellings. How many of these crea-tures were they dealing with? As she gripped the sword tighter, its leather handle slipped under her fingers.

One of the creatures slid down the wall, its claws sparking against the rocks. After landing, it shook its hide, much as a dog shakes its wet coat, and the scales along its back knocked off their dust. "Loos," the creature rumbled, "your forays into unknown lands have given me trouble before. Am I to believe that you do not deserve my wrath, and that these small creatures are laying false accusations against you?"

Something about the creature's manner of speaking and the tone it used, made Caritha realize that it was female. She looked at the creature that was called Loos. He had hunkered down a bit, and his dark eyes looked at the floor as if concocting a falsehood.

"If you cannot speak forthright, then keep silent!" the female screamed, filling the cavern with her voice and forcing Caritha and her sisters to cover their ears or go deaf.

Loos cringed and skirted the chamber. He ventured a step closer to the female and raised his eyes, but the other raced forward, swung her tail in a tight circle, and sent him crashing into the wall with one thwack.

The creature turned in Caritha's direction and strode forward. It raised a clawed hand, retracted its claws, and dipped its head ever so slightly to stare down at them. "I am Vectra. You need not fear me. This is my realm, and I welcome you to it." She sat back on her rear legs and gestured with her heavy hand. "State your errand."

Caritha bowed to the creature. "Our quarrel is not with you. We have come at the bidding of Lord Ilfedo, ruler of the Hemmed Land." Feeling emboldened by Vectra's request, she pointed her sword at Loos. "We have come to deal with this murderer, for he came by night into our land and slew our people, burning them in their homes and pouring his poisonous vapors upon them until they died."

Laura moved next to her and bowed as well. "We are messengers of death sent at the behest of our lord, Ilfedo, to stop the wicked in their tracks. When a creature threatens the Hemmed Land, we are called upon to seek it out."

Approving rumbles resonated from the creatures that observed from their caves.

Vectra cocked her head to one side and looked up at her companions. "You speak with uncommon strength for members of your race." She swiveled her massive head to gaze upon the Warrioresses. "It is a rare thing to find strength in your weak species, especially a strength that gains our praise."

Caritha lowered her blade. "Humanity, compared with you, *is* weak. At least, that is, if you are speaking of physical strength. But our strength is born of another race and our roots are not as they appear."

"Hmm, your speech is a riddle." Vectra dipped her head. "Far be it from me to unmask your secrets. I enjoy the manner of your speech."

Long moments of silence passed during which Vectra seemed to contemplate her next words. When she spoke, it was gentler, yet firm. "You need not fear me. I also seek justice. If Loos has indeed slain the innocent, he will pay at your hands for his wickedness."

Caritha relaxed, but the creature raised a cautionary finger and a long claw slid out of it.

"However, his condemnation must be according to the laws of my domain, not according to yours. If you do not abide by them, I will be forced to execute you. Loos must be proven guilty either by his own admission or by the testimony of no less than three witnesses. If this proof is not obtained then the accusers—in this case you—have the right to duel him in our great arena. Secondly, it is permitted under our law that if his guilt is in question, he has the right to procure aid in the duel from his relations and friends. If he wins, his record is cleared. If you defeat him, your actions are approved, and his destruction is declared just." Her dark round eyes bored into Caritha's. "Have you come with proof, or a mere accusation?"

"The proof lies in the distant border of our land, in the blood spilled there, and in the destroyed habitations." Caritha felt despair creeping over her. Was Vectra mocking her by making these demands? She could see it in the creature's eyes—a look that said Vectra knew Loos was in fact guilty. "How can we possibly offer three witnesses? They are severely injured; some are near death!"

"Nevertheless, it is our law and you must abide by it." Vectra turned to the accused. "Answer me truly, Loos, or I will see to it that your lies are bared before your brethren." She stood on all legs and crashed a foot into the stone floor. "Answer their accusation!"

He dipped his head to her and replied, "Among your servants I am faithful above many. My conduct both near and far *has* always—and always *will* be—honorable. It grieves me that these vermin have even dared to accuse me of these deeds." His gaze shifted to the Warrioresses. "Let me clear myself in the arena!"

"Presumptuous fool!" Vectra threw him again and spat upon him. "The great arena is the purest test of the heart. By your own words I believe you are guilty, and I will soon be proven right when these humans stand over your corpse." She pulled him up and drove him out of the cavern, yelling after him as he ran into a tunnel. "Choose those who will stand with you. The duel will begin within the hour."

Vectra thundered back to the Warrioresses. Her eyes were so fierce that they could have driven many a warrior to their knees. "I see the purity in your hearts," she said. "Do not fear the duel, for the wicked *never* win a battle in our arena. Win this fight, and you will have proved me right."

Caritha glanced over her shoulder at her sisters. Rose'el lipped four words: "Lose, and we're dead."

"Come." Vectra pivoted and stomped deeper into the cavern. "This tunnel leads to the arena."

They entered the dark passageway, and the stone floor shook repeatedly as the creatures climbed down the walls, thudded to the floor, and followed. Caritha tensed her arms and raised her chin. "Walk proud, my sisters. Remember our father, and fight as he would fight."

"Oh quit talking. Humph!" Rose'el folded her arms. "You're making me even more nervous than I already am."

Vectra led them out of the darkness into blinding daylight. Enormous stones ringed a flat section of desert ahead of them.

The creatures congregated to the stones from tunnels along the solid stone hill that rose behind them. "Looks as though the spectators are gathering," Laura said.

Levena looked down at her sword. "They look restless."

They were now standing at the arena's far end. Yimshi beat down without mercy, The movement of the surrounding creatures in the stone grandstands stirred a canopy of dust. "Prepare yourselves!" Caritha loosened her sword arm, swinging it in small arcs in front of her and facing into the wind. The dust stung her eyes, making it difficult to keep them open.

A loud commotion came from the tunnel through which they had entered. Loos and three other members of his species exploded into the arena.

"Great." Evela steadied herself by grasping Laura's shoulder. "Now we have to take on *four* of them?"

Laura bit her lip. "It certainly looks that way—"

"Silence!" Caritha scolded. "The time for doubts is long past. You've grown soft in the Hemmed Land, my little sister. Remember how you acquitted yourself against the Sea Serpents?"

Evela laughed nervously. "I've tried to forget."

"Focus! Only our combined powers and skills with a sword can bring us home in one piece. Do you want to die out here?"

"Of course not!" Evela's eyes flared, and she pointed her blade in Caritha's face. "Now stop haranguing me! I'm going to fight."

They raised their swords in unison. The creatures charged toward them, hints of yellow vapor in their nostrils. Tendrils of energy accumulated between their swords' blade-tips. A ball of electricity formed, radiating a bluish-white light as it grew in size. In a deft move, Caritha reached under the ball, plucked it off the blades, pulled her arm back, and threw the projectile at Loos. It struck squarely in his chest.

He stumbled, collapsing to his six knees. His companions closed in, compassed the women, and blew clouds of vapors upon them. Gasping for breath, Caritha reached out with her mind, calling upon the elements of nature to come and assist. A stiff wind blew from the north, dispersing the vapors harmlessly into the arena's stony grandstands.

Still, she could not catch enough fresh air to purify her lungs. Her strength seeped from her arms. She dropped her sword and grabbed her burning throat. Through the stirred dust she caught a glimpse of Laura dropping her weapon. One by one the remaining sisters fell to the desert floor. The whites of their eyes showed, and their eyelids closed.

"No—no!" Caritha fought to remain conscious. With trembling arms, she grasped for her sword. All she needed were a few moments longer. But her fingers did not find the hilt of her weapon. Instead they skipped over it and clutched sand. The light of day was veiled. She could feel death closing in on her.

# 12

# REDEEMING THE FALLEN

The seemingly endless natural wall of stone lay in the distance. Oganna watched the five figures begin to climb toward the opening high in the rock. Suddenly one of the women hesitated. "Fool," Oganna chided herself. "They probably spotted you!"

She laid flat on the ground, waved her hand in an arc, feeding the already hot air with her energy. Heat waves bounced in front of her, creating a curtain of illusion between herself and the Warrioresses. If all went as she hoped, the sisters would see a few mirages and then dismiss their doubts.

Within moments they began climbing again. Oganna remained on the ground, shielded from any prying eyes with more heat waves. The sisters filtered into the cave and disappeared within its dark recesses. She rose, shook the sand from her loose, golden hair, and raced to the wall.

She had never climbed a cliff before, but there seemed no better time to learn than the present. Reaching over her head, she grasped a crag and pulled herself up. The pack on her back offset her balance, making her task more difficult. She made steady progress until she was a few feet from the cave. She grabbed a loose stone and almost lost her balance when it broke free in her hand. But she regained a secure handhold and continued until she stood within the safety of the cave.

She licked her parched lips, pulled out her water canteen, and drank two long draughts. The straps of her pack bit into her shoulders. She hefted it down and leaned it against the wall. Her shoulders ached. She stretched her arms and twisted around to loosen her back. Ah, that felt better! Drawing her sword, she allowed it to transform her apparel. The crimson blade provided more than adequate lighting. She looked down the tunnel in the rear wall and glanced back at her pack. If she encountered the creature that inhabited this place, she would want to face it unencumbered. Thus decided, she left the pack and climbed down the tunnel. In the darkness her silver garb emitted a faint glow, making her look like a ghost.

When she reached the tunnel's end and stood in the creatures' underground home, she looked around. The ground shook, and she flattened herself against the tunnel wall. A stampede of terrible creatures passed by, racing into a tunnel at the cavern's opposite end. She made a quick evaluation, noting the crocodile-like heads and the thick hides. The creatures stood over ten feet tall. She had found a nest of the species that had destroyed Bordelin, but where were the sisters?

As soon as all the creatures had passed by, she followed them. Sounds of battle came from ahead and blinding sunlight drew her to a tunnel that led back to the desert floor on the opposite side of the natural wall. At last she came to the tunnel's end and peered outside. Enormous stones ringed a parcel of flat land. The creatures were, for the most part, lying on the stones. Their dark eyes gazed at the arena floor. Four of their species were blowing concentrated clouds of yellow vapor upon an unidentifiable target.

A wind blew, dispersing the vapors and revealing the target of the creatures' assault—the Warrioresses. Oganna's heart filled with rage. She spun her crimson blade in her hand as the last sister collapsed to the desert floor. She kept a firm grip on its handle. "Desist!" she screamed.

One of the creatures turned toward her and snarled.

"You scum of Subterran. You wicked creatures! Have you no honor? Are you afraid of these women? Come! Let us see if you dare to face my wrath." Sober and fearless, she strode forward, holding the crystalline sword before her with both hands. Its blade rose like a hovering spire of blood.

"Loos," one of the creatures called from the stadium, "your quarrel is not with the young human."

The creature disregarded the other and ambled toward Oganna, his head skimming the sand. "Come near, human, and I will show you how a megatrath deals with threats. I will crush you as we have crushed our other enemies—"

In the midst of his sentence, Oganna reached for her boomerang, spun around, and sent it sailing through the air. Her aim was perfect. The sharp crystal passed through his open mouth and severed his tongue. As the tongue fell to the sand, the arena went silent.

Loos's companions glanced at the tongue and took a couple of steps back. Oganna nodded and caught the returning boomerang in her left hand, holding it up for all to see. "Do any more of you have a word to share with me?" When the attackers didn't respond, she continued. "The next time I hear a tongue utter ill, it too will fall."

The megatraths shoved aside the unconscious sisters and charged toward her. Oganna firmed her hold on the sword. She closed her eyes, letting the rage within her burn and pouring it into the sword. When she was ready, she opened her eyes. "Give me fire, my sword," she whispered. "Give me a flame to scald the wicked." Flames sprouted from her blade, covered it, and shot out from its point.

The creature nearest her hunkered as it ran, while another opened its mouth to expose rows of teeth. She faced them, a new confidence arising within her and driving out all uncertainty. With a piercing yell, she sprang onto the head of the nearest creature and drove the burning blade into its eye. It screamed in pain as she pulled the white-hot metal from its socket. Red blood spurted from the wound as she dropped to the ground. An inferno of flames rolled from the other three creatures' mouths. They closed in around her. But her sword fed off their fire, enveloping her in a bubble of energy.

Tongue-less Loos poured vapors from his nostrils. She choked a bit, but recovered long enough to jump again and stab out his eye. He flung her from his head, smashing her into the ground. He reached for her and with his large hands began squeezing.

As her breath left her, she flipped her sword and stabbed it with all her strength into his wrist. Loos pulled away from her blade and reared into the air, making a horrible sound that probably would have been a scream if he had still possessed a tongue.

Oganna gasped for air. Her knees felt weak. She knelt on the ground. Yellow clouds covered her, cutting her off from the world of the living. Her shoulders drooped, the sword fell from her grasp, and she felt her eyes rolling to the back of her head.

⚛    ⚛    ⚛

"Rise, my daughter!" Albino's pink eyes were filled with love. His gaze was soft, and he reached out with a strong hand to steady her.

Caritha looked around, confused. She was in his throne room. "Father?" Her lungs burned, and she coughed. A vaporous ring of yellow came out of her mouth.

"Breath deeply, my daughter. Drink in the fresh air. Let it fill you with life anew." He heaved in, expanded his chest, then let it all out in a plume of fire. A smile curled his mouth.

She shook her head. "How . . . what . . . how did I get here?"

"I brought you back." He slapped his tail against the marble floor. "And it's a good thing I did, too. You would have been lost."

Warm, pure air cleansed her body. Caritha stood straighter and looked out of a large stained glass window to her right. "Why am I here?"

He lowered his head, drew her toward him, and looked into her eyes. "Oganna is making the ultimate sacrifice," he said. "She followed your path and now her life is on the line."

"Then you must send me back!" She trembled at the thought of her young charge facing all four of the terrible creatures alone. "She is not ready to fight on her own—you must let me return."

"Caritha, my dear child, I would like nothing better. But if I restored you and your sisters to the arena, you would follow a very bitter path." He shook his head. "I have seen the future, Caritha, and it is littered with pain. If you go back, you will reap sorrow as if you are drinking the rivers of the world—"

"But isn't there joy along with the pain?" she asked. "Surely there is hope for the future."

"There is hope." His eyes emptied of emotion, and his wings flexed. "Even now one of my faithful warriors stands, though all of you have fallen. She is ready at this moment to give Oganna the moments she needs to survive. You've lost one sister. What if returning you to the arena would destroy those that remain to you? You do not know if you can defeat the creatures. What if you could avoid the pain ahead? Would you stay with me, or would you still wish to return?" He sighed. "I have seen things far more evil than a mere megatrath. I have battled the forces of darkness since long before you were hatched."

She caressed his scaly chin. "Father, do you fear the future?"

"No. Dread it? Yes."

She held her chin high. "If my life must be given in exchange for Oganna's, then so be it. I see in her the makings of a woman who can change the world. Her heart follows righteousness, and her will is governed by selflessness. My own pain is inconsequential."

He cocked his head to the side. "You have grown over the years, my daughter. Once you were only concerned for the welfare of yourself and your sisters. Living with your sister's husband has matured and changed you—for the better."

She reached both hands around his long neck as he embraced her.

"Now." He released her. "If you are convinced of your decision, then I will return you to the battle. Your sisters have been given the same choice as you." He grinned from horn to horn. "They all gave similar answers and will return with you."

The white and gold walls of the palace around her, along with the dragon's image, began to fade. "I love you, Father!" She smiled as her sisters congealed around her and the desert sand reappeared under her feet. She and her sisters were truly one—one in purpose, one in motivation, and one in love. She ran her finger along her sword's rusted blade and laughed as it cut her finger. It was time to deal with these megatraths.

The sisters charged across the expanse, closing the distance between them and Loos and his companions. They leapt on the creatures' backs, striking futilely at their hides. The megatraths rolled over on their backs, rose, spun, and thwacked at the sisters with their tails. Laura, Evela, Levena, and Rose'el were sent flying, but Caritha dodged the blows and remained on the offensive. "Is that all you've got?"

Loos threw fire at her, and she noticed that Oganna had taken out his eye. Clever girl, she had aimed for the vulnerable spots instead of trying to take the creatures down all at once. She raced forward, holding back her sword until the last second. Loos's mouth opened to snap at her. She thrust with all her might, scraping her blade along the roof of his mouth. He stumbled, blood pouring onto the ground.

❈ ❈ ❈

As the battle raged around her, Oganna heaved in breaths of clean air until the poison in her system lost its potency. Still, her strength would not return, and she knew that she was not yet healed. What should she do? Her aunts were beginning to falter and the megatraths, though wounded, were still fierce.

She picked up her sword, pointed it toward the sky, and called out, "I cannot rise. Will no one come to my side in this time? Will not a savior show himself?"

"Oganna, hold still," a soft voice said from behind her. "Let me draw the poison."

Turning, Oganna looked into the fiercely beautiful face before her. Starfire held out her hand, palm up. Strains of yellow curled from Oganna's chest, creating a transparent sphere floating above the fire lady's hand.

"There," Starfire said. "Rise now and fight!" Flames enveloped her and she vanished.

Oganna arose a new person, her spirits high and her confidence growing. She divided the air with her blade. "My sword, from this day forth you will be called the Avenger. Prove now your worth." She lifted it above her head and threw it straight as an arrow into Loos's remaining eye.

Now completely blinded, Loos opened his jaws wide in a roar of pain. Oganna sent her boomerang sailing into his mouth. He clamped his jaws together, and the weapon's sharp edge sliced upward into his brain. He fell like a stone to the desert floor. The arena grew quiet. The Warrioresses and the remaining three megatraths stood still, staring at the grisly sight.

# 13

## TOMB OF THE ANCIENTS

Standing over Loos's corpse, Oganna pulled Avenger's blade from his eye and used it to pry open his jaws. The boomerang had been lodged deep into his head. She reached inside his mouth, feeling through the slimy saliva. When she found her weapon, she jerked it out. She pulled away her sword, and Loos's jaws snapped shut.

She looked down on him and shook her head. Slaying the creature should have brought some remorse to her heart, but though she tried to feel compassion or sorrow, she could not feel any for him. He had brought this end on himself by slaying the people of Bordelin. He was an unrepentant murderer, and she had been the agent of justice.

She waved a hand at Loos's companions. "It is over. He is dead. Get out of my sight before you meet similar fates." They dug their claws into the ground and bolted into the tunnel from whence they'd come.

"Oganna, are you all right?" Even as Caritha asked the question, she was beaming with pride. "You have done well."

Oganna pointed at the creatures around the arena. "Will they give us trouble?"

"The megatraths? No, I don't believe they'll give us any trouble. Their leader, Vectra, seemed to sympathize with us and showed bold dislike for the creature you just slew."

Nodding her head in the direction of an approaching megatrath, Oganna raised an eyebrow. "Is that Vectra?" Her aunt nodded and stood back.

The creature was over ten feet tall and walked with a confidence that seemed to frighten the sisters, but Oganna discerned admiration in the creature's eyes. Vectra neared and snorted a flame, then spoke to Caritha. "Who are you? Never before have I seen humans fight with such ferocity."

Caritha bowed and gestured toward her sisters. "We are the Warrioresses—"

"Welcome to my domain, Warrioresses." Vectra turned to Oganna. She bowed in the young woman's direction. "And who is this?"

Oganna sheathed Avenger and tucked away her boomerang. Her silver dress vanished, and her aunts gasped. "I am honored to meet you." She wiped sweat from her forehead and bowed low. "I am Oganna, princess of the Hemmed Land."

"I am also honored by your presence here, Princess. My name is Vectra, and these are my people, the megatraths."

"I am sorry for this intrusion, but it was necessary," Caritha said.

Vectra shrugged, kicked Loos's carcass, and returned her attention to Oganna. "Megatraths respect a valiant warrior who does not back down in the face of great odds. You have proved yourself to be most valiant and a superior combatant, unlike any human I have ever encountered. You have proved your worth to us today and have earned an eternal remembrance in our stories. From this day forward any megatrath that disgraces you or your subjects will bear eternal shame. Please, accept my friendship and join me for my evening meal."

Caritha raised a hand. "Thank you for your generosity, but—"

Knowing that her aunt's refusal would injure Vectra's feelings, Oganna cut her off. "You are most kind. We accept."

The creature's lips opened to reveal a long row of teeth. It lumbered into the arching tunnel opening. Its long legs quickly moved it deep into the dim subterranean habitation, outdistancing Oganna. It glanced back at her, as if realizing it needed to slow down, and reduced the length of its gait.

They passed through several caverns before coming to a dining chamber. Along the way, Oganna and the sisters were greeted by silent stares and deep bows from the megatraths. Oganna wondered how many of these creatures there were. They came from every tunnel and chamber, and many more lumbered out of sight into the caverns' dark recesses. She imagined that if these creatures were organized into a military force, they would be capable of incalculable destruction. They could probably tread entire forests, destroy fortresses, drink up lakes and, in the process, destroy nations.

She imagined hundreds of megatraths storming through the Hemmed Land and punching holes in Ilfedo's army. She shuddered. "It's a good thing that Vectra has taken a liking to us; otherwise she might pose a real threat to the Hemmed Land."

Laura pulled on her sleeve. "Oganna, what were you thinking? We don't know anything about these creatures."

"You are right." Oganna swallowed hard. "For all we know they might be planning to feast on us!"

Laura stared at the floor, worry creasing her brow. Then she turned up her nose and looked sidelong at Oganna. "That was not funny, young one." She dropped behind and spoke in a low voice to Rose'el.

Glancing about, Oganna realized that she was standing opposite a monstrous stone slab about six feet high, twelve feet wide, and nearly a hundred feet long. Vectra directed several megatraths to set another stone on one side of the table for her guests. "I apologize for the height of my table, but we rarely receive human visitors." She waited for them to sit atop the stone.

When everyone settled, a megatrath thrust its way through the creatures milling around the table. Its enormous hands plunked massive stone dishes onto the table. Desert fruits overflowed several bowls. The megatrath curled its lips up, showing its long rows of teeth as it plopped a stone platter in front of Oganna. Fat black fish of a variety unfamiliar to her ringed the platter.

"I hope you will enjoy these." Vectra tapped the fish with the tip of her claw. "My cook snatched them from our underground rivers. Also try this." From a bowl she extracted an oblong orange fruit as long as Oganna's arm and cracked it on the table. Taking a small piece, Oganna tasted it. The cream interior tasted like pears and, strangely enough, beef.

"This is delicious." She smiled at Vectra. "May I ask what it is?"

"Da'pra!" The megatrath rumbled, and it licked its lips. Then it grabbed at several bowls, moving each aside until it picked one up and sniffed at it. "Try this and let me know if it also pleases you."

Oganna stood on her seat to peer inside the bowl. Yellow leaves, brown grape-like things, and glowing red beans the size of carrots floated in a soupy mix. "What are the ingredients?"

Vectra rumbled for several minutes. At first Oganna thought she had inadvertently insulted her. Vectra scratched her thick chin then scraped her claw on the tabletop. "I'm sincerely sorry, princess. I have no idea how to describe this to you. It is composed of food indigenous to our underground realm."

Oganna dipped her fingers in the cold soup and slopped it in her mouth. Most of it tasted akin to grass, but a strong aftertaste almost forced her to gag. Apparently some things eaten by desert creatures, God never intended for human consumption.

During the meal an overwhelming sense of belonging filled Oganna. She had fallen upon her aunts' attackers with strength beyond her years, and she had triumphed. Her actions had saved their lives.

The sisters talked to her with respect. They responded when she spoke to them and even went out of their way to let her eat before they did. At last she had graduated from student to respected asset. Perhaps, in time, they would admit her into their group in the place that her mother had once filled.

Her thoughts then turned to her hostess. Vectra treated her as a hero and displayed confidence in her. Indeed, the other megatraths at their enormous table regarded her with near reverence. It was as if her victory over Loos had elevated her to a higher plane in their estimation than that of the Warrioresses.

Were they naïve enough to trust a complete stranger solely on the basis of that individual's combat skills? They seemed warlike and strong, yet maybe their culture was more vulnerable than it appeared. She imagined a smooth-spoken warrior, for instance, entering the megatraths' realm and using deceit and subterfuge to bring about a war among them. They might easily be taken advantage of.

She focused her attention on Vectra, seeking to understand the megatraths and whether or not they would be inclined to form an alliance with the Hemmed Land. She told Vectra of her people's customs, such as turning one's sword handle to the victor in friendly contests. More than this, she elaborated on the layout of the land and the difficulties her father had encountered while securing peace.

Vectra found the stories of Ilfedo's encounters with the Sea Serpents of particular interest. "Your father sounds like a worthy leader." She licked the food from one of her claws. "We megatraths respect one who proves his worth against such odds. I have never heard of a Sea Serpent before, but my people tell stories about the Sea of Serpents. Our ancestors said it is wild and untamable, with creatures that no being has dared disturb for two thousand years."

"I don't doubt it." Oganna grabbed a sharp stone and carved into an apple the size of her head. "Among my people there are stories of men who have left our land in favor of crossing the Sea—never to return. Although none of my father's people have attempted to cross, many of them now fish it, and some fishermen are venturing deeper into its uncharted waters where fish abound. Several of these fishermen have become rather prosperous."

The megatrath picked up a large basket of fruit, tilted it up against her open snout, and swallowed the contents in a single gulp. "*We* do not eat fish. The fruits of the desert and the water beneath it are all we require for sustenance."

"Have you ever tried fish?"

"I haven't, but some megatraths did, and they died shortly afterward. Though it is unclear whether or not the fish killed them, we have determined that the spirit of fish was not intended for our consumption. Thus we avoid it whenever possible."

"But you have served it today."

"Only when we have guests—non-megatrath guests, that is. The flesh of fish will not harm humans. Thus we serve it."

"Just as our desert can kill you but will not harm us, so is the way of fish with humans." Vectra looked into another basket and pulled out an oblong fruit almost five feet in length. "This is Prapra, a delicacy among my species, but to humans it is deadly."

"Curious. How do you know it is poisonous to us?"

The megatrath grinned a toothy smile. "An adventurer once came through this way and partook of my predecessor's hospitality. During the meal he was warned that the spirit of Prapra was poisonous to all except desert dwellers. As I'm sure you have figured out, he tried it anyway. Then"—Vectra snapped her enormous fingers—"he died."

"And who was this traveler? Do you know his name or where he came from?"

Vectra squinted at her and cocked her head to the side. "Come, let me show you something." She lumbered toward one of the tunnels.

Before following her, Oganna reassured her aunts. "Don't worry about me." she whispered. "We can trust her."

Caritha frowned at first and then nodded. "You may go." Her mouth formed more words, and Oganna read her lips: "You have your sword?"

Slipping her hand to her side, Oganna activated Avenger so that the blade turned crimson. She turned away and followed Vectra down the tunnel.

※　※　※

In the dimness, Oganna struggled to put one foot before the other without stumbling. She drew her sword and used it and the glow of her silver dress to show the way. The tunnel's stone walls were smooth and polished from centuries—perhaps even ages—of use, so much so that they could not have been smoother if an ocean had carved the passage. She ran her hand along the stone as she walked, feeling every dip and rise in its surface.

Ahead, Vectra spat a flame into a channel on the rock wall. It sparked in the oil and blazed, the flames spreading over a section of wall about twenty feet high and at least that broad. The fire-lights helped illuminate the upper interior of a vast cavern, but the cavern floor fell away in front of her into depths cloaked in shadow. How amazing that such a place existed. The air smelled damp, old, and somewhat stale.

Vectra stopped, her body rigid, her head held high as she looked, or waited, for something. From the dark abyss ahead of them rose a silver disc. It looked fluid, like water running over polished metal. It began to revolve clockwise, and various colors streamed from its edges. The stone under Oganna and Vectra's feet glowed pink in the shape of a rose.

From the shadows beside her a voice chuckled softly enough for only Oganna to hear. "I think I'll wait back in the dining chamber with the dragon's daughters. You have good instincts, child. This creature is no threat."

Oganna grinned into the shadows. Specter! She should have known—he had followed her through the desert and probably watched the entire battle. She heard his robe swish over the floor as he returned to the tunnel.

Kneeling on all six legs, Vectra rumbled deep in her throat. "We must respect the ancient spirit that guards this place, Princess. For it alone grants access to the Tomb of the Ancients."

Oganna stepped forward. "What is the—"

"Look at the rose!" Vectra's tail twitched. "Read the marks upon its petals. Then follow my example, and bow to honor the dead."

The marks etched on the rose's petals were foreign and she could not read them. She sheathed her sword, allowing her silver garb to dissipate. "I do not understand these runes."

Vectra turned in surprise. "Surely you must, for this is the original script of the Common Tongue, which both you and I speak. " After a pause, she snorted a yellow vapor. "You speak the truth, Oganna. I can see that. But," she pounded a fist on the floor. "But unless you come over here and kneel, the spirit will not open the tomb, and I will be unable to show you what we came here for."

Above the depths of the cavern the silver disc continued to hover in silence. Its lights mesmerized Oganna, and her curiosity grew. What was this strange contrivance? What was it guarding? At last she knelt. Then she waited.

"Princess, your head! Put it down."

Her head? Oganna looked in puzzlement to Vectra and observed that not only was she kneeling, she was bowing as well. Realizing her error, she tipped her head forward.

It was just in time too. The silver disc descending to the depths stopped and then rose to its previous elevation, spinning erratically. Vectra's eyes remained lowered during the process. Oganna kept her head lowered, too, but raised her eyes. That disc was no spirit.

The opposing cavern wall, once ordinary stone, now began to transform. Its face slid away, revealing the front of a building carved in the stone. Eight white pillars, four on either side of a broad doorway, fronted the structure. The pillars nearest the doorway radiated blinding white light, forcing her to look away.

She glanced back to the tunnel through which they had come. A rusted steel door started to slide from above, blocking it off. Before the door had fully closed, she caught sight of her aunts rushing through the tunnel with their glowing swords in hand. They were stopped short of the door by an invisible barrier. The door closed and Oganna turned back to see the wondrous cavern. She was alone now, with a megatrath, but she felt no need for concern. Vectra was a creature of honor, and she seemed to know this place like the back of her massive hand.

"Princess, the Tomb of the Ancients awaits us." Vectra was floating over the abyss in the place where the disc had been.

But no, she only had the appearance of floating. Just as the Warrioresses had bumped into an invisible barrier, so there was an invisible walkway stretching across the depths.

Taking a cautious step forward, Oganna set her foot upon the smooth, cool surface. Was it glass? She leaned down and tapped the surface with her fist. No, glass would feel firm, and this did not. She struck it but heard no resulting sound. It was as if it was there, yet not there. She stood, smiling reassurance to Vectra as she walked over the level surface toward the creature. The sensation felt odd—surreal. Each step felt lighter, and each stride sped her passage.

"Come." Vectra plodded forward.

They walked down the white path to the entrance. The megatrath growled and threw its weight against the hefty doors. The doors groaned inward, and Oganna breathed in sharply as she stepped into an endless corridor. The floor was stone and the ceiling gleamed of an unearthly light emitted by innumerable crystals implanted therein. Heavy wood beams crisscrossed high above, supporting the ceiling. This 'tomb' rivaled the splendor of a palace.

She pointed down the endless corridor. "How far back does this go?"

"I don't know. Some of us have tried to find out, but though we walked for hours, we never even glimpsed its end." She pointed to an inscription on an overhead beam. "And that reads,

'Some secrets are best left hidden.' From this we gather that we must be content with the knowledge we have and not venture into the depths of this place."

Oganna doubted that the inscription was supposed to be interpreted exactly that way. Nevertheless, since the issue did not matter, she did not pursue the subject. "Vectra, you call this place the 'Tomb of the Ancients.' Why?"

"The runes that you cannot decipher were passed on to my people by the remnants of the ancient humanoid race that built this place. We know little about them except that which has been passed down to us in the form of legends and myths told us by our ancestors. According to our stories, the Ancient Ones gave our ancestors this underground world as a reward for good deeds and taught them their language. As you entered this place, did you not see the writing above the doors?"

Oganna shook her head.

"Above the entrance is an inscription that reads, 'Tomb of the Ancients.' On the doors are several lines of verse that I have memorized:

Forever may the spirit of this tomb watch over these dead,
And forever may they rest in peace.
To those who come in hither:
Pray that the spirit herein enchained will not awaken."

A shiver ran up Oganna's spine at the final line. "Sounds kind of creepy."

"And it should," Vectra said. "Our stories tell of an evil creature of great might who was pulled into the depths by a creature of great good and chained in the darkness by the Ancient Ones. It is said that one day he will arise and avenge himself on Subterran."

"Who was this creature that brought him down? What was his name?"

Vectra sighed, her eyes moistened, and she smiled. "His name is too sacred to utter and too revered to be written."

Oganna inspected the tomb more closely. Numerous door-ways flanked by marble pillars along the arching walls led from the endless corridor into darkness. No doubt the entombed remains of the ancient people that had built this place lay some-where within the connecting chambers.

"Here, in this protected place"—Vectra's feet thudded on the stone floor as her gaze roved over the high ceiling—"my ances-tors have been buried along with anyone else we put to rest. Beside this, Oganna, you might have already guessed that the Tomb of the Ancients holds not only our remains and those we have buried here, but also those the Ancients buried." Ducking through a doorway, she led Oganna into a dark tunnel. Along the way she blew flames to ignite the many torches nestled along the walls.

When they arrived at one particular chamber, Vectra sat back on her haunches. "Notice that the floor is inscribed. It says, 'Here lie strangers.' Observe that the room is nearly a perfect circle. And these tablets—" She indicated stones set in the walls. "These mark the graves of the strangers that befriend us and die among us."

Oganna listened with rapt attention.

"Remember that adventurer that I told you about? The one that ate Prapra?" She pointed a claw at a stone tablet. "Well . . . that's him."

"Really?"

"Yes. This particular chamber is reserved for those who are not megatrath. Here the adventurer will be preserved for all time by the spirit of this place."

Vectra pressed a fist against the stone, and it slid forward. Inside, a peculiar sarcophagus coated in a translucent material lay on a stone slab. Clearly visible through its convex surface was a middle-aged man, lying as if in sleep. A smile was on his face, and his body was clothed in a snow-white robe.

"He does not look dead." Oganna ran her hand over the abrasive sarcophagus, lukewarm to the touch. "It's as if he is sleeping."

"I know what you mean, for I too have had that feeling. It does not matter who we bury in this place, or what their expression is at the moment of their death. When the spirit covers the body a smile lights the entombed one's face. All the dead can be seen as whole as the day they were laid to rest. They are dressed in the same white apparel, and they have the same joyous expression. It is a mystery I do not pretend to understand."

"How many of your people have been buried here?"

The creature shrugged. "The number is beyond reckoning. We are not even sure when the Ancient Ones gave this tomb to our forebears.

"Maybe a thousand years, maybe more."

Leading the way, Vectra returned to the endless corridor. She proceeded a couple dozen feet down the corridor, then turned to lumber through a larger doorway to the side. She spat flames against the walls. Torches flashed while the tunnel grew in proportion to the larger door. Instead of a small chamber, a vast room opened before them, its walls rising hundreds of feet high. Here the enshrined megatraths had been buried. Four circles inset in the ceiling shone down pillars of light to illuminate the area.

Oganna could see that the ancient architects had designed this room as a gift to their megatrath friends. Here the creatures' remains had not decayed. Within these walls they were safe.

Here no tomb robber could enter and strip the creatures of their dignity.

"Magnificent, isn't it?" Vectra scratched the floor then continued. "Someday I too will be buried here, but not until I have subjected all megatraths under my leadership and have led them to peace with one another. When my kingdom is greater than my forebears, I will rest here among them."

Oganna folded her hands over her abdomen. What did Vectra mean by subjecting all megatraths under her leadership? Were the megatraths a race divided into nations that Vectra wished to conquer? Oganna decided to wait and ask the question later when Vectra was not so preoccupied with thoughts of the past.

"Well, Princess, now that I have shown you the Tomb of the Ancients, it is time to leave." She led the way out of the tomb and closed the doors behind them.

Oganna looked at the doors. Yes, the inscription was there just as the megatrath had said. She turned and briskly walked off the edge, expecting that the invisible surface was still there—but she plunged foolishly into the dark abyss. Soon her fall slowed, and she ricocheted off an unseen force. In an instant she found herself standing where she had been.

She looked down the path at Vectra. The creature slammed shut the heavy doors. Oganna about faced. Not ten feet in front of her, a duplicate of herself stepped toward the precipice. Oganna dashed forward, grabbing for her duplicate's shirt, but her other self plunged into the dark abyss. She looked back at her guide. The megatrath seemed oblivious to what had happened. Vectra loomed beside her and knelt, again awaiting the tomb's 'spirit.' Oganna glanced over the precipice—into the deep shadows that played between barely visible cliffs and boulders. What had happened? Where had her other self fallen? Or had she somehow been thrown back several moments in time? She shivered and knelt beside Vectra. She'd had enough excitement for one day.

The silver disc rose, the lights shone, and once again they walked to the other side of the abyss on an invisible surface. Behind them the tomb's entrance was again sealed off, replaced by the wall of uncut stone. The silver disc descended into darkness, and the steel door that had blocked escape from the cavern now opened.

Oganna walked into the tunnel and greeted her aunts as they rushed toward her. They couldn't disguise their worry. Their foreheads were knit and their eyes were narrowed. Their hands sweated as they fingered their sheathed swords.

She wondered if she should tell them what she had seen. If she did, would they believe her? She decided that, for the time being, she would sort out the mysteries in her own mind and tell them no more than necessary.

# 14

# PART DRAGON

Oganna felt as though she had walked among gods and partaken of their former glory. Vivid recollections of her experience in the Tomb of the Ancients passed through her mind, and in her heart she understood more profoundly how little she really knew of the world.

"This ancient race," Oganna said to Vectra as they walked alone through the cavernous depths later that day, "they taught your ancestors to read their language?"

"Yes. We are not certain why. Some of us believe they wanted to leave clues for us to follow, clues that could lead us to a greater, more meaningful existence. Others among us say that the Ancient Ones simply left it with us as a way to understand how to bury our dead in the tomb."

Oganna stood still and looked into another seemingly bottomless cavern. "What do you believe?"

The creature smiled and peered into the cavern along with her. "You are very inquisitive about us."

"Yes, I suppose I am." Oganna turned her blue-gold eyes away from the depths and looked at the megatrath. "This language of the ancients—the script on the tomb—could you teach me to read it?"

"But you already speak it. Surely you are able to read it as well."

"It is true that we speak the same language. However, I do not understand the ancient script—"

Vectra swatted the air. "Perhaps, then, you use a different set of runes. Maybe our runes are simply another characterization of that which you are used to." She brushed the dirt from a section of flat stone and scratched twenty-six figures into it. "This is A," she said, indicating the first figure. From that point she recited the remainder of the alphabet for Oganna.

Beside the strange characters Vectra had written, Oganna scratched the letters that were familiar to her. Vectra was right— they had the same alphabet, just different characters to represent each letter. The ancients had not written in a foreign tongue; they had likely created one alphabet or the other as a code to confuse their enemies. It was either that or the Ancient Ones' runes were the originals, and her people used a modernized script.

A palm-sized granite stone lay nearby. Oganna picked it up and copied the cipher from the wall. "Now I can read the Ancient Ones' symbols and understand what they say." She slipped it into one of her pockets.

"Vectra, what did you mean at the Tomb of the Ancients when you said that you will 'subjugate' all megatraths under your leadership? Are there other megatrath nations with their own leaders?"

Vectra chuckled deep in her throat. "You *are* an inquisitive one, aren't you? You seem to remember every word I speak. And that is fine with me; in fact I welcome a keen mind such as yours." She paused before continuing. "There are several other underground megatrath nations, none of them equal in might to mine. They are scattered enough to make it difficult for me to reach them all. You see, in order to unite them I must prove myself to be the strongest in each of those nations, either by our nation conquering theirs in war or by me dueling their leaders. This takes, as I am sure you can imagine, a very long time.

"These caverns in which we stand were once ruled by my great grandfather, an exceptionally powerful megatrath. He was the last in a long line of strong-willed leaders who held the many factions together as one nation. After his death there were five megatraths of equal strength who fought for the kingdom, but none of them could overcome the others. So an agreement was reached that allowed each of them to rule a portion of the kingdom so long as they left the others alone.

"My race was once mighty and"—she gave a toothy grin and ran her claws down the wall—"we were feared by our enemies. Now we are divided and thus weakened. I intend to unite our factions once more and restore our former glory."

Oganna thought of her father and how he had taken the Hemmed Land's inhabitants from a loose network of vulnerable people to hope and unity. Vectra's desires seemed to be on the same, commendable plane. But were her motives?

"No doubt you are curious what my motives are in this matter." Vectra scratched her side with her claws. "Allow me to assure you that it is not for the glory of conquest, though I do enjoy a good fight! My kind have lived in the darkness for too long, and it has hardened us to the world above and to each other. It is time for the megatraths to follow me into a new era of peace, achieved through conflict."

The possibility of forming an alliance with Vectra had been at the back of Oganna's mind ever since the tour of the tomb.

With these desert monsters on her father's side, the Hemmed Land's southern border would no longer be a concern, and their assistance might prove helpful in Ilfedo's troubles with the desert north of the Hemmed Land. Had the time come to broach the subject, or should she wait?

A breath of damp air sent a shiver up her spine as she turned to gaze boldly into Vectra's eyes. "You and I have an opportunity here," she said. "To create an alliance between our two nations. Together we could change this part of Subterran by spreading civilization. Think of it—an ally on your northern doorstep! What better way to strengthen your position in the eyes of your fellow megatraths? If your rivals make war upon you, we will aid you. If we are attacked, then you will come to our aid."

"Hmm." Vectra paced back and forth.

"Vectra, why not? Surely the rival megatraths will hear of how the Warrioresses and I slew Loos. If you ally yourself with us—strengthening the bond of trust between us—they will fear you more than ever."

No answer.

Oganna smiled. "By showing me the Tomb of the Ancients you have proven that you trust me. Tomorrow my aunts and I must return to our homeland. It is my sincere desire that you will accompany me so that I may return your hospitality and acquaint my people with your kind."

With a sigh, Vectra looked at her. "Your people will remember my kind with bitterness for, though I did not wish it, one of my subjects invaded your territory and committed murder. His life has been justly extinguished, but his deed will forever haunt us."

"Then come with me to the Hemmed Land. My father is facing a strange sort of threat on our northern border. Winged men that fight like birds have invaded on occasion and now, it seems, desert vipers are going into our forests to slay people in their sleep.

If you were to come and assist him, the people would recognize the goodness in your heart, and you would earn their trust."

"I *would* like to earn their trust." Vectra rumbled in her throat long and low. "Loos's deeds are a blot that I want to rectify. I favor an alliance with your people." She puffed out her chest and growled her resolution. "Let us today and now make a pact—between us alone—to stand by each other as friends even if everyone else stands against us. And let us bind ourselves to this friendship with an unbreakable oath."

Oganna relaxed and nodded. "Agreed."

"Come with me." Vectra knelt and invited Oganna to hop on to ride. "The place that I should like to do this is a long run from here. It would be a rough walk for you, but for me it is nothing."

The creature's hide was rough, scaly, and uncomfortable. Oganna wasn't going to complain, but Vectra swiveled around to look at her. "A ride on my back will not be the easiest on your body. Slide up to my neck."

Oganna complied. Vectra's neck felt flexible and the scales smoother, and as Vectra started running, Oganna found that the ride was a lot smoother than she'd thought it would be. She held on tightly as they spiraled down a narrow path along the cavern walls. Total darkness soon enveloped them, and only an occasional flash of flame from Vectra's mouth lighted the way.

Vectra reached the cavern's floor, slid on her rear legs to break her momentum, and skidded to a halt. "I used to come down here when I was a *megling*. The darkness hides these depths from the firelights above, and few megtraths have ever ventured down here. It is their loss, for I have found wonders that they have not imagined."

She tilted her head back, her sides billowing as her lungs sucked in air, then she snapped her head forward and let out a deafening roar. Her bellow resounded through the unexplored depths, daring any to stand in her way. As the last echoes died out, she repeated the roar, eerily bouncing it throughout the chasms, chambers, and tunnels. Satisfied, she walked forward with Oganna still clinging to her neck.

The megatrath spat a stream of fire ahead, revealing a tunnel straight ahead. It had a circular opening, and its floor sloped deeper underground. Large tiles, most of them broken, covered the tunnel floor. A statue had fallen across the floor. Large stone pieces that once formed the image of a human—male or female, Oganna could not tell—lay scattered. The statue's base stood whole and a pair of stone-carved, sandaled human feet remained atop it, broken off at the ankles.

Vectra lumbered into the tunnel and stepped over the fallen statue.

"What is this place?" Oganna asked.

"Truthfully I do not really know." The creature walked into the deep darkness, still descending. Oganna could feel the powerful feet thud on the floor. "I really do not know the purpose of many of these ancient constructions. It is a pity. My race lives above all of this—and we know so few of the secrets these places hold. The Tomb of the Ancients we know, for it was a gift to the megatrath race. But beyond that there are depths, depths in the darkest, deepest places. I know that the Ancients constructed this—all of this. Yet why and how is beyond my knowledge.

"I am now taking you to a place of solitude that I discovered as a *megling*. I believe it also was constructed by the Ancient Ones—and one of their spirits still resides there. He is a wise guiding spirit of great power, as you will soon discern. If we do not anger him, he will bear witness to our oath of alliance and ensure that the oath is kept."

"So this spirit—is he someone you can see?" The megatrath barrelled forward. As the dark tunnel rushed past, Oganna cringed. She could only hope Vectra wouldn't blindly knock into a wall. She forced a smile, hoping it would influence her tone. She doubted very much this spirit could be real. "Vectra, have you ever touched this spirit? Like, is he able to physically manifest himself?"

The creature gasped. "Never! Once I tried to approach his form, but I will never do so again. He condemned my action, and my body suddenly felt as though it were boiling in lava. Fortunately I came to my senses and, in pardon, he permitted me to return from time to time to see his magnificence and hear his counsel."

Vectra rocked to a stop. Oganna felt the creature's body quiver.

A light shone upon them from high above. Its blinding radiance forced her to shield her face with her hand. She squinted between her fingers at a cream-colored orb attached to the ceiling by a twisted iron elbow.

A voice spoke out, a confident male voice that filled the room. "Megatrath, welcome." She looked about at the brightly lit walls constructed of rectangular blocks of stone. Vectra kept her gaze to the floor, but Oganna peered into the corners, trying to discern the voice's origin.

"What is your name megatrath?"

"It is I, Vectra. And I bring a friend."

Oganna still could see nothing to indicate where the speaker came from. She glanced up at the orb. Was it possible that the speaker could see through that illumination device?

"I assume, Vectra, that you desire entry into the chamber for counsel."

Vectra bowed her head toward the far wall. "This human wishes to ally herself with me."

A long silence, then the light extinguished. Darkness flooded back into the chamber, and Oganna strained to make her eyes adjust. Another light blazed from overhead, shining in a narrow beam upon Oganna's head. The sudden brightness stung her eyes.

"Ah, yes. I had not noticed," the voice said in a hushed tone. "She *is* human."

"She is also my friend," Vectra replied.

Oganna heard stones grating. The light shifted toward the far wall, shining upon a large square opening. Vectra plodded through the entrance a couple dozen feet and halted. The stones grated behind them, and the entry resealed itself behind them, leaving them in pitch-blackness.

"Human, step forward."

Oganna frowned. To what or to whom did the voice belong? Vectra's head lowered her to the floor. Her shoes cracked on what sounded like tile, and she groped forward in the darkness in the direction of the voice. "Why?"

She heard Vectra snort. The megatrath's voice hissed around her. "Do not anger the spirit!"

"I want to see what you look like, spirit. I want to see you for what you really are. Long ago you inflicted unnecessary pain on this megatrath." She dropped one hand to her side and curled her fingers around Avenger's crystalline hilt.

"Impudence!" the man shouted. The chamber reverberated with the sound. "Submit to my will, human. Do not anger me." Through the veiling blackness the ghostly image of a giant man strode toward her. In his hand he held a wicked-looking sword of enormous size, and a small helm crowned his head.

She drew Avenger from its sheath. Its crystal blade turned crimson, its power clothed her in silver, and she stood as an angel without fear. The light of her sword and garment lit the area. She stood in a room constructed of stone. The light revealed a small window set in the back wall. She glanced back at Vectra. The creature cowered on the floor, every muscle trembling. No doubt remembering the pain this "spirit" had inflicted on her as a *megling*.

The man pointed his gloved hand at Oganna. Her joints ached, and then her skin warmed as if with fever. But she set her face toward the small window. If the imposter had sequestered himself in there—

With a silent command, she doused the light of her sword and that of her clothing. She concealed herself in the shadows and ran along the wall, dragging her finger lightly over the stones until she found a deep notch. Carefully she spidered her fingers along the notch, tracing the rectangular outline. So this was a small door. Tensing her arm, she pushed against the stone barrier. It swung inward without so much as a squeak, and she slipped inside.

To her right curved a long narrow room, dimly lighted by glowing ceiling panels only five feet above her head. She calmed her beating heart and walked around the curve. There, she stepped onto a grid of muted, yellow lights, warm under her feet.

A grid of multi-colored buttons, along with a few levers, glowed on panels set in the walls. Green and blue strings stretched from the ceiling to the floor along the back wall. Each string pulsated light, and a steady hum filled the room. A sheet three feet wide and two feet high leaned against one of the lighted panels. An image of Vectra still cowering in the darkened chamber appeared on its face.

A bearded man stood on a white floor panel in front of the image display. He held the sword she had seen earlier in the ghostly image. But now both he and the sword were proportionally smaller. In fact, he stood a bit shorter than her father. The man scowled at the screen and muttered, "That little whelp. Where'd she go?"

Willing her sword to glow again, Oganna let it clothe her in the silver dress. The man spun and took a step back, eying her up and down.

"Despicable." She let her eyes bore into his. "It is hard for me to accept that some people are as cruel as you. How dare you torture a megatrath just to maintain this facade. You are no spirit!"

"What—you found your way in here?"

"You are coming with me, sir." She raised Avenger and frowned. "I want you to tell these creatures that you are mere flesh and blood! And I want you to repent of this evil you have done. Deceiving these creatures with this ancient technology— that is what this is, is it not? Some advanced machinery that you have learned to manipulate?"

"I do not have to answer your questions, child." He flipped his sword in his hand and scraped its tip on the floor. "Treat me with respect, or I will soon show you that tricks are not my only talent." With a swift motion he brought his sword toward her throat. She ducked under it and shoved his blade aside with the Avenger.

A smile curled his lips. His shoulder-length hair was gray, and his face was wrinkled, but he fought with great strength. Each time his sword smote hers she was forced to grip her hilt with both hands. He swung his sword in a V motion, always facing her, and steadily drove her back.

Beads of sweat moistened her forehead. She lost ground and struggled to keep her tired feet from slipping on the smooth panels. The recent journey through the desert and her encounter with Loos had drained her of energy. Her knees buckled, and she wavered in her defense.

"I *am* a spirit. You cannot win against a spirit." He held his sword in one hand and reached behind his back.

Too late, she saw him slide out a second sword. He swung it like a club and smote her on the head. Stars danced through her vision and, as she fell, she heard him laugh.

⚜ ⚜ ⚜

Bright green grass waved all around. Puffy white clouds dotted the blue sky overhead, and a gentle breeze moved the clean, warm air across Oganna's face. She blinked and raised her hand to her face. Yes, she had a welt where the pretender had hit her.

She shook her head. What had happened? Where was she? The field she was lying in extended as far as her eyes could see on all sides. A shadow fell upon her from behind. She turned.

"Hello." A wrinkled man with a long white beard that nearly reached the ground sidled in front of her and offered a hand. He was barefooted, and his body was wrapped with a snow-white toga, while on his head he wore an equally white turban. "Are you lost, child?"

Without answering, she accepted his hand and stood up. In her other hand the sword Avenger burned furiously, reflecting its red hues against her silver garment.

The elder who helped her up was short. His turban didn't even reach her shoulder. His eyes were bright blue and his ears were at least three times as large as hers.

He eyed her weapon and vestments. "What is your name?"

Ignoring his question, she responded, "Where am I? What has happened?" She squinted her eyes, looking skyward, and recalled the duel with the stranger.

The little man stroked his beard, then looked up at her. "Thoughts—your mind is full of them." He reached up with his hand and touched her forehead.

As he withdrew his hand, a web of light pulled from her forehead. Instinct told her to stop him, but another conflicting sense restrained her. If he had wanted to harm her, he could have done so while she was lying in the field.

For a moment the man held the web of light in his hand and stared at it as it glowed. Then he closed his fingers over his palm, stretched out his arm, shook his hand a few times, and threw the webbing into the wind. As soon as it left his hand, it burst into fine dust and settled on the ground. There an image formed— an image of pure light—of Oganna's recent duel. It replayed her struggle, then destabilized and disappeared.

The old man looked at Oganna. His eyes looked playful. "That is how you came here."

"Where am I?"

Once more he touched her forehead. "Does that feel better?"

She reached up to feel for her welt, but it was gone. "Thank you."

"It is not worth mentioning, my dear. Now, tell me, this man you were fighting, do you know him?"

She shook her head. "No."

"Good, then I will send you back so that you can finish your fight." He walked off at a brisk pace and called for her to follow.

Within half an hour they topped a rise and stared down a hill at a great lake rimmed by a vast city. "My home," said the man, "and your pathway back to Osira."

"Osira? What is Osira?"

The old man swallowed hard. "My mistake! I meant to say it is your pathway back to Subterran."

Her brow furrowed. "I am not on Subterran? Are you trying to say . . . what, that I am on *another* world?"

He laughed and pointed at the ground behind her. "You didn't notice that you have two shadows?" When she looked behind, she saw he was right. He told her to look at the sky again. "Does your world have two suns?"

She looked up and couldn't help gaping in astonishment. "I am on another world."

"Yes, you are on mine." He waved a hand toward the city and beamed with pride. "We have perfected our society. Unlike your world, we do not need instruments of war. We rest in the Creator's peace. But come! I mustn't reveal all mysteries to you, for then I would be at fault for interfering in your future."

"But how do you know of my world?"

"We are familiar with it—but little more than that." He halted and faced her. "Let me give you a word of advice."

"Certainly." She shook her head. The sudden transference to this place felt like a dream, dizzying.

"When you get back to your fight, don't rely as much on your physical strength." His eyes roved from the sword to her silver garb. "There is a lot of strength in you. Yes—much potential! I see that you can use the power of dragon blood, and you are not an amateur at it." Leaning closer, he winked. "I would say you must be part dragon."

She started in surprise, and he laughed. "When you return to your fight, use your dragon side—your powerful side—the side that grants you the use of potent energies unique to your blood."

They had not reached his city before he stopped, stooped, and pressed his hand on something in the ground. Then he stood up and waited as an exquisitely carved gazebo rose before them. "I regret not having the time to show you more," he said. "I have thoroughly enjoyed meeting you."

He led her onto the gazebo platform and ordered her to stand on a pad at its center. Then he bowed low, kissed her hand, pulled a lever, and she found herself lying at her opponent's feet in the subterranean antechamber.

The old man's words flashed through her mind. "Use your dragon side," she repeated.

The 'spirit' looked down in shock and his sword shook in his hand as he pointed it in her face. "How did you do that? You were out cold." As she rose, he struck at her.

This time she closed her eyes and felt the substance of everything in the surrounding area. She could feel the walls, the floor, and the electrical energy running through the ancient platform. She drew power from her sword and reached out with her mind. She raised her hand and clenched her fist, pulling the stones from the ceiling and from the walls so that they broke up.

Her opponent screamed and dropped one of his swords as the stones pinned him. "Please. Don't kill me! I beg of you, please let me live. I meant no harm to the megatraths."

She scowled. She wouldn't leave him to die. Besides, Vectra had to be shown the truth. She reached out with her mind, throwing the stones from his body with a mere thought, and then dragged him toward the door she'd entered previously. The anteroom collapsed. Stones fell on the wall panels and sparks sailed in all directions. A string of energy lashed at the man, drawing blood from his chest. As he grabbed at his wound, a stone slammed into his shoulder, cracking bone. A panel loosened from the wall and flipped end-over-end onto the lighted floor panels. Electrical current raced along the panels, snapping at her soles. Bolts zigzagged along the walls, and an explosion rocked the chamber floor.

After pulling the pretender through the door, she closed it behind her. Letting out a long breath, she leaned against the wall, slumped to the floor. Her shoulder hit an ancient lever that flipped and turned the lights on, illuminating the main chamber. Stones grated again and two more doorways slid open along the opposite wall.

The mighty Vectra raised her head slowly and stepped forward. The chamber was large and the ceiling high. She glanced at the tiled walls and squinted at the bulbous orb glaring from far above. Then she looked at Oganna, and bewilderment reigned in her eyes. She lumbered forward, towering over the wounded man.

Oganna kicked rubble to the side and shook her head at Vectra. "There is no spirit in these walls. There never was. He is only a man utilizing the strange mechanisms of this buried civilization to further his own esteem in your eyes." She looked at the humbled pretender. "I wonder how long he has lived down here—apparently alone. Vectra, you said that you came to this place as a *megling*. Did you see the spirit then, too?"

"Yes, I have seen him my whole life." She stared wide-eyed at the imposter. "And I have lived a *long* time. Longer than any human should."

"Well," Oganna said as she laid her hands on the man's wounds, "then he must be very old—for a *human* that is." Ignoring her exhaustion, she poured healing energy into the man. His bruises and wounds healed before her very eyes.

She patted his cheeks. "I think he's fainted. He has lost a lot of blood." The wrinkled man stirred, his eyelids fluttered open, and he looked in defeat upon her and the megatrath. "Well, sir," Oganna began, "you had better explain yourself."

"Please, wizard," he said. "I meant no harm." He swallowed hard. "Six hundred years ago I was a guest of the megatraths, and while I was exploring these ancient passageways I happened into this chamber. Please do not take me away. Let me die in the home I have found within these ruins."

"You have deceived me ever since I was young?" Vectra exhaled a noxious fume. "You do not deserve an honorable death. I should kill you here and now."

The gray-haired man grasped his sword and held it between him and the creature. "This weapon allows me to command these ancient workings to do whatsoever I will, and if I wish it I can destroy you."

Smoke roiled between Vectra's teeth. She pointed at Oganna, and her retracted claws slid out of her fingers. "This coming from you who failed to defeat a young woman? You should be in dread of me, deceiver. I can almost taste your blood in my mouth and feel your arms crushed between my jaws as I suspend you above the depths of my underground realm. I would drop you into the abandoned cities and, before your demise, you would curse the moment you challenged me."

Oganna stood between them and shook her head. She glanced at the megatrath and then at the man. "It was a cruel thing you did to Vectra when she was young. Was that your reward for her kind's hospitality?"

"But I did not do that on purpose. I swear!" He cupped his hands and looked at Vectra's toothy face. "There was a mechanism—I did not know what it would do, so I did not plan to touch it—but my elbow brushed against it and—"

"And my body burned with inner fire. Something I have not forgotten, deceiver." The megatrath exhaled yellow vapor.

"But I found a way to shut if off. The pain stopped. Didn't it?" His face brightened, and he brushed dust from his beard.

Vectra stared at him for a moment, then her jaws parted and a quick stream of fire shot out. It burned his beard and hand.

At first the man cried out, then he shook his singed hair out of his eyes and gritted his teeth. "I will accept that as your forgiveness, megatrath. My debt to you is paid."

"I concur." Vectra growled and scraped the floor with her claws. She glanced down at Oganna. "You have exposed him, and I am grateful. Name a request so that I may grant you a reward."

The creature's offer hung in the air for a few moments. Oganna circled the man and then faced the megatrath. "His debt to me has not yet been paid."

The man's mouth opened wide, and his eyes reflected fear.

She held her head high and gazed down at him. "Vectra and I have come here to make a pact of alliance, but I see now that her plan for binding it for eternity will not work. However, you can still serve as witness to this event. If you will serve as witness to our oaths, then I will forgive and forget your misconduct, and we will leave you to your solitude." She looked into Vectra's dark eyes. "He is harmless. I do not sense wickedness in his heart. What he has done is wrong, but I will forgive if he does this deed."

Gruffly, the creature grunted.

Oganna looked down at the man. He smiled his gratitude and mouthed a "Thank you."

"One thing, sir. I am *not* a wizard." She held her hand to her chest. "I am the human offspring of a dragon. Please do not make me cringe by associating me with demonic forces."

The man smacked his knee. "No. You are an angel." Thereupon, he stood as witness while Vectra and Oganna declared an alliance between their two peoples and pledged to hold to their vow no matter what the future might bring.

The man raised his sword with both hands. "This vow must be maintained." He snorted a laugh. "Or I will come back to haunt you." His whole person phased, the sword disappeared, and so did he.

The megatrath stepped back when he disappeared—as did Oganna. The creature dropped its voice to a whisper. "Maybe he *is* a spirit."

Oganna laughed. "If he is a spirit, then maybe I am too." She straddled Vectra's neck. The megatrath shook its hide and turned in the direction they'd come. With powerful strides it carried her up and out of the chambers. Behind them the lights flickered and extinguished, leaving the chamber once more in darkness. It took a while, but gradually Vectra climbed out of the subterranean world's depths. On the way Oganna occasionally peered into the deep crevices bordering the trail and wondered what mysteries remained to be solved in the still-deeper regions of this place. A shiver ran down her spine as an image of abandoned cities haunted by a creature dwarfing the megatraths painted itself in her mind. Deep, deep underground. She shuddered and forced her thoughts elsewhere.

This alliance that she had formed with the megatrath could greatly benefit her father's people. But what would he think of her committing herself to this pact without his prior consent? And what would Caritha and the other Warrioresses say? She ignored the doubts and determined that, whatever might happen, she would remain a faithful friend to the megatrath. She would keep her oath.

They reached a higher elevation where the firelights lit the way. She glanced back one time, wondering what had become of the man who lived down below. His wounds had been severe, and even though she had healed him, he was old and would likely die. But then again maybe she was wrong. After all, he had an extraordinary knowledge of the Ancient Ones' technology. Perhaps someday it would be possible for her to return. Perhaps one day the secrets buried here would be revealed to her. Perhaps.

# ALLIES

The narrow band of water that formed the underground stream flowed unhindered through the stones. Oganna, holding her sword in one hand to light the way, followed the stream from the chamber in which she'd slept. It bent around a corner and angled down, leading her into a tunnel she had not explored.

Before she saw the waterfall, she heard it thundering from high in its cavern. Soon it came into view, plummeting to a circular pool carved in the stone floor by centuries of erosion. A hole somewhere above allowed a band of light to beam on the pool. It reflected on the water and danced in white and silver patterns along the walls.

She sheathed her sword, knelt, and drank deeply, savoring the cool, refreshing liquid. Submerging her hands, she cupped them. Next she splashed water on her face and wiped it with a handkerchief.

Someone walked to the other side of the pool. She could hear footfalls on the stone, and she discerned the figure of a woman in the reflected light.

"Good morning, Oganna." It was Caritha's voice. "You were up late last night?"

"Vectra was showing me around."

"Um, hum. I see." She washed her face in the pool, then stood and came to Oganna. The reflected light created wild patterns on her dark hair and highlighted its reddish tinge. "Well, as soon as Laura, Rose'el, Levena, and Evela wake up, we can say our farewells to the megatraths and be on our way."

Oganna bit her lip. "No. No, I am afraid it will not be that simple." She folded her hands behind her back. "Last night I took an oath of alliance with these creatures, namely with Vectra." She told Caritha of the old man dwelling deep in the caverns, whom she'd fought—but left out the part where she ended up on another world—and she told her how the man had witnessed the pledge to ally with the megatraths. "So," she said, "today we will leave, but Vectra is coming with us."

"What?"

"She wants to meet Father and, if she is able, to help him with his troubles in the north. The megatraths are desert creatures after all."

"Oganna, I know that you did this with the best of intentions. But I do not believe you considered all the facts before you made this commitment. These creatures are a race bent on conflict, and they revel in testing one another's physical strength. You may respect Vectra, yet I see no reason to believe we can trust her followers." She put a hand on Oganna's shoulder. "However, you *are* the princess and thus the future queen of your father's people. The decision is not mine to make; it is yours. I may not fully agree with it, but I will support it."

Oganna smiled and stood. "Will you tell the others for me? They will not object if they know that you stand behind my decision."

"Of course." Caritha's hand slid off Oganna's shoulder and dropped into her pocket. She started to walk away.

Oganna held up her hand. "Oh yes, there is one more thing."

"Yes?"

"We leave within the hour. Tell them that you are all to meet me at the ledge where we first came into this place. And everyone should make sure to grab breakfast first. Bring your packs with you to the ledge."

Caritha nodded, smiled, then pulled her hand out of her pocket to wave as she left. Something shiny clattered to the stone. She knelt on the floor, searching for it.

"Aunt Caritha, did you drop something?" She stepped toward her, but the woman held up a hand.

"Yes—please do not come any closer." The woman laughed with relief and picked something off the stone surface. She stood and clutched it to her breast, then raced out of the cavern.

※　※　※

Sparks flew from the stones above Oganna's head as Vectra dug in with her claws, swung her body out of her cave, and slid down the cavern wall. "A good morning to you, Princess. Did you sleep well?"

Oganna bowed as the creature thudded to the ground and loomed before her. "Very well, thank you. Is everything ready?"

"Yes." The creature stretched and yawned. "I've already set things in motion."

"Good. The Warrioresses will meet us at the rendezvous within the hour."

Vectra hunkered on the stone floor and rumbled an invitation. "Care to ride on me to the ledge?"

"No, thank you. I think I'll stretch my legs before the trip."

Vectra lumbered to the tunnel that led out of her subterranean home. Oganna followed close on her heels. The megatrath dug her claws into the stone walls, and her powerful legs pulled her at an astonishing pace up the tunnel. When they reached the cave at the tunnel's end and stood on the ledge that overlooked the desert, Vectra angled her long head to look down at her. "What do you call my desert, Oganna?"

"We don't have a name for it." Oganna walked forward, feeling the mighty creature's gaze follow her. She looked out over the sands stretching to the horizon. "It is known to my people as the southern desert." She looked to the creature. "Why? Do you have a name for it?"

Vectra chortled. "When all megatraths were united as one nation, we called it Resgeria."

"Then Resgeria it is." Oganna peered over the ledge. Several dozen megatraths lumbered onto the baking sand, aiming their long bodies in the direction of the Hemmed Land. "How many are coming with us, Vectra?"

The creature threw the front half of her body over the ledge. Her rear legs dug into the cave floor, holding her in place. The creature counted on her claws. "One hundred of my finest followers."

The Warrioresses stepped up on either side of her. Their mouths dropped open, and Rose'el looked at Oganna and clacked her tongue. She edged closer and spoke so only Oganna could hear. "I hope you know what you are doing, young lady."

"Wait a minute, Oganna." Laura glanced at the megatrath force and swallowed hard. "You can't bring all of them with you. What would your father say? The people will be frightened beyond belief."

"This is a token of Vectra's commitment to our alliance." Oganna rested a hand on Vectra's side. "They will bring us to the Hemmed Land, and we will bring them to meet Father."

Vectra spun around, jumped backwards, and grasped the rock face with her great claws. "Coming?" She skidded down the cliff, leaving fresh scratches in her wake.

Oganna and the sisters followed her to the desert floor with all due speed, but compared to the megatrath they made slow progress. Oganna looked at the remaining descent and clambered back to the cave opening, ignoring the quizzical expressions on her aunts' faces. After pulling a thin rope from her pack, she tied it around a boulder in the cave, pulled it taut, backed over the ledge, and rappelled down the rock's face. In this way she passed the sisters and reached the desert floor ahead of them.

The Warrioresses descended foot by foot and finally arrived on the desert floor. Rose'el looked at the rope and shook her head. "Humph! You could have saved that. It's stuck up there now."

"Maybe not." She held the rope out to Vectra. "Do you think you can snap it for me?"

"With pleasure." The creature jerked the rope and it fell to the ground. Its end had ripped, but the rest of it was still good.

Vectra bent low and addressed the Warrioresses while Oganna climbed to the nape of her neck. "You may ride on my back or on the necks of other megatraths if you so choose."

"Riding the neck is smoother." Oganna tucked her skirts under her bottom and bounced a little. "Believe me. I've tried both."

In a graceful move, Caritha sidled up to another of the creatures and bowed to it. "May I?"

A pleased rumble came from the creature's mouth, and it bent down. She clambered on, the creature stood, and she spoke to her sisters. "It really is quite comfortable up here."

Laura and Rose'el murmured to each other, then led the others to Vectra. They sat on the hard scales of her back and held on to the short horns protruding from her spine. Oganna shrugged. "All right, but I think you'll regret it!"

Having all her passengers on board, Vectra dug in her heels and dashed northward. A strong wind bit the sand, spinning it in thick clouds. Visibility fell to zero, but the megatrath charged through.

Oganna put her cheek against the creature's neck, reached to her back, and pulled a shawl from her pack to wrap around her head. The sand stung without relenting. When at last the wind let up, Oganna unwound the shawl from her head. Hot, dry air chapped her face.

One glance at the sisters riding Vectra's back, and she smirked. Sand had attached itself to their sweating faces. They bounced with each stride and clung tightly to the creature's body. Caritha's mount ran fast on Vectra's heels.

Yelling over the din of six hundred pounding feet, Oganna twisted to look back. "Comfortable back there?"

"Very funny." Evela spat sand from her mouth. "Just you wait. Once we get off, I'll teach you a lesson or two in manners, young lady."

The megatraths did not stop until midday, and then it was only to take a short rest. Several of them ripped up a portion of the desert floor with their claws until they reached clay about fifteen feet down. Digging a little farther, they hit an underground spring. A pool of water formed, and everyone drank. Afterward the megatraths rolled in the mud.

Oganna watched with fascination, then looked up at Vectra. "Why are they doing that?"

Vectra rolled herself in the mud before replying. "Yimshi's rays will bake a crust of mud over our scales, allowing us to maintain a cooler body temperature for a longer period of time." She motioned over to one of her followers and ordered him to clean the mud off her neck and back. "Unless you prefer to sit in mud—," she said to the women. They assured her they were indeed more comfortable without the mud.

Their response was not fair to the creature, so Oganna objected, insisting that the mud must remain. "Do not worry about us, Vectra. We can clean our clothes later." She stared meaningfully at Laura, Rose'el, Evela, and Levena. "Isn't that so?"

They nodded their heads vigorously, and she could see that they felt ashamed of their selfish behavior. Without further ado, all of the sisters with the exception of Rose'el humbly approached separate megatraths and requested rides on their necks. Each of the creatures hunkered on the sand so they could climb on. Rose'el held her head high and took a lonely spot on Vectra's back, grasping a horn.

Oganna swung her legs over Vectra's neck while the creatures lined up behind her. She caught sight of Caritha conversing with her mount before getting on its neck. The creature looked very pleased with her company. In an instant the cavalcade took off. They raced on through the heat, never slowing, never stopping, until nightfall. The air chilled, and then they slowed.

As the stars began to stud the sky, the megatraths lay down in a protective circle with Vectra, Oganna, and the Warrioresses at its center. The exertions of the day had exhausted them and before long everyone, with the exception of Oganna and Caritha, had fallen into deep slumber.

Lying there under the stars awakened Oganna's imagination and brought to mind some questions she had been meaning to ask. She waited until Caritha comfortably situated herself before initiating a conversation.

They talked on insignificant matters for several minutes, until Caritha propped herself on one elbow and raised her eyebrows. "You are trying to lead the conversation around to something, aren't you? What did you really want to talk about?"

"Father once told me that the dragon who is called Albino made my mother and all of you. Is that true?"

"Ah, I think I see where this is leading." Caritha adjusted the rolled blanket under her head.

"You want to know where we came from, or more specifically where your mother came from. Very well, only bear in mind that there are some things I am not at liberty to tell you. I wish I could reveal everything, for your sake, but I am bound by the dragon's wishes." She ran her finger in the sand. "The Albino is our father, Oganna. He alone is responsible for our existence."

The cold desert wind breathed across the sand, sending shivers down Oganna's spine.

"You are probably wondering where Albino comes from." Caritha shook her head. "To that question I can only give a vague answer because neither I nor any of my sisters knows exactly where. He has his own domain—a wonderful land rich with happiness and full of nature's marvels. So strong is he that his land has never been invaded and no one who lives there, to my knowledge, has ever died. Only he and those closest to him know its location. I myself do not know how to reach it—even if I wanted to."

Oganna pushed herself up on her elbows. "What can you tell me about my mother?"

"She was the closest of us to the Albino, and she spent a great deal of time with him. I attribute her greater power to that fact above all, for if I and the others had also focused on spending time with him, no doubt we would have learned a greater mastery of our powers. But as it is, we did not, and I am ashamed to admit, his fondness for Dantress caused us to grow a little jealous.

"When we were young, the dragon gave us these rusty swords, and later, when we were not much older than you, he set us in the forest where your father and mother met. He intended us to use our weapons and powers to defend the helpless and destroy any wicked creatures we came across, and for a time, we intended to.

"Then we grew lazy and stayed very near to our woodland cave. Your mother, though, continued to seek ways to fulfill our mission. She had a soft heart and would often go alone on long trips to find creatures in need and aid them.

"Then your father came along and stole her from us. We felt she had betrayed us by leaving, so we followed her and hid ourselves in the forests of the Hemmed Land. There we bided our time, waiting to kill your father and take back Dantress." Caritha paused to glance at the ground. She sighed and covered her face with her hands.

"We believed that your father had deceived Dantress, leading her to believe he loved her when he only planned to use her. Because our blood is that of our dragon father, none of us can give birth to a living child without giving up the life in our blood. We knew that giving birth would kill her. But when your mother died to bring you into the world and your father wept, I saw in his face a greater devastation than I have ever seen a person endure.

"Guilt finally caught up with us. Our presumptions had led us to false conclusions, and we'd nearly killed a good man. That day we revealed ourselves to him and followed him to bury your mother."

Tears welled in Caritha's eyes. "Dantress defended you against *us*. She told us not to interfere, and when we did, she received power that I cannot explain—unless it came from our father." She folded her hands. "She had such conviction, such fury in her eyes, but at the time I could not see it. Now, so many years later, I understand what she meant. I look at you and know that her sacrifice was not in vain."

She sighed and reached out to pat Oganna's cheek. "I am tired and we have a good way longer to go tomorrow. Get some sleep."

As she lay back, Oganna listened to the heavy breathing of the creatures around her. It sounded like a constant wind protectively encompassing her. She thought of her mother, wondered what it would be like to know her, and promised herself that she would live worthy of her sacrifice.

The unmarked trail to the Hemmed Land's southern border proved wearying. When they came in sight of a town, Oganna ordered a halt. "I think it would be wise if I went on ahead with the Warrioresses." She patted Vectra's side. "The people will probably be shivering in their shoes, wondering if you have come to destroy them."

The creature dipped its head and growled. "Do what you think is best, Princess. My guard and I will wait until you call for us."

Caritha kept pace beside Oganna as she led the Warrioresses into town. "This is really embarrassing." She patted her dress and a cloud of dust arose. She coughed. "I am *not* at all presentable."

"What about me?" Rose'el brushed sand off her cheeks. "I've been bouncing on Vectra's back for an intolerable period of time, and I can't walk straight. And did I forget to mention that the seat of my dress is covered in mud?"

Oganna shook her head at Rose'el. "That creature saved us a lot of walking through a harsh environment. Come, we must arrange accommodations for the megatraths and calm a throng of terrified people. *Then* we can worry about ourselves."

The town's main street was deserted, except for a couple cats and a yellow dog. The dog came up to them and lolled its tongue while Oganna scratched its head. The air felt good, refreshingly moist and cool after the desert heat. "We do look quite dirty." Oganna dropped her hand from the dog's head. "I wonder where everyone is. Perhaps they don't recognize us?"

"Who doesn't recognize us? I don't see anyone around." Rose'el crossed her arms.

Out of the corner of her eye, Oganna caught movement in a second-story window. She drew her sword and raised it above her head, sending streams of energy throughout her body to transform her filthy attire into that of her silver-clad self. The dog stuck its tail between its legs and darted into an alley, but the townsfolk rushed from their dwellings and businesses.

"It is Princess Oganna and the Warrioresses!" They gathered around and knelt before her. "We saw the creatures come from the desert, and we feared the worst." . . . "Why have they come and why are you with them?" The questions poured in like rain until she raised her hand for silence.

"The creature that destroyed Bordelin has been slain. His blood stained my sword. No more will that creature invade our land. No longer will you live in fear. And in appreciation to the murderer's race for their help in bringing justice upon him, I have extended a hand of friendship to the leader of the megatraths. Her name is Vectra, and the desert she rules is called Resgeria. I proclaim a formal alliance now exists between Resgeria and the Hemmed Land.

"Treat these creatures as you would your closest friends. You will find that they are gentle giants and intelligent beings of remarkable potential." She scanned the crowd. "Who here speaks for this town?"

A short man, clad in loose tan trousers and a white collared shirt, stepped forward. "I do." He bowed low. "I am Mayor Gregory, at your service, my lady."

"Mayor Gregory, will you be so kind as to find accommodations for the megatraths? They have had a long and exhausting trip."

"Of course, if it is your wish it will be done." He turned to some men standing nearby. "Organize everyone and have a tent made to shelter our princess and the Warrioresses. Prepare food for them and these creatures."

Splitting up, the people went to their assigned tasks. The mayor came forward again. "If it would please my lady, may I offer lodging in my home to you and the Warrioresses?" He puffed out his chest. "My wife is a superb cook!"

She accepted and told the sisters that she would meet them at the mayor's home later. "Mayor Gregory, is there any news of my father?"

"Afraid there is, my lady. But it doesn't sound encouraging. Seems that he hasn't been able to stop the vipers from killing people, and the army is still patrolling the border. It's a mystery and many people are panicking. Some say only half the original population remains up north, some having been slain by vipers and others moving out of the territory."

Thanking him for the information, she walked out of town. "I must see to it that Vectra knows what is going on."

She found Vectra in a large field by the town. Townsfolk ran hither and thither laying straw inside large tents. They glanced up at the enormous creatures, but for the most part ignored them. Vectra raised her long mouth out of a creek and let the water run down her neck.

"Ah, my friend." Vectra's teeth chattered as she spoke. "Your people have been very kind and are taking good care of us."

Oganna chuckled as the creature shivered. "Are you cold?"

"Goodness, yes! How can you bear this temperature? It is as cold as nighttime in the desert, and yet the sun is still up." She grimaced as a strong gust of wind cooled her hide. "I'd heard that you humans like lower temperatures, but until now I didn't know it was true."

Oganna looked out over the field and changed the subject. "Tomorrow we must proceed north. I've been told that my father is still engaged in some sort of trouble along our border with the northern desert."

"Ah, a desert! That sounds better." She licked her scaly lips. "Then tomorrow we will accompany you into the north."

The next day the megatrath horde followed Oganna and Vectra northward. At Caritha's suggestion, the Warrioresses went on ahead to tell people of the new alliance and spread good will toward the creatures among the populace.

Vectra seemed fascinated by the Hemmed Land's culture, and she inquired into many things that she saw as they passed. "It is serene here, and beautiful," she remarked after passing several large fields of flowers. "My race has not striven to create beauty. Instead we have worked to harden ourselves and cast off fleshly frailties. Perhaps this is a weakness?"

"Perhaps it is serene." Oganna plucked a flower and held it up for Vectra to sniff. "However, your race has preserved a far longer history than mine has maintained. In that area my people could learn from yours."

"We don't laugh very much." Vectra rumbled in her throat. "Your people seem to laugh a great deal of the time. It would be good for my people to learn again to love life through things other than combat."

Several people stood behind a white picket fence, watching the procession pass. Vectra grinned with her snoutful of teeth.

The humans' faces paled, and they stepped back. The creature sighed heavily, her head drooped, and her gait lost its enthusiasm.

Seeing this, Oganna went to the fence and called a young lad over. "Can you run?"

His eyes shone, and he bowed. "Yes. I am the quickest in the land!"

No doubt this was a mere boast, but she did not care. He would do. "Very well, then listen carefully to what I have to say. Go ahead of us along the roads and spread the word that any megatrath that makes an attempt at a friendly smile or gesture should be regarded with the utmost courtesy. I want everyone to make them feel wanted. I want everyone to welcome these creatures!"

"Yes, my lady!" He vaulted a fence and raced like a deer across a field to the north. Oganna smiled. He might not be the fastest in the whole of the Hemmed Land, but perhaps someday he would prove that his boast had carried a grain of truth.

On the next day as they passed through a smaller town of wood and stone houses, Vectra curled back her lips to reveal her teeth to an onlooker. The people waved, grinning up at her, and the megatrath's face lit up. She swung around, facing Oganna. "Now *that* is what I call a good beginning to a long relationship!"

Oganna, riding on Vectra's neck, waved back to the townsmen, but she hardly noticed them. The closer they came to Fort North, the more she wondered why her father had not yet been able to stop the vipers from attacking human settlements. Had he run into a deeper problem than he'd anticipated, or were there simply more of the creatures than he'd assumed?

Surely with the sword given him by the dragon, mere desert vipers did not present a continuing threat. If, however, the Art'en had returned—

# 16

# LOVE'S WATCHFUL HALO

Darkness shrouded the forest as Ilfedo watched silent and still, beside a large oak tree. Beyond the trees the late evening mist curled its blue fingers over the desert sand. The viper snakes were not known to leave the safety of the desert climate, but for some time now they had been seen within the Hemmed Land's border. The reports had come in sporadically at first, then deaths were reported, and people were found poisoned in their beds with viper's fang marks on their necks.

Something strange was afoot. Ilfedo could feel it. Ever since he had first organized an ambush for the vipers, he had felt moody. The slightest remark from a close friend sometimes made him angry. His shortness of temper started after his first night—when he had been standing guard—just as he was now. A feeling of evil had loomed over him, only for a moment, but it was long enough to make the hair on his head prickle.

He blinked his eyes as a splash of cold wind blew across his face. His ears listened for a sound, and with his eyes he searched the forest floor. The leaves by his feet rustled, and he discerned a reptilian head tasting his boot with its tongue. He slid his hand over the pommel of his sword and wrapped his fingers around the handle. The sound of the viper's soft, dreadful hissing caused him to tense. The creature reared its head back and moved to strike.

In a flash he slid the sword of the dragon from its sheath. The living fire leaped forth, and he severed the snake's head in a precise stroke. The armor of living fire covered his body as he scanned the ground. It was as he'd suspected—the forest floor's leafy carpet teemed with desert vipers. Their hissing grew in volume as they sighted him. He dove to the side as several flung themselves from the trees. Their fanged jaws snapped as they struck where his head had been.

He held his sword at arm's length, pointed its blazing tip at the invaders, and spun. The fire of his sword spewed forth, set the ground ablaze, and drove the serpents back. Hundreds of smoking snake corpses twisted on the ground. He walked forward, sidestepped a burning log, and continued to burn out the vipers.

Once the vipers had begun to retreat, he raised his left arm and motioned for his hidden warriors to join him. He had two hundred men with him that had been trained by the Warrioresses. Each of them drew a sword made by the master sword smith Linsair, and armor of light covered their bodies. The light from their swords combined with his own and blazed beneath the trees as if a thousand lanterns hung from the branches.

Ilfedo wrinkled his nose at the smell of burnt flesh mixed with the freshly spilled blood of those serpents chopped up by his men. An oppressive darkness began to cloud his mind. It bore down on him as if stifling his ability to think for himself. He felt enraged, furious—yet he could not explain why. The men had moved a little distance off. He could see them combing the forest and slaying vipers as they went.

The feeling of darkness maddened him, and he found himself gritting his teeth. "Get out!" For a moment he felt relief, but the oppression returned, and he spotted a serpent slithering up a tree. He gripped the sword of the dragon in both hands and swung it with all his strength. The blade glowed white and severed the tree's trunk. He stepped back and breathed deeply as the tree toppled and crashed to the ground.

Enraged that the darkness still stuck in his mind, he rushed into the forest, joined the fray, and slew every serpent he came upon. The remaining vipers rushed toward the desert, and he scorched them with his weapon.

Ombre came to him then and pulled him aside.

The oppression didn't seem to be affecting him any more. Ilfedo calmed himself enough to talk. "What is it, Ombre? I am a little busy right now."

Ombre slid his drawn sword into his sheath and nodded. "These vipers are acting possessed. What do you know about them?"

"Know about them? What do you mean *know?* They are poisonous serpents, reptilian—"

"And they are *intelligent*." Ombre jabbed his thumb over his shoulder. "One of our men claims that one of these *serpents* just begged for its life."

"Impossible!" Ilfedo felt a growing frustration. He fought it in order to retain control over his actions.

Ombre beckoned to a young man standing a short distance from them. His head hung as if in shame, his sword lowered so that its point rested on the ground, and the light of his armor dimmed. As he stepped forward, he gave Ilfedo a quick bow.

"Dispense with the pleasantries, warrior." Ilfedo thwacked a tree root with his sword. "Tell me what happened."

"Well, my lord, I found a viper in a tree as it attempted to evade our attack. I swung my sword to cut off its head, but before I killed it, the serpent gave me a piteous look and cried out, 'Mercy! Oh, please have mercy!' It was too late to withhold my blade, and I ended up killing it. I once vowed, as did all warriors trained by the Warrioresses, that I 'will bear the sword of light with wisdom, that I will live to serve justice, and that I will die for the innocent. I live to serve justice, and I am committed to showing mercy rather than vengeance.' It is our code of honor, and I have shamed it."

Ombre patted the younger man's shoulder. "You have not shamed it," he said. "The remorse you have shown proves to me that your heart is right. Now, go back to the fort. We are about finished here."

"Yes, my lord." Sheathing his weapon, the young man ran into the forest and was lost to sight.

"Well, what do you think of that?" Ombre shook his head.

"Of what?"

Ombre laughed nervously. "You are kidding me, right? Ilfedo, this alters our perception of these creatures. If they are intelligent, then we could consider negotiating with them and finding out what has driven them here. If nothing else, the fact that they are intelligent means we should consider alternatives to exterminating them."

"It changes *nothing*, Ombre!" Ilfedo recognized how wrong his words were as soon as he said them. Yet, somehow, he could not change his attitude. He jumped up a nearby tree and snagged a four-foot-long viper that was hiding in the crook of a branch.

"Well now, if these creatures are intelligent, and they can talk, then I think it's about time we took a prisoner." He ignored his friend's frown and squeezed the viper so that it could not move.

"Ilfedo, what's wrong with you? Why would we make a prisoner of this creature? If they are intelligent, then we need to find out why they have come."

"Before, I would have said no. Now, I say *yes*." He laughed uncomfortably. The oppression filled his mind again. It weighed like a burden on his shoulders. He shook it off and faced his friend. "War is war, Ombre. If these creatures *are* intelligent, then they also have a choice. They have made theirs, and I have made mine."

The viper in his hands opened its fanged jaws. Its round eyes looked desperate, and its plea sounded almost like a whimper. "Mercy?"

Ilfedo shook his head at Ombre. "See what I mean? Even hint at going soft on our enemies, and they take advantage of us."

Ombre glared. "You *are* in command, Ilfedo, so what are your orders?"

Glancing back toward the desert, Ilfedo laughed. "Eradicate them." He handed the viper to his friend and ordered him to bring it to Fort North.

His friend growled at him through gritted teeth. Ilfedo couldn't blame him. Why was he acting this way? What was this dark oppression that wouldn't release him? He knelt with his sword and held it as if begging for it to drive away the darkness in his soul.

A halo of white light surrounded him and peace filled him. He felt a woman's hands caress his neck, he heard the sound of her breathing in his ear, and he recognized the voice of his wife. "Take care, my love, for the wicked are seeking your destruction."

Daylight replaced the night, and a lush field stretched as far as his eye could see. Dantress stood before him, just as lovely as the day he'd met her. Her smooth, olive skin felt warm to his touch, and her lips dripped with sweetness. She smelled like spring flowers and a fresh breeze. He wrapped her in his arms, wishing with all his heart that this was not a dream.

She laughed, and a smile spread over her face as she tickled him until he laughed too. He knew that he should not get carried away with this dream, but he couldn't help it. He did not care. The world meant nothing to him when she had been in his life and now . . . now that she was dead, he cared even less. Often he'd hoped and prayed for death because it alone could reunite him with her.

Dantress embraced him and looked up into his eyes. "This moment cannot last much longer, my love. I am here now, not because I wished it, but because it was allowed. You are in grave danger and so is our child. You must not let anything happen to her."

"Danger." He looked around. "Danger from what?"

She leaned against his chest, and her eyes burned with flames. "Beware of them, Ilfedo. They are an ancient race, full of evil." She directed his attention to the darkening sky.

Creatures having the bodies of men and the wings of eagles dove toward him. He felt their evil pressing upon him, yet he could also feel *her* body against his. He clutched her close, shut his eyes, and kissed her.

"The Art'en will not harm you as long as I am with you," he said as he stroked her long, dark hair.

She laughed a quiet laugh, then turned to him with sober eyes. "No, my love, they will not harm *you*, so long as *I* am at your side. And I will be with you whenever you need me, even when you don't believe that it is possible."

The creatures and the daylight dissolved around him, replaced by the forest where he knelt. He rose, sheathed his sword, and then fixed his eyes on the desert. Something moved from behind a tree, then hid behind another. A dark-featured man sprinted out of the forest and raced across the sand. The fellow glanced behind him and leaned on a tall staff with an orb at its head. Ilfedo knit his brow. The figure stopped for only a moment, then ran on. But Ilfedo knew that wasn't one of his men. He puzzled over it for a few moments as the man disappeared across the distant sands. He shrugged, and walked away. There would be another day to find out who or what that was.

# WHEN A
# GOOD MAN FALLS

Ilfedo strode down the main hallway on his way through Fort North's primary structure, his boots clapping the rough-hewn wood floors. The smell of pine lay heavy in the air. He waited for the guards to open the door to his right, then entered and shut the door behind him.

"Well, my little prisoner, welcome to Fort North." He took a seat opposite a metal cage.

The four-foot viper curled in a corner of the small prison, the metal bars set close together in order to keep the creature from escaping. It stared back at him with wide, black eyes.

"Do you have a name?"

The creature remained silent.

Ilfedo crossed his arms and shook his head. "You've already been in that cage for several days. Do you want to remain there?" He paused before continuing. "I can get you out—back to your little home in the sand. But first you have to answer my questions."

It cocked its head and opened its mouth. "Mercy?"

"No. No *mercy* today, my little enemy. At least, not until you help me learn what I want to know. You and your friends have been thorns in my side, viper, and I want to know why."

The viper lunged against the bars, showed its fangs, and snapped its jaws.

Ilfedo stood and kicked the cage to vent his frustration. "Have it your way, viper. But you may regret it." He left the room. In the hallway he pushed the guards against the wall. "Make sure that *thing* stays locked up!"

"Of . . . of course, my lord. That is why we are here."

Ilfedo returned to his quarters, the room that also served as his office. Animal pelts draped the large chair behind his desk, and an embroidered rug covered the floor. Furs overlaid the sofa against the back wall just under the window. Two chairs for guests sat across from his desk. He'd had the walls, made of oak boards, painted a cheerful white and hung the heads of some of his kills thereon. Behind his chair he had tacked a map of the Hemmed Land.

His finger traced the northern boundary until it rested on their current location, and he sighed. "Cursed creatures. What could they possibly want here? They belong"—he jabbed his index finger into the map—"in the desert."

He sat down and looked out the window. Thunderheads rolled from the eastern sky, and a stiff wind bent the treetops. Rain was sure to follow. He watched Yimshi's yellow disc fight with the clouds until it gave up and cast brilliant rays between the billows hiding it. He remembered how the white dragon shot away into the sky.

His hand touched the pommel of his sword. He ran his fingers over it, feeling the superior craftsmanship. He thought back to the day that Albino had given him the sword. What a dark day that had been for him.

Why, of all people, had the dragon given the weapon to him? Of course, he knew the answer—because of Oganna. The Warrioresses had told him that the dragon created Dantress. If that was true, then that would make his daughter the dragon's granddaughter. *My daughter, the descendant of a dragon.* Sometimes he worried about that. If she was not fully human, then there was an element to her being that surpassed his comprehension. She possessed abilities that could not be explained, such as the time that she had shot an arrow without a bow, and when she had eased his sorrow almost at the expense of her life.

"Deep in thought?" Ombre stepped through the door and sat in one of the guest chairs across from him, stretching his arms behind his head as he leaned back.

"You might say that."

"When in doubt ask a friend." Ombre nodded to the map on the wall. "It's been almost a week since we took that viper as prisoner, and I still don't see what good it did."

Ilfedo gave him a wry look. "I already apologized for my behavior. Can you please let the issue go?"

"Well, seeing as I *am* a soft-hearted individual." Ombre chuckled. "All right, I forgive you."

Ilfedo glanced out of the window. In the distance a bolt of lighting zipped to the ground, and shortly afterward a clap of thunder followed. He turned from the window and leaned against his desk.

"Ombre, that night when we captured the viper, did you see anything odd?"

His friend leaned forward. "No. Why? Did you?"

At that moment, Honer came in, and Ganning limped after him.

"The wind is kicking hard out there." Ganning crossed the room, dropped his sheathed sword onto the couch, and sat down. "Do you think we should call off our night patrol? The vipers have not been seen since you scorched them that last time, and it doesn't seem likely they will come in this weather."

Ilfedo drew his sword and let it clothe him in the armor of living fire. "If you were the enemy, Ombre, when would *you* make your next attack?"

"On a stormy night."

"Exactly." Ilfedo sheathed his sword, and his attire returned to normal. Then he directed his friends' attention to the map. "That same night we took a viper prisoner, I saw a man retreat from the forest and escape into the desert. I did not get a very good look at him, but he carried a staff with a sort of ball on top. I suspect he is somehow connected with the vipers." He paced back and forth across the floor as he spoke, his sheath clinking against his leg.

Ombre stood and scratched his chin. "And you think this man may return tonight?"

"It seems to be a fair assumption, because he was hiding, and what better time for him to return than in the midst of a lightning storm?" He paused for effect. "Tonight, I suspect, the vipers will attack, and I am hoping the mystery man will be there as well. You, my friends, are my best chance of catching him. I do not care if he is dead or alive, though it might be useful to take him prisoner."

Honer looked confused. "Why do you need us? You have a good many of the Elite Thousand—"

"Yes, their service will be invaluable, but I will need men who are able to hunt as well as I can, and men that I can trust to work rogue. If you all help me, I am sure we can bag our prey."

The final flash of lightning disappeared in a distant rumble. Ilfedo, Ombre, Honer, and Ganning stood in the shelter of darkness, awaiting the vipers' attack. It came soon enough. Wave after wave of the slithering vermin glided through the trees. The glowing swordsmen attacked with vehemence. Warriors with the swords of light swarmed through the trees. Keeping the serpents in front of them, they formed an impenetrable line and marched forward, driving them into the desert.

Sheathing his sword, Ilfedo snuck toward the forest boundary in search of the strange dark-featured man he felt certain waited for the vipers somewhere nearby. He kept as quiet as possible and left his sword sheathed so that the living fire would not betray his location.

At last, having explored the ground, he peered into the trees. To his horror he recognized an Art'en perched high in the branches. Ilfedo approached through the darkness until he stood by the base of the tree. "Ho, there!" He drew his sword. "Come down peacefully, and I will let you live."

The wild-haired man lighted down gracefully—too gracefully, even for an Art'en. He had a grayish face chiseled as if from stone. Ilfedo tensed as the figure crept toward him. The wild-haired man bowed and a feeling of utter darkness bore down on Ilfedo. He dropped his sword, then picked it up again. He had to rid himself of the evil oppression. His head felt like it would collapse under the pressure, and he felt his mind leaving this world and sailing to the next, as if he was dying.

Through delirium he saw dark, feathered wings spread from his opponent's back. Just as he'd seen in the vision—Dantress had tried to warn him. The wings snapped against his face, and he fell to the ground. Nausea overcame him as the winged creature stood over him. "The vipers will soon return," it hissed. "Maybe I should let *them* finish you. Ah, but no. This will be very pleasurable to do myself, and Razes will be most pleased."

"You will not slay him." A dark-featured man stood next to the Art'en, and the creature bowed away, spitting on the ground. The man stepped closer to Ilfedo and lowered the glowing black head of his staff. "I will finish the spell and all will be well with you. Do not fight—hear the spirits that you have denied. They are calling to you."

Whispers filled the air, and a plume of smoke fell through the trees. The Grim Reaper rose from the smoke and pulled back its serrated scythe, though it had only one arm with which to wield the weapon.

"No!" The dark-haired man with the staff jabbed his finger at the Reaper, though it trembled. "He must live in order for the full plan to succeed."

The Reaper's hood turned into smoke, and it flew around Ilfedo and the man. Its skull emerged from the smoke, and its empty eye sockets stared at the man.

"Oh, you know I fear you," the man said as his body quivered. "But there is one I fear more, and there is nothing you can do because of that."

Spinning in a tornado of smoke, Death vanished. But the voices ceaselessly, though unintelligibly, hissed and whispered in Ilfedo's ears.

The oppression filled his being, latched onto his heart, and ripped it apart. His mind flashed back to the day his wife died, and the bitterness of defeat clung to him. He felt separated from himself and unable to connect to his actions. The darkness of this creature's soul spread over him, and he felt powerless to stop it.

In another moment he lost all sense of where—or *when*—he was, and he found himself in the same field that he had seen in his vision. Once again, Dantress reached out, this time to comfort him. "Stay with me, my love," she said as he knelt and wept against her body. "Do not let the evil control you. Fight it, stay with me. Do not let him control you!"

He heeded her words, though anxiety clouded his mind. Looking into her face gave him the strength he needed to hold onto his sanity, to hold onto life. In her eyes he saw peace; in her eyes he saw hope. And that hope carried him as his mind screamed that he had stepped into a nightmare.

Ombre stood back-to-back with Honer as a dozen bold vipers attacked them from the ground and the trees. His skill with a sword had developed over the last years. He moved his blade with speed and precision, cutting the creatures to shreds in moments, and then looked around. "Honer, have you seen Ilfedo?"

Lopping off another viper's head, Honer turned to him with a look of consternation on his face. "He's gone off alone?"

They called Ganning over, and he pointed to the desert. "I think he went that way."

Ombre wiped the multi-colored stains off his blade and beckoned for them to follow as he set off in pursuit of his missing comrade. He looked through the trees ahead, stopped dead in his tracks, and shushed his companions.

Ilfedo stood next to a large tree at the forest's perimeter and his sword was not drawn. Suddenly a man dropped from one of the trees, approached Ilfedo, and spread dark, feathered wings from his back. The wings snapped forward, throwing Ilfedo to the ground. The man folded his wings back and stood over their

Lord Warrior. His hands were moving in circular patterns, and he muttered something unintelligible.

"Now!" Ombre rushed toward the creature with sword raised. But his head slammed into an invisible barrier, and he fell back. Honer and Ganning fell beside him. Shaking his head, he rose but could no longer see his fallen friend. Smoke filled the space between them.

"Something very strange is going on. Honer, Ganning! Come on get up. Ilfedo's in serious trouble." He pulled both men to their feet and stabbed his sword forward. It hesitated at the barrier then pierced it. He grunted and slashed at it. Feeling for an opening, he slipped through and ran toward the smoke.

When he reached the spot, the smoke vanished. The Art'en spun on him, but he twisted around as the winged man moved and slashed his blade along its back. Deep red blood drained from the wound. With a screech that sounded more like a bird than an injured human, the creature dashed into the desert and flapped its wings until it achieved a low altitude. Gaining speed, it receded from view.

Honer and Ganning grasped Ilfedo's shoulders and helped him to his feet. "Whoa, there. Take it easy," Ombre told him.

Ilfedo shook himself. "You see. The Art'en returned."

"Yes, but only one of them. Thank the Creator for that." Against the backdrop of stars over the sand Ombre's eyes detected the dark marauder's winged form. "I hope it doesn't bring back its relatives."

"It is only a single creature," Ilfedo said. "Surely nothing we need to burden our minds with at this time."

Ombre turned and looked into Ilfedo's eyes. They did not return his gaze. "Are you all right, Ilfedo? Your eyes look glassy."

"Yeah, Ombre's right. Your eyes are kind of glassy." Honer and Ganning held on to their friend's shoulders and steadied him as he teetered.

Ilfedo hung his head and shoved them aside. He walked off without another word.

Matching his friend's pace, Ombre followed. "Ilfedo, where are you going?"

"Since *when* do I have to answer to you, warrior?"

"Answer *to me?* What are you talking about?"

"Never mind, warrior. Goodnight."

Speechless, Ombre shrugged at Honer and Ganning. They seemed not to notice. They stared wide-mouthed into the distance. He followed their gazes to the forest's edge.

The warriors that bore swords of light chased the remaining vipers back to the desert. Their glowing ranks formed a line of light that was a perfect backdrop against which he discerned another Art'en flexing its wings. He blinked his eyes and watched the creature follow its accomplice into the desert. More than one Art'en had come back to the Hemmed Land. And where two survived there could be many more.

Other warriors of the Hemmed Land pushed through the forest and, when he glanced that way, yet another winged human took to the skies. "Three?" Ombre was incredulous. "What is going on here?"

Unable to answer his own question, Ombre left the area, gathered the warriors of light, and marched them back to Fort North. Along the way he kept an eye out for Ilfedo. Something sinister had clapped its hand on this place. He could feel it. Ilfedo had been acting strange of late, very strange. And now he'd encountered an Art'en alone. Ombre remembered the glassy appearance of the Lord Warrior's eyes, and he shuddered.

Ombre breathed in the crisp night air. The dew had wet his clothing, and he was looking forward to changing into some dry clothes. He said goodnight to Honer and Ganning as he entered the fort, went to the main building, and entered his quarters. He lay in bed and tried to sleep. Troubling questions ravaged his mind and his dreams were filled with screaming Art'en. At last, in the midst of his troubled imaginings, he turned his thoughts to Caritha, and with her lovely face in his mind he was at last able to rest.

The dinner bell rang through the compound, and Ombre got out of his bed. He donned a black shirt and trousers, threw a white sash over his left shoulder, and tied it to his belt. The leather strap for his sword's sheath lay nearby. He put it on his other shoulder and dropped the sheath to his left hip so that he could easily reach for his sword with his right hand.

He paused at the door to fix his eyes on the gray wolf head hanging on the wall. The days of hunting with Ilfedo had long ago passed, and he missed them. He'd kept the trophy as a proud reminder of how he'd saved his best friend's life. Best friend, brother—Ilfedo was both to him.

With a frustrated growl he left the room, slammed the door behind him. He made his way to the parade grounds where most of the warriors had gathered to eat at long tables. Homer and Ganning sat among them.

"Ombre!" Ganning beckoned with a grin. "Hurry along; we've saved a seat for you."

Ombre walked to the barrack's far end. A tall young man with dark, curly hair flipped eggs on an outdoor stove and stacked them on the table. His other arm skillfully stirred sliced potato and blueberries in a pan. Thick slices of bread soaked in a bowl of milk. The man flopped the slices onto the stove and chuckled to several warriors with plates in hand, as if sharing in a joke Ombre hadn't heard.

"There's plenty, plenty, plenty for everyone. Take your fill and take your pick!" He sounded like an auctioneer, only he wasn't getting paid for this.

"James McCormick," Ombre interrupted him, pushing his plate forward. He grinned. "How's it going?"

"Pretty good. I can't complain." James wiped his goatee with a sleeve and picked up the plate. "You want something fresh?"

"Watching you, I just know you do love to cook."

"Yes. I don't do it too often, but I have to admit, I do enjoy it." He flipped eggs and toast onto Ombre's plate and sprinkled cinnamon on top. "Are you feeling all right, Ombre?"

"To be honest . . ." Ombre shook his head and sighed.

James set the plate down and glanced at the line of waiting men. He reached for a selection of spices and held a straight face. "I could spice up your toast with a little jalapeño pepper."

Ombre picked up the plate and chuckled. "I'll be fine without that. But thanks for trying to boost my spirits." He started walking away, but the cook held up a hand.

"Here." He stabbed a fork into a thick steak at the rear of the stove and set it on Ombre's plate, holding up his forefinger. "You've gotta have steak."

"Thank you, James." He left the line and walked to the table, sitting next to Ganning. The morning chill refreshed him, though the heat of the rising sun warmed his back. Honer and Ganning, between mouthfuls, talked about the Hemmed Land and reminisced about their hunting days.

"Seems like it was only yesterday that we could travel for hours through the forest and never run into anyone." Ganning let the steak juices drip between his lips and closed his eyes with a grin. "Oh, James knows how to make these."

Ombre played his fork in his eggs. "Now . . . now there are people every few miles."

Honer dug his fork into a stack of two pancakes. Butter oozed between them. "I miss those days. Back then we hunted to our heart's content and roamed freely. Sometimes I worry about our children—"

Ganning paused midway through his steak. "How do you mean?"

"They are growing up in a changing culture, a society that is gradually rejecting its heritage in favor of a more comfortable life. People are chopping down the trees and trampling the wild animals' habitats without a second thought. They build new homes, new towns, and new roads. They are making for themselves an *easier* life. Yet they are forgetting that nature is not their slave to be used and abused. It should be cared for, respected."

"In all fairness, I must point out that nature *is* our slave and without its resources we would be unable to live. We kill the creatures and eat them. We take timber from the forests and build homes."

"But, Ganning, how long do you think this prosperity will last? The trees we take down are not being replaced, and the animals are being driven farther from us. Unless we conserve the Hemmed Land's resources, we will end up exhausting them. There will be nothing left for our children. Do you see what I mean?"

Ombre felt compelled by Honer's postulations to break into the conversation. He put his half-emptied plate to the side. "There will be new challenges and different lessons for the next generation. They will face new frontiers and build on what we have started."

"Ah!" Honer raised his finger to emphasize his point. "But the question is, are we laying a proper foundation?"

"How do you mean?"

"If we continue to destroy the forests and kill off the animals, there will be *nothing left* for the next generation. Will the Hemmed Land be able to sustain our growing population, or will subsequent generations drain its resources? In fact, at the current rate, I foresee that our country's natural resources will reach a critical low even before I'm an old man. To our north is desert, to the south is desert, and the Sea of Serpents guards our eastern border. The western forests may permit a little expansion, but that is a small territory. We are cut off from the rest of the world, and we know little to nothing about it. We are *hemmed in.*"

He bit into his last pancake and swallowed. "I mean, if we ever need to expand, I suppose we could explore beyond our borders and scope out the territory. But if hearsay is true, the western forest is cut off by a vast swamp, in the midst of which is an active volcano."

"I never knew you had such an interest in geography," Ombre said. "Since when have you become an expert on these matters?"

"Since I finished the National Archive building. There are all sorts of little-known facts in our ancient scrolls, and I've been reading through them." He shoved his plate to the side and wiped his mouth. Crumbs fell from his pants as he got out of his seat. "We'd better get going, Ganning."

"Get going?" Ombre stood up and started toward the kitchen. "Why the rush?"

"Haven't you heard?" Ganning grabbed his plate, took Honer's, and waved him away.

After putting away his dishes, Ombre turned to his friend. "All right, Ganning, *what* was Honer referring to?"

"Ilfedo called for a special meeting this morning with all his counselors. You weren't informed?"

Ombre frowned and stomped toward the main building. Ganning limped after him and whispered into his ear as they walked into headquarters. "Take it from me, Ombre, Ilfedo is acting strangely."

"Yeah, I'm beginning to notice."

"Do you think it has anything to do with that Art'en creature we saw last night?"

Ombre shook his head. "I wish I knew." He stepped into the council chamber. He wished the Warrioresses would make a surprise visit. They would know what to do.

The room wherein he now stood contained a circle of high-backed, wooden chairs, one for each of Ilfedo's military commanders and a few extras for invited guests. Ombre sat with Honer and Ganning, fairly close to the seat Ilfedo occupied.

"My subjects." Ilfedo rose from his chair. "It has been brought to my attention that we have a certain prisoner and that that prisoner refuses to talk. Therefore I have called this meeting to give permission to torture the creature."

The members of the council looked horrified, and each and every one, much to Ombre's relief, rose and offered objection. "This goes against our moral standards, our laws, and your policies," they cried. "Why do you even suggest such an evil?"

"Silence!" Ilfedo roared. "Sit down, all of you! *I* am in charge here."

Ombre gazed at the enraged man's eyes. They reflected the light as if they had been made of glass. It was even more apparent now than it had been last night. He stood and addressed Ilfedo. "My lord, as commander of your army and your friend I formally add my objection to your proposal—"

"Sit down!" Ilfedo's face reddened, and he breathed rapid, short breaths. "Your objection is noted, but my plan goes forward. Order the guards to do as they please with the creature."

Ganning rose and put up his hand, opening his mouth as if to speak. But Ilfedo pounded his fist on the wall. "Any more objections, and I will consider it an act of betrayal to me and the country. I did not call you all in here to voice your opinions! Now, go. All of you."

Heaving a sigh, Ombre left the room. Outside the door to the viper's prison he spoke to the guards. "Lord Ilfedo wants you to torture the prisoner, then report any and all information that you learn directly to him." He started to walk away, thought better of it, and added a final word of advice. "For your own good I recommend that you disregard this order. The Warrioresses will not be silent on this matter when they return."

The men nodded their heads, but their eyes told him that they did not mean it. He shook his head and left the fort. He strode through the south gate and walked into the fields. A lot of the forest in this part of the country had been cleared long ago to construct the fort. He was alone at last, and he breathed deeply of the air to let it clear his troubled mind.

To the south a flock of black birds rose from the trees with loud cries. He strained his eyes. What was that coming over the rise? He could just pick out several massive forms lumbering into view. Was this a new enemy? At a time like this? He turned to the fort and called to the watchmen. "Summon the Lord Warrior, Honer, and Ganning . . . and hurry!"

# 18

# A PRESENCE OF EVIL

Fight, my love! Fight! Don't let it win!" Dantress's tears splattered on his neck as he knelt at her feet and clutched her to him.

Ilfedo felt the warmth of her body against his. He could feel a cold darkness surrounding and choking his will, but with her so close he fought on, determined to win the battle. "What is happening to me? Why am I here?" He looked into her eyes for an answer. "Am I dead?"

Dantress pulled him roughly to his feet, laced her arms around his neck, and held his gaze. "You are not dead—not yet." She sniffled. "Fight it, Ilfedo, don't stop resisting, or you *will* die!"

He put his fingers in her hair and ran them through the soft, silken strands. It smelled like freshly cut roses in spring. His resolve faltered. In his being he longed to let the darkness win. Then he would die—and be with her again. "I am tired of fighting, my love," he said. "I want to be with you. Don't you see that

I am wearied and sick of the world? It is filled with violence. The Hemmed Land . . . it is a speck in the vast stretches of existence, a glass that may easily be broken. I want to get away from it all, to leave and be rid of the physical elements. *You* are all that matters, and all that has ever mattered since I met you."

Waving her hand in a semicircle, Dantress created an image of their daughter. "There is *nothing* there for you? What of Oganna? Are you ready to leave her alone?"

He pressed her closer to his body. "She has your sisters and Ombre. What can I give her that they cannot?"

"Hope."

"You mean that I am a beacon . . ."

"The future is dark, Ilfedo, and without you this world will fall without hope of redemption." Her eyes pleaded with him. "Do this for me. Do this for our child. Fight this evil, and vow to do so until the day you die."

"What do you say, Ilfedo?" In a flash, the albino dragon loomed beside them. A gentle smile showed on his boney face. "Are you up to the challenge?"

Ilfedo's jaw dropped open in astonishment. "How are you here?"

"Never mind the details when death is on the line, my friend." The magnificent creature dipped his head, and smoke curled from its nostrils. "Just answer the question."

"First, we need a moment more of privacy."

The dragon looked away.

Bending over Dantress's tear-streaked face, Ilfedo kissed her with all the pent up passion in his heart. "We will be together again, someday," he whispered in her ear. "A love like ours will never end."

The dragon grabbed him from behind. "Brace yourself, Ilfedo. The battle for your soul has only begun!" Albino's claws clasped Ilfedo's body and lit up with fire. Searing heat shot through him. The pain was immense and then it grew unbearable. Tears sprang from his eyes, and he dug his fingernails into his palm until he drew blood. The darkness within now became more apparent. It was a presence, an evil, trying to drag him into despair. A name appeared in his mind—the name of his oppressor.

"You don't want to live," his unseen adversary told him. "Stay here, die here, live here, and be with the one you love."

A growl from Albino shook the ground. "Show thyself to me, sorcerer! Show yourself to me and release this man."

Mist rose from the ground. It twisted into the form of a man that cried in torturous pain. "Oh I will not reveal that," the mist cried. It bowed to the dragon. Albino's scales radiated light, and it roared at the mist. "Revealed you will be, for you have a twisted soul and have rejected thy God."

The misty form screamed again, and this time it solidified into the form of a dark-featured man. The dragon roared again, and the claws of his other hand split the ground, causing the mist to fall therein. "Auron! You have fallen too far this time and retribution is upon thee."

Ilfedo cursed himself. This being, whatever it was, had tried to get him out of its way. It wanted to dispose of him, to rid itself of the threat he posed, and it was assaulting his soul to attain victory. How selfish he'd been to entertain such a thought! "You cannot win," he told it. "I'm coming back, and I will stop you!" He struggled against the presence, wishing it would give up the fight. But it only grew stronger, and he weaker.

❈   ❈   ❈

Oganna alighted from Vectra's back and ran ahead of the mega-trath horde to the fort gates. "Father!" She wrapped her arms around him, and he stiffened. She backed away, hurt by his apparent disinterest.

Ombre walked over and clutched her in a bear hug. "What are you doing here?" He looked past her, and a look of relief passed over his face. "Ah, you came with your aunts."

The five sisters lined up beside her and greeted the men. But Ilfedo did not respond to them either, and Oganna frowned. His eyes did not meet hers when she glanced at him, and there was something strange about the way he studied the approaching megatraths.

"Father, what is wrong?"

He glared at Vectra as she came to stand behind Oganna. "Aren't these the creatures that I wanted you to slay?"

"Slay?" Caritha turned a withering gaze upon him. "You sent us to deal with the creature that murdered the people of Bordelin, not to wipe out its species. This is Vectra, leader of the megatraths and ruler of Resgeria, the land of the southern desert. She has come in peace as your ally."

Ilfedo kicked his boot into the dirt. "Oganna, why are *you* here? I sent the sisters, not you, in pursuit of the creature. Yet here you are as if you took part in their mission."

The sisters spoke up, taking turns in their eagerness to show how well their pupil had performed. They told him, from start to finish, how Oganna had followed them, and later rescued them from death in the arena. "If she had not engaged Loos and his cohorts in combat, we would not have been able to recover from the first attack." After they had finished their story, they stood silent, waiting for him to reply.

When Ilfedo did not speak up, Vectra did. She rested her right hand on Oganna's shoulders and spoke to him. "It is as the

Warrioresses have told you—your daughter achieved a great victory against discouraging odds. She has earned a place of legend among my people, and I was honored to join with your great nation as allies."

"And you think that *I* will go along with this alliance?" He tilted his head back and laughed harshly. "I would die before joining forces with a low, dirty race of desert dwellers!" In the stunned silence that followed, Ilfedo spun around and reentered the fort. He shot out a final insult as he departed. "The sooner you all leave us, the better it will be for you."

Oganna turned to the megatrath and tried not to cry. "I'm so sorry. I don't know what has happened. Believe me, please believe me. That is not like him, at all." She gritted her teeth and glared at the fort. "Do not worry, Vectra. The Warrioresses will find out what is bothering father. He always listens to them."

"Humph! It did not seem to me that he was in the mood to listen to anyone." The creature thundered away after a stiff bow, muttering something under her breath about how dumb Ilfedo was compared to his daughter. "A fighter without honor."

With a sigh, Oganna shrugged and shook her head at Caritha. "What did I do? I truly did not think he would respond like that."

"Leave him to me and my sisters." The woman grasped Oganna's shoulder and whispered in her ear. "Just wander the fort and find out if anything seems amiss. I feel that something strange is going on here, almost evil, and it may have something to do with your father. We will speak to him, and if Ombre is willing, he will go with us."

"There *is* something strange about Ilfedo." Ombre joined the conversation with a furious eye. He fingered his sword's pommel. "He hasn't been right ever since we started making nightly ambushes on the desert vipers. On the last attack he encountered an Art'en." Oganna's jaw dropped. He nodded his head and raised an eyebrow. "This one targeted your father on our last raid. I'm not sure why, but he has been exceedingly moody and indifferent ever since."

Ombre crooked his arm, and Caritha took it, letting him lead her into the fort. Laura and Evela chattered back and forth as they followed. Rose'el went too, her arms crossed again. Levena paid them no heed, though she trailed along. She had her sword unsheathed and was picking at the rust with a cloth. Oganna watched them enter the main building, then started to wander the fort. If her aunts found out nothing, *she* would.

⚹ ⚹ ⚹

There was no answer to Caritha's knock at Ilfedo's office door. She could feel the tension hanging in the air as Ombre and her sisters hovered behind her. They all felt as she did—uneasy, confused, and concerned. Ombre's recounting of Ilfedo's behavior in front of the council earlier that day greatly troubled her.

She shoved aside the questions that were pummeling her mind and braced herself as she opened the door. Ilfedo was sitting at his desk, his head buried in his hands. He was digging his knuckles into his skull. If she hadn't known better, Caritha might have attributed this to a severe headache. However, when he looked up, she put her hand over her mouth and gasped, for Ilfedo's face twisted in a sneer, and his eyes gazed without seeing.

"My brother, what has happened to you?" She skirted his desk, bent over him, and grasped his right arm. Laura, Evela, Rose'el, and Levena filed into the room and stood in a line facing him. Ombre stepped past them and leaned against the wall, looking out the window.

Rose'el leaned over the desk and stared into Ilfedo's eyes. After a few moments she frowned at him and raised a fist in his face. "Just give the word, Caritha, and I'll gladly slap him."

Caritha rested her hands on the desk. "That won't be necessary. Stand back. Let's talk civil."

"You mean that you will *try*." Laura twisted her mouth uncomfortably.

Caritha ignored her. "Ilfedo, what is wrong? Let us help you. You know we can."

For an instant his face softened and his gaze relaxed. "Help—help. Pull me from this. Pull me out." His eyes hardened again, and he stood up. "Get out! Leave me be."

"Ilfedo," she said, "you can't mean it."

"Oh yes, I do. Leave now, or I will call for the guards." He glowered at Ombre. "You too, get out of my sight before I thrust you through."

Caritha frowned deeply. "What's wrong with you?"

His body twitched, and his eyes looked normal again, then they reverted to their former condition, and he clenched his fists. "Do not make me hurt you."

She rose to go, but he grabbed her and slapped her across the face. As tears spilled, Ombre rushed over. His fist smashed with brutal strength into Ilfedo's head. He sprawled over the desk. Caritha wept as she stared at her unconscious brother-in-law.

Wiping her tears with a handkerchief, Ombre kissed her stinging cheek, reached his arm around her waist, and guided her out of the room. Her sisters followed, though Rose'el held on to the desk, as she said, "I'll teach him."

"Come on, Rose'el. Can you not see? Ilfedo is not himself."

The sisters pulled her out of the room. She cursed Ilfedo and growled. "Let me kick him. Just one kick, and I'll bring him to his senses!"

"Enough, Rose'el." Laura grabbed her arm. "Let it rest."

Ombre ran a hand over Caritha's cheek. "Are you all right?"

"Yes, but shaken." She hung her head. "What will we do now? He doesn't even want to speak to us and—"

"He seems evil," Evela offered.

"Well, does anyone have a suggestion how we can help him?"

A lad ran past them into Ilfedo's office and emerged a minute later. Ombre pulled him aside and inquired what he'd been doing.

"The Lord Warrior is furious about something." The lad's voice trembled. "He is demanding to meet with his counselors right away. I'd better go now and do as he told me. He started to run down the corridor.

"Thank you, my boy." Ombre turned him about and knelt to face him. "Now, was there anything else?"

In a whisper the messenger told him more. As the lad left, Ombre folded his hands behind his back. "Well, ladies, it seems that our *friend* has stipulated that we are not invited to attend this forthcoming meeting."

"Of all the nerve!" Rose'el started marching down the hall.

"Where are you going?" Caritha asked.

"To the council chamber. Where else?"

The council chamber had been constructed on the fort's ground level. It was rectangular, and a circle of wooden chairs occupied its far end. Animal skins draped the chairs, and a handsome array of swords hung on the walls.

The double doors swung open, and Ilfedo's commanders trooped in. Each of their eyes popped open upon seeing Caritha with her sisters and Ombre, but they also nodded at them and smiled. Laura sat next to Caritha, but Ombre switched with her and gave Caritha's hand a comforting squeeze. "Don't worry," he said. "Every man here will stand with us. Just do what you feel is necessary. Honer and Ganning will back me up one hundred percent."

Honer and Ganning sat across from Caritha. She acknowledged them with a nod, hoping to lighten the tense atmosphere. Both of the men smiled back.

Ganning cleared his throat. "It's good to have you with us again."

"Yes." Honer breathed deeply and exhaled slowly. "We've missed you all."

Ilfedo slammed the chamber doors open. He glowered in Ombre and Caritha's direction, then went to his seat. The sword of the dragon was still girt at his side. His eyes were darker now, yet hazed. After sitting down he gestured to two men by the door. "Guards, bring in the prisoner."

All heads turned to the open doors as a cage was borne into the room. Caritha could hear the caged viper hissing and snapping its jaws before she could see it.

"Behold our enemy," Ilfedo said. "This creature is a low, desert dweller, and it is capable of communicating with us. So far, it has refused to tell us what I want to know. It repeatedly asks for mercy." He let out a sardonic laugh before continuing. "Lord Ombre and other members of this council have opposed the use of torture to get the information that we need from this creature, and so I have personally accepted responsibility for the task. He strode to the center of the ring of chairs and waved a hand in the guards' directions. "These two men have performed the task for me—and, so far, I am very pleased with their work."

He pointed a finger at Ombre. "You, my commander, should have obeyed me. For the time being your command will be handed over to another man." He looked around the room. "Are any of you—" his body twitched and his face contorted in pain before he could go on. "Are any of you ready to obey me without question? If you are, then I will give to you the rank that Ombre now holds."

Ilfedo's counselors gasped in horror at his words. They talked amongst themselves, seeming to debate the truth of Ilfedo's words and looking at him as if he were a ghost. Ilfedo rushed forward, smote one of his counselors on the face, drew the sword of the dragon, and poised it against the man's throat. Caritha felt faint as Ombre stood to his feet with his hand on his sword's pommel. The sword of the dragon, given to Ilfedo by the dragon, did not blaze; the living fire did not come forth, and the light did not shine. If Ilfedo killed that man the sword would, of its own accord, turn around and slay him.

☙ ☙ ☙

Oganna stepped through the doorway and dropped her hand to her side. "Have I missed something?" She took a step toward her father and slapped him across the face.

His eyes and mouth widened and, again, the assembly gasped. "This is none of your concern, young one." Ilfedo leaned over her.

"Oh, I think it is. After all, the leadership of the Hemmed Land will one day fall into my lap."

"Hah!" Ilfedo spat on the floor. "Then I do, here and now, take away your right of succession."

Suddenly she noticed the cage and the viper. Blood caked the creature's head, and its lower jaw hung loose. A fire burned in her soul, and she turned to the guards. Her hand tightened around her sword as she spoke. "Who has done this?"

"It refused to talk, and Lord Ilfedo gave us permission to torture it," they answered.

It would have been better for them if they had remained silent. Oganna drew out her sword and transformed herself into a goddess in silver, wielding a blade that glowed red. She thrust the nearest guard straight through his heart, pulled out her blood-stained blade as he fell to the floor, and struck the floor with her blade's tip. "Behold, the Avenger!" She burned her gaze into the faces of those around her. "With it I *have* and I *will* execute justice upon all. Honored members of this council, are you so blinded by the chain of command that you have lost all sense of moral responsibility? Why did you wait for me to come before putting a stop to this wickedness?"

Out of the corner of her eye she caught sight of the remaining guard jabbing the viper with his sword. She slid her blade around and struck at him, but her father drew his sword and parried the blow. "Do not make me hurt you, little child."

As soon as his blade touched hers it melded to it and, together, the sword of the dragon and the Avenger slew the guard. Oganna reached out with both hands and took back the swords. As she grasped the sword of the dragon, it blazed with brilliant light, and a jab of current touched her mind.

"Oganna, my daughter, I am here." It was Ilfedo's voice inside her mind. She felt the presence of another with him, between him and her, blocking her path to bring him back. "Father," she said, stepping close to him, "I can feel the darkness waging war inside of you. I can see—something wicked—controlling you. Let me help."

Before he could react, she dropped the swords, reached up, and pressed her hands on either side of his head. Her hands glowed, and she felt the powers of her mother surge against the tide of darkness and attack the evil that had rooted itself in his being. The resistance was strong, too strong. She closed her eyes against despair, and the pain that suddenly assailed her mind. She held her ground. Yet the darkness, though not overcoming her, would not be overcome. She opened her eyes and strained to cry out. "I—can't do this alone."

The Warrioresses dashed to her side. Caritha spoke to the members of the council, though Oganna could not hear what she said. Ilfedo's counselors rose off their seats, bowed their heads, and knelt on the floor with hands folded in prayer.

The Warrioresses laid their hands on Ilfedo and on her, strengthening her powers with their own. Together they melded into a potent force that forced the indwelling presence into a corner of Ilfedo's subconscious. Then they surrounded it and pressed in until it suffocated and deceased.

Oganna's exhausted arms fell to her sides, and her legs gave out under her. Beside her, Caritha, Laura, Evela, Levena, and Rose'el followed suit. The last thing she remembered seeing was Ombre as he and other members of the council stumbled to catch them before they hit the floor.

# 19

# RENEWED MAN

I lfedo was still struggling against the evil trying to overcome him. The dragon remained beside him, as did his
deceased wife. But he felt an infusion of holy love beat
back the evil one. His chest heaved in rhythm with his labored
breathing. He felt disoriented, yet energetic. He flexed his arms
and shouted triumph to the sky. Though he could not see them
in his vision, he knew that, somewhere in the world where he'd
left his body, his wife's sisters and his own beloved daughter
fought to bring him back.

The dragon rested a hand around his shoulders and spoke
in rumbling tones. "You have seen through your own eyes the
harm that your possessed body has done to your alliance with
the megatraths. Vectra is a proud creature and a powerful one.
Make it your priority to mend your relationship and treat her
with respect."

"I will."

"One more thing, Ilfedo. Don't ever again be caught in battle without your sword, for it alone can prevent this incident from recurring." The dragon stepped back and moved his hand in a circle over Ilfedo's head. Blue-white light streamed from his claws and fell in waves to the ground until a bubble of swirling light surrounded Ilfedo.

He blew a kiss to his wife and mouthed, "I will be with you again. I promise." She and the dragon dissipated, and he found himself standing in the council chamber at Fort North. He stumbled and fell to his hands and knees. To his side lay his sword on the wood floor. He reached out and grasped it, then rose to his feet. The living fire sprouted from his weapon and decked him in the magnificent armor.

His counselors stepped back and then knelt before him. Ombre came forward, grinning from ear to ear. "It's good to have you back, my friend."

"It's good to be back." Ilfedo embraced the man, then nodded at his unconscious daughter and sisters. "They need rest. See to it that they are cared for." He turned to leave.

"Ilfedo, where are you going?"

"Do not worry, Ombre. I will be back in due time. First I have to mend a wrong done to the megatraths."

He sheathed his sword, left the fort, and found the mega-traths camped to the south around a stand of widely spaced trees. The creatures stirred and raised their heads as he passed between them. Evening was falling, and the cool air felt moist.

"Explain your errand, sir." One of the creatures rose to its full height and peered down its nose at him.

"I have come to speak to your leader, Vectra."

The creature snarled. "She is busy right now, *Ilfedo*. I suggest you leave before I remember your insult to our noble leader."

At that moment Ilfedo was ready to apologize, but he decided that the creature would view this as a weakness. After all, had not Oganna won their respect through combat? He growled up at the megatrath and stared boldly into its eyes. "Do you think that I fear *you*?"

"Yes."

Ilfedo laughed and drew his sword. The flames sprang forth and covered him, and the megatrath stumbled back. "This weapon bears great power, megatrath. I suggest that you permit me to pass before I am forced to make a scene."

"Enough!" Vectra lumbered around her loyal follower and gazed upon Ilfedo. "You are not a friend of ours, Ilfedo. The child you had may be pure, but I have seen that you are not."

"I was not myself." Ilfedo bowed. "A dark spell had been cast over me, and I could no longer control what my body did." He took a step forward and raised his sword in both hands. "This weapon is an instrument of the pure and will only respond to those that are worthy. Surely if I were deceiving you this weapon would not now clothe me in light."

"Humph, for all I know you could be a sorcerer. This sword proves nothing!"

"If you do not believe me." He extended the sword's handle to her. "Take it and see if it will discern your heart."

"What? Is this a trick?" She rumbled deep in her throat and yellow vapors drifted into the air while flames burst from her mouth. "Father of Oganna or not, you will die!" She charged into him, spun around, and hit him broadside with her tail.

He flew through the air and felt the trunk of a tree meet his back. He fell to the ground and gasped for air. The megatrath wanted a fight, so he would have to test himself against her. Very well, he would give her a duel she would not be able to forget.

Waving the sword over his head, he blasted the surrounding trees with fire until the other megatraths backed a safe distance away from him.

Vectra charged in spite of the fire and spun around. This time, instead of hitting with her tail, she crushed him with her back. She stood, grabbed one of his legs, and flung him through the trees. As the branches scraped along his armor, he clung to his sword and sent a torrent of flames behind him. The fire slowed his plunge and he landed softly on the ground.

He raced back to the burning ring of trees, faced the megatrath, and poised his sword into the flood of fire she flung at him. He felt himself at one with the sword. He could feel the heat of Vectra's blaze touch its point, and he heard it crackle as the sword redirected and threw it into the creature's face.

Vectra shook her head and roared. "Is that all you can do, Lord of the Hemmed Land?" She advanced, pouring vapors over him.

Coughing, Ilfedo slipped around her flank and stabbed his blade into the scales on her tail. Vectra screamed in pain, and the sword's power siphoned the energy from her body until she lay on the ground, helpless and weary. He withdrew the sword from her body and circled to her head. "I will not slay you, Vectra. I have need of your friendship and of your respect."

The other megatraths surrounded them. He looked into their eyes, trying to read their expressions. "Do not worry, my friend." Vectra parted her lips to reveal rows of deadly teeth. "You have earned our respect and reclaimed your honor."

He nodded and passed his sword over her body. "Then rise, my ally. We have work to do."

The creature stood and shook her tail and then her whole body. "How did you do that? I feel well again."

He glanced over the weapon in his hand, confused. "I don't know. It just came to me."

⁂ ⁂ ⁂

That same night, beneath the trees, Ilfedo stood at the ready. He did not bother to look at the ground; instead he searched the trees' branches. At last he spotted his quarry—the winged man perched, as he had been before, in a tree on the edge of the desert. "Ho, up there. Do you dare try me again, this time alone? Where is that human master of yours? Auron I believe his name was."

The creature dropped on top of him, knocking him to the ground. "The spell was not strong enough last time," it hissed. "This time I will try it myself."

"That was," rumbled a voice from the shadows, "if you got to him before I got to you." The alligator-like head came into view and snapped its jaws over the creature's head, picked it up, and growled deep in its throat. Ilfedo cringed as he watched yellow vapors drift from Vectra's mouth around her struggling victim. Vectra shook her head vigorously and dropped the limp body.

"Well done." Ilfedo perked his ears and glanced to the east and west where the sand ended and the forest began. Yellow clouds of the megatraths' poisonous vapors wafted through the tree line.

Vectra picked up her victim with one hand as if he were a doll and stepped out of the forest. Several of the Art'en flitted from the trees and flew in vain toward the desert, but the vapors had robbed them of oxygen. The megatraths plunged into the desert, caught them, and slew them. The ground shook as the creatures roared their victory and beat the sand. A few others chased the surviving vipers into the desert.

"My people will follow the vipers for a couple miles. That should give us a good idea in which direction to look for the perpetrator behind these assaults. However, I doubt the vipers will *ever* return after tonight. And it looks like"—she nudged the dead creature she had dropped—"we killed the last of these."

Together they examined the creature. His clothes were black, and about his waist a rope had been tied. His face was dark, and his nails were as long as bird claws. Flipping it over, they noted that his feathered wings were dark brown.

Ilfedo scratched his chin thoughtfully. "Before they appeared in these forests several years ago, I had never heard of creatures such as these. Not even in my ancestors' legends. Have you?"

"No." She lumbered farther on, and they looked at the next body. "This one's face is different, and he looks shorter. Other than that, he is almost identical to the first one." She turned to Ilfedo. "What should we do with the bodies?"

He considered for a moment before indicating the desert. "Pile them over there and burn them."

Lines of men emerged from the forest. They carried seven Art'en into the desert, and the megatraths picked up another five. The creatures tossed the bodies into a heap, then ringed it and poured flames from their mouths. The bodies smoked, and the clothing blazed.

Using the sword of the dragon, Ilfedo disintegrated the heap with fervent fire shot from the blade. As he finished, the remaining megatraths returned from chasing the vipers and reported to Vectra. She in turn lumbered over to Ilfedo and growled. "The vipers are fleeing to the north. Their lair must lie somewhere in that direction."

"Then we will need to plan a campaign to hunt them down and discover if there is anything beyond this desert that provokes these attacks."

"The vipers will perish for what they have done to your people." Vectra stomped her foot in the sand.

Ilfedo sheathed his sword and gazed back into her dark eyes. "My primary concern is to find the man behind the reins. Who is creating this conflict and why? Someone is masterminding all of this, and I don't think it was the sorcerer Auron. But how to find that individual I do not know."

Vectra roared into the night, and the megatraths pivoted to face her. "We are finished here. Return to the place of our lodging."

The creatures lumbered together, formed a group, and thundered into the forest. The stars shone brilliantly that night as Ilfedo and Vectra returned to Fort North. Every now and again a shooting star burst in the heavens, and they stopped to watch. Once, a fireball blasted from the west and blazed a bold trail in the velvety sky as they passed through a meadow. It exploded without a sound.

"Looks like a good night for stargazing," Ilfedo said as they passed into the trees on the other side of the meadow.

The megatrath bent a tree to the side so that she could pass without breaking it. "Indeed, it does."

He frowned, thinking of the campaign he would need to organize into the north desert. "Vectra, it will take a few days for me to assemble my army and prepare it for a campaign through the desert. I don't want to pack light for this trip. Whatever lies out there, we must be ready to deal with it at first encounter. Supplies must be organized, distributed, and packed. Equipment has to be readied, and I must arrange for matters to be tended to in my absence. By the time I set out to find my enemy, they will be ready and waiting for me. I would prefer to take the offensive and strike before they have time to prepare."

"Then I and my guard will move out tomorrow morning in advance of your army. There are one hundred megatraths at hand, a significant enough force to follow the vipers and scout

out potential hostiles. Besides, desert travel is what we are made for. It will not take us long to track down the serpents, and it will be easier for you to follow our tracks than the viper trails. If we wait even one day, the wind may erase the trail, and we would be unable to follow them."

Ilfedo thought for a moment. If he refused her offer, she would likely take offense. If he sent her ahead of his army, it would give him the time he needed to prepare a substantial force, but it might also place his new-found ally in great jeopardy. He took one look at her thick, scaled hide and laughed inwardly. What was he thinking? A force of one hundred megatraths could easily deal with a small army and stand a fair chance of victory.

He bowed to her. "Very well, we will do as you suggest."

Oganna's eyelids felt heavy. She yawned as someone stroked her brow and grinned when her father's frowning face came into focus. "Father, you are better?"

"Yes, Oganna. Thanks to you, the spell was broken, and I am myself again." He took her hand and held it in his larger ones. "I've patched up things with Vectra, too. She and the other megatraths have once again driven the vipers into the desert."

She sat up slowly and put a hand on her head to soothe its ache. "I discovered a presence—an evil presence—that was fighting with me as I sought to release its control of you. He must be very strong with sorceries if he was able to control you from afar."

"Well, you don't have to worry about him anymore. Vectra killed him, and her companions took care of his partners."

"No." She withdrew her hand from his and held it palm up toward the ceiling. "I can sense the presence still. It is no longer in you, and it is far weaker, but whoever our enemy is, he is still a very great threat. I can sense it. He is lying in wait for whoever first searches for him. I am certain of it."

He shifted in the chair by her bedside. "The megatraths are leaving in the morning to track the vipers. I need a couple days to ready the army, so it will be a little while before I catch up with them."

"Then I will go with the megatraths."

"I don't know, Oganna. You look weak."

She squeezed his hand and looked into his eyes. "Father, please do not try to stop me. Vectra will need me, and have you heard how I slew Loos?"

He nodded. "Caritha informed me a little while ago."

"Then you know that I can do this."

He rose from the chair, kissed her forehead, and smoothed back her hair. "Your mother would be so proud of you." He walked to the door, and she saw him shift his shoulders before he answered her. "All right, my daughter. I will not stop you. But be careful. I will follow with the army as soon as possible."

"Thank you, Father."

Instead of going back to sleep, she threw on a robe and strode to the council chamber where the prisoner lay in its cage. She lifted the viper out. The creature offered no resistance. She brought it to her room, closed the door, and laid it on the bed. Gently she placed her hands on its skin. "Do not be afraid. I am not going to hurt you."

As she began to heal its wounds, she felt resistance. At first she didn't know what it was, then she recognized an oppressive darkness. Some kind of spell was eating at the creature's free will, in the same way that Ilfedo had been ruined. "Oh no, you don't!" she cried as the presence attacked her.

Forcing her will to concentrate, she sought to cast out the presence. But, though it could not overcome her, she could not overcome it. She brought the Avenger, laid it against the creature and, adding its power to her own, surrounded the evil seed and killed it. Weakened, she slumped over in a faint.

&#10087; &#10087; &#10087;

"Psst! Mistress?"

Oganna rubbed her eyes. Who had called her?

The viper slithered to her arm and raised its venomous head. At first she cringed, believing that it would strike her, but she saw that its mouth framed a rather cute grin. "Mistress?"

She pointed at her chest. "Me? You are talking to me."

"Psst! Who else?" The snake coiled its tail around her arm.

She stood and smiled back at it. "You have changed."

The viper rubbed its head against her skin. "Psst! Mistress, you saved my life. That makes me your lifetime friend. Do you know what that means?"

Oganna laughed inwardly. She felt funny talking to a serpent. "No, what does it mean?"

"I will be with you until the day I die. I am called Neneila, and I will protect you with my life and offer advice if you want it." The creature curled the remaining couple feet of its length around her arm and tasted her sleeve with its forked tongue. "Mistressssss you are very pretty."

Suppressing a giggle, Oganna left her room with the viper wrapped around her arm. This arrangement suited her. She could imagine it would be nice to have a constant companion to share her thoughts with. She left the fort and found her father, the Warrioresses, Ombre, and Vectra conferring by a stand of trees. The members of Ilfedo's council stood nearby. The mega-traths lumbered into line behind Vectra.

A murmur passed through the air as she approached. The men pointed to the viper on her arm and whispered to one another. Ilfedo glanced at her arm. "Well, my dear. You have worked another miracle overnight." He smiled and patted her shoulder. "If your little friend is comfortable, let's get down to business."

"Psst! Mistress, I don't like being called 'little.'" The viper raised its head in disdain and eyed Ilfedo. "Psst! Psst! Psst!"

But Ilfedo did not seem to hear the creature. He addressed those assembled and introduced Vectra. "Please welcome our ally, Vectra, ruler of Resgeria."

"Men of the Hemmed Land," Vectra growled. "Let your enemies be mine, and mine yours. I have brought a force strong enough to search out and discover your enemy. We will repay them for all the harm they have done to you." She held up her hand, and her claws emerged from the fingers.

The counselors raised their hands and cheered.

Vectra gazed upon Oganna. "Your father informed me of your decision to accompany us. All I can say is, I will be honored to have you by my side."

"Psst! What's this?" the viper hissed. It twisted its head around in order to see the megatrath from head to tail. "Big, bad, ugly, scaled—"

"Shush, Neneila." Oganna tapped the little creature's head and glanced at Vectra, hoping no insult had been perceived.

"Look who's talking," the megatrath grunted. "A tiny, insignificant, beady-eyed—"

The viper slipped its tongue in and out of its mouth and showed its fangs. "Psst!" Venom glittered on its fangs. "I am also *poisonous*. Sssince I will be traveling with you—treat me with respect."

"Please, stop, both of you." Oganna shrugged her shoulders, gazing into Vectra's face. "Can't we all get along?"

The megatrath drew back her head and crouched to the earth. "You are right, princess. I shouldn't let such a small creature bother me."

"Small! Psst, you rude, fat—"

Oganna clamped her fingers over the viper's mouth. "No more insults. Okay?" She swung her leg over Vectra's neck and held on as the creature stood to her full height. She spotted her father. His brow furrowed as if questioning the wisdom of her decision. "Don't worry, Father. I will be careful."

Vectra lumbered up to her fellow megatraths and opened her jaws wide, emitting a series of high-pitched shrieks that rolled across the fields until answering calls from the other megatraths filled the morning air and sent shivers up Oganna's spine. She imagined that the forests and hills of the Hemmed Land continued to ring with the megatraths' cries, and at the sound the inhabitants fled in fear. The great creatures formed a line with Vectra at its head.

"Hang on to me, Oganna." Vectra's body tensed, mighty muscles rippled. "This is going to be a rough ride."

Like a flood, they raced through the fields and crashed through the forests until they passed out of the Hemmed Land and into the northern desert. They kept up a fierce pace for a couple hours and then slowed whilst Oganna roasted in Yimshi's rays.

"Ah, this heat feels wonderful." Vectra rumbled in her throat, and she stretched. "This is more like my land. Except there are far fewer boulders in Resgeria."

Oganna sneezed as Vectra stirred the sand. "This climate may be all right for you, Vectra. But to me it is stifling!" The viper slithered up her arm and settled around her neck. The collar of her garment provided some shade for its body.

# NETROTH, CITY OF
# THE GIANTS

After enduring three days of travel through the boulder-strewn wastes of the northern desert, Oganna felt relieved to see green hills rise from the distant horizon. She dismounted and ran until her feet touched grass, and a tree shaded her. The cooler air kissed her dry skin. A few trees stood out on the grassy rises. She climbed to the crest of the first hill and gazed down the opposite side. A deep blue stream gurgled out of its base and ribboned through the flat landscape.

Leaving her shoes and socks on the stream's bank, she waded into the gentle current, splashed the water on her face, and washed the dust from her hair.

The megatraths lumbered over the hill, drank of the fresh water, drained the barrels of now-warm water that they had brought with them, and filled them anew. Oganna wrung the liquid from her hair and washed her legs off whilst the viper dropped to the ground and curled up on the stream's bank. "Psst, Mistress what's all the fuss?"

Oganna did not answer, instead laughing as she lay back on the grass. The green blades tickled her bare feet, and the ground received her in its soft cushion. The sun was setting in the west. The sky in that direction turned orange and purple. Wispy clouds dotted the sky, each one a different shape.

"We'll rest here for now." Vectra sloshed in the stream. "Tomorrow we continue north."

One by one the megatraths curled beside the stream, and soon their labored breathing filled Oganna's ears. Vectra brought over a pack and set it by Oganna's feet. "Goodnight, Princess."

"Goodnight." She watched the creature curl up nearby and smiled when Vectra's snoring reached her ears. The viper slithered under her legs and came up by her side. "Are you ready for sleep too, Neneila?"

The viper stretched its jaws, until the fangs were fully exposed, then yawned.

Oganna pulled her bedroll from the pack, rolled it out, and snuggled into it while the viper curled beside her head and dozed off. Soon she too would fall asleep with the sounds of crickets singing in the night. To her their songs were not mere vibrations wrought in the delicate tapestry of their wings, for she could hear the words. Now, as the crickets sang, she hummed along and repeated their words in her mind:

In the darkness, Netroth's bell tolls for the dead:
The unavenged slain that once roamed her streets.
They toll for the mighty king that into doom was led,
And the citadel that stands in the wake of his defeats.

Oh, hearken to the pleas of the cities' murdered inhabitants.
Cry now for children torn from play,
For mothers slain by the corrupted giants,
Weep for the king that should not have lived to see this day.

Will not a champion rise to stay the wizard's hand?
When will justice be dealt to end his dread?
Who will save this burning land?
Who will rise to deal justice upon the wizard's head?

It seemed a strange thing for crickets to sing. She whispered their phrases into the night, then closed her eyes and fell asleep.

⊗    ⊗    ⊗

The next morning Oganna rose with the dawn. The air felt strangely warm for so early an hour. Putting away her bedding, she roused the viper. "I'm going to explore. Do you want to come along?"

"Certainly, Mistress. Psst! I wouldn't miss this." It wrapped itself around her outstretched arm and settled its head over her right shoulder.

Oganna walked over the next hill and the next until she came to the top of a rise that stood higher than all the land ahead of her. To her astonishment she saw a vast stretch of rolling hills that extended from the base of the hills on which she stood to a trio of mountains in the distance. Smoke rose from the smoldering ruins of innumerable buildings throughout the region, and geometrically laid out roads converged from the horizon, allowing access to the buildings and a main highway that drew a straight line to the mountains.

A multitude of dead domesticated animals dotted the landscape in dried pools of their own blood. Arrows lay strewn on the ground with broken spears and an occasional sword. She descended the hill and tried to pick up one of the swords by its handle. But it was twice the size of Avenger and at least three times as heavy. She released her hold.

Kneeling next to an arrow, she ran her finger along its shaft. It was as long as a man, and its head dwarfed any she'd ever seen. Not far off lay a spear with a shaft at least sixteen feet long! She stood and walked to the nearest structure, a four-walled home with its roof caved in. The doorway rose five feet higher above her head.

"Oganna!" Vectra's massive foot splintered the spear. Behind her the other megatraths lumbered over the hills, and suddenly the objects scattered about seemed small.

Vectra picked up the sword and stabbed its blade into the ground. Then she raised the front third of her body and picked up a couple arrows in each hand. The megatrath cracked them in her teeth. "I was worried about you, Princess. You should not wander off alone. This land is foreign. We do not know what creatures inhabit it."

"I had no idea that there were people living this far north." Oganna shook her head and gaped at the structure. "Look at this place. It's as if giants built it."

"And fought a war here." Vectra lumbered through the field, picking up various weapons. She lifted a shield and smashed her fist into it. But the shield held, and she pulled back her hand, shaking it and growling.

Vectra hunched down beside Oganna and eyed her quizzically. "Did you imagine that this part of the world would be any less interesting than ours? Take my word for this." She wiggled her claws at the territory ahead of them. "Subterran is full of other civilizations, some old, some young, some wicked and some good."

Oganna nodded thoughtfully. "It looks as if someone burned this place out and it *wasn't* with the consent of the inhabitants. Look at the weapons and livestock. Someone made war on these people."

"It does look that way." Vectra kicked another shield aside. "And I have little doubt that this devastation is somehow linked to the viper raids on the Hemmed Land."

"No doubt." Oganna walked to the main highway and followed it toward a large hill. Vectra lumbered beside her, a comforting reminder of a mighty ally. Smoke rose from behind the hill, and the point of a spire stabbed at the sky. The highway disappeared over the hilltop. Without warning her companions, she ran to the crest and peered beyond.

In a very deep and wide valley rested the ruins of a mighty city constructed of stone. A wall rose over forty feet high around its perimeter. Streets lined the city in the shape of a sailing ship wheel, with four highways as spokes running from the center to the four gates below the valley's rim. A wooden archway, inscribed with letters from the ancient alphabet, crowned the nearest gate.

" 'Netroth.' "

Vectra, coming up from behind, caught her breath and laid a restraining hand on Oganna's shoulders. "Take care, Princess. I have heard of this place. It is a city of the giants. Little bodes well with those creatures, for they are warlike and powerful."

Oganna couldn't help smiling at that. "Sounds like another race I know."

They descended into the valley and passed under the arch into the city. The one hundred megatraths pounded after them. Every footstep resounded through the empty streets, and the air smelled mildly of rotten eggs. Dead animals lay everywhere, and most of the buildings had been burned.

The spire that Oganna had seen belonged to a citadel at the city's heart. It spiked above the four highways that led to the gates and intersected beneath it. A gargantuan stone ramp appeared to be the only way to enter the structure. This ramp dropped one hundred feet from the citadel entrance to the highway ahead of her and descended on either side of an arch, allowing passage underneath to the rest of the city. Deep chips in the citadel walls and chunks of stone lying around it indicated it had endured bombardment.

Nevertheless, the city itself had fared far worse. Whether that was due to its weaker construction or an enemy's wrath she could not determine. Oganna felt as if she was walking through a land of ghosts.

She climbed an enormous stone step into one of the houses and gazed at the ceiling rafters ten feet above her head. Spiders crawled over thinly spread webs between the rafters and two beams crossed beneath them for support. It didn't smell musty, but something putrid made her pinch her nose. She wandered past the kitchen table with two large wooden chairs on either end. A third lay on the floor with a broken leg. An iron stove sat against the one wall. She stood on tip toe to see the stovetop. Burned eggs and bacon filled a pan. And to the side a raw egg had broken on the cooling shelf.

Leaving the cooking area, she spotted an open door in the far wall. In the room beyond, she could see an enormous bunk bed with sheets neatly tucked under the mattress and fluffed pillows. She left the building to peer into the next one. A broken table and chairs littered the wood floor and red splotches dotted the planks. The plaster wall had cracked, and a telltale red stain streaked from above her head to the floor. A torn shirt large enough for three men to fit in lay on the floor before her.

In each home that she searched she found not a soul. She found meals left uncooked, and others with tables set and the dinner unfinished. Either the giants had fled, or they'd been forced to leave.

She stood on the steps of one huge mansion, feeling like a midget, and watched the daylight fade. "It appears as though the citadel is the sturdiest structure remaining in this city." She glanced back at Vectra as the creature stuck its head in another doorway. She waited until the megatrath pulled its head out and returned her gaze. "We should take residence inside it for the night . . . just in case whoever did this comes back."

Vectra nodded and roared down the city streets. The other megatraths emerged from various buildings, and walls collapsed in their wake. They came at her summons and stood while she pointed out the citadel. "We will take refuge in there for the night. Tomorrow we will do a more thorough search of these buildings."

One megatrath lumbered out of line. "Vectra, I don't think that would be the wisest course of action."

Vectra wheeled on the creature, grabbing its neck in her claws and driving its head into the stone pavement. "Dare to question my word again, and I will personally crush you into this rubble."

"But Vectra, I only wanted—"

She spun in a tight circle, crashed her bulk into his, and sent him flying into a pile of loose stones. He shook himself and rose. She roared in his face, spewed fire until he cried for mercy, and thwacked him with her boney tail before eyeing the others. "Any more objections?"

Oganna shook her head and set off after Vectra in the direction of the great ramp. The megatrath's ways seemed strange. Effective—and yet strange. She observed the creatures' expressions. In spite of their leader's apparent insensitivity or, perhaps because of it, they were smiling.

The viper's tongue tickled her ear. "Psst, Mistress! Your companions are very strange."

"Shush, now." She stroked Neneila's head. "You are also a strange companion."

"Psst, no I am not."

"Oh? What makes you say that?"

"You will see, Mistress. I am not the first viper that has bound myself to a human, and you will find it to be very advantageous. Psst! Wait, and you will see what I mean."

The citadel ramp rose before her. Oganna strode up it with Vectra and two other megatraths leading the way. The stone construction fascinated her. Stone tiles cut in the shape of diamonds covered the walkway. She peeked over the edge. There were no railings along the side, in spite of the dangerous plunge anyone who stumbled would take over the edge. A blast of cold air threatened to throw her off, and she shuddered, imagining herself slipping and then falling over fifty feet into the streets below.

She followed Vectra to the citadel's entrance. "Goodness!" Vectra exclaimed as she threw her weight against the hefty iron doors. "How did the *giants* open these?" The megatraths struggled against them until they finally opened noiselessly inward.

The megatraths pushed inside and unpiled an assortment of heavy objects blocking the entry. Oganna pointed to a heavy, square stone that had been set against the inside of the doors. "There's your answer, Vectra. I don't think the giants intended for these to be opened."

The citadel was incredible. It could have defined the word 'incredible.' A pillar rose from the center of the floor to a junction where eight arches met high in the structure. Several stairways recessed into the walls, and each of them spiraled upward. Doorways opened in the walls along the stairs. All around her, she saw furniture strewn on the cold floor.

"Oganna, come over here." Vectra stood in the doorway to an adjoining chamber.

Peering around the megatrath, Oganna let out a long breath. "Wow." Ornately carved wood covered the room's high walls. Wooden flowers, swords, spears, scrolls, and people adorned the upper half and the ceiling. Wooden rods ran parallel lines several feet off the floor, until they were hidden at the far side of the room behind an empty stone throne. Chiseled into the wall above was a sentence written in the ancient alphabet. "Vectra, what does it say?"

"'The voice of the One speaks for all.'"

Oganna stepped into the room. "One thing is now certain: this place *was* built by giants. I don't know if we should be thankful that they aren't here, or if we should pity their apparent demise."

She ran her fingers down the wood panels that formed the walls. Each one was covered with a unique carving. Some depicted battles, others showed ceremonies, and others showed families fitted in fancy clothing. "So many souls," she said in a hushed voice. "So many nameless faces." She gazed upon the image of a father holding his infant child in his arms and she glanced at her feet. How many innocent lives had been ruined in this place?

The viper reached out with the tip of its tail and caught her tear. "Psst! Mistress, you should get some rest."

"For once I agree with the serpent." Vectra growled and beckoned with a massive hand. "Come. We'll need your help to set up the tent your father packed for you."

An enormous fireplace had been built into a wall in the main chamber. Several megatraths left the citadel via the ramp and reappeared minutes later with armloads of timber. They stacked some of it in the fireplace and breathed gentle flames on the wood. The fire flickered and burned hot, warding off the night chill.

Oganna pulled out her bedroll and placed it near the fire. Vectra started to take out the tent from one of the packs they'd trundled along, but Oganna raised her hand to stop her. "This will do fine." She and the viper slipped under the bedding, and the heat from the fire filled her with toasty warmth.

With all the megatraths inside the citadel, she expected to sleep sound in the knowledge that she was safe. Yet every shifting stone she heard startled her wide-awake, and every howl of the wind against the citadel sent shivers down her spine. The place seemed to invite her worst nightmares to come true.

She thought of the empty city. What had happened to the people? Even if most of them had been killed in a war, shouldn't there be *some* survivors in such a large city? And why weren't there any human bodies? They could not simply vanish. She pulled the blanket closer to her chin and steeled herself against morbid thoughts.

Tomorrow she would get a fresh start and find out what happened here. Maybe if she discovered what had become of the giants' civilization, she would find out who had sent the vipers and the Art'en to attack the Hemmed Land. Her father had called the wizard responsible for placing him under a spell by a certain name, but it escaped her. Feeling tired from her long day, she rested her mind.

⚛ ⚛ ⚛

The next day a cold drizzle fell on the city. Vectra punched several megatraths in their sides. They roused, growling as they rose to their feet, and lumbered to the enormous citadel doors. Other megatraths pulled the doors open, and the megatraths plodded down the ramp.

Oganna stepped onto the walkway. Neneila the viper draped over her shoulders and lashed a forked tongue into the air. The megatraths thudded into the city and spread through the streets, poking in and out of buildings. Another line of them passed her and followed the first group into the streets.

Oganna craned her neck to see the entirety of the citadel. The stone structure rose majestically, almost touching a dark cloud. She returned inside, gazing around the interior. At the stairs she lifted her foot to the first step, twice as large as the ones in her father's house.

"Be careful." Vectra rose next to her, her dark eyes probing the stairwell. "If there *are* any survivors, they may be up there."

"Don't worry, I'll be fine. I have my weapons with me." She climbed each of the stone steps to the second level, a wide-open room with a floor of stone blocks. No wonder the arches in the main chamber were necessary. Anything less could not support the weight of this floor.

Continuing to the third level, she entered a broad hallway. On the right a wooden door with a heavy iron latch at eye level blocked her way.

Drawing Avenger from its sheath, she waited for it to turn crimson before thrusting it through the wood and cutting a hole large enough for her to pass through. The room into which she stepped turned out to be the giants' armory . . . and what an armory it was. Swords, ranging in size from six to nine feet long rested in velvet-lined, wood cases along the walls. Each of the weapons shone like polished silver. The room smelled stale, as if it had not been opened for some time, and a layer of dust hung in the corners.

An assortment of spears hung at the far end, their shafts decorated with dyed feathers and streamers. Wood and leather shields lined the left- and right-hand walls, and a few maces lay on a table in the center. She imagined what it must have been like to see an army of giants wielding these weapons in battle. What a magnificent and terrible sight they must have made!

She left the armory and found more stairs leading up. They brought her above the armory to the interior of the citadel's spire. It was breathtaking. Steel beams rose on all sides, crisscrossing one another to a great height before joining at the roof's peak, at least a couple hundred feet up. Along the interior of this structure another staircase snaked upward, its steps clinging to the inside walls as they circled the spherical interior. "Here we go," she said as the viper gaped at the ascent.

"Psst! Mistress, are you sure this is a good idea?"

"Of course it is." She started climbing the stairs, grunting with the ache in her leg muscles. "Why do you ask?"

The viper tightened around her arm and gulped. "If we fall. Psst—splat!"

Oganna laughed and continued the climb. There was a railing, but it rested just above her head, so she kept as close as possible to the wall in order to avoid the steps' edges.

As she climbed the stairs she gained a more intimate view of the awesome structure. The roof appeared to be of stone construction, though it may have been a compound, such as clay. Steel reinforcements held it together. It took her a while to reach the top. Standing on that final step, she faced a metal door set in the roof. Pushing the iron latch upward to open the door proved impossible, for it was exceedingly heavy. Instead she wedged her sword under it and broke the latch. She waited for the severed metal to fall, then opened the door with relative ease and stepped through onto an observation platform on the roof.

From this vantage point the city buildings looked like miniatures. The smoke mixed with a steady rain to form a haze. The highway by which she had come to Netroth shot out of the valley to the hilly region where smoke still rose from some of the burned dwellings in that direction.

Bringing her attention back to the citadel, she examined the platform on which she stood. It circled the steeply inclined roof near the top of the spire. She walked to the opposite side of the observation platform and looked to the north. Things appeared to be much the same, except for the mountains arising in the distance. Smoldering, ruined buildings and slaughtered livestock dotted the landscape.

Just beyond the grass-covered terrain, a dark hill stabbed skyward. Try as she might she could not see it clearly, partly because it was so far away and partly because smoke rose from it at several points.

"Neneila, do you see that?" She pointed as best she could toward the distant dark hill. "Can you make out what that is?"

The creature squinted and stretched out its neck, then wrapped itself over her shoulders. "Psst! If only I could remember what happened to me after the spell took hold. Then I might know. After all, if it *is* your enemy that did this, then I was likely involved."

"Perhaps." Oganna left the platform, returning into the citadel. "Perhaps Vectra can help us find out what it is."

She descended into the citadel's main chamber and described as best she could what she'd seen from the platform. Vectra scratched her head. "Mm, you say it was burning?"

"It appeared to be."

"It would take us too long to go there if you walk. I will carry you." Vectra hunkered to the floor and waited for Oganna to get on her neck.

After gathering her guards on the ramp, Vectra raced north along the highway until she passed out of the city. The megatrath shook the rain out of her face, Oganna shielding her own face. Her clothes clung to her body.

They ignored the buildings smoking around them and came within sight of the smoking, black hill. Machines of war littered the hills for as far as Oganna could see. Along with the hand weapons and shields stood several trebuchets of extraordinary size and equally large catapults standing like sentinels in the wake of a battle.

The rain slackened, and the smoke rose more thickly from the heap. Oganna turned up her nose as they approached. The stench of burning flesh overpowered her senses. Her horror intensified when Vectra began to tremble and growled a stream of curses. "Oganna, look. It is the giants. We have found them." The dark heap of tangled bodies of the giants stretched for a long distance. Their arms and legs stuck out from the pile, and fire licked at their corpses. Women and children, warriors young and old, lay together in death, their faces frozen in fear.

Oganna gritted her teeth, dismounted, and picked a child's doll out of the mud. Here lay the inhabitants of Netroth, slain without consideration of age, gender, or social standing. This was a *massacre*. She looked at the ground around the heap. Rage boiled in her heart, and she clenched her fists, drew out Avenger, and sent a wave of energy from her hand to the sky. "Before I leave this land, I swear that justice will be carried out upon whoever did this." She turned to the milling megatraths. "The rain has all but quenched the flames. Burn this heap before the rotting flesh finishes poisoning the ground."

The creatures hesitated as they waited for Vectra to confirm the order.

Vectra spun upon them and drove them toward the heap. "You heard her. Burn it!"

The megatraths drew in deep breaths and poured steady streams of fire on the bodies. The smoldering wood ignited, the flames wrapped around the heap, and before long the bloated funeral pyre roared heavenward.

# THE TOLLING BELL

Upon returning to the citadel in Netroth, Oganna saw uncertainty in the megatraths' eyes as their gazes shifted back and forth. She understood how they felt, for she felt it too—fear of an unknown enemy that had brutally wiped out an entire city. What kind of enemy were they dealing with? They must have been strong in order to besiege and take a city as great as this one.

Vectra shivered in her hide and forced a smile at her companions. "Don't look so depressed, my brothers and sisters. We are safe. We have food to last several more days." She threw wood into the fireplace and shot a lazy flame into the midst. "And we have heat." The others gathered around, and soon the warmth from so many bodies filled the massive room, driving away the dampness.

First one megatrath and then another brought more wood to the fire until it roared. They heaped the excess wood to the side and settled down for a nap while Oganna and Vectra stayed alert. They did not want to be caught unprepared if the enemy showed himself.

Suddenly the citadel doors burst open, and a blast of wet air surged into the citadel. Oganna and the megatraths shot to their feet. She half-expected to face an army of foes. Instead a lone giant stumbled inside. He was dressed in elaborate armor, and a tattered yellow cape fell from his broad shoulders. He leaned on a sword held in his right hand. His eyes blazed with hatred and blood ran from his many wounds. On his head rested a silver crown with a large diamond set in its face.

His eyes darted about. Pain twisted his expression. He staggered toward them and lowered his head, spreading his legs wide and holding his sword with both hands. "Wh-what? How did you come to be here? I know none of your faces, nor am I familiar with your race. If you follow the wizard, then stand ready, because you will fall by my sword!"

Vectra growled and the other megatraths pressed closer to the giant.

"I have given all of you fair warning. Now speak!" His eyes rolled back into his head, and he breathed deeply before shaking his head and refocusing his gaze.

Gazing up at the imposing figure, Oganna stepped forward and laid her sword on the floor. "If you are not here to harm us, then we intend you none." She edged closer.

In a deft motion he grasped her by the throat. Vectra rushed forward, clamped her claws on the man's arm, and forced him to release his hold. His head drooped, his eyes rolled back in their sockets, and he collapsed.

Oganna bent over, grabbed her throat, and gagged. "Whew! Thanks, Vectra, he has a fist of iron."

They laid the giant on the floor by the fire, and Oganna unbundled the tent that she had brought along. She glanced at the citadel doors. They remained open after the giant's unexpected arrival. "I would close those doors if I were you," she said to a nearby megatrath.

The creature lumbered to the entrance, closed them, and leaned against them.

As Oganna looked at the giant, she gasped. "What in Subterran happened to this man? It looks as though someone sliced him all over with razor blades!" Dried blood caked the man's body, and fresh blood ran from numerous deep gashes. In several places his bones lay exposed.

"This man must be someone of great importance," Vectra said as she helped Oganna set up the tent and slide the giant inside. Oganna had intended to set up the tent for her own privacy, but giving it to him—it felt right. "Look at his crown. That is no mere decoration. It is possible that the throne we found is his."

Oganna slipped the weighty ornament off his head and set it aside. "I must tend to his wounds. Otherwise, he will die."

"Take care, Princess. This giant could be the very villain we have come to find."

"No. I don't think so. Our enemy would not have come alone to this place if he had won the battle. However, if I can heal this man, then he should be able to tell us what is going on around here."

The megatrath chortled. "And what if he doesn't know? What if we are chasing a ghost, and there is no villain to be found?"

"Then we have come here for naught, and the answer to the mystery of the winged men and viper attacks lies elsewhere. But I do not believe this devastation is coincidence; rather, I think that we have stumbled upon the place my father is seeking. All that remains is to find and deal with the sorcerer."

"An admirable analogy, Oganna, and I hope you are right. I too would like to *deal* with the perpetrator. I'd like to give him a piece of my mind, a sniff of my vapor, a scalding by fire, and I'd like to tear him limb from limb with my claws."

As the megatrath spoke, Oganna set to work carefully cleaning and sewing the unconscious giant's wounds. "Vectra, would you send out some of your guards in search of water? There must be wells in this city and barrels that they can use to bring the water back here. I will need lots of it." As her friend moved away, Oganna said, "And tell them that any clean cloth they can find will be greatly appreciated."

"Hmm, will there be anything else?" Vectra raised her eyes in mock sarcasm. "Perhaps you want them to find food as well?"

"That *would* be nice. Thank you, Vectra." She laughed and drew the needle through the giant's skin, pulling together his sliced skin.

Over the next couple hours, Vectra sent search parties into Netroth, and they brought back all that Oganna had required and more. They gathered more wood for the fireplace, too. Soon the citadel felt nice and toasty. It had been a long day for the megatraths. As the room heated, the flames glistened off their hides and they fell contentedly asleep.

Oganna stayed awake, tending to the giant's wounds. Several cuts proved too deep and ragged for her to sew together. These she laid her hands on and probed with her mind to find that source of extraordinary strength and power within her blood. *There!* She pulled with her mind, feeding off the strength and healing with the powers therein. Energy surged through her and blossomed, its aura enveloped her, and the giant's deep wounds healed. The exposed flesh turned pink, and the skin closed over it.

Exhausted by her labors, she sat back. "Now, Mr. Giant, your body must heal the remainder on its own." She rose and left the tent. Within the shadow of Vectra's bulk she unrolled her bedding. The firelight flickered cheerily as she lay down.

The megatrath stuck her snout in Oganna's face. "You don't trust him, do you?"

The viper slid from around Oganna's neck and onto the blanket. "Psst! What do you take Mistress for, a fool? She won't trust unless she *knows* she can." The creature slipped out its tongue in a derogatory gesture. "Psst! You may have a large brain, megatrath, but sometimes I wonder if you know how to use it properly."

"True, I do not trust easily." Oganna folded her hands behind her head. "I don't trust the giant because I do not know him." She chuckled as she continued. "Would *you* trust him if you were *my* size?"

The megatrath grunted, settled her head to the floor, and fell asleep, breathing rhythmically. Oganna lay down as well, while the serpent remained on top of her blanket. She stared up at the citadel's stone walls. The flames in the fireplace threw a flickering light over the interior. These sturdy walls were a comfort to her, standing watch as a guardian, never resting—needing none.

In her mind's eye she saw night close in over the city of Netroth. It was full of haunting sounds that echoed down the abandoned streets and traversed the empty buildings. She saw a knife that had never finished cutting a loaf of bread, and a child's doll neglected and alone. The entire city dressed in black, mourning its children, mothers, and fathers. In its sorrow a city bell tolled eerily in the darkness.

She opened her eyes, stunned. The bell *was* tolling! On its own? She doubted it. She glanced at the doors to the ramp. Two megatraths, sleeping soundly, were resting against them. If someone tried to sneak in they would be unable to. Vectra jerked up her head, then curled tighter around Oganna. "Don't worry, Princess. Nothing will happen to you on my watch."

The bell ceased tolling. A restless megatrath stirred, rose, and stoked the fire before curling up again. Oganna glanced up at Vectra. The bell tolled again. Had the giants' enemy returned? She looked again at the citadel. They were safe within these walls . . . she hoped.

In the middle of the night she still could not calm herself. She felt as if a pair of eyes was spying on her and her alone. She glanced at the citadel doors and the door to the giant's throne-room. No one in sight, and she breathed a sigh of relief. She turned toward the fireplace, and a man's hand clamped over her mouth.

"Shhh, dragon child. It is only I." Specter released his hold on her mouth and stood before her, shimmering in and out of sight. "It took me a long while to find you. You are becoming quite skilled at protecting yourself." He smiled.

"What are you doing here?" she whispered.

"I am looking out for you, little one. And a quest of my own is intertwined with my duty to the dragon." He stepped close to the fire and stretched his hand toward the blaze.

Oganna gazed upon the warrior. How in Subterran he had managed to slip in unnoticed was beyond her. But he was here now, and her heart had slowed its wild pounding. Somehow, even though creatures as large as dragons surrounded her, this invisible guardian allayed her fears more than they. "What do you mean by a quest of your own?"

He stared into the flames and for a time said nothing. Then he closed his eyes. "The wizard who placed your father under a spell is familiar to me. I have waited for so long to meet him again. And now your path and his have crossed. If they cross again, I will be ready."

Turning to her, Specter looked at her with bright eyes and a grim expression. "I need to ask that, if you come across him, you leave him to me. Nothing would please me more than to end his evil."

"But"—she frowned—"you don't have any powers. Do you? If he serves the powers of evil, then I should face him, not you."

"Please," he whispered, "I will ask nothing else of you. Only this one thing do I require. Leave the wizard Auron to me."

Something about his manner made her cringe. "You mean to kill him, don't you?"

Specter turned back to the fire.

"If you do that, you will die." Oganna shook her head. "No, I'm sorry, but I cannot let you do that."

"What makes you so sure that I would die in combat with him? Did I not protect your mother and your aunts all the days of their youth? I stood with them when they faced a witch and a wizard." He gazed over his shoulder, meeting her eyes. "You are young, Oganna. Trust that I know what is best. For I would do nothing to harm you."

"But you wouldn't care if you are harmed in the process." She frowned as the viper blinked its eyes, then glanced at Specter and popped them open. Its mouth opened in a little scream. Oganna clamped her fingers over its mouth and put a finger to her lips. "Silence, Neneila! He is with us. Now go back to sleep."

The viper took another look at the cloaked warrior with the scythe. It slithered under the blanket.

"You don't care if you live or die. Do you?" Oganna burned her gaze into the silent guardian. "But I do."

At last he dropped to one knee and looked down at her with a smile. "I have lived two lifetimes, child. I have seen the ancient fall and this generation rise. Long ago a great sin was committed against a pupil of mine, and today you live in a darkening world that is a direct result of that event."

He waved his hand at the sleeping megatraths, the citadel, and the doors. "These creatures would not be here, and this land would not have fallen if I had long ago seen the coming evil. Everything is a direct result of what he did a day long, long before you, your father, or even his father were born. Auron knows this, and I must bring him to justice!" He clenched his fist and vanished.

"Specter?" She called his name softly over and over again, but he did not respond. And when she spread her other senses into the surrounding room she found nothing except megatraths and Neneila. With a resigned sigh, she lay down.

# WRATH OF THE MEGATRATH

The heat from the fireplace felt good on Oganna's back as she opened the tent flap and peered inside. The giant, wrapped in cloth bandages from head to toe, stirred and groaned. His eyes blinked open, and he raised himself on his elbows before calling out in a weak voice, "Hello? Is anyone here?"

She stepped into the tent, gave him a warm smile, and rested a hand on his shoulder. "Easy there, you are still very weak. You've been out for two days, and your wounds are still healing."

He gazed around the tent. She had neatly stacked his crown, cape, and boots in one corner. His sword lay next to him. "Where am I?"

"You are in my tent." She knelt beside him and dipped a cloth into a nearby bucket of water. "Lean forward please."

The giant glanced at her face. Then he bent forward. She wiped the cold cloth over his forehead and felt his temperature with her hand. "You are healing better than I expected."

The giant's tense arms relaxed. He stretched his shoulders and looked at her with eyes as soft as a bed of Night Grass on a cool evening. Even sitting up, he was a little taller than Oganna. He had shoulder-length, brown hair, a handsome face, and muscles like wrought iron. "Well, young lady. It appears to me that you have saved my life. And I don't even know your name."

She felt her cheeks flush and smiled. "I am Oganna—*Princess* Oganna of the Hemmed Land."

"Strange. I have never heard of such a place. But it is my pleasure to meet you, Princess. Now would you mind telling me *where* I am?"

Wondering if his injuries had affected his memory, Oganna returned his gaze. "You are in Netroth. Don't you remember?"

"But I was entering—" He closed his eyes and bit his lip, holding his head in his hands. "The day before last I came into the city. I was entering the doors to Ar'lenon when—"

"Ar'lenon?" She hesitated. What was Ar'lenon? But of course he must have meant the fortress. "Is that what you call this citadel? Ar'lenon?"

"We are in the citadel?"

"Yes."

A relieved smile curled his lips, and he clenched his fist. "Then Ar'lenon does still stand . . . despite everything, it still stands." He sighed. "Forgive me, I have not answered your question. The answer is yes, I *am* referring to this citadel."

"It is a remarkable structure. Did your people build it?"

He skirted her question. "What does it matter now? They are—gone."

She wrung the cloth, returned it to the bucket, then stood. "I have told you my name. Will you tell me yours?"

"You may call me Gabel."

"It is a pleasure to meet you, Gabel." She curtsied. "I couldn't help noticing that you wore a crown, and your cape is sewn from a rather rich material. Are you the lord of this land?"

"Yes, I am—I was. But now I am nothing. The land has been destroyed, and no one remains alive. I—" His lips quivered. "I don't have anyone left." She could tell that he was struggling with memories she could not share, that he wanted to appear strong. The man inside lost the battle, and he wept.

She reached out and embraced his neck. "It's all right," she whispered. "You are among friends now and thus you are safe. Do not be ashamed to cry."

Gabel sobbed, then choked and cleared his throat, shaking his head. He lay back, growling. "Oh, Razes! I will make you pay for the evil you have done. You will beg for mercy at the end and regret the day that you slaughtered the innocent and brought ruin to my land. *I* will *make* you pay with your life for this evil." Weakened, he lay back and fell into a fitful sleep.

Oganna left the tent, tiptoeing so as not to disturb him. "He is asleep," she said before Vectra could ask.

"That I guessed." The megatrath carved a circle in the stone floor with her claw.

Oganna reached down, and Neneila slithered around her arm. She held the viper in front of her face and lightly stroked its head. The viper closed its eyes. She looked past the viper into Vectra's enormous face. "Did you hear him ranting about the massacre?"

"Yes. Whoever this *Razes* character is, he must be bad news to incur such bitterness."

Oganna began to pace the floor. "If Gabel is right, Razes is responsible for butchering the inhabitants of this region. I suspect he is also the villain behind the attacks on the Hemmed Land. Gabel mentioned winged men fighting for Razes." She stood still and nodded in the tent's direction. "At least Gabel bears no hostility toward us; in fact he seems to feel indebted because we are caring for him. If Razes is enemy to us both, then we share a mutual problem. Perhaps when he is feeling stronger, Gabel will be able to tell us more."

Vectra cocked her head and listened to the monotonous sound of rain pummeling Ar'lenon. Oganna kicked a pebble on the floor and watched it roll over the stones. "The rain is not letting up, is it?"

The megatrath sighed. "Two days of constant downpour. I'm beginning to wonder if Yimshi will ever come out again. Surely this will delay your father as well."

Twisting her head around, Vectra barked an order to one of her guards and gazed up one of the stairways that led into the spire of Ar'lenon. "If I was certain that those steps could hold my weight, I would go to that observation platform you told me about and stand watch. If Razes pummeled this city before, he might come back to search for survivors . . . and he might bring friends."

"Setting a watch up there wouldn't do much good." Oganna set Neneila around her shoulders. "The climb is too long, and it would take a long time for you to come back down and warn us if you spotted trouble. Besides, if Razes came here, he would have to come by way of the ramp and knock on the doors to find us."

"Then I will post guards outside the citadel doors on the ramp. At least then we will have warning of trouble."

Oganna thought for a moment. "That would be a risk. Anyone standing out there will present an inviting target."

"Nevertheless I am willing to take the risk. Besides, if anyone did attack, they would have to do so first from a distance, and our scaled hides are too thick for a mere arrow to pierce." Having thus decided, Vectra posted two megatraths on the ramp and set up a rotating schedule to change the guard frequently. "Do not worry, Princess." She curled up on the floor. "My guards are more than capable of this task. They will not be caught by surprise."

Deep down Oganna hoped the megatrath was right. It would be a shame to lose two megatraths before a fight even began. Then again, maybe Razes would not return to Netroth. Even if he did, one hundred megatraths garrisoned within Ar'lenon posed a formidable force. She should stop worrying and just pray her father arrived before Razes.

The next morning Gabel's face displayed more color. Oganna brought him oatmeal for breakfast, and he dug into the bowl with a vengeance. "Thank you so much for everything you have done for me." He grinned at her, and she laughed.

"It feels good to see you doing so well."

Vectra's enormous head poked through the tent flap. "How is he this morning?" Her question had been directed to Oganna. Then the creature's dark eyes focused on the giant. "Oh, I see you are awake and feeling better now. Good!" She backed out of sight, and the flap fell back in place.

Gabel's eyes almost popped out of their sockets. "What was that?"

Oganna could not help it—she laughed at his reaction. "That was a megatrath. Her name is Vectra, and she came with me to find out what is causing the viper raids along my land's northern border."

He chuckled. "You keep interesting company, Princess."

"I prefer to think of it as making interesting friends. My father and I are very grateful to have the megatraths as allies.

They are fierce fighters. I fought them once, and I hope I will never have to do so again."

The man looked thoughtful as he stared at the tent flap. "How many of those creatures have you brought with you?"

"It would be more accurate to say that they brought me. But why do you ask?"

"Because if my enemy returns, he will try to kill you, too."

"Gabel, who is this enemy of yours? Tell me all you know so that I can make a fair judgment on what happened here."

"There is a lot to tell," he began wearily. He clenched his fist and looked into her eyes. "Where is my sword?"

In answer, she pointed to where it lay by his side. The weapon was longer than she was tall. "It is a wonderful piece," she said.

He clutched it to his chest, then relaxed his grip and lay it across his knees.

"This sword has belonged to every king of Burloi since my great, great-grandfather built this city and established the monarchy. From generation to generation it has passed from father to son as a symbol of our strength to deter those who would destroy us." He paused and lovingly eyed the blood-stained blade "But that was before Razes's rebellion—"

"You mentioned him the other day, though only in passing. Who is this Razes?" She pulled away one of his bandages, saw that the wound was healing well, and smothered it with fresh salve.

Gabel eyed his injury as well. "You have the hands of a healer, little lady. I wish there was some way I could reward you."

"You can." She sat back. "You can tell me what happened here."

"Oganna. That *is* your name?" After she nodded he continued. "Razes is another giant, though younger than myself. When he was a youth I incorporated him into the Ar'lenon guard. But he was very ambitious and, desiring power, he led an uprising to dethrone me. It failed and I, in an attempt to show mercy, sent him into exile instead of to the guillotine as he deserved."

He gritted his teeth, then spat on the stones. "He and his followers fled Burloi and disappeared into the east, we thought for good. That was a little more than two years ago. Then, just a year and a half after his disappearance, Razes returned from the east. He was not the same youth that had left us. He had acquired a terrible weapon that gave him seemingly unlimited power. With a word he was able to demolish a building and with another he could control the weather.

"My people have long known that there are evil beings that practice magic, but we had never been face to face with such blatant proof of their abilities. Razes declared that he had become an agent of wizardry in our land and that this entitled him to whatever he desired. 'Those who resist will die,' he declared.

"The population split over loyalty to me and fear of the sorcery. Almost half of them sided with Razes because they believed that it would be useless to resist him. Burloi erupted in civil war. I fought tooth and nail for every part of my land, but he repeatedly defeated me." Gabel spread his arms and gazed up as if seeing through the tent fabric to the stone ceiling. "Here in Ar'lenon, I and my counselors made our last stand.

"In his wrath, Razes destroyed Netroth. Then he and his wizard apprentice, a human, ascended the great ramp. I fought them. However, Razes's companion also wielded magic. I was outmatched and defeated. They threw me off the ramp and the last thing I remember is seeing my remaining counselors struggling against them. If they survived, I would know it, for they would never have abandoned me even if they thought that I was a lifeless corpse." Striking the ground with his fist, he said, "Those who use magic should be cast into fire!"

Oganna folded her hands in her lap. "There are powers for good and powers for evil. For example, some would call the things I can do magic." She held up her hand, and it pulsated white and blue light. "But all good things come from God. That is what my father taught me."

"You—you are a sorceress."

"I am not. I am the blood descendant of a dragon, and as such I have their seemingly magical abilities. It is my inheritance, and it is a blessing."

"Inheritance?"

"Yes, a parting gift from my mother. She died shortly after giving birth to me. In order for me to live she had to give up the life energy in her blood. But she followed the Creator's will." She stood to her feet and parted a fold of her garment to reveal the crystalline blade of Avenger. "I made this using the power in my blood." Gabel looked skeptical, so she proceeded to draw the weapon and array herself in silver.

He drew in his breath. "Whew! What I wouldn't give to have a weapon that could do that." Chuckling, he glanced down at his sword. "Actually, there is a legend among my people that our northern brethren once had swords that could render them invisible and that there was no sorcery involved. So, I suppose, it is possible that—as you say—God can give his creatures special abilities."

"And I honestly believe that, because the power was bestowed by God, he could take it away from me at any moment He chose." Oganna slid the Avenger back into its sheath and returned to her normal state. "We will talk more later, Gabel. Your wounds have not finished healing, so for now I want you to rest."

He leaned forward and lightly kissed her forehead. "For a normal-sized human, you are quite interesting. I have enjoyed our discussion."

As she left the tent, Oganna glanced over her shoulder and shook her head with a laugh. "I can't help but wonder. How tall are you?"

"Last I measured"—he laid his head back—"ten feet, two inches. Scurry along now, little lady. As you said, I should rest."

Oganna went to the fireplace. The viper untangled itself from a broken chair, slithered up her outstretched arm, and rested about her neck. "Psst! Mistress, when can we leave this place? In case you haven't noticed, the megatraths' body odors are increasingly stronger."

Vectra lumbered over and nodded at the tent. "How is King Gabel doing?"

"He is doing a lot better. His wounds are healing well. He shouldn't need bed rest for much longer."

"Good, he seems like a nice man, and I would like to get to know him better." Vectra jerked up her head, and she stretched her neck toward the ceiling. "Did you hear that?"

"Hear what?"

Vectra lumbered to the citadel doors, threw them open, and walked out on the ramp. The rain had stopped. "Do you hear it now, Oganna?"

"Hear what?" But the viper spoke into her ear, and she bit her lip. "The vipers are coming."

Vectra shook her head and stamped her feet in impatience. "No, no! Quit listening to that little creature for a moment, and you will hear something else." She swiveled her head toward the north.

Over the valley's rim poured a dark flood of giant men. Their tramping resounded through Netroth's vacated streets, a terrifying unison of clanging armor, rattling shields, and stamping feet.

"I don't think—" Oganna was about to say that the enemy had not spotted them when a screech from behind made her duck just as an arrow shot over her head. She spun to find a winged man swooping through the moist air. "Never mind. They've found us. Come on! Vectra, you must warn the others."

Oganna parted the fold of her garment and slid the boomerang into her hand. A dozen Art'en dove from the dark clouds, joining the first. She threw the boomerang into their midst, watching its trajectory as it severed several heads before returning to her palm.

In the distance line upon line of armed giants descended into Netroth from the north. Like a wave they rolled into the city, onto its streets.

Another winged man, a shield and sword in its hands, swooped around Ar'lenon Citadel, its brown wings fanned out. It landed on the ramp and sprang at her.

"The Art'en will reign again," it hissed. "Die, human!" But it had landed between her and Vectra. The megatrath's clawed foot crushed the man's wings to his sides and raised him off the stone ramp. The Art'en struggled in the mighty grip.

"Not on my watch!" Vectra hissed back. Her mouth opened and clamped down on his midsection. Then she cast the Art'en off the ramp so that he fell into the city.

Oganna turned toward the sky and raised her sword as two others spiraled to the ramp and rained blows upon her. They each bore a shield and a sword. She parried their blows and struck back in rapid succession until one of them slipped around behind her. She raised her boomerang to block his attack, but Vectra rolled into him. The megatrath's six legs worked methodically, tearing the Art'en into bloody pieces before she scorched that which remained with fire.

The other creature proved agile and a capable fighter. He dropped his weapons and avoided every thrust Oganna attempted.

Then he kicked her jaw with his foot and smote her face with his wings so that she fell.

"At last I have you." It grabbed for her neck.

In an instant, Vectra stood over her and smashed her fist into the creature's chest. "I don't think so." She skidded around and pulled him back by the wings, then held him suspended in the air.

Oganna ran back to the citadel doors and shouted to the two megatraths standing guard. "Hurry, that army is getting nearer, and they far outnumber us. We must get these doors closed." She turned and looked for Vectra.

The megatrath leader gave the Art'en a rigorous shake. "So you like heights?" she screamed. "I'll give you one to remember me by!" Before Oganna could say anything to stop her, she barreled into the citadel with her captive in hand. Without thought to the damage she was causing she punched through the stairway entrance, and the stones crumbled away, leaving a space large enough for her to pass through. There was just enough time for Oganna to grab onto Vectra's tail and vault onto her neck.

Vectra rushed up the stairs as if her life depended upon it. In her fury she did not heed Oganna's protests. The ascent, which had taken Oganna a long time, lasted for what seemed like only moments. Vectra burst onto the observation platform and screamed her victory to the encroaching enemies before breaking her captive's wings and tossing him to his death. His body crashed onto a roof and rolled onto the street.

Art'en swarmed through the air toward the platform, screeching and clawing at the wind. They ascended and circled Oganna and the megatrath before drawing bows and arrows. A hail of arrows sped through the air. Oganna dismounted. Vectra stood in between the arrows and her. The projectiles bounced off Vectra's scales.

The Art'en flipped through the air. Several landed on the platform and a couple on Vectra's back. They drew swords, stabbed at the megatrath. Vectra bellowed the louder and caught a couple of them with her forearms. A tornado of flames issued from her mouth, turning the others into living torches. After breaking those in her arms, she threw them over the platform. Their screams echoed into the city and faded.

"Vectra!" Oganna beat her fist into the creature's neck to get her attention. "Enough of this." The creature hunkered down, and she remounted.

Another Art'en swooped over Vectra's head, and she swiped her claws at it, but missed. The creature hovered just out of her reach. "Oganna, now! Decimate them."

More Art'en dove from above. Oganna gritted her teeth. Vectra was right. It was time to show the enemy what they were capable of. She raised Avenger and fed it her power and rage. Electrical current enveloped its blade, knifed into the air, and struck the Art'en. They froze in the air, their feathers started to smoke, and their hair stood on end as they crashed into the roof. They grabbed at the tiles but rolled off and fell into the city.

# 23

# BATTLE FOR AR'LENON

Far below, on the ramp to Ar'lenon, the stones changed color, starting with the end touching the city streets and progressing toward the citadel doors. Vectra and Oganna both looked down. "Oganna, what is that?"

"Psst!" Neneila's forked tongue tickled Oganna's ear. "I was right. Those vipers that are still under the wizard's spell are coming."

After one more glance, Oganna clung tighter to the megatrath's neck and leaned forward. "Come on, Vectra. We have to get down there *now!*"

Vectra lowered her head and smashed through the stone walls of the citadel. Oganna cringed as shattered stones sprayed over her face and body. The megatrath thrust the front of its body through the hole. Its rear feet held to the platform while its head and forearms angled dangerously into the gaping heart of Ar'lenon. The stairs curved some twenty feet beneath them.

"No, Vectra, don't!"

But the megatrath leaped, dropping them through the massive structure. As the walls streamed by, Oganna gritted her teeth and stiffened her body around the creature's neck. Landing with a thud that shook but did not break the massive stone steps, Vectra raced down the remaining stairs. As they careened around the structure's interior, Oganna prayed she would not fall and held on for her life. Every jolt of Vectra's body threatened to throw them into the heart of Ar'lenon and to certain death. They dropped beneath the spire and descended the next stairs, passed the armory, and jumped into the main chamber wherein they'd encamped.

The megatraths rose on their thick legs and shook their hides. Vectra rumbled in her throat and flashed her bloodied claws in their faces. "Today let this city be shaken with the cries of our victory. Let this citadel ring with the battle we bring to the giants, the Art'en, and the vipers. Teach them to never again oppose a megatrath!"

Roars of approval deafened Oganna, forcing her to cover her ears with her hands until the megatraths quieted. Hisses filled room, and she turned as vipers slipped through the arrow slits along the citadel wall nearest the ramp and swarmed inside.

"Burn them out!" Vectra rose on her rear legs to an imposing height. Flames sprang from her tooth-ridden mouth and splashed against the arrow slits, turning squirming vipers into blackened, smoking skeletons. From either side of her the megatraths lumbered forward, opened their jaws, and took turns burning the vipers until they blackened the ancient walls.

Oganna sprang to the floor, her sword swiveling in her hand. Its blade turned crimson, and her glowing silver dress replaced her former garment. The megatraths growled, rumbled in their throats, and threw open the heavy doors. She stepped into the doorway, drew on her powers, and blasted the ramp before her.

A mass of desert vipers slithered around and over one another to reach the citadel. They covered the ramp a foot thick.

"Take them!" She advanced with the megatraths lined up behind her.

Everywhere she aimed, her sword sprayed fire upon the vipers. Megatraths flanked her, Vectra to her right, and another to her left. They added their flames to hers until half the length of the ramp had been charred black and the air smelled like steam and wet, burned wood. Before long many of the vipers receded from before her, disappearing into the maze of ruined buildings.

The giants plowed into the streets, a thick mass of humanity that increased in number every moment. They raised their shields and advanced toward the ramp.

Oganna parted a fold of her silver skirt, reached inside, and took her boomerang in hand. She drew back her arm and threw the crystalline weapon with all her might. It shot in a long arc, descended through the giants' ranks, and lopped off several heads before it returned to her hand.

Vectra shook her head and stumbled, shaking her head again. The creature collapsed beside her. Six more of the megatraths fell. Vipers swarmed over their bodies.

"No!" With a single thought she reached out her hand and willed destruction on the vipers. Balls of energy gathered before her hand, then shot against the ramp, blasting with such force that the stones trembled.

Fearless and angry, she raised Avenger and charged down the ramp. The standing megatraths roared and raced past her. They lowered their heads and spun into the first rows of giants, sending the large men flying over their companions' heads. Oganna blasted the ramp with balls of energy. The glow in her hands spread up her arms, and most of the vipers perished at her hand.

Vectra's side heaved; her nostrils quivered. Oganna knelt at her side and laid a hand on the creature's cooling body. She had to do something, but what? The poison had rooted itself in the creature's blood.

The giants lowered spears and pressed upon the megatraths, forcing them back to the ramp. Time was running out. Oganna raced to the ramp's base and pulled aside a couple of the mega-traths. She pointed up the ramp. "Bring those wounded into a circle around me." The megatraths bowed to her and barreled up the ramp. They dragged each of their sickened companions into a circle, and Oganna stepped inside and raised the Avenger.

As she held the sword in her hands, a pillar of smoke fell into the circle, and Death congealed before her. His bashed skull peered at her from beneath his cavernous hood. He raised his scythe with his only arm. She froze. Terror seized her like the morbid cold of a plague.

The Reaper stabbed his blade into a fallen megatrath, and his black robe swung around his skeleton legs. The megatrath's body convulsed, and its eyes glazed.

"You vile creature!" She ran forward and swept Avenger's blade from his head to his foot.

He stood his ground, his jaws open in a soundless laugh, as her blade cut through him without so much as touching him.

"No, no, no!" Oganna drew back, stunned.

The giants grappled with the megatraths at the ramp's base. They sank their huge blades into the creatures' bodies and speared their sides. Two megatraths roared and threw themselves into the giants' midst. And the giants speared them and marched over their corpses with a shout that rang in her ear. The remaining megatraths, except for the two with her on the ramp, fought under the insurmountable assault, but one by one the giants cut them down.

Deep down Oganna realized that the battle could not be won. As she turned to face Death, she was powerless to stop him. His bashed in skull—a gift from her father—grew back as his blade sucked the dying breaths from the megatrath.

As she stared helplessly, a figure coalesced between her and the reaper, a figure that held another scythe in its hand. Specter's gray cloak shimmered as he faced Death. "At last we meet again." Specter swung his blade toward the Reaper's whole arm.

With a quick twist, Death pulled its scythe out of the megatrath, and floated to the side. The two scythe blades clashed together. Specter dropped to the ground, spun, and kicked the Reaper's feet. The specter of death fell, and Specter crashed his boot into its ribs.

"Dragon child, tend to the megatraths." Specter fell to the stones as the Reaper pulled his legs from under him, but Oganna knew he had spoken to her. Her eyes followed him as he rolled across the stone ramp, grappling with the dark being. He tumbled over the ramp's side, pulling Death with him.

Oganna focused on the megatraths. Back in the desert arena, Starfire had drawn the poison from her body and saved her life, but how had she done it? Oganna held out her hand, palm up, just as she'd seen Starfire do. She closed her eyes for an instant to strengthen her focus. When she opened them, she knew what she must do.

Pointing her sword at the sky, she reached out with all her might to the heavens. Thunder rumbled; lightning cracked and then split the air. Another bolt of lighting followed, spiked toward her, and fastened itself to Avenger's blade as if it were a lightning rod. The portion of clouds directly overhead parted, and Yimshi's warm rays poured through onto Oganna and the wounded. Avenger's blade glistened in the sunlight, and absorbed the tremendous energy the storm unleashed.

Tendrils of electricity spiked from her crimson blade and latched onto the prone megatraths. The poison drained from their bodies, forming a sphere of venom above her hand. Their life forces were restored. Against all visible odds, the megatraths rose to their feet and shook themselves.

She felt a thrill pass down her spine as the clouds continued to clear in the wake of her miracle. "Rise, my friends," she told the megatraths. "Let us send retribution upon these vermin." Thereupon she spun around, the sphere of venom hovering above her hands. Of its own accord, Avenger slid into its sheath. She lifted the sphere and flung it into the oncoming giants. It burst like an egg on a giant's helmet and sprayed its poisonous contents over the line of the giants.

Vectra and the other megatraths reared on their four legs and clawed the air, roaring. But Oganna focused cold eyes on the assembling giants. They had halted as if waiting for someone. She only hoped they weren't waiting for Gabel's enemy, Razes.

Their ranks parted, and a human strode through the gap to the ramp's base. He was clean-shaven and dark-featured. Scars spider-webbed over his face. Unlike the giants, decked out in heavy armor, he wore only chain mail protection on his head and around his neck to his shoulders, pitch-black leather pants, and an equally black breastplate. In his left hand he held a long handle. Serrated sword blades speared from both ends of the handle.

He walked over the dead megatraths onto the ramp, gripping the leather handled weapon in both hands. A staff with a dark orb at its head was strapped to his back.

Oganna held her breath. The effort it had taken for her to draw raw energy from the sky had taxed her strength. She needed rest. But she rebuked herself. Rest would not come any time soon. She might as well settle in and pray she and the remaining megatraths could withstand this horde. She glanced again at the man's weapon and hoped he couldn't handle it as proficiently as her father handled the sword of the dragon.

A sneer curled the dark-haired man's lips. "A *girl?* Ha! Battles have no places for women."

The viper reared its head and slicked its tongue at him. "Psst! Get closer leather-brain, and I'll stick my fangs into you."

"So, I see that you are in the habit of keeping snakes. My master also enjoys their company. They can be—useful—for the dirty work. Maybe after I show you a trick or two in combat techniques he will see fit to give you some lessons of his own."

She searched the crowding giants' faces. "Your master. Ah, you must mean Razes. I know of one particular individual that is not too happy with him."

For a moment the man faltered, then he narrowed his eyes at her. "I don't know how you know my master's name, little waif. But I'll soon show you that making light of him is not a wise course of action."

The giants charged up the ramp and around her. They collided with the megatraths while the man sprinted toward her. Vectra would have to fight alone this time.

The man swung his double-sword. She parried and followed through with a thrust at his abdomen. He also parried, but she swung around, drawing her boomerang, and sliced it along his arm.

As the man's blood oozed from the cut, the viper sprang from Oganna's neck and inflicted its deadly bite on his neck. "Sssweet!" the viper slurred in his ear. "Taste death at the bite of one of your master's victims." It swung around his neck and sprang back to Oganna.

Oganna sidestepped as the man stabbed at her.

His blades whirled expertly in his hands, and he was adept at keeping her off balance. Nimbly she avoided him, letting him wear himself out and allowing the poison to do its work. He cursed profusely and stumbled back. "You are insignificant beside my master. He will have vengeance, and beneath his fury you *will* fall!"

Not bothering to answer, she drew back and threw the Avenger through his leg. "Mark what I say." The villain spat as his eyes grew bloodshot, and he dropped to his knees. "You think you're strong. You think you can win? The battle has not even begun." Drawing the staff from his back, the man held the sphere against his body, and his flesh closed around his wounds.

She kicked his head and held Avenger's point to his throat. "I could kill you, Auron. I recognize you now. You were responsible for my father's insanity. I recognize your presence in my mind."

He cackled. "Truly the powers of darkness are harnessing Subterran for me and those like me." He raised himself enough to spit on her blade.

"With God as my witness, I must save this duel for someone else." She twisted the blade in his skin, drawing blood. "Specter will deal with you. Your fate is in *his* hands." Then she kicked the side of his head as hard as possible. His body went limp, and his eyes closed.

She glanced at his scarred face as she held her blade inches from him. What a waste! A surge of hate for the enemy poured into her heart, but she suppressed the feeling before it took root in her soul. Hate, the mother of great wickedness—she would not give in to it.

All around her the battle for Ar'lenon raged. The megatraths rolled into the midst of the giants' forces, struck with their tails and claws, threw vapors and fire, yet they were heavily outnumbered and began to lose ground. Oganna retreated with them.

"We cannot continue like this, Princess." Vectra blew a weak flame and coughed. "We must retake ground."

Oganna raised Avenger and sprinted into the advancing giants. She slashed two giants' legs and, as they fell, pierced her blade through another's breastplate into his heart.

Vectra swung her tail into the men, killing two more. She whipped it back, stabbing its boney point into a giant's abdomen. Another megatrath rose to a great height on its hind legs and fell upon the giants, raking them with its claws. The remaining megatraths poured a mixture of flames and vapor in one direction and charged down the ramp.

Standing alongside her monstrous allies, Oganna struck down giants on every hand. But, though dozens fell, more took their place. Thousands of them filled the city, yelling at one another and pushing past each other for a part in the fight. They poured through Netroth's northern gates and flooded through the buildings.

Oganna slashed a giant's arm, then ducked as another stabbed his spear at her, sticking it into the street. Its shaft, as large as a small tree, quivered.

But while she struggled to maintain her ground, the giants pulled down several megatraths. One giant rose above his fellows and swung a hammer of tremendous size, smashing several megatraths' heads.

"Vectra, we cannot win this battle." Oganna blasted energy from her hand, killing another giant. "Help me onto your neck."

The creature knocked down several giants that stormed between them. She lowered her head and fire issued from her mouth onto the enemy ranks. "Climb aboard!" She slashed at their nearest enemies.

As Oganna rose from the street on Vectra's neck, she looked over the milling heads of the giants and pulled out her boomerang. With all her strength she flung it at the level of their necks. It spun through the masses and decapitated a dozen or more giants. It arced through the air and returned to her hand light as a feather. She secured it under her belt. Other giants were getting too close to Vectra and, in such tight quarters, the boomerang was less than effective.

She held Avenger with both hands and dug her knees into Vectra's scales to maintain balance. Yelling for all they were worth, they charged toward the giants, Vectra blowing fire and Oganna striking with her sword. They left a mass of wounded and dying giants in their wake, and finally a number of them fled.

One giant swung a sword at Vectra's side, and as Oganna blocked him with Avenger, she braced for the impact. The sword he was using had to be at least eight feet long. He pulled back and attacked again. This time she fed her power into her sword. Avenger's blade became almost invisible, and when it met the enemy's blade, it cut it in half. Her weapon flamed, and the attacker retreated into the sea of other giants.

Several giants managed to separate another megatrath from its fellows. With halberds, swords, and battle hammers they pummeled it. Oganna directed Avenger's blade in their direction and sent out a devastating fire that washed over their backs and burned them alive. Still, the megatrath fell.

Vectra rumbled and snapped her jaws at her fellows. "Everyone get into the citadel! Now!" She stood alone with Oganna on her neck. Her claws opened giants' arms, and she ripped their bodies apart as her faithful guards raced up the ramp into Ar'lenon. Oganna counted the survivors—there were only fifty left.

Vectra drove the giants back from the entrance to the ramp with a cloud of vapors, then spun on her rear four legs, and dashed up to the citadel. The megatraths met them at the doors. Once they were inside, they closed them and barricaded the entrance. Oganna wiped her brow and dismounted. "This battle is lost unless we get reinforcements."

Vectra heaved a sigh. "Even if they did come, I doubt they could break through those lines to rescue us. No, I think we are on our own."

Oganna did not want to admit that, but it seemed to be the truth. But she said to herself, Father, if you are coming, please hurry! We need you.

Ilfedo patted his Evenshadow's neck. "Whoa, boy." He sat up in the saddle and wiped his sweaty palm on his trouser leg. He would be glad to get out of the desert heat. Ahead of him lay a line of green hills, a welcome sight after the rocky wastes behind him. He held his saddle horn with his left hand and turned to the right. "What do you think, Ombre? Journey's end?"

Ombre smiled, but as he did, thunder clapped. His jaw dropped, and he pointed toward the sky. "Look!"

In the distance, over the green land, heavy rain clouds stretched into the north. The clouds split open and a beam of sunlight followed a bolt of lightning toward the ground, only to be hidden behind the hills.

The Warrioresses walked up between the men and gazed at the sight. "That storm is not of natural causes." Caritha swallowed. "The power of the heavens has been drawn upon."

Ilfedo turned her way. "Do you think that is the direction in which we should head?"

She did not immediately answer. She gathered her sisters in a circle. "If we unite our minds, then we may learn more." She drew her rusted sword, and the others followed her example. The five weapons touched at the tips, and static energy buzzed along their blades. The sisters drew back their weapons.

"Ilfedo!" She grabbed his arm and pointed north. "We must go now! Oganna and the megatraths are in serious danger. I sense a great darkness closing around her. We must get to her before it is too late!"

He spun in his saddle, drew the sword of the dragon, and held it above his head. Flames licked from the blade and a torrent of fire spat into the air. Before him, stretching back into the desert as far as he could see, line upon line of sword-wielding men cheered. Seven thousand voices shook the earth.

One thousand men emerged from the main force. In a steady, practiced line they marched forward. He raced his stallion to their lead. "Draw your swords, warriors of light!" The sweet sound of one thousand metal blades slipping out of their sheaths answered him. The desert rang with the warriors' shout, and Yimshi glinted on their blades. A flash of light followed, and Ilfedo's magnificent army was arrayed in white armor. Their blades glowed.

Division after division of men stretched into the distance as far as he could see. Eight thousand men ready to follow his bidding. A tremor of reality struck him, but he wheeled his mount and urged it toward the green hills.

He waved his hand at Ombre. "Will you do the honors, Commander?"

"Gladly." Behind him Ombre called to the regular troops, and a man clad in green armor brought forward the lord's personal mount. Midnight whinnied as Ombre slid onto his back and shouted at the top of his lungs, "Forward!"

The order passed from mouth to mouth with growing enthusiasm, and the army followed Ilfedo toward the rising terrain. He rode into the hills, stopping only a moment to cool his face in a stream and let his horse drink. The sound of eight thousand men tramping into the foreign land filled his ears as he left the stream and walked off alone into the hills. His army would need to refresh themselves at this stream before going farther.

The clouds continued to dissipate. He thought he smelled a whiff of smoke. He came to a rise taller than those around it and climbed to the top. Smoldering ruins stretched across the rolling hills, and in the distance a dark mass coming from the north descended into a valley.

"Like ants swarming on their prey." Caritha stepped up beside him and laid a hand on his shoulder. "Oganna is in that city. I'm certain of it."

"What? In there!"

He dashed back to his Evenshadow and drew the sword of the dragon. The living fire lit him like a match and then returned into the blade, leaving him decked in the armor that only he wore. The warriors of light raced with him toward the valley—a line that seemed to stretch endlessly in either direction. He raised his sword and wheeled his stallion before them.

"March, men! March!" Their enthusiastic cheers deafened him, and the Warrioresses stepped up beside him. They drew their swords and walked toward the main highway. In the distance the din of battle grew. Ilfedo dug his heels into the Evenshadow's flanks.

Patience was no longer a virtue.

# 24

# THE ULTIMATE SACRIFICE

The double doors trembled as the giants tried to break inside Ar'lenon. The surviving megatraths shook their bloodstained hides. Oganna massaged her sword arm. As sore as it was, how would she handle another assault if the giants broke down the doors? Could she and the megatraths hold them back?

The giants set up a cheer that filled Ar'lenon.

With Vectra's help, Oganna climbed to one of the arrow slits that overlooked the ramp. Giants packed the ramp. Five of them swung spiked battle hammers against the doors.

She unfastened her boomerang, held it out the opening, and flicked it into the giants. Once again it brought down several of them before settling back in her palm. Hopefully that would make the others think before attempting to bring down the doors. "All right, Vectra, you can let me down now. They have backed away."

Taking advantage of the giants' hesitation, the megatraths opened the doors and sent a tornado of fire and vapors onto the ramp. The enemy retreated, and the megatraths closed the doors and rebuilt the barricade.

"Oganna, you look exhausted." Vectra rolled Oganna's bedding outside the tent by the fireplace. "Catch some sleep. I'll keep watch."

Oganna peered into her tent for a moment. Gabel lay fast asleep. She dropped the flap over the opening and went to the water barrels. She poured the cool liquid over her arm and cringed as she rolled up her sleeve. The dried blood came with it. It wasn't a terrible wound, but it was enough to weaken her even more. Exhausted, she bandaged her wound and fell asleep.

Ilfedo raised his hand, even as he reigned in his mount. Far ahead of him, coming out of the valley and from hills to the northwest, marched an unbroken line of giant men clad for battle.

Ombre rode up beside him.

"How many do you think there are, Ombre?"

"It's difficult to say. A few thousand at least, and there could be more in the valley."

The Warrioresses lined up beside him.

"My sisters." Ilfedo gazed upon them. He had to make certain they stayed safe. Caritha's eyes narrowed, and Rose'el slapped the flat of her sword into her palm. They looked ready to do something rash. "I want you to stay by my side, Caritha. If we are going to find out what is happening in that valley, then we will first have to break through these giants."

Caritha nodded and scanned the advancing enemies. "Night is falling."

He glanced at the reddening western horizon. "Good. That works to our advantage." He twisted in his saddle to face Ombre. "Send the Elite Thousand ahead of the regular troops. Their swords will give them an advantage, as will their superior training."

Drawing his sword, Ombre signaled to Honer and Ganning. They in turn signaled to the sub-commanders, who in turn led the warriors of light by two-hundred man divisions. Two of these fanned out to the east, one formed an arrowhead to strike the enemy's opposite flank, and the remaining two divisions proceeded toward the valley.

Ilfedo kept his eye on the two moving to attack in the east. Suddenly the giants cheered, and the hills trembled as more marched from the valley. Their ranks swelled to the east and directly ahead. "Well, Ombre, how many are there now?"

His friend hesitated and started counting. At last he stopped. "Who cares?" He adjusted his breastplate. "Let's go get them!"

The Warrioresses stretched their arms and twirled their swords. "The battle favors the bold." Caritha's blade glowed. "I second Ombre's motion."

"Yeah, and I'm hungry for a good fight with whoever has done anything to Oganna." Rose'el grunted. "If we stay here we'll end up on the defensive—and I *hate* being on the defense."

Ilfedo rode ahead, and the Warrioresses ran after him. Ombre, Honer, and Ganning led the Elite warriors in their wake directly toward the heart of the opposing force. Ilfedo reached the giants first and cut into their ranks but found that he had left everyone else behind. Alone he battled the enemy, and on every side the large men fell beneath his sword.

He hacked and burned his way back to his own force. His warriors were locked in battle, unable to get past the giants and into the city.

"Fall back!" He led an ordered withdrawal and then summoned messengers. "It is time to bring all our forces to bear."

The messengers ran to carry out his orders. The Elite Thousand regrouped, and the regular army stormed into position
behind them. Their ranks covered the hills. He set his mouth in
a firm line. The army of giants was formidable. He wanted every
one of his warriors to go home to his wife and children. But to
the army of giants he shook his head. A heavy price would be
paid for the future queen today.

Dismounting, he sent his Evenshadow to the rear of the army
and unsheathed his sword. With the living fire licking his armor,
he marched down the highway. Eight thousand men shouted
behind him.

The giants marched toward him, then broke into a run. He
let them eat up their energy. As they drew near, he sprang upon
their front line. His sword cleaved the first giant's shield in
half, and he stabbed him through the heart, then spun his blade
behind him, impaling another.

Caritha sprang to his side, and Rose'el followed. Laura,
Evela, and Levena brought down three giants simultaneously.
Six strong, they advanced at the front of the army, stabbing
and slashing until the giants' hammering blows slowed the
Warrioresses.

Ilfedo stabbed his sword into another giant and grabbed a
fallen spear. The sapling-thick shaft made him stagger under its
weight. He felt the sword of the dragon infuse his muscles with
energy. He lifted the spear with a shout and threw it into his
foes. It pierced a giant's breastplate, passed through the body, and
impaled another standing behind the first.

Several giants leered down at him and cracked their hammers
and swords against his sword, driving him to the ground. The
darkness of night settled around him. He could see the divisions

of warriors with swords of light pressing upon the giants, but they battled beyond his reach.

He drove his fiery blade into a giant's chest and severed the man's head before his body hit the ground. Another giant stepped up and stabbed at him with a sword. He brought his blade down and cut it in two. Fire shot from his sword's blade and set the giant's head aflame. He ran the man through and turned to the next opponent.

Suddenly a wave of winged men sprang from deep in the giants' ranks. They soared high, a hundred of them at least. Ilfedo grimly watched as another hundred Art'en sprang into the air, joining their fellows. Their screeches shot across the field of battle as they dove in one massive horde toward his army.

"Archers!" the call rang through his army. "Take aim! Fire!" A cloud of arrows rose over the warriors of light. The Art'en flapped their wings as if trying to stem their descent. The arrows found their marks, and the wave of flying creatures fell from the sky into the giants' ranks.

Blood ran down Ilfedo's blade and collected at its tip, dripping to the ground in a red stream. The light of his armor lit the area around him as bright as day. One of the giants came at him from behind and smashed its battleaxe into his helmet. He fell to the ground as his opponent pulled out a sword to run him through. Twisting away, he jumped back up, grasped the giant's arm, and thrust him through his heart, dropping him like an oversized bear.

He felt his helmet with his fingers, running them along its unmarred surface. If he hadn't had the dragon's armor protecting him, that blow would have killed him. Three giants raced upon him. He arced his sword behind his back, holding it with both hands, then brought it to forward at their knees. They too fell, and Ilfedo drove deeper into the enemy lines.

❦   ❦   ❦

It seemed that mere moments had passed when a dreadful cheer startled Oganna awake. Neneila the viper slipped around her neck. She rose and made her way out of the tent. Morning light streamed through the windows and arrow slits along the citadel walls. "Vectra?"

The megatraths stood facing the doors, their claws digging into the stone floor. Vectra ambled over to her side and spoke so low that only Oganna heard her. "I happened to look out the slit in that wall when the giants cheered. There is a new arrival in their ranks. I think this is the one Gabel called Razes."

"Razes?" Oganna rubbed the sleep from her eyes and drew the Avenger from its sheath.

The doors groaned and shook. Outside the cheer rose again, stronger, and then the wood splintered into millions of tiny chips. A cloud of dust hindered her view for a moment. When it cleared, the figure of a giant stood alone on the ramp.

He was at least ten feet tall, though he seemed taller because of a steel helmet on his head. He cleared his throat and looked down on her. "There now, you must be the little dame about which I have heard so much." He curled his fingers tighter around the long metal staff in his hand.

Oganna advanced onto the ramp. He pointed his staff at her, its head twisted into blades around a small white globe. Too late, she realized his intent. A wave of energy rippled against her, throwing her down and throwing several megatraths to the floor.

"He is mine!" Vectra spat. She and her companions charged onto the ramp.

Oganna struggled to rise but invisible bands forced her shoulders down. She could hear Razes cackling as he backed down the ramp, just out of Vectra's range. "You are such loathsome creatures." He waved his hand, and the other giants collided with the megatraths and knocked them into the street. Now nothing stood between her and him.

The wizard sauntered up the ramp, stepping over bodies. "So this is the mighty and beautiful princess of the Hemmed Land. Too bad your father isn't around to save you from me—he's *busy* elsewhere."

In Yimshi's light his black armor shimmered. Oganna stared in horror. Every surface of his apparel had been outfitted with protruding blades. Even the back of his leather gloves were barbed with razor-sharp metal. She struggled to rise and fought to lift her sword. The bands holding her broke, but she felt too weak to stand.

Razes twirled his staff in a circle, built speed, and brought it to bear against her head. The impact nearly knocked her out. Blood ran down her face. Pain knifed from her skull to her nose. The wizard swung again, and she cringed, unable to stop him.

An enormous sword slipped in front of her and parried the wizard's blow. Gabel stepped over her and snarled at his nemesis. "Seeking to add yet another crime to your sins, Razes? Does it please you to see the innocent suffer?"

"Ah, *Your Majesty*." The wizard mocked a bow. "So, you have survived the purging of Burloi. I should have guessed that you would come back." He spun his staff around his waist. "The Valley of Death has made me strong. Very strong."

Gabel took a step toward him. "If you are referring to the dark magic you wield, then you are mistaken, for it has allowed you to do terrible things and taken from you that which is most important: your soul. This power has consumed you and *you* are a slave to *it*, not the other way around."

Razes grinned. "You are the one that has nothing, Gabel." He spread his arms. "Look around you, old man. I have everything."

"Everything? What you have is the support of a blind mob that destroys everything in its path."

"Ah, but even a mob can serve a purpose." He thumped his staff against the stone floor. "Just to show you how *good* of a person I am, I will give you one last chance to join forces with me. If you refuse me, then I will cut you up *before* I set to work on your little lady friend. Now step aside and prove your new allegiance by watching her die."

Gabel's knuckles turned white as he held the sword more firmly. "You have killed all the people that I loved, Razes. Except for this little angel. Your corruption ends here."

The wizard guffawed. "You could not end it before—"

"Don't act so confident, you slime pit! When you beat me, you had your apprentice with you. Now it is as it should have been—just you and me!" Gabel circled left. His eyes resembled cold steel, and every muscle in his body tensed. Oganna could only imagine the hate that swelled in his heart as he slashed viciously at his adversary. He stabbed his sword into stones, and they blew up in the wizard's face.

Oganna sat in shock. Gabel's sword had powers. Why had he not mentioned it to her?

Razes leapt out of the way, pointed his staff in the king's direction, and hit him with a blinding flash of light. He laughed as Gabel stumbled, and despair crept into Oganna's heart. The wizard spread his arms. "Are you having trouble with your eyes, old man?"

Gabel staggered closer to Razes and then sank his sword into the wizard's leg. His gaze shifted to the wizard's face. "Sorry, my mistake, I guess I wasn't stunned by your blast after all."

Screaming in pain and anger, the wizard grasped Gabel's neck and raked his blades down the length of his chest. Blood pooled on the stones as Gabel dropped his sword. Razes brought his knee up, driving its blades into the king's abdomen. He let him drop to the floor. "Did you *really* think you stood a chance, old king?"

Still weak and a little dizzy, Oganna struggled to her feet and held her sword. Avenger's blade turned crimson, and the silver garments covered her. She looked upon her fallen defender with all the love she could have given a second father, and tears flooded her eyes. Gabel's eyes looked back at her from his mutilated face. They were sad, yet fulfilled, then as they closed forever, he murmured, "There *is* great potential in you, Princess Oganna. Don't let anyone tell you differently, little lady."

Gathering her last strength, she darted behind Razes and stabbed wherever his body presented a target.

"Is that all you can do?" He dodged her blows and thwacked her sides with his staff. She felt Neneila fall limp under her shirt.

Razes growled at the sky and hit his wounded leg with the head of his staff. The wound cauterized, and he thrust his blade-ridden fist at her.

She stumbled, and then stood still. Desperately she tried to understand why her senses seemed impaired. Why couldn't she attack him? An oppressive darkness crept over her. At last she recognized the spell he was using against her. Her mind was in a panic. His power bound her, reached inside her, and stole her will. Then it struck something else, a residual strength innate and untamable: her dragon side.

With all her will she pushed back and fought against the spell. "Depart!"

The force of her refusal threw Razes backward, and he screamed in frustration. "You little imp! Resistance is useless."

Oganna cast fire from her blade, but his staff absorbed it. She struck with lightning, yet his staff resisted, and he remained unharmed. "Your powers cannot match mine. I have been trained by the greatest of wizards in all deadly arts. Now, witness my power." He stretched his hands to the sky. Far above lightning flashed in the clouds. The wind whipped through the city and swirled the clouds until they spun far above. Lightning flashed, zipped beneath and into the clouds, then spiked toward the earth. The bolts wove through one another, gathered speed, and headed toward the place where she stood.

The bolts blasted against her head and shoulders, but she pulled the first one down and wrapped it around her body as a shield so that the other bolts entwined themselves about her, then simply dissipated. "How little you know of the power of good." She gazed up at Razes and frowned. "It *will* overcome you." Thereupon she pummeled him with blows from the Avenger. On every side she poured her fury like rain and sought to find a weakness.

Razes blocked her sword, and the head of his staff slipped past her defenses, landing blows on her thighs, shoulders, and then her chest. She gasped for air, drew back Avenger, and charged him with her blade aimed for his chest. But Avenger's point clinked against his armor and slid over it. She widened her stance, seeking to rebalance herself.

Raising his staff above his head in both hands and pointing it at her, Razes sneered. Black and red energy blasted from the staff's end, striking the ramp at her feet. The stones trembled and cracked. They crumbled into dust beneath her, and she fell. A moment of weightlessness and a glance downward; the ruins of stone buildings rose to meet her. Her spine impacted a large stone block, snapping her head toward the ground. Every muscle in her body burned as she tried to raise her head. She screamed.

Razes leapt down after her, and his staff appeared to absorb the shock of his fall. "Poor, poor thing." He clacked his tongue and held the razors on the back of his hand against her face. "What a pity."

Her vision blurred, and she breathed in rapid, short bursts that seemed void of air. She glimpsed his evil face as he sliced into her skin. The pain compared to nothing she had ever experienced. If she could have cried out she would have, but she had run out of tears. Before she lost consciousness, she felt his staff crush into her face and then chest. No longer could she feel pain.

⚜ ⚜ ⚜

Specter had been grappling with his adversary through the night inside a ruined building. Now in the daylight he gritted his teeth and drove his blade into the Reaper's leg, pushed him against the stone walls. Death fell again, and this time Specter fell upon him and tore his scythe out of the Reaper's boney fingers.

He lifted his face toward the sky and laughed as the Reaper squirmed beneath him. Its feet and hand transformed into smoke. "Oh, you cannot run forever! I have seen the wickedness you and your kind would unleash on this world, and I loathe you. Now with the help of God, I bring you to a just end."

Holding the scythes tightly, he clubbed the Reaper's skull until cracks spread through it. He hammered the scythes into the skull in quick succession. Fury filled his arms, and Death's skull broke into a thousand fragments.

Something exploded on the ramp above, and he stood to his feet, holding the Grim Reaper's headless body in his hand. Oganna fell off the ramp, and Avenger slipped from her hand. She crashed into a ruined building, stirring a cloud of dust.

A giant arrayed in armor unlike anything Specter had ever seen dropped after her. The giant raised a wizard's staff in its hand and crouched over the dragon's offspring. He held his blade-ridden fist against the young woman's lovely face and viciously cut it open. Oganna's body collapsed and, in the stones beside her, Avenger's blade ceased to glow.

"Master! Let me finish her." A dark-featured human stumbled up the heap of stones to the ruins, leaning on a dark staff.

Razes glanced down at the man and laughed. "You have a lot to learn, Auron. You fell at the hand of a girl? Wait until Letrias hears of this." He stood aside and pointed at Oganna. "She's all yours."

Specter roared with rage and dragged Death's carcass into the sunlight. He raised his scythe and faced the giant, rolling the Reaper's remains down the rubble. The carcass slid to Razes's feet.

The giant picked up the carcass, and his eyes narrowed.

Specter caused his cloak to render him partially visible and set his feet in the debris, frowning at Auron. "Rise, traitor!"

The man spun, glanced at Specter, and stumbled back. He pointed the staff at him. "W . . . what? Who are *you*? I do not know you."

"Think again, Auron. You know me better than your new master knows you." He slipped the hood off his head and smiled. "Brian's blood stains your soul, and now I will exact retribution on you so that none will forget the cost of shedding innocent blood."

"No!" Auron's lips trembled, and he shook his head vigorously as Specter advanced, rattling his chain mail. "I saw you fall. I saw you die."

"Hmm." Razes laughed and kicked his pupil toward Specter. "It looks like you have a fresh opportunity to prove yourself, Auron."

"This man—he died long ago—I saw him die." He stepped back. "Master, do not make me face him. You must slay him now, before he brings death upon us both."

Razes shrugged his enormous shoulders. "Very well." He swung his staff, but it passed through Specter as though he were a ghost.

Specter swung his scythe, cutting the traitor's arm. Auron screamed and then struck back with such speed that his staff cracked Specter on his cheek, and he fell into the rubble.

Auron sprinted after him, thrusting his staff into Specter's mid-section. But Specter kicked the man in the chest and, when he had fallen, laughed. "God has shown me favor today, Auron. Your master cannot touch me while your traitorous debt remains unpaid. Did you believe escape from the Creator's retribution would be possible? Were you fool enough to rank yourself above the will of Providence?"

The traitor stood and swung his staff at Specter's legs. Specter blocked it with his scythe's handle. "You can never beat me trading blow for blow, Auron. Or have you forgotten?" He spun, cutting the man's side with his scythe blade.

⚜ ⚜ ⚜

Ilfedo wiped his brow and paused a moment to allow the sword of the dragon to reenergize him. All night he had been fighting. All night the sword had kept him from tiring, and now he stood far ahead of his army and his friends. He thrust through another giant, and another, and another. One more approached, and he jumped into the air, holding the sword above his head, and cracked the giant's helm. After landing in a crouch, he spun. Fire spewed from the blade, and he straightened and stepped past giant human torches.

He crested the valley's rim and glimpsed the megatraths fighting around the ramp to the citadel. Dead and dying littered the city. The knowledge that Oganna was there too drove him mad, and he continued on without consideration for the danger. He descended into the city by way of the roads and fought within visual range of the ramp.

Then he saw her glowing silver figure, and the giant man opposing her. The giant blasted the ramp, and she fell a long, deadly distance into one of the demolished buildings. Her adversary leapt down after her.

His daughter, his most precious companion! He cried out, and his sword burned those closest to him. He stabbed and hacked all in his path as if they were hay in a field until at last he stood at the base of the ruined structure. The giant with his back to Ilfedo laughed hysterically and pounded the now-almost-unrecognizable body of Oganna. The wizard spun his staff to strike again and spoke to the motionless body. "You have failed, young one! But at least you died at the hand of I, Razes."

Ilfedo smashed his fist into the giant's lower back and toppled him with a stiff kick to the back of his leg. Razes's head crashed into a large stone, and when he picked himself up, he had to wipe blood from his mouth.

# A JUST RECOMPENSE

In Ilfedo's hand the sword of the dragon blazed as never before, and the living fire upon his armor burned with unparalleled fervor. He felt the rage boiling inside of him, and when he looked again at his daughter, he was filled with hate. He stepped over a foundation stone and held his sword with both hands before his face. Only one thing mattered to him now: vengeance.

The giant looked down at Ilfedo and spat. The staff in his hand dripped with Oganna's blood.

Ilfedo stepped closer. "Don't you dare touch my daughter again."

"And what if I do?" the wizard mocked. "Will you kill me?" He spun his staff and scoffed. "Do you think that I fear you? You are lower than the dust and worthy only to be ground into powder. Your body will hang in my hall alongside that of your daughter, and it will be a warning to all that oppose me in the future."

"You are mistaken, wizard, for it is you that will be an example to *my* enemies. And when this day is done and your soul has fallen into eternal darkness, then I will laugh at your corpse and feed you to the birds."

Razes stomped toward him and sneered. "Prepare to die!"

A series of cries and roars echoed around him. Caritha appeared from behind a pile of rubble. She pulled her rusted blade from a giant's breast and let him fall beside her. Another rushed her from behind, but his eyes opened wide, and he fell forward. Laura took her blade from his back and stood side-by-side with her sister. Beyond them, cutting a path through the enemy masses, charged Levena, Evela, and Rose'el. They reached Caritha and Laura, then formed a line.

Rose'el eyed the wizard. "So, *this* is the big, bad enemy. I'd expected more than a coward that cripples young women!"

"Just say the word, Ilfedo, and we'll help you cut him into a thousand pieces." Caritha stepped through the rubble, and her sisters formed a half-circle around the giant.

"Yeah." Rose'el pointed her blade at the giant's head. "I'll take *that* off!"

Razes advanced and spread his arms. "Is this supposed to make me afraid? You are like insects beside me." He beckoned to his forces, and a line of giants stamped toward the Warrioresses.

The sisters touched the tips of their blades together and sent out wave after wave of energy into the giants' midst. The wizard's forces fell back, their hair smoking and their faces red. Ilfedo let his sword shoot fire from its tip and addressed the giant. "It looks to me like you are outnumbered."

Cackling, the wizard raised his staff at the sky, and lightning struck the ground, opening a large hole. Razes sneered and looked into its depths. "Come, *my children*, you have work to do."

Out of the hole slithered a multitude of vipers that swarmed around him in a protective circle.

Ilfedo dashed to Caritha's side and shook her shoulder. "Get Oganna out of here! I'll keep him busy."

※ ※ ※

The sisters climbed the rubble into the ruins and looked upon their young charge. "No, it cannot be!" Levena clamped her hand over her mouth.

Evela screamed and tears ran down her cheeks. Laura closed her eyes and knelt in front of Oganna.

Rose'el swallowed hard. Her body trembled, her shoulders quaked, and her eyes moistened. "Is she already gone?"

"Hurry, she isn't breathing!" Caritha grabbed Oganna's blood-soaked legs, and Laura held her arms. Both of them gasped and stared in horror at the mutilated face.

"Is she, is she, is she dead?" Laura choked back a sob.

"Not yet. Come on!" Caritha said.

Levena, Rose'el, and Evela charged into another wave of giants, stabbing every which way. Caritha and Laura grunted under their burden as they followed the path over the dead and dying that the sisters created. They carried Oganna along the highway. As they approached the valley's rim, a shout caused them to look up.

Ombre and the Elite Thousand crested the hill. The warriors of light stretched in both directions for as far as Caritha could see. The giants were losing ground, and the swords of light could be seen everywhere, piercing hearts and severing limbs.

The regular army charged into the city, leaving heaps of dead giants in its wake. When they reached the citadel, they protectively surrounded the surviving megatraths. Hopefully Oganna's friend, Vectra, was among them.

Caritha helped Laura set Oganna down on soft grass. All five sisters knelt around her. "What can we do?" Evela cried. "She looks dead already."

"But she isn't. Not yet." Caritha drew her sword and touched it to Oganna's chest. The others followed her lead. "Draw upon the strength that Father gave us, the powers within—use it up if necessary—drain yourself completely of it if necessary—feed it into her."

The viper's head peeked from under Oganna's collar. It rubbed its head gently on the young woman's neck.

Caritha sent the powers within into her sword, and the weapon glowed. Tendrils of blue and red light latched on to Oganna's chest from all five swords. Caritha screamed in pain and her sisters soon followed. It felt as if the fabric of her existence was ripping out her heart. But she held on as the power left her blood.

A cocoon of light cascaded around the body, and through its veil she saw Oganna's wounds close and the blood dry. The energy receded and snapped back against the swords, throwing Caritha against the ground. When she sat back up, Oganna's chest heaved steadily, and her eyelids fluttered open.

Caritha embraced her and cried on her shoulder. The others wept too, for Oganna's beauty was forever gone. Her face and arms bore the ugly scars inflicted on her by Razes.

⸎ ⸎ ⸎

"It's all right," Oganna said through her own tears. "I'm here. I'm alive." She gazed heavenward. "Thank God for that."

The sisters looked at each other, unable to reveal the horrible truth. Oganna's eyes froze on her arms. Her skin felt rough, rather than smooth. She felt her face and the realization hit her. "I'm—ugly." She buried her face in her hands and wept.

Caritha and her sisters tried to comfort Oganna, but they could offer no consolation. How could they? They hadn't lost *their* beauty. And so they cried with her until a tremendous explosion rocked the earth and they spun around.

Rose'el pointed to the base of Ar'lenon. "*Ilfedo!* What does he think he's doing?"

Ilfedo drove his flaming blade into the ground at Razes's feet and blasted the rocks out from under him. As the wizard's vipers sailed through the air, he directed the sword of the dragon at them and roasted them alive before they touched the ground. He slammed his shoulder into the wizard's abdomen and brought his blade around in a swift arc, slitting the giant's arm just above the elbow.

Ilfedo's army swarmed into the street, and the wave of giants fled. Razes screamed at them, "Back you fools! Destroy them." He cocked his arm and thrust his blade-ridden fist into Ilfedo's chest.

Ilfedo stumbled. He glanced down at the deep wound. But how had the wizard penetrated the armor of living fire? Ilfedo felt faint. The world spun around him, and he fell. As the world darkened, Razes cackled.

Suddenly the sword burned his hand, forcing him to drop it. It hovered in the air above him and shot the living fire into his body. It felt as if he had gone from a frigid night's chill to the warmth of a sunny day. The blood stopped flowing, and his flesh healed without so much as a scar to show for the deadly wound.

Razes stepped back, and Ilfedo saw astonishment in the wizard's face.

He grinned. "Nice try." He rose, took his sword in hand, and stabbed into the ground. The stones and dirt blew up again in the wizard's face and threw him into a wall of stone. Before the giant could rise, Ilfedo shot fire from the sword of the dragon. The wizard held his staff in the flame's path, and it absorbed the living fire.

Ilfedo jumped forward, smote him on the chin, and cut the wizard's staff in two. He stepped back, hoping to receive the giant's surrender. Instead, small orbs of energy formed in the wizard's hands.

"You think that you have defeated me?" The wizard eyed his orbs greedily and then chucked them in rapid succession in Ilfedo's direction.

As the orbs broke harmlessly on the sword of the dragon, the sword left Ilfedo's hands and hovered before him. He felt as though he had left his body and lay inside the sword. He shot like an arrow straight into his opponent's heart. When it was over, he returned to his body and opened his eyes.

Razes slumped against the wall, and his remaining orbs fizzled out of existence in his hands. His eyes froze open and his breathing stopped.

Ilfedo grabbed hold of his sword, drew it from the corpse, and sheathed it at his side. The armor of living fire gave way to his everyday apparel, and he walked out into the city. He could see the last of the giants scrambling out of the valley, heading north, and he knew that they would not be coming back. Several Art'en flew above the giants, yet they too did not glance back. Heaving a sigh, he walked down the highway, stepping over the bodies of the giants on his way.

Ombre rode toward him and wiped his dirty blade on his trouser leg. "It is done, Ilfedo. I don't think those giants will give us any more trouble. The Hemmed Land is safe."

"How did our troops fare?"

"They did well."

"Casualties?"

Ombre shook his head and lowered his gaze. "Yes, there were some."

Caritha tapped him on the shoulder, and he realized that all five sisters and his daughter were standing by him. Oganna's scarred face startled him, but he caught himself, reached out, and clutched her to himself. "It's all right, my daughter. The wizard is dead."

"Father, I am—I am ugly!"

Tears poured from his eyes, for he knew that it was true. "The blame rests with me." He choked on his words. "I should not have allowed you to come here."

"No!" another voice rumbled from the streets. "*I* am to blame." Vectra stumbled toward him with her head lowered. Blood ran from the many wounds she'd received, and her eyes overflowed until she too wept.

Oganna broke free of her father and ran to the trembling creature. She reached out and laid her hand gently on Vectra's snout. "It is no one's fault, Vectra. What is done is done." She wiped her cheeks and continued. "Though I am ashamed to show this face in public, I do not hold you or anyone else here responsible for it. Did you draw the blades across my face and mutilate me? No. You would never. Razes alone carries the blame."

Ilfedo counted the megatraths gathering behind Vectra. Twenty-four remained out of one hundred. He shook his head. Seventy-six dead.

"Oganna, Vectra . . . let's gather the dead and head home. Tonight we will camp along the border with the northern desert. There is fresh water there and space for our numbers to spread out."

Oganna shook her head and looked at him with her blue-gold eyes. They were still as beautiful as the day she was born. "I want to stay here for a while. There is one giant in this city that deserves a proper burial, and I intend to give it to him."

Vectra sniffled. "Indeed he does."

He started to beckon the Warrioresses over, but she stopped him. "Please, Father, I want to do this alone—unless—unless Vectra is willing to stay with me."

The megatrath rested a hand around Oganna's shoulders. "I would have it no other way." Vectra bent down, and Oganna straddled her neck. As the pair went off, Ilfedo heard Vectra command the remaining megatraths to follow his orders and leave her behind.

He organized his troops and the megatraths into bands to collect the dead. Using material from the demolished buildings, they constructed large sleds, then they laid the dead on them and hauled them toward the desert. Ombre sent messengers ahead of them to the Hemmed Land and to Resgeria to both report the battle's outcome and to bring more manpower.

Within two days reinforcements came and the last of the dead were hauled out of Netroth. Ilfedo mounted his Even-shadow and rode out of the valley. Only once did he stop to look back. The mighty citadel, where he had last spotted his daughter and the megatrath, stood as a grim reminder to him that all great things that have a beginning also have an end.

He wheeled the Evenshadow stallion and rode after his army. Maybe during this time alone Oganna would find peace with her new condition and realize that the love of those around her did not depend on her physical appearance. He had survived, and so had she. What more could he ask for?

⊗  ⊗  ⊗

"Die, Xavion! Why can't you just die?"

The traitor and his captain battled in one of the city's larger remaining buildings. Twilight lengthened and deepened the shadows. A warm wind whistled through the rafters.

Specter smiled as Auron stabbed at him again with the wizard staff. "That staff can only rejuvenate you for so long." He cut the ancient traitor's leg, and Auron fell back, touched his staff to the wound, and it healed—but much more slowly than it had a day ago. "You see? While your dark powers falter, I remain unchanged. While you grow desperate, I grow confident. You should have learned from me all those years ago instead of betraying me." He grabbed the chain mail headdress and yanked it off Auron's head, throwing it ten feet away.

Auron sneered and looked back up at him. "I didn't want to be someone's servant!"

"Ha! Everyone is a servant. We only choose what master to serve. And we know why we are both here, at this place, now." He spun, and the blade of his scythe slipped behind Auron's legs and cut them behind the knees. With a cry the traitor collapsed. Specter knelt beside him. "You chose your master, and I chose mine, and now we must each face the consequences."

"No. No, this cannot be. Letrias promised."

Specter stood and pressed his scythe blade against the man's throat. Then he kicked the staff out of Auron's hand. "I am a more honorable man than you, my fallen apprentice. I remember that you used to care for righteousness. It was not all an act. And for that reason I am going to show you mercy today."

He grabbed the man's neck and pulled him bodily off the floor, holding him there with his feet dangling in the air. "Consider whom you serve and choose wisely, for the next time we meet in this way, I will come as the specter of death and your judge."

Specter dropped the man to the floor. He pulled the hood over his head and faded into invisibility. Auron wept and wiped at his bloody nose, then he whispered. "If only I knew that repentance could bring me forgiveness, then I would." He frowned, jumped for his staff and broke it across his knee.

A pulse of energy shot down the broken sorcerer's tool, exploding through Auron's leg. The traitor grabbed his leg and screamed and wept.

Specter grasped a fallen beam and hung his head. And he let a tear slip down his face. For there, not twenty feet away, groaned a man he had once loved as a brother and treated as a son. But maybe this time mercy would pave the way to repentance. Maybe a traitor who betrayed his new master could resurrect to new life.

Turning, he stepped down onto the street and knelt with hands folded. "Send thy prophet, my Maker. I pray."

# THE END OF SORROW

Vectra motioned for Oganna to come closer to the wall of stone as she threw her weight against it. The stones grated, and the hidden door opened inward to reveal a dark corridor beyond. Oganna stepped inside as Vectra closed the door behind them.

"Vectra, do you see any torches in here?"

The megatrath grunted. "It's pitch black. I can't see anything."

Oganna drew Avenger and let the silver robes adorn her sore, scarred body. The air smelled stale, and the light from her weapon showed thick cobwebs on the walls. It had taken two days of searching for them to find this place. It had been cleverly concealed in one of the buildings around Ar'lenon by a false wall in what appeared to be a distinguished home.

"This place looks as though it could use a good cleaning." She ran her finger along the grimy wall. "I wonder why the giants didn't maintain it."

Vectra grunted again as they entered a large, square room decorated with runes and carvings. A long, flat stone table adorned the room's center. Gently she laid the linen-wrapped body of the brave giant king onto the tabletop. Next she heaved aside a blank square stone from the front of one of the tomb's many recessed chambers. Behind the stone lay a hole large and long enough for the body.

"Here, Princess, the epitaph has not been written." She leaned the stone against the table.

An oversized chisel and a hammer rested in one of the walls. Oganna fetched them to the blank stone slab standing as high as her head. The giants' tools were almost too big for her to manipulate, but she chipped away at the stone for the next few hours until she had engraved the words she wanted:

Here lies Gabel, King of Burloi
In life he was magnificent
In death he was immortalized
In memory he will be loved
Our friend, may you rest here in peace,
Undisturbed, until the eternal God claims this world.

"It is a fitting monument for a brave man." Vectra scraped her claws on the floor. "Now, let us put him to rest." She slid the wrapped body—feet first—into its chamber, and then reached to a pack tied on her back and set it on the floor.

Oganna opened it and pulled out a rich purple cloth. This she laid over Gabel's body, then drew out his cumbersome sword. She had spent the better part of three hours cleaning it the other day when she had found it, and now the blade and handle shone as if new.

Vectra accepted the weapon from Oganna. Balancing its blade in her claws, the megatrath rested it lengthwise on the purple cloth.

Oganna reached into the pack for one final item: the giant's silver crown. "He said he was *king* of Burloi," she whispered. "No king should be buried without his crown." As she lifted the crown onto the king's chest, the diamond augmented the light flowing from her sword.

Vectra heaved the heavy tombstone with Oganna's epitaph in front of the chamber, sealing it against prying eyes. Oganna melted the seams together with Avenger's fire.

She knelt on the floor, and Vectra followed her example. They remained like this for a long while, paid their respect to the dead, then rose to go. Oganna glanced around the tomb, noting the other stones along its walls. She pulled her cipher from her pocket and translated several of the ancient writings. "Vectra, am I getting this right? Most of it is gibberish to me."

"That's because most of the things written on these stones are names and titles."

Oganna put away her cipher and walked out with Vectra. The creature closed the secret door behind them and together they built a false wall out of the rubble to conceal it from any future explorers. Oganna, now that she stood in the light of day again, veiled her face with a white cloth and walked in silence up the ramp to Ar'lenon. She paused for a moment to admire the colors of the sky as Yimshi set toward the west.

Tomorrow she and the megatrath would start the return journey to the Hemmed Land. Oh how she dreaded what people would think when they looked at her. Would they keep their distance and avert their eyes, or would they gape and stare until she was embarrassed to tears? The 'hideous freak,' that's what they might call her. A freak! She scolded herself for wallowing in self-pity and reminded herself that she still had much to be grateful for. But though she tried to convince herself otherwise, she knew that her scars would forever change her.

&#9767;  &#9767;  &#9767;

That night Oganna watched Vectra lie beside the enormous fireplace in the main chamber. Neneila coiled next to the creature. It seemed the two had bonded. The megatrath closed its eyes and breathed deeply and slowly.

Oganna rose from the fireplace and wandered one last time up the steps to the observation deck of Ar'lenon Citadel. There she screamed out her pain to the sky. There she cried anew for her brave martyr Gabel—he was but one of many that had died in her defense, but he had done so without a hint of regret. Evil had risen and claimed the life of a noble king.

"Why did this have to happen?" She leaned back against the roof and covered her face with her hands, but as soon as she touched her scarred self, she ripped the veil from her face and threw it off the platform.

In that moment the clouds flashed with white light and, looking up, she saw great wings spread in the sky. Albino descended upon the citadel and settled on its pinnacle. His claws gripped the roof's steep surface and held him with seeming ease in spite of his great size. His pink eyes glinted as they gazed into hers, as if seeing through the flesh to search her soul.

She caught herself staring, and she marveled at how calm she suddenly felt with him nearby. Even before he said a word, she felt as if he had done a world of good. She basked in his presence.

The dragon wrapped his white tail around the roof, and his boney lips curled into a smile. "Do not grieve for Gabel, my daughter, for what he did, he was pleased to do for you. Seeing you brought him hope for the future, and your innocence reminded him of the worth of sacrifice." Albino reached out one clawed hand and lifted her chin. "Your mother would be proud of you."

She lowered her eyes, ashamed to let him see what she had become. "It—it was not only for him that I was crying."

He slid down the roof. His claws cracked the tiles, and their pieces slid off, rolling over the platform and falling into the city as he came to rest on the platform. She could sense his penetrating gaze still upon her as he rumbled in his chest. "Hold still, my dear, this may hurt."

Oganna felt as if her skin burned with fire. She cried out as the pain increased and clutched her hands over her face. Between her fingers she lifted her gaze to the noble white face. The mighty creature returned her gaze, unwavering.

Cracks formed on the dragon's facial scales and glowing red blood oozed forth. The dragon growled, shook his head. It grasped the citadel's roof with one hand and bent the metal supports, still growling softly. Suddenly she knew what he had done, what he was still doing—all for her.

The wounds Razes had inflicted, the horrendous disfigurement, spread across the dragon's face and raced down his neck, even to his chest. But not a single tear fell from the dragon's eyes, though every fiber of his body trembled.

She ran to him, ignoring his glowing blood flowing over her body. His arm clasped her against his chest. And she wept. His cool scales soothed her skin. The pain in her face melted into warmth.

"Now." He held her at arm's length and ran his eyes from her feet to her head. "Ah, yes! That is *much* better."

At first she reached to feel her face, then she hesitated and gazed up. But a brilliant glow radiated from his face, forcing her to avert her gaze. She knew that scars had destroyed his image, and she wanted to weep on.

The dragon, however, whipped his clawed fingers around and held up a silver mirror. "You are the offspring of a dragon, my child. We are a beautiful race. Scars do not become you."

She beheld her face in the mirror—restored, whole, and beautiful. She jumped up and wrapped her arms around his neck. Deep in his chest Albino rumbled, and then he laughed. His mighty arms held her in a tight embrace. The gratitude she felt could not be expressed in words, so she didn't say anything. Instead she let him feel it.

At last he set her feet on the platform. She gazed up at him with tears of joy in her eyes and made the request that now burned her heart. "What of Gabel? Would it be possible—to restore his life?"

"Oganna, my child, your heart is good, and you have kept your mind pure. But though I could restore his life, yet for your sake I will not. The Creator has a plan for everything, and even this sorry event had to come to pass. The loss of a friend is a hard thing to bear, but in dealing with it you will be strengthened, for you must learn now how to cope with the loss of those to whom you are the closest.

"Nevertheless do not fear. You will see Gabel again." He angled his magnificent face toward the sky and snorted a gentle flame. "Just look at how those stars are shining tonight."

A tear for Gabel slipped down her cheek.

"There, there, enough weeping." His glowing face smiled as he flexed his wings. "This is the end of sorrow in this place, Oganna. Yet, this is not the end of your journey. Hard times lie ahead. Remember always that you are mine, for I will be watching over you through it all." With a final smile he spread his magnificent white wings. They seemed to cover the entire sky, and she wished he would stay and wrap her in them. His leg muscles rippled, his wings beat downward, and he ascended into the night.

As she watched him go, she ran her hand over her smooth skin before calling after him. "Goodnight . . . *Grandfather*."

Somersaulting through the air, his whole body glowing, he glanced back. "Goodnight, my precious granddaughter. And know that I am always watching out for you, even when it seems I am not near." Then he shot into the night sky, streaming away like a blazing comet of white over the distant horizon.

The cool night wind howled through the city streets, bearing a sad note of finality. A formerly powerful nation had been overturned, its people slain, and its buildings burned. Only Ar'lenon and its damaged ramp stood whole. She looked around one last time and then entered the citadel to descend the stairs.

❀    ❀    ❀

In the morning Oganna packed her tent and goods and put them on Vectra's back. The megatrath glowed with ecstasy. "My goodness, don't *you* look lovely today." She gave a toothy grin, and Oganna smiled back. She had revealed the truth of her heritage to the creature, and the megatrath treated her with all the more respect.

Whatever the dragon had done to her had not only healed her body but had revived her spirits as well. His blood stains covered her clothes, reminding her of the pain he suffered on her behalf.

She slapped the megatrath in a playful manner, then waited for her to lower her neck so she could climb aboard.

When Vectra swung open the doors, fresh morning air filled Oganna's lungs. The megatrath bounced onto the dimly lit ramp and rumbled contentedly in her throat. "We are finished here."

Down the ramp and onto the highway they raced. The eastern horizon brightened, blazing orange and yellow streaks across the sky. Not a single word more passed between them as they left the city. Oganna felt Yimshi's rays warm her blood, and her hand dropped to the Avenger's hilt. She fingered it for a moment and then, as Vectra crested the rise out of the valley, she turned for one last look.

The bodies of the giants lay in the streets, on the collapsed buildings, and on the ramp to Ar'lenon. A dark cloud rose from the north and grew in size as it approached the city. The sounds of scolding birds fighting with one another to reach the corpses soon filled the valley as flocks of vultures and ravens came to the feast.

"The wizard has fallen, and now the birds will pluck the flesh from his bones." Vectra stamped her feet with satisfaction, pivoted on her rear four feet, and galloped to the south. Her six legs beat against the ground, carrying Oganna quickly away.

Oganna drew her sword and held it aloft. The silver robes covered her again, and her blade turned crimson. Whatever the future held, she would face it with the knowledge that she was the grandchild of a dragon. Around her neck the viper slept. Oganna sheathed the sword and leaned forward so that Vectra could hear her. "Let's go home!"

## THE END

# ACKNOWLEDGMENTS

It is an amazing feeling to look at my second completed novel, knowing that God has blessed me in letting me fulfill my writing dream. This particular work was been in-progress for several years. Originally it was going to be the first novel in The Sword of the Dragon series.

I want to thank my wife for her steady support. Truly I believe she is my number one fan and she is a wonderful mother to our son.

To my son, Andrew. Someday, when you're old enough, I hope that you will pick up these books and know how passionate your dad is about stories. They can educate and teach, just as Jesus taught us.

To the wonderful people at AMG, thank you for making my publishing dreams a reality!

Thank you also to Robert 'Treskillard' for accidentally suggesting the fantastic change to Albino's interaction with Oganna after the battle for Ar'lenon. That scene is now one of my favorites in this novel.

And lastly to all my wonderful fans! This journey would not be as much fun without you.